"And now, m... it's time to p...

Rafer's arms went around Suzanne again, and he gave her a kiss. Warmth rushed through her, made her melt against him, her wrists locked behind his neck. She felt the heat of his lips shifting to the arch of her throat. The next thing she knew, he was carrying her to the bed.

"You wouldn't take advantage of an inebriated lady, would you?" she protested as he lowered her.

"Only with the most considerate devotion," he breathed as his lips grazed her neck and shoulders. His hands shaped her, gentled her, distracted her from everything but his touch. He was finding softness, more softness, discovering a mysterious need in her that was becoming immediate. His tongue had gone from teasing to erotic plunder, his fingers sliding up her thigh beneath the silk of her underthings. When he kissed her again, she kissed him back with a growing heat that made his hands quicken upon her body until she cried out, wanting something more . . .

〜〜〜〜

GOLDEN NIGHTS

GOLDEN NIGHTS

CHRISTINE MONSON

WARNER BOOKS

A Warner Communications Company

WARNER BOOKS EDITION

Cover design by Jackie Merri Meyer
Cover illustration by John Ennis

Warner Books, Inc.
666 Fifth Avenue
New York, N.Y. 10103

 A Warner Communications Company

Printed in the United States of America

First Printing: January, 1990

10 9 8 7 6 5 4 3 2 1

To the sun-kissed heights of Colorado,
our many good Colorado friends,
Tomcat and Lord Gore, as well as my bears,
most particularly, Jon.

Also with gratitude to Louis Dupuy's Hotel de Paris,
whose gracious doors did not open in time to be
enjoyed by the characters of this book.

ONE

Oh, Father, Dear Father

New York City: September 17, 1869.

"Father, when Aunt Francis came to tea yesterday, she asked if I had padded the attic for you. When I told her you'd gone to Bar Harbor to fish, she fixed her monocle on me with a gimlet-eyed stare and brayed, 'Nobody can keep a nut on ice forever, even the Maintrees.' " Suzanne Maintree raised her hands in exasperation. "When an old lady who doesn't know enough to clean marmalade from her mustache perceives my lies, how can you expect me to go on assuring the world that you're not eating the attic wallpaper?" Suzanne's tasselled Balmoral boot tapped the alley cobbles near a garbage scrap alive with vermin.

"You've a perfect right to tell the world anything you like, my dear, but Aunt Francis is correct," replied her father, fastidiously arranging a rag pile into a pillow for his back. "You may as well tell the truth. I am neither coming back from Bar Harbor nor descending from the attic." Edward Maintree could trace his lineage and aplomb back to a bastard son of Edward I of England. The Maintrees' American fortune stemmed from a small land grant awarded by Elizabeth I to a doughty ancestor who managed to survive Sir Franc Drake's circumnavigation of the globe. Despite his forebears

no swashbuckling lingered about Edward. A courtly, restrained man, he reminded many people of an Episcopalian
minister; even now, in his weathered black suit, he might
have been sitting crosslegged upon his pulpit, bizarrely at
ease. His tranquility provoked Suzanne to the end of her
patience.

"Do you want me to say that you have become"—she
struggled futilely for a polite phrase— "a drunken derelict?
That if anyone would care to call, you've moved to the second
alley off Bloomingdale Road and Tompkins Square?" Her
dark-lashed green eyes flashed as her contralto voice rose.
"Shall I suggest that if the gentlemen wish to join you for a
smoke at your new club, they must pass muster of the members?" Although she was too well bred to point at the drunken
derelicts lazing nearby, her fingers twitched. "Imagine being
blackballed by a level of society unable to decipher the al-
phabet unless it appears on a liquor label?"

Strung along the tenement alley, the Tompkins Square
bums watched with interest. Periodically, one of the respectable establishment assaulted their ranks to wrest a lost soul
from degradation. The retrievers displayed energy; the
quarry, a rheumy indifference. Today, as was common, the
miserable degenerate was an embarrassment to the retriever's
family. Most retrievers rated not a second glance; this one
was a four-star spectacle. A redhead, and no Fido. In the
garbage-strewn alley behind Hoffenstahl's Biergarten, one
saw few platinum-grade socialites. Ignoring the mud spat-
tering the white cashmere polonaise of her walking dress, she
stormed to and fro, the agitated, feline swish of her bustle
rousing a few reprobates to nostalgic lechery. Ignoring their
half-hearted mating invitations, she had been worrying her
tired, old dad for nearly two hours. She had hit all the familiar
persuasive notes, several corkers, and was reaching her final
resort.

A bum scratched the flea skimming his ribs. Final resort
heralded the heart render: the crux of the fray when the would-
be rescuer finally took the outcast seriously, and the outcast
either won or lost his dignity. That should be a Fourth of
July show; the looker had a hellish temper.

"Father, for the last time, hand over that liquor!" Alert and angry as a frustrated cat eyeing an indifferent fish in an inaccessible bowl, Suzanne Maintree circled her sire. The rustle of her green-and-white-striped skirt stilled with an ominous pause. "If you refuse, I shall throw myself under the wheels of the first carriage that passes. My death will be on your head!"

Over the rim of his schnapps bottle, Edward Maintree observed his daughter with the fatalism of a disappointed philosopher and the imperturbability of an experienced parent. At twenty, Suzanne had the magnificent looks and determination of her late mother. What charm and guile would not avail her, sheer obstinacy generally achieved. This afternoon, to the fascination of the curbside bums, she had pleaded, debated, and tiraded with an eloquence the famed actress, Adelaide Ristori, would have envied. Her battle to return him to the tattered dignity of the family fold was now lost, and she had retrenched to desperation. Her threat to dispatch herself might be melodramatic, but not entirely idle: she loved him staunchly and the brutal strain of his financial ruin made them both unpredictable. When he disappeared on the night of July 12, 1869, from their Lafayette Square townhouse into the bleak oblivion of the gutters, Edward knew his relatives considered him unhinged. Suzanne was obliged to face the family alone, as she must face society's scorn when his disgrace became public. At the moment, when he most longed to shield his daughter, her best chance for survival lay in his disappearance.

Judging by his daughter's white face, his lack of reaction to her threat had finally convinced her that all efforts were useless. Her golden complexion lacked its renowned glow, her green eyes their hypnotic allure. Her skin was sallow, her eyes glazed with growing despair. Like every young woman of status, Suzanne was overprotected. She was only now beginning to comprehend the hard reality, not only of his ruin, but of life. To overcome the hardships that must soon rain upon her, her hopelessness must be replaced with her customary dauntless energy. "My dear girl," he murmured with deflating practicality, "what if you threw yourself beneath a carriage and the wheels simply ruined your face?"

Suzanne's eyes shot sparks of indignation. "How can you ridicule me, papa! Have you so lost yourself in liquor and self-pity that you no longer care for anyone?" In three short steps she was upon him and the bottle. The bottle went crashing against the bricks of the Biergarten wall. Cowering bums shielded their heads.

Heedless of the splatter, Suzanne stared at the splotch on the bricks above her father's head. She sniffed the wall. "Water!" she gritted. "You haven't even the backbone to be a real drunk!"

Edward's eyes took on a glint of their own. "I have not yet cultivated a taste for fivepenny-a-gallon liquor, but if you would care to dispense the price of a good bottle of cognac before leaving, I shall endeavor to achieve an appropriate stupor."

The fight seeped out of Suzanne. The pearl-eyed white dove perched upon her tilted hat dipped low as she stooped to take his hands. "Oh, papa, do forgive me, but I am at wit's end. Why did you wait so long to tell me that you were losing everything? I might have sold mother's jewels. You might have endured another year, reversed your losses . . ."

"But more likely have lost every last penny. Besides, most of the jewels are paste; Mr. Charles Tiffany already owns the best of them." Edward smiled faintly. "Darling, your grandfather was the first gentleman in our family to evade the drudgery of business. Grandfather lived well and generously. He gave to every public foundation who approached him, and maintained your grandmother like a queen." He patted her hand. "In sum, he spent $9 million in his lifetime and left a debt of $3 million. I managed to pay off three-quarters of that debt. Unfortunately, last year, I lost that Pennsylvania trunk railroad to Jay Gould because he persuaded several of your grandfather's creditors to recall their loans. My levelling 'teeter' tottered." He tidied the water flecks from Suzanne's skirt. "The remaining jewels are your insurance; if you are thrifty, they will maintain you decently until you marry Marcus." His eyes held hers. "If you still mean to marry him."

"Of course, I do," Suzanne replied without a shred of doubt. Marcus Hampton was the last problem on her mind. To see her gentle father sitting straight among these huddled, hopeless men broke her heart. Her father's posture held a subtle defiance never previously evidenced. Edward Maintree was a scholar bred not only to a sheltered life, but to duty.

Although beyond Suzanne's appreciation, dereliction held philosophical luxuries for Edward. Now he had time to think and dream, time to write poetry in penny notebooks. He pitied Suzanne, but not himself. His life had been full despite its heartaches. Two years after Suzanne's birth, his vibrant young wife, Marguerite, died trying to bear him a son. Yet the joy that she had loved him endured all his life.

Yes, Edward reflected as he regarded his distraught daughter, I have been blessed, but I wonder if Suzanne will be as fortunate. Without a mother's guidance, she has grown headstrong and too certain of her looks and position. She means to marry a man as proud.

And with equally depressing ambition, she first meant to salvage his pride.

"You must come home with me now, papa," she coaxed with a winsome charm leavened by partly recovered assurance. From her first dewy-eyed gurgle in the crib, Suzanne had never been obliged to pick up so much as a rattle if a man was convenient. "Marcus and his mother are escorting me to one of Mrs. Margaret Astor's balls tonight. I shall take the opportunity to tell Marcus you have been ill, that there have been difficulties. We shall move the wedding to November first rather than wait until Christmas."

"Why do that?" Edward asked sharply.

"Because Marcus will want to help. He can spare enough money to cover those remaining loans . . ."

"Because he is fond of me," Edward finished dryly.

"Papa, I know you were disinclined to Marcus's suit, but he has always wanted to earn your regard."

"Darling, I'm not sure he is inclined to purchase it."

"Papa"—Suzanne pressed his arm reassuringly—"the loan is temporary. You will repay him as faithfully as you did grandfather's creditors for twenty years. Why is Marcus so different from a bank?''

"A bank can invade only a portion of my privacy, while Marcus Hampton will feast upon it all. Because he will have my daughter and my humiliation as collateral. Because''— Edward's normally serene blue eyes hardened—"I cannot abide the man.''

Suzanne stared at him. "Papa, you agreed to Marcus. Besides, you were rarely taken with any of the men who pursued me.''

"Because they were either weak or frock-coated brutes like Gould; Marcus is neither one nor the other. For all his fine manners and looks, he's shapeless, secretive. Do you notice he never really says anything? He talks of art, the latest divas, flatters the women, is clever with the men, but he never enters the conversation.''

"Papa, I prefer Marcus's subtlety," Suzanne countered with only faint indignation. Edward's flat rejection of Marcus at this late date bemused her. Virtually every eligible bachelor in New York had courted her during the past two years. She was not only the city's most beautiful debutante, but one of the most cultivated, having been schooled in Paris. She had glamour, intelligence, and a fine bloodline as prestigious as the Van Rensselaers, Brevoorts, and other great patroon families. Enjoying her reign to the hilt, she had been in no rush to choose a husband. Edward had neither pressed her to choose nor commented upon her choice this spring. Why should he now object so vehemently to Marcus? Was he attempting to cushion the blow should Marcus prove reluctant to wed a dowerless bride?

Suzanne forced herself to be patient. Her father's world had been overturned; quite naturally, he feared hers might be toppled as well. Marcus assuredly wanted her. Secretive or not, he could barely restrain his desire when they were alone. She excited him, and he excited her. So far, she had yielded nothing she should not, but she wanted his kisses, to hear his breathless words of impatience for their wedding night. How could she confide such unmaidenly eagerness to her father? Besides, her attachment to Marcus was not merely one of passion.

"Marcus has been educated in England and seen more of the continent than Vanderbilt's ships. He's also far from frivolous. Marcus has increased his inheritance twofold in the past seven years. There is more to Marcus than meets the eye and that is why I find him intriguing."

"A pickpocket is intriguing. Marcus has increased his fortune by helping the Jerome brothers destroy other businessmen."

Suzanne sighed with growing exasperation. Across the alley's sliver of sky, the afternoon light was waning, but had her surroundings been as notorious as Murderers' Alley, she would not have budged. "Papa, jealous gossip has always circulated about the Jeromes, and if you disapprove of Marcus, why did you not say so when he asked for my hand?"

"Because you would have eloped. How can a man say no when he has said yes too often?"

The point struck home, eliciting a wince. "Have I been dreadful, papa?" Suzanne whispered, her self-assurance vanishing. "A disappointment to you?"

"Do thorns make a rose less sweet?" he asked softly. His hands clasped hers with increased firmness. "I ask only if you love Marcus."

Her lovely green eyes were startled, her hands steady. She had good hands for a horsewoman, with never a false message from them. "Of course, I do. What woman would not?"

Your mother would not, Edward reflected. Suzanne's love for Marcus Hampton was not the sort that endured a lifetime, but she was too young to be convinced of it. Long ago, he had learned the folly of attempting to force her from a course upon which she was determined. She required a strong, but clever hand, and he had never been clever in the world's eyes. "Go home to Marcus, darling," he whispered. "I wish you both every happiness."

Her hands tightened on his. "You are not coming?" she breathed, tears filling her eyes.

He shook his head.

"Then I shall come to you," she replied defiantly.

"No," he said firmly. "If you come again, I shall not be here. I am where I wish to be. I have endured more than I liked of a gentleman's existence. Believe that, and go on with your life."

"No," was the staunch reply. "I shall not leave you."

With a sigh, he pondered the shapeless pouches of men slack against the filthy walls; many reclined on garbage. The tenement deathtraps advanced across New York like a monstrous plague. Men like John Jacob Astor, Goelet, and his own father had created this misery by leasing the land to landlords as grasping as themselves, then looking the other way. He had written much in his penny notebooks besides poetry, but wondered if he would ever have the courage to let Suzanne read, far less experience, this horror.

How could he ever abandon her again? He saw again her small child's face pressed against the nursery windows when his carriage entered the drive at Lafayette Square. His responsibilities so usurped his time that she pattered after him at home like a kitten begging to play.

No matter how pressed he was by his schedule in New York, he had supper with her three times a week, even if he planned to dine again elsewhere. From the age of eight, she conferred with the cook to ensure his favorite dishes and polished her conversation to suit what she imagined to be his tastes. The polish increased, and her beguiling awkwardness became expertise. A consummate, if naive, seductress, her accomplished wiles had won her Marcus Hampton. He had only himself to blame. During those swiftly passing, precious years while she tried almost pathetically to lure him into sharing her young life, he had been able to spare only a fortnight at each summer's end at Broadacre, their Connecticut country house. And now, he had all the time in the world.

"Very well, you have won." A hired carriage waited for Suzanne at the distant alley entrance. She had risked much to come here, but not the discretion of the family driver. "Ask the hackman for the loan of his coat. I can hardly be driven to my front door in these soiled clothes."

Elated by her victory, Suzanne hugged him, ignoring the

damage to her dress. She whirled and ran toward the hackman, then abruptly halted. Fiercely, she turned to meet the bums' impassive stares.

As she feared, Edward was already gone.

With transparent envy, Bradford Hoth watched Marcus whirl Suzanne around the ballroom of the Astor's new mansion on Fifth Avenue and Forty-fifth Street. In her white satin gown, and with a small diamond and pearl tiara glittering in her titian hair, she resembled a marvelous, spinning taper. Compared to Suzanne's vibrance, the marble perfection of the nude Psyche mirrored at the far end of the ballroom faded to that of pretentious rock. Suzanne was said to have English skin, but although he had never been nearer to England than a Walter Scott novel, Brad was certain few ladies of that misty isle could rival her glorious ivory and rose complexion.

Bradford was not alone in his admiration. Fully a dozen bachelors were gazing at her graceful figure as morosely as he. We're a sad lot of hounds thwarted by the fox, he reflected, with me the runt of the pack. His auburn hair and ruddy features were passable, but Maintrees did not marry common meatpackers from Chicago like the Hoths. His father's millions merely bought social invitations that permitted him to bay at the moon. Some months after his being introduced to her at a Goelet ball, Suzanne permitted him into her circle of admirers. Brad was smitten. Not only was Suzanne breathtaking and exciting, she refrained from making parvenues miserable. Such compassion, he had come to believe, had vanished like the dodo from the highest elevations of society.

Brad arranged to meet her by seeming happenstance when she occasionally went driving alone on rainy afternoons. Renting horses day after day to catch a glimpse of her was not inexpensive, but Brad counted his money well spent. Once, they conversed about horses and the West until she laughed and said he reminded her of her father. "His eyes light up like yours when he imagines travelling to Stratford-on-Avon." Her betrothal to Marcus Hampton was the blight upon his comparatively lonely life in New York.

She appears unhappy tonight, Bradford thought as Suzanne and Marcus danced past him. She loves the polka, yet appears to take no joy in it. Something is the matter. I wonder if she has had a spat with Marcus.

Foolish, irrepressible hope surged in his heart. Could Suzanne mean to end the engagement? But hope quickly faded. What if she did jilt Marcus Hampton? Hampton's loss would not improve his own chances. Still, he could not help being concerned—and madly curious.

Marcus Hampton was less so. He was preoccupied.

Marcus seems miles away tonight, thought Suzanne as her handsome fiancé nimbly skipped her through the polka. His conversation was as deft as his feet, but his dark eyes were abstractedly drawn to surrounding faces, and walls lined with mediocre Barbizon School paintings. I did not think speaking of father would prove so difficult. She felt shy and awkward, sensations new to one who customarily braved haughty doyennes in their dens without a tremor. Still depressed from seeing her father that afternoon, she scarcely wanted to talk to anyone . . . yet surely she could vent her feelings to Marcus. His perceptiveness was sometimes unnerving. They often laughed at the elaborate facades of dignity constructed by the New York elite, the shams of cultivation and gentility that overlay private scandals and quarrels. Now she was feigning serenity while a nightmare of apprehension reeled through her mind. Where is my father tonight? she wondered in distraction. In what cold, miserable alley will he sleep? What if I truly never see him again?

She stumbled, felt Marcus's unfaltering support cover the error. "Marcus, I . . . really don't care to finish this dance. May we please find a quiet salon and sit through the next set?"

"Won't our retiring appear rather strange?" he countered. "You rarely miss a waltz, far less a whole set."

When have we ever cared what people thought? Suzanne was tempted to retort, but held her tongue. Tonight of all nights, honey must prevail over vinegar. "I am rather tired, Marcus. I was at Madame Arnaud's most of the afternoon."

She was not about to admit she had passed the afternoon trying to lure her father from a drain gutter.

Marcus's smooth, olive face was guileless, too guileless for his innate subtlety. "Ah, yes, your trousseau fitting. Women do endure so much to make a perfect presentation." He kissed her hand as he led her from the floor. "You poor darling, you should have told me. Of course, we'll have a rest."

All right, you know I'm lying; don't belabor it, Suzanne bridled distractedly

He escorted her to a salon bordering the ballroom, where only discipline kept her from sagging onto a plush Lawford sofa. Despite heavy curtains at the closed windows, the muted rattle of carriages was audible from Fifth Avenue. Three massive arrangements of *Gloire de Paris* roses were vased on claw-footed gilt *etagères* between the windows. *I feel I am attending papa's funeral,* Suzanne thought, *and Marcus means to bill me for the coffin.* She stole a peek at him through her eyelashes. Hovering solicitously in his black tuxedo, he did resemble an undertaker—a slightly impatient undertaker. Her father's warning flickered through her mind.

"Shall I fetch a punch, darling?" Marcus offered.

"No, but please do sit down, dear." *Don't loom.* With an effort, Suzanne pulled herself together and banished her misgivings. Marcus had been her confidant before becoming her fiancé. He was too clever to be managed by the usual feminine methods, which made him a pleasurable challenge. She decided to be charming, but direct; playing the tragedienne tonight might permanently concede him the upper hand in their relationship. She had no intention of grovelling under any man's heel, least of all Marcus's. Mutual respect was the keystone of marriage. She assumed a decorous, but seductive posture, calculated to the rise and fall of her decolletage. "I need your advice, Marcus, about a grievous matter. I have come to rely upon your strength and good judgement."

"Of course." Marcus settled into the tufted cushions about six inches away. Generally, in such circumstances he was close enough to kiss her neck.

"My father has come into financial trouble," she began with resolution. She described the recalled loans.

"I see," responded Marcus soberly. "How frightful for him."

Encouraged by his sympathetic tone, she continued. "Father needs money, Marcus; not a great deal as these transactions go . . . perhaps $220,000."

"That isn't a trifling amount." The same sober tone.

"But certainly not an impossible sum," she stonewalled, "and father's credit record was impeccable before losing that trunk line." She looked at him with an expression of entreaty only flint-hearted old John Jacob Astor himself could have denied. "Marcus, I know it's a great deal to ask, but would you loan him the money? You would be repaid with interest within the next five years." Four hours with Edward's banker yesterday had provided her a rude education. The counter bribes to the creditors alone would cost in excess of $50,000.

Marcus looked faintly amused. "Darling, where did you ever get the idea that I could afford such a sum?"

Her assurance was jolted. "Everyone knows you're well off, Marcus."

He wagged his head. "I have a few millions, yes, but they are almost entirely tied up in real estate. Actually, I live on a fairly modest personal income."

"Keeping polo ponies at the Westchester Polo Club . . . and a ninety-foot sloop doesn't precisely entail dwelling beneath a mushroom."

"I absorb losses on those nags, you know." He idly stroked the long, white curve of her neck. "Georgia Brown lost in the ninth just last week, cost me nearly $5,000."

She tensed beneath his fingertips. "Does Georgia's laggard pace mean that my father cannot expect your help?"

"Did he ask you to approach me?" Marcus inquired languidly.

"You know he didn't."

"No, he never liked me. Just as well we aren't financially entangled, I suppose."

Suzanne suddenly went cold, as if encountering a coiled

cobra. "Why do I have the feeling that you relish father's misfortune?"

His fondling halted. "Darling, what a thing to say. You know I never bear grudges. Live and let live."

She detached his fingers from her neck. "Your generosity is commendable." Ignoring his wounded expression, she rose from the divan to angrily confront him. "Had you already heard of father's loss before I told you?"

Marcus rested his arm along the sofa's curved back. "As a matter of fact, yes " His apologetic smile was as smoothly arranged as his pomaded black locks. "These things do get about all too quickly, you know. The Union League is as gossipy as a sewing circle, and as for the Observatory Club, well, you know how they are."

Numb, she walked away from him. "Those Union League war hawks are already stabbing the needle into father because he refused to desert the old Union Club when they allowed the Southern members to resign rather than be ejected. And the Jerome brothers' Observatory clique deliberately destroys reputations for profit." She turned. "Dare I hope you refrained from joining them, Marcus?"

"Darling, I have the greatest respect for your father . . . despite our differences. I should have preferred to deny the gossip flung at him, but then I could hardly lie, could I? By the end of the week, the real facts will be out." Marcus sighed. "I see you are disappointed in me."

With a pensive frown, he rose, tucked his hands into his pockets, and began to slowly pace as if perturbed. "Your father never really thought I was good enough for you. Considering that I am in no position to help you now, I fear you have reached the same conclusion as he." Pausing, he contemplated her with the genuine regret of a mink cheated of all but a whiff of his ladylove's civet. "What can I say? I understand your lack of confidence, yet foresee no possible peace can issue from its poison. In truth, my own honor and nature disincline me to bear such undeserved scorn." He clasped her shoulders. "My dearest love, my lost love, although it wounds me to the heart, I must bid you farewell."

Suzanne buried her small, hard fist in his stomach. "You execrable actor," she hissed with satisfaction at his pained explosion of breath. "You snivelling, vindictive eel." Dancing out of reach of his angry grab for her wrist, she wrenched up a flower vase. Blouson roses and swamp-tainted water transformed her dapper fiancé into a sodden arbor ornament. Scarlet with rage, he squelched in long strides after her when she ran for another vase. His hands missed her chignoned curls by a hair as a firm male hand caught him by the scruff.

"You, sir, have clearly wearied this young lady's forbearance," said Bradford Hoth curtly, his freckles standing out brightly on his incensed face. "Not only that, you have attempted to lay violent hands upon her person. If you care to preserve your farcical reputation as a gentleman, you will immediately leave this room." All this was dictated as Bradford forcefully propelled Marcus toward the door.

"The bitch attacked me," protested the struggling Marcus in dumbfounded outrage.

"Bitch!" Suzanne rounded after him, but not before Bradford twirled Marcus in his tracks and with a smash to the nose, spread him upon the carpeting. Suzanne gaped in wide-eyed dismay at his slack, unconscious jaw. "Oh, Marcus."

Bradford was tempted to step on Marcus's face as he helped Suzanne to the sofa; instead, he sidestepped the body as if it were a pig dropping. He settled Suzanne against the cushions, but took care to take her into his arms again as he sat beside her. Closing his eyes, he rested his cheek against her marvelous hair. "Dear, darling Suzanne, I know how you must feel. The rotter ought to be horsewhipped. He must have been looking for a way to break the engagement once he learned about your father. How terrible for you."

Suzanne's eyes opened dazedly as he stroked her hair. "How do you know about papa? How could you? . . ."

He flushed, his freckles brightening again in his honest young face. When embarrassed, he resembled a square-jawed mastiff, healthy and full of energy, yet fearful of reproof for tumbling over furniture. "I sensed something was wrong tonight. I thought I could help. Well . . . I knew Marcus was with you, of course, but somehow . . ."

"You listened." She finished rather succinctly for one choking on tears.

His flush deepened to the roots of his curly auburn hair. "I'm afraid so. I am dreadfully sorry."

She sat up. "I'm not. At least, not dreadfully. Everyone is bound to know by tomorrow; Marcus will delight in telling them. Father will appear as some sort of swindler and I shall be a hatchet murderess."

"Not necessarily," Brad comforted, glumly aware she was right. Marcus would hasten to cover his own reprehensible conduct. Suzanne and her father would be humiliated. He tried to think. "Miss Maintree, if I may ask, does your father plan to issue a statement regarding his losses?"

"My father," she said with hollow finality, "is gone. He saw his ruin as irretrievable and his continued presence a liability to me. Aside from a few relatives with modest incomes, I am alone."

Bradford's attention fixed upon Marcus's ignominiously limp figure. "Miss Maintree, forgive me, but did your father leave you any means of support?"

She laughed shortly. "Enough to last until I married Marcus. I should say I shall be a long time in marrying anyone."

His brown eyes lighting with inspiration, he clasped her hand. "See here, your situation need not be so bad as all that . . . I mean, well . . ." He hesitated, then plunged on. "Would you consider marrying me?"

The droop disappeared from her shoulders as if he had dropped a mouse down her bodice. She blinked. "You, Mr. Hoth? Are you serious?"

Brad dug a finger into his choking collar. "I do realize my proposal is rather sudden and I'm not the sort of husband you might have envisioned, but . . ."—his voice trickled off— "but . . . I love you." The shock on her faced jarred into confusion, then sobriety. His fragile hope crumpled. She must be seeking a tactful way to escape his rash importunity. He could almost hear his father's derisive summation of his smitten stratagem. Nitwit. Brad smiled weakly. "Well, now, the horrible truth is out, and you can laugh."

"I do not think you are amusing, Mr. Hoth," Suzanne

responded in soft wonder, her lustrous eyes warming with gratitude, "but . . . truly, I do not see how you could love me when we have spoken of little together but horses and cactus."

"I loved you before you said a word to me," he replied faintly. "I'm afraid I found the cactus discussion more memorable than you realize."

"But Mr. Hoth . . . Bradford"—she fell silent, then gazed with sad conviction into his eyes—"don't you see you are merely infatuated, that tomorrow's reality must bring disillusionment? I am unsure of my ability to make any man a good wife." Her eyes faltered. "Father had quite a stern talk with me . . . when I saw him last. I am vain and selfish, you know . . . and I have a vile temper." She waved wanly at the broken vase. "There lies the proof. No, you do not want me."

From Brad's point of view, her brave honesty elevated her onto a pedestal in the dreamy reaches of myth. Never had Suzanne's radiant beauty seemed more perfect to him, more compelling. Filled with desperation, he caught her hands. "I do want you. I just never had any hope of having you before. Why should you look at me when there were so many others?"

Distraught, she pulled away. "There are no others now, and unlikely to be. Beauty is a short-lived commodity, I realize now. Wealth endures. No man in New York society will marry me for my looks alone, particularly after Marcus sullies my reputation. I cannot marry you, Mr. Hoth."

Bradford's mind worked frantically. He had to persuade her. Fate must have intended this moment; otherwise, how could he be given such an opportunity? He must succeed.

"Miss Maintree, listen to me. You need money: I have money. A married woman has some protection from scandal, and if Marcus Hampton attempts slander, I shall silence him in court. Between my banking contacts and my father's friends, I can ensure your father a new business position, a chance to redeem his losses. Don't you see this is a splendid opportunity for him? If we act immediately, he can say he

has merely altered his business direction, not forsaken it."
He made her face him again. "You can also counter Marcus
Hampton's accusations by declaring he has turned vindictive
because you ended the engagement to marry me. No one will
approve of me, of course, and they will think you are misled,
but your course of action will be believable." He took a deep
breath. "Oh, please, Suzanne; dearest Suzanne, don't refuse
me. If all this mess hadn't happened, you might have married
Hampton. Some good fortune has come out of your misfortune. A gaming man might say you are on a roll."

Her daze diminishing, Suzanne listened with mixed confusion and reluctant fascination. Bradford Hoth was mad, of
course, but he meant well. And he was kind. He would never
know what such kindness meant to her at this moment. Probably he was ten times Marcus Hampton's worth for all Marcus's millions and calculating charm. Still . . .

Touching Bradford's cheek regretfully, Suzanne rose from
the sofa with a sweep of her skirts that heralded a final rejection as delicately practiced as the graceful waft of a gei-
sha's fan. And then, as he gazed up at her with misery mounting in his eyes, she found herself reconsidering. His offer
had undeniable advantages, particularly for her father. And
for once in her life, she had to admit she needed male support
and protection. New York was a man's preserve and without
a man, she was bearbait. Bradford Hoth was reasonably attractive, personable, and if not well educated by her standards, willing to learn. On the other hand, she was not blind
to the advantages she could bring to the Hoths. She had looks,
polish, brains, youth, and the Maintree bloodline. She was
—the word gagged her—breedable. As rough-hewn Chica-
goans were not finicky about skeletons in family closets,
Bradford Hoth could do a great deal worse.

And so could she.

Bradford's fervent kiss at their wedding the following Fri-
day was not altogether reassuring. His hands were damp with
anxious anticipation; his embrace was awkward, yet his lack
of finesse concerned Suzanne less than his ardor. Keeping

Bradford at bay in the bedroom would require some skill. While she meant to honor her marital obligations, she had no intention of producing a dozen children.

They left the justice of the peace's modest office over-flowing with flowers. Bradford was fairly skipping with anticipation; Suzanne was, if not precisely tranquil, resigned. After he handed her into the enormous, rented four plus and directed the cabbie to the Marquis Hotel, she conversed with him comfortably, even with a degree of affection, but her mind was elsewhere. Her fingers locked about her bridal bouquet, she stoically surveyed her future. Unlike Bradford, Suzanne had no illusions about the marriage. Residence in Chicago might as well be exile in Tibet. Windy City society would be barbarous, their chief topic of conversation the acquisition of money. But why be hypocritical? New York society might shun mention of money to the point of being ludicrous, but they concentrated on it as relentlessly as their raw Chicago rivals. With luck, she and Bradford would lead a pleasant, if predictable life into a ripe old age. In due time, they might each take discreet lovers and follow their separate pursuits; she was willing to compromise, although certain requirements must be met. Their house would be situated on Lake Shore Drive and decorated by a respectable New York firm; she would not have some puffed up haberdasher turning her house into a gilded saloon. They must join the best art and literary guilds to advance and improve the local cultural climate. Her children would not inherit an uncultivated society.

Bradford would undoubtedly be amenable. His solicitor called on Marcus the morning after the war of the roses. Whether bullied or bluffed by threat of court suit, Marcus agreed to hold his tongue about the broken engagement. Also, Bradford hired a detective to return her father to the fold. Whatever happened, Edward Maintree would be cared for, and once his safety was assured, she could stand anything.

Feeling Bradford trying to inveigle his fingers through hers, she dutifully unlocked her grip on the bouquet to accept his hand. "You have become very quiet these past minutes," he said, his voice holding a note of nervousness. Then he laughed awkwardly. His hair was still wet from his comb, his square face as scrubbed as a boy hoping for an extra dessert. "You are not reconsidering, I hope."

"Oh, no," she reassured him with a forced smile beneath her hat veil, "I am entirely committed to you, Bradford."

Vastly relieved, he patted her kid-gloved hand shyly and readmired her pale pink silk bridal costume as if she were an endless supply of gilt-wrapped petits fours. "Are you thinking of tonight?"

Dear me, no, she wanted to blurt; I want to think of anything but that. Where intimacy with Marcus Hampton had once spun swan's-down illusions of exquisite seduction, wine and roses, the same experience with Bradford implied the grate of squeaking bedsprings. A Parisian schoolmate had described the sounds that accompanied them. Between a man's legs was *l'équipage* that stallions sported so shamelessly. According to the schoolmate's more worldly sister, *l'équipage* was inserted *là*, where the little ponies were produced. The procedure was *très* overwhelming. Considering the grandeur of equine development, Suzanne was suitably overwhelmed and still unconvinced the whole *delicieusement* was merely concocted from the languishing imaginings of prepubescent Parisiennes.

"Perhaps . . ."—her voice seemed to emerge improperly —"perhaps I am the slightest bit nervous, Bradford." She hesitated. "I . . . do not suppose you . . . do you have any experience?"

He was taken aback. She could almost hear him debating whether to lie, fabricate a fairy tale, or admit the awful truth that he was, or was not, a virgin. "Well, I have had a trifling experience," he finally conceded, then patted her hand consolingly. "You really needn't worry, you know. It's rather like rowing a dinghy."

A dinghy. Suzanne weakly closed her eyes.

A liveried room service captain ushered dinner into the white-brocaded bridal suite at the hotel. Suzanne waited in the dressing room until Bradford dismissed him, then sidling through the sitting room door, gave her bridegroom a resolutely brilliant smile. He lit up at the cling of her lilac silk dinner dress. Hand-stitched by Madame Arnaud, the high-necked bodice had filmy panels of Alençon lace that displayed demurely alluring glimpses of her shoulders and arms. Coming forward, he held out his hands. "You look like a goddess, darling. I'm the luckiest man in the world."

Clasping his hands, she forced herself not to flinch from his kiss. "I'm fortunate, too, Bradford," she said honestly. "You have been unfailingly kind and considerate. I hope to make you a good wife."

"Darling, how could such a paragon do anything else? I'll be the envy of every man in Chicago!" His eyes took on an unfamiliar glint of gloating triumph. "My father will be pea green when I bring back a Maintree. I'll show him!"

Suddenly wondering whether he had married her for love or display, she was both dismayed and affronted. "Does such acclaim mean a great deal to you, Bradford?"

"It does to everyone, I suppose. Don't you enjoy wearing the prettiest dress at the ball?"

"Yes, but on the other hand"—she affected a teasing pout to hide her growing alarm—"I doubt if one of my frocks would fit a tennis trophy."

"You mustn't mind my showing you off." With a tolerant chuckle he pinched her cheek. "You're quite a prize for a modest fellow like me."

Although his expression was reassuring, she could not banish a lingering trace of disillusionment and distaste at being patronized. "Very well, if it pleases you, but Bradford dear"—her green eyes curved up at him with a hint of warning—"unruly brat that I was at the age of four, I once pinched back an uncle who pinched my cheek." At his blanch, she amended mildly, "We got along very well after the boundaries were established. He did not pinch, and I did not let my cat sleep on his lawn chair."

A rueful smile slanted his lips. "I promise I won't pinch in the future." He wound his arm in hers, his eyes filled with adoration. "And I shall try not to be too proud of you."

Attributing her fears to wedding night nerves, she squeezed

his arm in affectionate reassurance. "Then I promise not to empty ink pens into your watch pockets. Shall we have dinner now?"

Either Bradford had exerted a great deal of consideration on the menu or relied upon the acumen of the maître d'; the meal was perfect. Consommé, peppered oysters, hothouse asparagus hollandaise, and veal marquis were accompanied by three excellent wines and two champagnes. Nothing was excessive; the coffee and truffled chocolates made a light finish. Suzanne wondered if a preoccupied digestion interfered with lovemaking; if so, Bradford might be more experienced than he claimed.

With leering Cupids festooned about her imagination, she attempted to prolong the coffee finale as long as possible. "What a pity your father could not be here for the wedding," she ventured, "but then a week was not much notice."

Brad's attention came up quickly from his coffeecup. "No . . . I daresay his reply to the telegram I sent him in San Francisco may be some days yet in arrival. He had business in California."

"Yes, you told me." A trace of anxiety darkened her eyes. "You don't suppose he will be displeased by your choice of a penniless bride, do you? My being a Maintree may be insufficient. . . ."

"No, no, he'll be delighted, I'm sure . . . once he's met you." The last comment emerged from under the linen napkin as Bradford blotted at his skimpy mustache. He smiled awkwardly. "Father likes his way, but he also admires a pretty ankle." His boyish features turned pink. "From my slight observation, yours are superb . . . if you don't mind my saying so."

"I don't mind," she replied gently, "and thank you for the compliment." Bradford really was sweet. She liked his ingenuousness, his shyness. Her father would like him, too. Bradford was genuine, without a calculating notion in his head. Why had she not recognized his decency before now?

Because, dear girl, dame conscience reminded, you were too vain a peacock. You presumed character to be a preserve of the elderly. Do not cheat this fine, young Galahad of the illusion that he loves you. Poor boy, he looks as nervous as you feel.

Fortified by generations of enterprising ancestry, she returned her cup for the final time to its saucer and ventured faintly, "Do you suppose it is too early to retire, Bradford?"

He blinked, swallowed. "No," he croaked. Then, almost comical relief passed over his reddening face. "No, I should be delighted . . . I mean . . . well . . . oh!" He bolted to his feet, then hastened around the table to help her from her chair. As if she were made of glass, he escorted her to the bedchamber door. "I suppose you would like a few minutes alone, so I'll have a cigar . . . more if you like."

"I imagine one cigar should prove adequate." Suzanne delicately closed the door.

Why didn't I ask him to smoke twenty cigars? she railed a bare half-hour later. Panting from the exertion of shoving her corset and bustle frame under the bed to conceal them from view, she slumped on the carpet in a pool of French lace. Her bustle resolutely refused to fit into the hotel drawers and she could scarcely hang the thing in the armoire next to Bradford's frock coats. As for French lace—she railed at the Gauls with feeling—the French were a lascivious lot whose civilization was in deserved decline due to their unprincipled morality. Her peignoir and nightgown were a racy, beribboned disgrace. Righteously forgetting her insistence upon diaphanous ecru lingerie for her trousseau upon her engagement to Marcus Hampton, she resolved to write the *atelier* in the morning!

But until then . . . Bradford Hoth would be treated to an unhindered view of his new Maintree property. Suzanne snatched an angora shawl from the back of a rocker. "Brad, dear," she called tremulously.

In two seconds flat, he came through the door and saw the shawl. "Oh, my delectable darling, you won't need that," he breathed. Then whisked the shawl to the floor.

At two A.M., a bellboy knocked at the suite door. A disheveled Bradford jerked the door open with ill concealed impatience. "Can't you read a 'do not disturb' sign?"

The bellboy handed him a telegram. "Sorry, sir, but this is marked urgent."

Bradford ripped open the envelope. "Oh, God," he whispered.

TWO

Baa, Baa, Black Sheep

When Suzanne opened her eyes the next morning, she was alone. She did not need to call for Bradford. The silent suite held that inhuman emptiness hotels engender despite their passing throngs of inhabitants. Brad's absence brought dull relief. Last night had been shameful, dreadful. She did not hate him, but she never wanted him to come near her again. The bellboy's interruption had been her salvation; only horror of creating more scandal had prevented her from darting under Bradford's arm at the door and fleeing the hotel.

She flung back the bedclothes and began to pack. Camisoles, petticoats, fox furs: everything funneled into yawning carpetbags dragged from the dressing room. Then as she dashed into the bathroom, the icy marble under her bare feet chilled her to a halt, her sturdy boar bristle toothbrush dropping into the sink. No . . . no, she would not run. She was Mrs. Bradford Hoth, with all the prerogatives that position entailed. She would live with Bradford, but not share his bed; he owed her a decent privacy, at least. She would dress and wait for him. Dreading the scene that must follow, she ran back to the bedroom and dug her bustle from beneath the bed.

Twelve hours passed without sign of Bradford. Having twice sent room service away, she was now starved . . . and furious. How dare he humiliate her, then leave her alone so long without a word, without even saying where he was going? The rocker jarred back and forth to the tedious tick of the mantelpiece clock.

Early the next morning, a knock at the suite door jerked Suzanne awake. Groggily, she stumbled through the dawn gloom to answer the summons. A whiskered man in a bowler hat and cheap suit appraised her. "You with Bradford Hoth?" he rasped.

"I am Mrs. Hoth. What do you want?" In no mood to be polite to a creature who smelled of mouldy cheese, she closed the door a fraction.

He chewed a toothpick. "I'm a detective. Your husband hired me day before yesterday to find a certain party . . ."

Grasping his arm, she pulled him into the sitting room. "Where is he?"

His bushy eyebrow lifted. "Hoth?"

"Bother Bradford Hoth! Where is the man you were sent to find: Edward Maintree?"

"Dunno. Ain't had time to find him yet." The detective glanced past her shoulder at the half-packed valises visible through the open bedroom door. "Checking out this morning?"

"What?" Suzanne collected herself. This man was paid to find answers, not ask questions. "No, we have not yet unpacked."

"Occupied, huh?" He smiled suggestively.

Perceiving his drift, she gave him an Astor-like stare. "Please state your business, sir."

"Sure." The toothpick shifted. "Where's your husband?"

"You may discuss any information that concerns Edward Maintree with me," Suzanne replied with mounting impatience. "My husband employed your services at my behest."

The detective drifted past her toward the bedroom door. She blocked him. He sighed. "Look, lady, if Hoth's in there, you may as well tell me. I'm gonna collect one way or another."

"You wish to be paid after scarcely two days on the job?" Suzanne's tone was withering. "Sir, you have scant cause for alarm. I am a Maintree and my husband is a . . ."

"Skipperdee." The detective's toothpick took on a deprecating slant. "He's skipped, ain't he?" At her questioning frown, he elaborated. "Scooted. Left town. Dodged the bill collector."

"Why should he?" demanded Suzanne, fed up. She measured the yardage to the suite door. A few dollars should foist the nasty brute out. Before she hoisted her lance, the detective interrupted again.

"Where've you been, lady?" Leer. "Besides slappin' the springs with your skipperdee?" Perceiving her intent to slap him, he edged away. He also sensed her genuine bewilderment. "Ain't you heard? As of yesterday, the gold market flushed down the drain. Jim Fisk got caught out trying to corner the whole show when President Ulysses S. Grant pulled the plug, had his treasury secretary drop $4 million in government gold on the exchange. Fisk lost his underwear and so did everybody who put in their oar with him. Your husband promised to pay me in gold shares. I'll bet he dropped a bundle."

The bellboy, Suzanne recalled in growing chagrin. The bellboy must have informed Bradford of the crash on their wedding night. Good heavens, had Bradford "skipped"?

Inconceivable. Being from Chicago did not make him a crooked carnival act.

"Just how much does Mr. Hoth owe you, Mr. . . . ?" Once rid of this detective, she would make her own inquiries.

He appraised the canary diamond brooch at the throat of her cinnamon silk dress. "Fifty dollars . . . plus expenses."

The amount was absurd. "You have receipts?"

"Sure," he lied.

"Then I shall pay you twenty-five dollars and the rest when you return with those receipts. As I was not party to your financial arrangements with my husband, I mean to establish the customary rate for investigative services. I shall speak with the chief of police to that effect this afternoon. He is a personal friend of my father's. Apply tomorrow to Sergeant Masterson of the First Precinct and he will settle your bill." She regally waved him to the door. "And now, I must bid you good morning."

He was suitably chastened, but disgruntled. And immovable. "I don't leave without my twenty-five dollars."

"Then please wait by the door." As he plodded to the door, she went to the bedroom dresser to fetch her reticule. Once containing twenty gold pieces, the reticule was empty except for a hastily folded sheet of hotel stationery. "Gone to Mexico. Matter of life and death. If you love me, burn this . . . Brad."

Love you? *Love You!* Her teeth gritted, Suzanne wadded the stationery into a shrunken ball she wished was Bradford's head. With all the dignity she could muster, she yielded Detective Cheese her brooch. He leered again before he left.

She slung on her furs and went directly to Bradford's bank, Gilstrap and Mather. As Bradford was a bank officer and board member, she anticipated no difficulty in speaking privately to the bank president. She was correct, but for the wrong reason. After twenty minutes and a great many more terse words, Mr. Roberts Holgarth, the bank president, informed her that Bradford's father, Ramsey Hoth, was a board member; Bradford was little more than a glorified clerk. Upon the morning of September 20, Bradford had embezzled $30,000 which the bank believed he invested in gold futures as his security box still held the now worthless certificates. Bradford could look forward to twenty years of prison porridge.

Ramsey Hoth stalked into the office while Suzanne's jaw was still sagging. "I see you told her," he snarled, his flaming red hair and Grant-style beard bristling. "This the gold-digging chippie you telegraphed me about, Bobby?" A broad block of a man, he wheeled on her, his black cashmere overcoat billowing like a variety show villain's. He had been a handsome man before whiskey and power settled his eyes back into puffy creases which blurred the strong slabs of facial bone and predatory nose like fat across a cut of raw meat. Petulance tinged the determination that compressed his generous mouth into an irascible, granite line. "Come to pick the bones, have you?" She caught an odor of Havana cigars as he bent over the swivel chair with a contemptuous glare. "Well, the bones are picked and the marriage is off. Scram." `

"Whom do you think you're addressing?" she snapped, still tremulous from reaction to his offspring's perfidy. "Your son may be a criminal, but I am certainly not! How can you hold me responsible . . ."

He chopped a curt hand in front of her indignant face. "Shut up. Your old man lost his money and you got dumped by a rich mark, so you latched onto my boy. Why the hell do you think he took that bank money, eh?" His broad beard jutted as if preparing to sweep her under the carpet. "To buy you. And you sold like a whorehouse floosie. So don't give me hoity-toity. You're back on the sidewalk, girl." He wheeled on the balding Holgarth. "You say nothing, Bobby. Hear? I'll cover the loss, but if you or any of your flunkies opens his mouth about this mess, I'll cram it down your throats. I'll pull so many assets out of this bank your heads will spin. Got me?"

Holgarth nodded with ministerial gravity. "I guarantee the discretion of Gilstrap and Mather . . . provided the sum is immediately settled."

Hoth slapped a money belt on Holgarth's desk. "In cash. No record. I want those certificates and I want to see those corrected ledgers before I catch the midnight train back to Chicago."

"Not San Francisco?" demanded Suzanne shakenly.

He stared at her. "Why the hell would I want to go all the way to San Francisco?"

She stood up, her clefted chin lifted. "Because Bradford led me to believe you were in San Francisco at the time the wedding took place. Your boy tells a great many lies, and I begin to see why. I can certainly understand why you might be upset with him, but you have no comprehension of justice. You're a rough-necked bully, Mr. Hoth; as blindly single-minded as an angry bull. I am vastly relieved that I shall not have to endure you at my dinner table for the next twenty years."

Hoth's glower deepened at her rebuke, but by the end of it, his mood altered to sardonic amusement. "Well, aren't you the persnickety little cowbird. Think you can flit right up to the old bull and polish the flies right off his horns."

His brawny hand slapped the money belt on the desk. "Just don't think you can hit on the old bull for any cash."

"I shouldn't think of living off your flies, Mr. Hoth," Suzanne retorted icily. Her green eyes glacial, she headed for the door. "And I shall be little troubled to avoid your company in future merely by watching for . . . bullpies on the carpeting."

"Well, I'll be damned," Ramsey Hoth swore with a tinge of admiration as the door slammed. "Brad got himself a doily-trimmed heller."

The heller dismally contemplated throwing herself in the river as she walked the twelve blocks home in a downpour. She dared not return to the Marquis Hotel without money to pay the bill. The account would be settled, as sufficient cash remained in her father's wall safe to last for a few weeks, but after that reserve expired, she must sell private belongings. Like the drenching rain, reality was a fast descending, blackening storm. The gossips would take to the deluge like ducks. She had been jilted by one man, and deserted by another on her wedding night. She was minus family, husband, income, and reputation; all because of the men in her life. Men who said they loved her!

With tears running down her cheeks, she glared wrathfully up at the lightning. God help the next rotten sneak who pretends to love me!

At the moment, the next rotten sneak had a more pressing matter than romance on his mind. Had Suzanne thrown herself naked into his arms, Kimberly Smith-Gordon would have dropped her on her delectable without time for apologies. His *cojones* were in immediate danger of being razored off by a machete and exhibited on an anthill by a gentleman named Juan Michaelo Luiz Sanchez Jesus di Montoya and a number of *vaqueros* sporting equally lengthy names and short tolerance for being cheated.

To the huge harpy eagle kiting the jungle-swathed plain between the Sierra Madre Oriental Mountains and the Mexican coast, Kimberly Smith-Gordon and the thirty specks in pursuit resembled an irregular stream of ants. Undiverted on its downward sail toward the sun-baked palm trees, the harpy was intent on the rabbit skittering the rutted road ahead of the first pell-mell rider.

With perspiration pouring into his eyes, Kim swore under his breath at the rabbit scrambling nearly beneath his straining horse's hooves. "Make way, you long-eared little turd! If this nag trips over you, I'll cram your tail up your tiny arse!"

His Spanich was fluent, but perhaps his British accent confused the Mexican rabbit. The horse tripped, the rabbit squealed, and Kim went head over keester. The sky spun like a cloudy toy top. In time, he lifted his head, surveyed the struggling horse, the flat rabbit, the nearing pursuers, and mumbled, "Shit."

All of which was the rabbit's and spread a surprising distance.

After a woozy struggle to his knees, Kim peered between his thighs at the approaching dust cloud which proclaimed his doom. "Mother, your brightest child will never go to Oxford." His being a decade past entry age was irrelevant. He preferred to please women whenever possible. An immediate lie usually satisfied a female so long as one never lingered to contend with her disappointment.

This *Senor* Juan di Montoya was as temperamental as a woman, and very disappointed in him. The proud *hidalgo* was also overreacting. By dint of a golden ore sample, Kim had attempted to persuade Montoya to come up with $20,000 for several shares in the Colorado claim that produced it. Montoya's enthusiasm stopped lamentably short of faith in his fellow man. Kim's collection call upon the faithless *haciendado* was met with rifles and machetes. Fortunately, noticing the sun's gleam on the welcoming party's armaments, Kim turned shrewd tail and ran for his life.

He was used to running since the age of six, but by the age of twenty-six, had grown somewhat weary of it. Kim's sigh was choked off by the dust rising from his horse wreck. Coughing, he clambered unsteadily to his feet, then with a heartfelt wince of regret, shot his mount. Not worth a damn, the nag was as dumb as the rabbit that downed it, but he never liked killing animals. "You're too sensitive to go into business," his father used to tell him proudly, "but with luck, you'll make a first-rate safecracker."

Luck. He had lost a half-dozen fortunes in a breath. Lady Luck was fond of him, but no clinging vine. Now he was stuck in the middle of a mosquito-infested jungle with a toy Mexican army on his tail, while Lady Luck's unladylike mirth echoed through the palms. He jerked his rifle from the saddle scabbard, wrenched his saddlebags free of the horse's lax bulk, and dove into the brush just as the first riders bore down on him. The dust resettled, the harpy scouted the dead rabbit, then soared away in disgust.

"*Que pasó?*" demanded Esmerelda, her strong peasant's fingers curiously tracing a red scratch that transected the faded white scar along Kim's tanned collarbone. Among the network of livid scratches were other scars, occasionally in places that fascinated even Esmerelda, who was as excited by goring as a matador.

Kim stretched his long, brown body, luxuriating on cool, clean sheets. Esmerelda provided the best in amenities and *amore*, in sleepy, seaside Alvarado. She was unreasonably priced, but upon their first sultry night together, he put all idea of reimbursement from her head. Like most women, Esmerelda adored him, and like most whores, was a good listener. After a bottle of tequila, he still had phony names in his story straight. Esmerelda would probably sell him to the real Montoya for a pinata. Resting his shaggy blonde head on her shoulder, Kim continued his tale. "*El Lobo*'s men rode after me until the undergrowth became impenetrable, then hacked through the jungle with their machetes."

Another pull at the tequila failed to dim his recollection of the real, grinding fear of clawing through the Orientale's suffocating rainforest. With thorn-shredded clothing exposing his hide to leeching garrapata ticks, he wormed through liana-laced jungle into a mangrove swamp that exhibited an exhilarating display of poisonous snakes and ominously agitated

dung-green water. At every sweltering second, he expected
either his head to be cleaved by a machete or his leg to be
bitten off by something whose teeth outnumbered his own.
Close shaves were nothing new, but he was paying entirely
too many visits to the barber.

Terror scuttled through his life as frequently as the roaches
across Esmerelda's floor; such roaches preceded black-
carapaced nightmares whose mandibles gnawed the nerves.
As a philosophical El Paso lady once described him, "You're
an alley cat who's been in too many fights, Jack. You're all
balls, claws and no character . . . but you got a hell of a
twinkle in your eye."

Few women could precisely describe what they saw in him.
In his grandest flight of vainglory, he would not have called
himself handsome. Weathering made him appear half a
decade older than his age and the recurring realignment of
his nose ran aslant of a drowsy, scapegrace smile. He was
mostly one color, tawny brown with golden points, like a
sun-loving mountain lion: he moved like one. Where the
puma's eyes were yellow, Kim's were the cobalt blue of a
cloudless desert. His rare show of teeth led the unwary to
presume he was tame, until presented with bitemarks on whatever part of them had prodded him too far.

The empty tequila bottle sliding from his relaxed fingers
to the floor, Kim's lean, beard-stubbled cheek settled comfortably into the impatient Esmerelda's plump neck. With a
mutter of exasperation, she climbed astride his flat stomach.
"Hey!"—a less than playful bounce in his midsection accompanied by a protest in Spanish obliterated his inclination
to sleep.

With considerable effort, he shoved her weighty rear down
to his pelvic bones to save his stomach from collapse. "Forgive me . . . where was I?"

"Up to here in the jungle." She sliced meaningfully at her
neck.

"Oh, yes . . . finally, I stumbled into a swamp restless
with crocodiles to sink beneath the ooze amid the jeers of *El
Lobo* and his gang. I am only alive because they were too

miserably hot to wait for my scraps to surface." Well warmed with tequila, he polished off the tale by knifing a monster crocodile before walking all the way to Alvarado without a drop to drink.

Appropriately impressed, Esmerelda showed her admiration by fucking him silly for another free hour. With a sigh of gratification, he finally flopped onto his back to smile happily up at Juan di Montoya's murderously patient face. Kim's hand shot beneath the pillow for his gun, only to discover it poised in the dainty hand that ten minutes ago had been expertly wringing his equipment with farm bred vigor. "Esmerelda," he sighed, "you are the bride of a donkey's heart."

She cuffed him daintily with the gun muzzle, then kicked him out of bed so he would not bloody her sheets. She was more annoyed when he carried most of the bedclothes with him. "You owe me 720 pesos for two days this week and sixteen nights last month, Smith-Gordon. Plus two hours Sunday afternoon, the twelfth of May. You think I screw *per niente*?"

Deliberately, the naked Kim applied the corner of her lace bedspread to his damaged head. "You might have gritted your teeth one night while you bit the buttons off my fly for *niente, chiquita*, but sixteen nights? Come, confess you like me the least little bit."

"I kill you!" Her large breasts swinging, she swiped at the bedspread with one hand, and at his head with the gun.

A hair ahead of Kim, Montoya snatched the gun. "Enough. I have no patience for squabbling."

"When you had patience enough to watch me boff this sow for God knows how long?" Kim ducked Esmerelda again to confront the *hidalgo*'s menacing gun. Distraction was definitely not working. Perspiration beading his brow, he hastily reshaped his strategy as fear nosed a cold, wet trail down his spine. Montoya was *muy macho*, but not *muy* bright. Hauling the sheet to his neck, the lanky Kim exuded the indignant distaste of a virgin appraising an elderly bridegroom. "Not sporting, old man. A lady's boudoir may be within blood-letting bounds but a whore's is neutral territory." His sandy head swivelled toward Esmerelda. "Tell him, Sugar. If he shoots me wrapped in your sheets, they'll never be virginal again."

"Outside, Montoya," Esmerelda ordered regally, "then chop him into little bits."

"Thank you, sweet." Kim's gratitude was sardonically saccharine as Montoya grimly allowed him to rise. "You always were a sentimental harpy."

Unable to define *harpy*, Esmerelda registered *insult*. "I tell Montoya your mine is a fake, you toad," she hissed victoriously in dismayingly clear English. "Who you think you kidding, walking around Alvarado with an ore sample the size of a bull's balls. Nobody with a good claim would waste two minutes in a pigsty like Alvarado. Eh?"

Kim longed to give Esmerelda's truculent jaw a good crack, but he had ignored that one transparent discrepancy in his scam. With rueful gallantry, he kissed her hand. "I salute you, Madame. You're a credit to cottage industry."

Wondering if she had been reinsulted, Esmerelda frowned as he headed to the armoire for his clothes.

"No, Smith-Gordon," snapped Montoya. "You go as you are. We shall see how you enjoy being made the buffoon."

His stomach knotting in frustration, Kim tensely halted in mid-stride. His .38 revolver was in the armoire and the rusty key required about three bullets in the back to turn. He eyed Montoya with genuine impatience. "I have considered you a man of principle, Montoya. Do you mean me to stroll from this bordello wearing nothing but the best of this lady's hope chest?"

"I do," stated the *hidalgo*, who received an immediate argument from the lady. Kim hoisted the flag of Esmerelda's habitual surrender about his loins. "You will also carry the saddlebag, Smith-Gordon," Montoya added as a fillip to his victory, "like a pack animal, but I promise"—his voice acquired a vindictive ring—"your public humiliation will be brief. When I have you alone, you will wish I had paraded you to Mexico City."

"You want to be alone with me?" Kim lifted a suggestive eyebrow as he swung the saddlebags over his bare shoulder.

"Move!" Montoya fairly screamed at him. "Move or I blow your balls off!"

Kim blew a kiss to Esmerelda, plucked up his sheet hem, and moved.

Partway down the narrow stairway to the bordello's cantina, Kim glanced over his shoulder at Montoya, who was on his heels. "Tell me something, Montoya. Why chase me so diligently because of a paltry failed swindle?"

"Pride," snarled Montoya. "A sentiment for which you have no understanding."

"Oh, I daresay my education is somewhat lacking compared to yours, but in our rustic *yanqui* lexicon, there is a saying. Pride goeth . . ." Dropping his sheet, he stepped aside as Montoya tripped over it and crashed headfirst down the stairs to lie inert at its foot. "Ah, you do know how that tired old saw goes . . ."

Minutes later, Kim emerged from the bordello into Alvarado's dusty main street. He was wearing Montoya's *caballero* attire with Montoya's bare rump neatly folded over the shoulder not occupied by his saddlebag. Montoya's men exploded in hoots of laughter. After all, when the *padrone* in his silver-embroidered black suit and his splendid sombrero tipped low against the broiling sun, emerges from a bordello with a bare-assed *yanqui* swinging limply from his shoulder like a plucked monkey, one must give vent to amusement. The *padrone* always gets his man, *si*?

Kim's saddlebag arm laboriously lifted to acknowledge the cheers. The saddlebag was heavy, Montoya heavier still. He had better exit before a ribald *vaquero* noticed that the limp head sifting powdered wall plaster into the dust was not a natural blonde. He issued two more matador salutes to the thirty surrounding men and strode resolutely down the street to the harbor. Although confused, they instantly started to follow him. Kim wheeled, Montoya's head circling like a *bola*, and jabbed out his hand, palm out. Comprehending, the men halted. Their formidable *padrone* meant to dump the dead *yanqui* in the drink. New murmurs of admiration trailed after the figure staggering with the weight of his naked victim. The bordello fight was as silent as a jaguar's attack . . . the *padrone* must have strangled the *yanqui* in his squalid bed of pleasure. Several of them hurried into the bordello to test the squalor of the beds.

Upon arrival at the waterfront, Kim fought for breath and against the impulse to heave Montoya into the harbor. Dispatching a helpless man like a rat would be unjust. Also, Montoya might be able to swim. *"Hola!"* he croaked up at the Portuguese shipmaster peering down with fascination at Montoya's fuzzy buttocks. "I've bagged a fine, plump ship jumper."

"Not mine." The Portuguese spat a yellow stream of tobacco juice over the gunnel.

"Yours," Kim panted insistently. "For free. *Comprendes?*"

The Portuguese's gold teeth gleamed. *"Comprendes.* Not mine."

Kim fished in his pocket for some of Montoya's money, and awkwardly brandished it. "Yours. Any more negotiation and I drown the hairy fart." He dumped Montoya in the dust, which rose in a little gasp of protest.

The Portuguese tallied the upstretched pesos, then his arm jerked at the heap in the dust. *"Si, si,* I know that ass anywhere. Hoist it up." When the heap betrayed a hint of protest, Kim dropped his ore-weighted saddlebag on its head. The heap resettled.

In due time, the *vaqueros* came in search of their *padrone,* but did not find him. The Portuguese ship was *vamos* up the coast, to drop Kim at Vera Cruz before proceeding to Montoya's next port of call: Liberia, North Africa.

The first person Kim encountered on the Vera Cruz quay was Bradford Hoth. With a wolfish smile, Kim appraised Bradford's earnest face, banker's suit, and hangdog air. A lamb on the lam, ready to be fleeced. Kim approached, shears poised.

THREE

Bullpies and Broomsticks

"Ho! *Senora!*"

Unaccustomed to being addressed in terms of *ho*, or *senora*, Suzanne did not turn. Lowering her parasol against the sweep of wind from New York harbor, she crossed Fourth Street after another disheartening search for Edward Maintree. As she dodged a spotted dog pursuing a cat, the cry came again. "Ho! *Senora* Hoth!" Curbing her impulse to either bolt from her pursuer or pelt him with a rock, she maintained a steady pace.

In the month after Bradford's disappearance, she held her head high, albeit with stern effort. Once the gold crash hullaballoo died down, civic interest pounced upon the unhappy wretches in its rubble. Not that the newspapers picked up Bradford's embezzlement. For all the public knew, Bradford Hoth had found his new bride lacking in some horrendous way and vanished to drown his disappointment. The *Herald Tribune* inferred he joined the French Foreign Legion; the *New York Monitor* that he was gambling away his father's millions in Monte Carlo. The *Penny Spender*, a pedestrian rag, insisted he was drinking himself to death on Canal Street.

Edward Maintree's ruin was picayune compared to some of the crashed fortunes, so his mention was mercifully rare. Suzanne might have gone equally unnoticed, except for her marriage to Bradford Hoth. Inner circle gossip, abetted by Marcus Hampton, hinted that she was afflicted with some peculiar deformity or disease, even with galloping imbecility. If she had encountered her missing bridegroom on the street, she would have ripped out his every fingernail and bitten for his heart.

"*Senora*," a swarthy man hissed so closely at her ear that she nearly leaped in fright, "I have word from your husband."

Every ounce of discipline was called upon to prevent her grasping the burly Latin by his lapels and snarling, "Tell me where the bastard is so I can kill him!" Instead, she said, "Really?" and regally waited.

The Latin, who wore a seaman's uniform, did not introduce himself, but appraised her with marked appreciation. "I have a package and letter from your husband. He says not to worry. He is well."

How disappointing, thought Suzanne. Do you mean this package does not contain his ear or preferably some other, more intimate part of his anatomy? My whole sense of justice denies that blithering Bradford is "well"! Aloud, she said, "How nice, and who are you?"

"I cannot say." He shoved the package at her and darted back into the carriage traffic.

Suzanne dropped the package like a bomb, only to snatch it up again for fear someone else might want it. After hurrying home to tremulously unwrap the box in privacy, she discovered it contained a rock. She contemplated the rock for some time, her ambitions horrible. Then, relenting somewhat, she decided Bradford was demented. His insanity would explain everything and relieve her of the crippling burden of revenge. Almost genially, she scanned his letter without a hope in the world of its proposing an end of their marriage and relieving her of him. She was right. He still loved her madly, and would make everything up to her.

Only a photograph of you, my own, displayed in a straitjacket, on the front page of the *Tribune*, she estimated fondly, would make everything up to me.

After four pages of ardor and apology, but no reference to his address, Suzanne concluded Bradford was a lost cause. She must initiate her own divorce proceedings. In seven years, she would be free; also, middle-aged, penniless, de-

serted, and divorced. She would have to trek to Alaska for
a husband who wanted a wife to crack his socks out of the
icy wash basin and pull his sled.

The letter's fifth page blotted her tears. Bradford had found
a gold mine; that is, he had purchased a Colorado gold mine
partnership with his private funds.

My private funds, she rephrased judiciously, and the dredg-
ings from the funds stolen from the bank. Bradford did not
dwell upon his income source. According to his letter, the
mine assay was splendidly promising, and production from
his share would repay his bank losses. He means to ask me
for more money, she decided, proceeding to page six. Page
six advised her to examine the rock. A wry, reluctant smile
curved her lips. No doubt, the rock was a crystal ball which
reflected Brad's adoring face. She tolerantly rotated the rock
. . . to see lovely threads of gold flicker like a tempting web.
Mesmerized, she revolved the rock, staring at the gleaming
tracery of precious metal.

For many nights thereafter, Suzanne saw that web in her
dreams: a lure of gold bedewed in diamonds shivering beneath
waltzing spiders of emerald, pearl, and ruby.

Kim swore, then kicked Bill Howard's valise across the
room. The valise careened an impressive distance, for nothing
was in it. The valise was a decoy, its owner flown. For nearly
a month, Kim had shared this shabby hotel room with Bill,
carefully sized him up, won his trust, and confided to him
the secret of his Colorado gold claim. He was convinced Bill
was ducking some minor offense, because Bill had no criminal expertise. Bill's mooning neglect of the local whores
suggested the problem was female. His family was probably
peeved because he had rendered some girl pregnant. He paid
his hotel tab on time, kept his suits pressed and shoes shined.
He wore a half-carat diamond ring, a sapphire stickpin, and
kept $5,300 in U.S. currency and $8,000 in Erie Railroad
stock tucked underneath his mattress. Bill was well worth
Kim's while, for his own rusty-hulled passage from Alvarado
had nearly emptied his pockets. Bill was not as prosperous

as Juan di Montoya, but far more naive. And his name was probably as bogus as Kim's own.

"I don't mind telling you, I'm in a jam," Kim complained somberly to Bill one night after they had polished off a bottle of tequila in a waterfront cantina. His voice lowered to a convincing note of bleary despair. "My throat would be cut in a second if anyone suspected I had this ore sample; the gold in it alone is worth $600. I can't risk selling it in Vera Cruz, but lack the price of a boat ticket back to the States. Like Midas, I'm starving while I'm stinking with money."

"I've never seen gold in the raw. Would you show me the ore?" whispered Bill eagerly.

Like I could show a pup his buttered biscuit, Kim conceded benevolently. Upon displaying the gold, he was only slightly disappointed when Bill offered the price of a steamship ticket as down payment on a claim share. A good hunter never discouraged a willing retriever. To clinch the deal, Kim provided an impressively engraved certificate of mining stock, identical down to the serial number, to the share held by Montoya. Bill's sudden chagrin about his inability to forge his alias on claim shares was mildly intriguing. Application of the alias "Bill Howard" to a legal document was a waste of ink to one unaccustomed to forgery. If Bill were afraid of inviting legal trouble by signing his real name, he might have done more than diddle where he ought not.

Bill dodged the issue. "Suppose we leave the certificate blank for the time being," he proposed. "I'll pay your ship passage as proof of my good faith if I, say, want to buy more than just a quarter interest in the claim when we reach Colorado."

Kim patted him on the back. "Well, I declare, Bill, that sounds decent. I knew you were square when we first met." He should have remembered excessive decency trails a whiff of deceit. Bill was as asymmetrical as a trapezoid.

After filching the ore sample and blank gold claim certificates, Bill departed on the next ship to New Orleans without purchasing a ticket for his new partner who was down to his last stolen centavo.

If matters continued at this jerkwater level, Kim decided in disgust, he might have to sell the other half of the ore sample cached under the hotel room floorboards.

Suzanne Maintree's straits became only slightly less dire than Kimberly Smith-Gordon's. Six months passed without word from either Bradford or her father. She had searched most of New York for Edward Maintree until sick with worry. She feared he might be dead. The most valuable household items were sold, the servants were let go, and the house itself was to be auctioned. Her relatives discreetly hinted that her notoriety might decline in California, preferably the Baha Peninsula where the sea gulls fancied Maintrees were a form of bird perch. In short, she was on the streets.

Suzanne was in a panic.

Her mind dwelt upon the gold-threaded ore hidden in her sewing box. The ore became a darkling promise of hope, albeit tainted by the possibility of deceit. When had Bradford done other than lie? After cheating her of home and respectability, why should he not continue his charade to prevent her from taking him to court and claiming a settlement?

And yet, what if Bradford were not lying? What if he was bamboozled into buying part of a fraudulent claim? Such hoaxes were perpetrated every day, particularly upon would-be highfliers like Bradford. If an honest man could not be cheated, Suzanne reflected grimly, then her beloved was the prime patsy of New York. She had learned words like *patsy*, *shill*, and *shyster* from the street bums she still plied for information about Edward. Her once lofty view of their plight had plummeted to pity, particularly after she ventured inside the tenements; residence upon a newspaper was preferable to a rickety hellhole where people were crammed nine to a closet. Now she never ventured to the slums without generously dispensing her dwindling food and clothing.

She was far more concerned for Edward's future than her own, although her notoriety and the scarcity of respectable employment after the crash blighted possibilities. Her essential courage and resourcefulness asserted she could support herself, and she would have whored if necessary to save her father. Her anguished heart and tattered sense of justice denied he should be reduced to miserable starvation while greedy monsters like Jay Gould and the Jerome brothers profited from his ruin.

All the while, a golden glimmer beckoned from the sewing box. What if Bradford's gold claim were real?

Suzanne realized how fully her waning hope was pinned on the claim when, a fortnight before the house auction, a telegram arrived to state that Bradford Hoth was dead. Drowned in a mining camp flash flood. If anyone had predicted Suzanne would one day weep for Bradford, she would have laughed. But penny dreadful imaginings of revenge were one thing, death was another. Now Suzanne wholeheartedly mourned a man who could do nothing right. Poor, deluded Bradford, who died still chasing rainbows. Who was he trying to impress? The world? His father? Or his wife who did not love him?

She stayed in her room for two days. On the first, she thought little about the rock in the sewing box; on the second, she pondered it a great deal. Brad's death hit hard, but the accompanying loss of hope was hideous. Unless . . .

Brad was alive. Her mind at bay, she explored every avenue of escape, so utterly did she distrust her—perhaps less than departed—husband.

Question: was the Colorado gold strike real or a ruse to initiate a goose chase? If the strike were a hoax, Brad would have sent those in pursuit of him yapping in the wrong direction and silenced her long enough to manage a comfortable escape to Tangier. But why would news of a man hunting gold in Colorado have come from Vera Cruz, Mexico? Why had a Mexican sea captain—his uniform was depicted in one of her father's books—deliver that ore package? And why had Bradford left that wedding night note that said he had gone to Mexico? Unless he *had* gone to Mexico.

Suppose Bradford had really purchased a partnership in a gold mine, not in Colorado, perhaps, but somewhere. Elated, he must have impulsively written her before venturing in search of the claim. Suppose he discovered the claim to be valuable, but reconsidered wading through the peril and expense of returning to the bosom of bank and family. Might he not prefer to play dead?

Suzanne speculatively tossed the ore sample in the air. Whether Bradford was alive or not, she meant to have a bit of her own back from him. She sent a telegram to Ramsey Hoth calculated to bring that gentleman roaring from Chicago in a hot rage.

"Threaten me, will you?" Ramsey bellowed as he paced before the auction podium in the Maintree parlor. "Come to New York or I'll regret it! I can have your silly neck snapped on any Sunday afternoon, what do you say to that, you cheeky bitch?"

"I should say you are more stupid than you are rude," replied Suzanne calmly. When he came for her, his long, fur-collared sack coat flapping, she quickly stepped with a stir of black crepe pleats behind a row of chairs. "You might listen. My proposal may mean money for you."

He halted, nostrils flared. "You mean the other way around."

"No, I mean all the way round, as in merry-go. I shouldn't bother with you if it weren't worth my while."

He glanced mockingly at the near empty rooms. "You're missing a few props for this medicine show, lady."

"Only the coffin, Mr. Hoth," she amended soberly. "Your son is dead."

Ramsey Hoth stared at her, his first confused disbelief giving way to denial, dismay, and outrage that passed like a blackening storm gust over a turbulent sea. For a bleak moment, an evanescent resemblance to his uncertain, desperate son transformed his pugnacious face, his eyes rounding like a stricken boy's. Moved by sympathy, Suzanne started to step toward him, but her impulse to offer comfort was dampened by the infuriated undercurrent that contended with his shock. Unable to tell which pained him more: his son's death or its occurrence without his permission, she concealed her impulse to pity. He felt for a chair and started to sit down, then did not, as she described the telegram from Colorado. "Is that what you wanted to tell me?" he demanded hoarsely. "You wanted revenge?"

"Not this kind of revenge. I should be glad if Bradford were alive. In fact, I think he is alive and laughing at all of us." She outlined her reasoning.

Ramsey scoffed. "You give that boy more brains than he ever had in his life." He went to the window, brushed back the heavy curtain to look out at the drizzle. "I'll concede Brad was gull enough to go for a phoney gold claim and blab about it to a scheming woman, but he had no real guile, no head for luring off the hounds." Letting the curtain drop, he smoothed its velvet as if erasing unwanted recollections. "He was a cheat who was outcheated, and now he's dead."

Shoving his big hands into his pockets, he peered dispassionately toward the dining room where there was an English sideboard carved with hounds in pursuit of a fleet hind. "We ought to drink to widowhood. You wouldn't have liked being married to my boy long." He arched a brow at the stylish black weeds rendered more severe by her slender, ramrod figure. "Brad's better off buried. You'd have gobbled him up like a tea sandwich."

"You must have been surprised when he married without your consent."

"I was that," he said flatly. "I never let him have enough money to cross me."

"And even more surprised that he became an embezzler."

His head turned slowly, his eyes icy. "He turned embezzler to support you, missy. If I'd figured he'd shove his hand in the till, I never would have put him in a bank to earn his living." By now he was catching the drift of her questions. "You figure he might surprise me again, don't you? That the kid's smarter than his old man thinks. How long did you know him before conning him into marrying you?" He smiled cynically at her closed face. "Surprised you, too, didn't he?"

"Your son proposed to me, Mr. Hoth, not the other way around." She clasped the carved rim of a chair. "But while Bradford fooled us both, he may conceivably do so again . . . if he is alive. If so, he has either found a claim or he has not. I say that the odds are probable that he is hale and hearty and having a large ho-ho at our expense." Moving down the aisle of chairs like a hunting cat, she watched him. "If Brad is alive without a claim, he should be punished; if he is alive with a claim, he should share it. If he is dead without a claim, we shall both mourn him; but, if he is dead with a claim, I should inherit."

Ramsey snorted. "What happened to 'we' on the last one?"

"I am Bradford's widow and by law, direct heiress to his estate. You cannot claim his claim without me; however, I am willing to share, for a certain price."

He dropped into a chair and stretched out his check-trousered legs with a dubious air. "What claim?"

"According to my reckoning, Bradford's gold claim has at least a modest chance of being real, and Bradford a better than average chance of being alive. Now you may not care about sharing a lode assayed at 1,000 ounces per ton, but I very much doubt if you will allow Bradford to put another one over on his 'old man.' "

His eyes narrowed, their skepticism touched with calculation. "Did Brad supply the assay figure?"

"I commissioned the assay." She hoisted the piece of ore from the podium dais and presented it to him like Cleopatra appraising Caesar.

He examined the ore. "Any two bit swindler could peddle this rock."

"So he could." Suzanne waited, her hands icy as her father's future dispassionately revolved in Ramsey Hoth's hand. If he tossed the rock back to her, she could plan on learning to make artificial flowers for ladies' hats . . . and didn't Ramsey know it.

His smile baited her. "Just what do you expect this bullpie to do for a share in your modestly authentic gold claim?"

Having expected he would not forget her original summation of him, she did not flinch. "I expect you to help me find Brad—publicly."

His dubious smile took on a glint of appreciation. "Not bad. Whether my boy turns up or not, you can't lose. You figure if I back you openly, I have to shove back your creditors for a while so people don't accuse me of letting my son's widow starve. Besides, how bad can the lovelorn bitch be, if old dad takes her into the family bosom. You get what you married Brad for: a name and a stake.''

"I have a name, Mr. Hoth; it's Maintree,'' Suzanne replied coolly, ''and I mean to resume it, whether I become a widow or a divorcée. As for a stake, I have no illusions about your extended benevolence. Once Bradford grants me a fair settlement, you will see the last of me.''

"I could see the last of you now by walking out that door and leaving it open for the auction vultures,'' he retorted. "Or I could find that claim myself and let you beat your head against the courthouse doors trying to collect it. With no money to pay a law firm for all the years I could keep the case running, you'd go gray before seeing a penny . . . particularly if I set a match to the marriage records.'' He eyed her sleepily. ''I could even have you killed.''

"Not quietly, Mr. Hoth. If anything happens to me, I have arranged for the story of Bradford's embezzlement to find its sordid way into the newspapers. Given sufficient annoyance, I may suffer a distraught lapse of discretion in advance.'' She looked down at him. ''Now, Mr. Hoth, do we do business?''

She expected him to explode; he did not. ''Do you know how to play poker, Mrs. Hoth?''

She sat down, because her knees would no longer hold her up. ''No. Will you teach me, Mr. Hoth?''

He nodded. ''Expect I will, considering we'll be spending some time together. Your only ace is blackmail, which is amateurish, but enterprising. You're trying to turn a pair of deuces into a full house; whether you turn out dumb and land on your bustle, or smart enough to find my boy alive, I'd like to see the last show of the cards. Be a real satisfaction to me, either way. But don't try cheating too soon. I generally shoot cheats and repent later.'' He smiled at her like a surfeited lion. ''Just one of my bullpie habits.''

FOUR

Tequila Flambé

Vera Cruz: June 15, 1879.

Ramsey Hoth's bullpie philosophy excluded sluggishness. Once decided upon a course of action, he followed it with alarming rapidity. Twenty minutes after leaving Suzanne to cancel her house auction, he telegraphed Denver; two hours after the wires stopped singing, Colorado began to crawl with Pinkertons in search of Brad and his gold mining claim. The logical place to begin the other end of the hunt was Vera Cruz. Three weeks after joining forces with Ramsey, Suzanne was in sunny Mexico, killing time and sweltering in the heat.

She refused to wait in the hotel while Ramsey made the rounds of Vera Cruz. Once the flying fur settled upon reunion of father and son, they would ally against her. She must wrest control of Brad from Ramsey by pitting her wiles against Ramsey's wrath. Ramsey would be some time in learning her threat of divorce was a bluff. Why slap another millstone around her neck when her current one could be converted into a life preserver?

I may never live with Bradford Hoth, she swore, but I'll be tinkered if I leave him. That miserable cheat owes me a respectable name and a roof over my head. A parasol the size of a salad bowl was certainly insufficient.

Beneath the parasol's rim, she grimly peered through the sopping lace of the handkerchief pressed to her brow. The swinging doors of Rosa's Cantina were unchanged in an hour; their neglected paint continued to peel in the briny Gulf of Mexico air; the men at the bar murmured in incomprehensible Spanish; the flies drifted in and out of the windows, around and about her face. In her stingy circle of shade, she swatted, and swore under her breath as perspiration pooled tranquilly in the dust around her pinching, patent-toed hightops. The heat was swelling her feet and her pink linen ruffles were wilting almost as pathetically as the curls across her flushed forehead. Ramsey must be having another drink, one of several at several waterfront dives. His advances into these iniquitous dens were now irregularly measured, but his benign salutes upon his emergences were as two-faced as Balaam's. He was deliberately making an ass of her

She would show him. She marched into the cantina and met the hot, blue-eyed gaze of a highly attractive *vaquero* seated at a poker table in the rear of the cantina. As her head lifted imperiously, but also with a trace of interest, he grinned in wicked invitation; one that she half regretted her inability to accept. She liked his face; there was something irresistibly engaging about his mischievous smile, that they shared a delicious, irreverent secret—an impression that was regrettably cut short.

As though her intruding toe set off a trip wire, a torrent of luminous, florid Spanish broke violently into English. "*Gordone*, you cheating *bastardo*, I'm going to break your face!" rattled across the gloomy, crowded cantina. An incensed, beefy poker player heaved over a table, then sailed his chair at the tall *yanqui* dressed like a Mexican *vaquero*.

The *yanqui* ducked without rancor, disengaging his long legs from his chair and several scrambling players. "Oh, come off it, Pedro," he cajoled with British tranquility, "you won seven hands. Do you want to turn into a bloody octopus?"

Unplacated, Pedro retaliated by seizing another chair. In seconds, the cantina became a melee of flying furniture and fists as the patrons became annoyed at the errant debris. The accused *bastardo* submarined from view. Alarmed, but undeterred, Suzanne clapped a hand to her rose-trimmed hat and ventured cautiously through the jostling slam of flesh in search of Ramsey. The racket and vehemence of the brawl soon reached epic proportions. The floor was slippery with spilled liquor and treacherous with fallen bodies, some still

thrashing in sodden struggle. Hearing a second huge crash
of the blackened mirror, Suzanne anxiously craned through
the flailing of a pair of old men, snapping and tearing at one
another's clothing like irate Pomeranians.

Suzanne's green eyes widened at a tequila bottle rocketing
for her head. As the bottle mouth assumed the width of a
shotgun bore, a hard arm locked around her neck and yanked
her to the floor. "Duck, darlin'!"

Suzanne recognized the British accent and white Mexican
camiso, but that was all. Devilish, phosphorescent cobalt eyes
in a tanned, beard-stubbled face blurred overhead before an
expert mouth that tasted of tequila closed over her own. Her
senses reacted as if a match had been set to the tequila. The
flame trail shot straight to the base of her belly. She was too
shocked to fight, too shocked to find she did not want to
fight. She felt only the scrape of his beard, the mobile, sultry
insistence of his mouth and whipcord body weighting her
down on the cracked tile. A long way from sober, Kim had
his leg between her thighs and a hand locked in her hair, but
she was as unprotesting as a hooded quail. His wide-brimmed
sombrero shut out the world. As tables, chairs, and glassware
smashed about them, she was oblivious. This was the un-
bridled, reckless excitement she expected from Marcus
Hampton, the elemental assurance missing in Bradford Hoth.
Why shouldn't a man make love to a hundred women on
barroom floors if practice made him perfect? Not even the
gunbelt digging into her hip distracted her concentration. She
was mastered, mesmerized, then . . . somewhere in her daze,
she realized this barroom soak was not only kissing her with
the rapture of an inspired artist, his hand was possessively
planted on her breast. Although his gunbelt had not shifted,
the *pistole* so shamelessly prominent beneath his loose *calzones* suggested the development of a hair trigger. Dim shadows of propriety skulked the edge of her bedazzlement, reared
up with a vengeance inspired by rebellious independence and
past pain. What did this Piccadilly cowboy think he was
doing! What if Ramsey Hoth saw him doing it? She grabbed
a fistful of his shaggy blonde hair and yanked.

Despite a muted sound of protest, Kim kept her firmly

pinned until he was done kissing her. Finally, his gilt-lashed blue eyes looked down into her flaring, outraged green eyes with a quizzical grin. "You and I have a problem, my sweet."

"What is that?" In angry futility, she pawed at his hand on her breast.

He peered glassily through the legs of the struggling men. "How do we wade through all this muck to the nearest bed?"

Her indignant retort was jostled out of her and cut short when he hauled her to her feet and hoisted her piggy-back. To her horror, he began to wade through the fray toward the stairs. He had long legs and a longer reach that calmly plucked combatants from his path. The man was serious! "Put me down!" she shrieked. "Are you crazy?"

"Don't worry, I used to cadge pennies in bars as a boy," he reassured her, his forearm fending off a bottle. "I'm good at this."

She had little doubt of it, and none that when availed of a bed, he would be altogether too good. Judging from the bulge in his *calzones*, boyhood was a dim memory. She had endured enough craziness this past year to fly into the embrace of a limey cock who merely wanted a giddy roll in the hay!

Planting the lace parasol strapped to her wrist across his throat, Suzanne cut off his air. His free hand caught at the parasol, but while unable to budge it, he refused to drop her. Victory neared when he began to stagger. Catching sight of Ramsey toe to toe with a bulky U.S. sailor near the bar, she steered her struggling steed through the melee. When he balked, she strangled him. He began to sag at Ramsey's side, and she prepared to dismount.

Unfortunately, Rosa, the cantina proprietress, battling with a chair at Suzanne's side, was struck down by a flying bottle. The torpedoed Rosa dropped her broad beam atop Suzanne, collapsing the stifled Kim beneath the petticoated pile.

While Ramsey pommelled away overhead, Suzanne heaved desperately at Rosa's inert bulk. Not only were her own corsetted ribs being crushed, Gordon showed no sign of breathing. He might be a lecherous sot, but his intrepid talents did not deserve to be squeezed out of existence by the elephantine posterior of a Mexican madame. She levered at Rosa with her parasol; it broke. "Ramsey!" she gasped. "Remove this horrid old bag!"

Ramsey's ears perked, but as Suzanne's bleat was but a drop in the din, he continued to smash face. A member of the assaulting force sailed across a table to remain under another one.

Her lace-mitted hands pressed upon the liquor-soaked floor, Suzanne gathered her diminished wind for another try, only to have a fallen gold watch fob snag her mitt. She tried to shake it loose, and between flurries, realized she had seen it before—dangling handsomely from Bradford Hoth's watch chain. Ramsey must have dropped it, except the chain led to the Briton lying on his face. The trail continued under the *camiso* pulled free of his dusty *vaquero* breeches into an untanned territory she hesitated to explore. Holding the little breath she had left, she slipped her fingers along the underside of his flat belly and probed inside his breeches.

"Jesus," murmured Kim faintly, "you are impetuous."

Her hand snaked out of his pants as if bitten.

"I'm not objecting, divine one," he drawled languuorously. "Just a trifle more down front and center, if you please."

"Ramsey!" she howled.

Upon noticing her, sheer delight at her frantic dishevelment crossed his face. He delivered a gleeful slam to his opponent's jaw that Suzanne would have found insulting had she been less eager to apply his brawn to her predicament. Leaving her to stew, he briskly turned to seek another adversary. "Ramsey," her voice soared another octave, "I've found your weasely brat!"

Wheeling, Ramsey boomed, "Where is he? I'll kill the little turd!"

She batted the sombrero from her captive's bemused face. "The trail begins here, provided"—her head jerked toward the unconscious Rosa—"you remove this cow."

A thrust from Ramsey's foot spilled Rosa over Kim's legs. "The trail"—Kim advised mildly—"leads nowhere, crippled."

Hooking his hands under Rosa's unsavory armpits, Ramsey

heaved her up. His face red from exertion, he toppled her like a redwood into the last of the battered, staggering brawlers. When Rosa's length crushed two men, the rest lost heart. With swollen faces, they wandered vaguely in search of felled *compadres*, pocket change, and unbroken bottles behind the bar. Ramsey righted a table, hoisted Kim, and dropped the groggy Briton face up on the table's surface as a brawny boy would a sack of groceries. "Now," Ramsey addressed his victim, "I butchered my first steer when I was six years old. I now own the biggest meatpacking plant in Chicago. If you don't tell me where my boy is, I'll chop you into low-grade hamburger. Got me?"

"Three cheers for luck and pluck," mocked the indomitable Briton, "Horatio Alger stories so inspire a poor lad like me."

Ramsey's jaw twitched. "I can take a hint. How much?"

Kim woozily sat up and brushed his thick, fair hair from his face. "How much is he worth?"

Ramsey shoved him back down again. "Your skin. Any more questions?"

Kim frowned in puzzlement. "Just one. Who are we talking about?"

"Bradford Hoth," gritted Ramsey.

Kim smiled apologetically, his teeth a quick, white flash against his tan. "You're never going to believe this . . . but I don't know Bradford Hoth from Miles Standish."

Suzanne caught Ramsey's descending fist. "Brad may have employed an alias."

Kim's bemused smile turned appreciative. "Thank you for enlightening your hamburger impresario. Tell me, why are you both being so decent, when we only met a paltry quarter of an hour ago?"

Suzanne almost smiled back. His narrow, aquiline face was not quite handsome, but extremely attractive, although she was unable to think why. His manner, if not his looks, reminded her of a choir boy secreting a frog beneath his cassock. No virgin to brawling, his once refined profile had gone rogue, the engaging slant to his grin counterpointing the skew to his nose. Sun-bleached nearly white, his tousled blonde hair looked as if his mother had forgotten to cut it. Those were the last of his boyish traits. Through his half-grown mustache and beard stubble, a thin, white scar curved the left side of his mouth. His genial blue eyes burned holes in her.

Defiantly meeting his bold gaze, Suzanne hooked a distasteful finger about the watch chain trailing across his thigh and swung the watch like a golden pendulum. "Does this look familiar, Mr. Hoth?"

Ramsey's meaty hand shot for Kim's throat. Before it connected, Kim adroitly rolled off the table to land lightly on his feet with a bowie knife from nowhere in his hand. While he was still amiable, he also appeared a good deal less drunk.

"Do refrain from snatching, Mr. Hamburger; I become jittery." The knife flicked into throwing position as Ramsey's hand darted forward.

"Don't." Smith-Gordon's British accent was now clipped. "I first resorted to mayhem when I was six years old, and today I own the largest collection of severed fingers in Mexico." Smith-Gordon smiled as Ramsey hesitated. "Ah, you also appreciate Mr. Alger's common sense. Now"—his foot hooked a chair and slid it toward Suzanne—"shall we sit down and discuss the mysterious Mr. Bradford Hoth."

Everyone warily sat, but no one said anything. Kim leaned back in his chair. "Well, here we are at the altar with the wedding off." He signalled the bartender who was sullenly taking inventory of damaged and stolen stock. "Bring your best, Malcolm, whatever it is. Mr. Hamburger is paying."

Ramsey glared. "Hoth, you smart ass. Mister Hoth."

Kim's impish blue gaze slid to Suzanne. "Heaven forfend this rumpled goddess should be Mrs. Hoth."

Suzanne could not help laughing at Ramsey's furious reaction to the affront. "I am the other Mrs. Hoth: Mrs. Bradford Hoth."

Kim's lips curved. "Suddenly, I am fascinated with Mr. Bradford Hoth. I assume he is departed; the question is whether only somewhat or altogether. While you must pardon my envious hope that he has reverted to the latter condition, why suppose I possess more information than you on the subject?''

She dangled the watch. "This belongs to Bradford."

"Ah." He glanced up as the barkeep planted three dirty shot glasses of rye whiskey on the table. "You mean Bill Howard."

"Bill Howard?" echoed Ramsey.

Kim kept looking at the bartender, who kept looking at him until Kim shifted his attention to Ramsey. "Malcolm won't go until he's paid. He knows I haven't a ringing centavo."

"Look, here," snapped Ramsey as the reimbursed Malcolm retired to his inventory, "where's my boy?"

"You mean Bill."

"I mean Bradford Hoth." Ramsey seized his whiskey, tossed it down. "Did you rob him?"

"The pilferage ran the other way." Delicately, Kim explained, enshrining his own pure character in a halo of lilies. Bill Howard, alias Bradford Hoth, had answered a legitimate mining stock deal by robbing him to the very camiso on his back, leaving him stranded and destitute.

"You, sir," said Ramsey flatly, "are the biggest liar that ever licked a barroom floor. The Pike's Peak gold fields are played out. You tried to cheat my boy, and you took his watch." He stood, towering over the grimy table. "Knife or no, I'm going to thrash the hell out of you."

The rattlesnake light that slithered into Kim's placid eyes pulsed fear down Suzanne's spine. "There's rather more hell to me than meets the eye, Mr. Hoth. Besides, if I were to become disgruntled, you might never see your son again." His stillness was that of a desert day without wind; a dry, deadly waiting that warned Ramsey would scarcely register the flick of the bowie's fang.

"Mr. Hoth . . . Ramsey," she intervened, "might we not learn more from this gentleman without resorting to threats? Particularly if he has proof of what he says."

Neither man moved. Finally, Ramsey carefully resumed his seat. "You have any proof, Mr . . . ?" He had cooled to an edge as hard and sharp as the bowie's.

"No," was the unruffled reply, "and my name is Smith-Gordon. Kimberly Smith-Gordon."

"Bradford left you nothing but this watch, Mr. Smith-Gordon?" queried Suzanne.

"Only because he forgot it," replied Kim, telling the truth for once. The watch chain had broken when Bradford Hoth rifled his bed for the claim certificates. "He also left behind 58 percent of the claim."

Sipping his rye, Kim waited for another storm of accusation from Ramsey. When the tycoon merely snorted his disbelief, Kim continued softly, "I know where your son has gone, Mr. Hoth. You'll find him only by transporting me out of Vera Cruz."

"Your price is a ship ticket?" Ramsey's voice held a note of contempt.

"I also expect ten dollars a day to act as your guide."

Ramsey scoffed. "A bum like you couldn't earn that in two weeks. Besides, I'm interested in information, not your company."

"You'll need both, Mr. Hoth"—Kim's eyes were level over the rye glass—"but you won't get either one if your manners don't improve."

"Why, you . . ." Ramsey's heavy shoulders strained the linen of his double-breasted sack coat, then relaxed. "Look," he grated, "I'll pay you a flat fee of $500 to tell me where he headed. You can buy a lot of coffee whores and hooch in New Orleans for $500."

Smith-Gordon glanced at Suzanne. Her cheekbones white, she was staring past his ear. "Your son owes me a hundred times that for the claim shares he stole, Mr. Hoth," he said gently, "and you owe Mrs. Hoth an apology."

The Chicago magnate's breath whistled through his teeth. "I'll reimburse you for $1,000, but Mrs. Hoth is no business of yours."

"Apologize, Mr. Hoth, or kiss off."

Suzanne had to admire Smith-Gordon or whatever his name really was. He was obliging the powerful Ramsey Hoth to grovel for a son who had disgraced him, a property he considered worthless, and the sensibilities of a woman he despised. Not only that, Smith-Gordon was threatening to sink back into poverty unless Ramsey gave in. The memory of his impudent, rakehell kiss still played havoc with her concentration, played upon her senses with the enveloping intensity of a sultry summer tempest. She must not let him distract her! She had to keep Ramsey in the game, because he was seeking a reason to throw in his hand. "This is a poker player," she advised her scarlet father-in-law. "Shall we let him deal the hand?"

Two days later, Kim let out a soft whistle as he strolled the quay amidship of Ramsey Hoth's *Spangled Lady*. Rocking peacefully at anchor, the steam-powered yacht stretched for 110 feet of glossy white paint and varnished mahogany. Eight crewmen in snappy blue and white middy uniforms wilted at their deck posts. Cooks and stewards presumably fried below. The *Spangled Lady* promised a full larder and empty staterooms . . . except for the one occupied by the ravishing Mrs. Hoth. Mr. Hoth was redundant, his absent son more so, and deserving of a small retribution. Kim did not debate long. With $300 advance on wages in his pocket, he could afford to return to Colorado, but not in comfort . . . and not in Mrs. Hoth's silken embrace.

Few women could wear pink without risking either insipidity or indiscretion, but his first glimpse of Suzanne Hoth banished the first possibility like a soaring Roman candle, and the last . . . well, that flushed, imperious face might be a first water Romanoff pearl, but he had never been so bent upon playing oyster in his life. In that frothy Irish lace and linen, she was delectable, delicious, a delight to the senses, and best of all, off guard. Restraint never entered his mind. She had the bearing of a swan, the shape of an angel, and eyes out of Coco La Tienne's cathouse that made him want to be indiscreet as quickly as possible if it meant luring her under the bar. He dismissed her late effort to strangle him. Any woman worth having was worth some inconvenience.

"I'm back!" announced Kim blithely as Suzanne responded to his knock.

Taking in his scent of English soap and cologne, she surveyed his expensively tailored white linen suit and rakish straw planter's hat. His haircut, his shave, his manicure. His Moroccan leather valises. "You look splendid, Mr. Smith-Gordon. Going somewhere?"

Having played cat and mouse often enough to discern a delicate claw, Kim attributed her swat to a shift in the game. "I hope to return to that paradise in those green eyes of yours, Mrs. Hoth," he murmured, "with any luck."

As Suzanne colored, Ramsey Hoth appeared behind her shoulder. "Your luck's run out, Mr. Con Man. Too bad you put your money on your back. You're the fanciest bum in Vera Cruz."

Nonchalantly doffing his hat, Kim lounged against the door frame. "I thought we had agreed not to be rude, Mr. Hoth."

"My manners have headed in the same westerly direction as my boy"—Ramsey's jaw shot forward—"and you can go kiss a pig."

"Don't know any." Kim smiled at the defiant Suzanne. "You two have decided that Bradford Hoth has gone to Colorado to jump my claim, thereby concluding that you don't need me. Am I right?"

"Right." Ramsey started to slam the door.

Kim inserted his foot in the crack. "I have something that belongs to your son, Mr. Hoth."

"Oh, hell," sighed Ramsey.

A quarter of an hour later, two ore samples sat side by side on the sitting room table of Suzanne's suite. Suzanne's ore half perfectly matched Kimberly Smith-Gordon's. "Well," conceded Suzanne reluctantly, "this proves there is a thread of truth in Mr. Smith-Gordon's tale, although none that Bradford stole the ore fragment he sent me."

"There's also no proof that this ore didn't come out of a Mexico City shop window," said Ramsey, "or would be worth a drat if it didn't. Five years ago, two hundred Colorado mining companies were listed on the eastern stock exchanges. In spring of '64, the bottom fell out. With easy placer gold panned out of the streams and riverbanks, everybody went crazy trying to figure out how to reach hard stuff deep in the ground, not like this easy stuff.'' He held up one of the ore fragments. "Every cockamamie contraption that came down the pike was sold to every dumb prospector that came along. Bunk. Nothing but bunk.''

"Ever hear of the Boston and Colorado Smelting Company, Mr. Hoth?'' countered Kim, sitting on the table edge.

"I expect you to tell me about it, Mr. Smith-Gordon.'' Ramsey's tone implied that if the company were worthy of note, he would have noted it.

"Professor Nathaniel Hill of Brown University formed the Boston and Colorado three years ago in Black Hawk, Colorado. He successfully applied Welsh techniques of smelting ore into mattes with copper bases to Colorado gold. The Boston and Colorado is an established firm that doesn't deal in bunk. Many mining engineers believe placer mining barely scratched the surface of the gold hidden in the Rocky Mountains.''

Well, Mr. Smith-Gordon,'' said Ramsey, "I also know a little something about the Boston and Colorado Smelting Company. Those copper mattes still have to be shipped to Wales to be processed. Costs a fortune and isn't likely to become cheaper for at least a decade. The best deep lode in Colorado costs too much to process.'' He tossed Kim the ore. "Peddle your gold somewhere else, Mr. Smith-Gordon.''

"How old will you be in a decade, Mr. Hoth?'' queried Kim softly. "Surely not too decrepit to spend a fortune.'' He placed the ore on the table.

"Colorado Territory has over 100,000 square miles of Indian-infested forest, ghastly desert and snowbound tundra. You might spend the next ten years looking for my claim, and consequently, your son . . . without my help.'' Noting Ramsey's attention lingering on the ore fragments, he smiled at Suzanne again. "Now, shall we discuss the liquor I prefer in my stateroom?''

FIVE

Stars and Garters

Compatibility on a boat is crucial to the pleasure of a passage. While the butcher, baker, and candlestick maker might have tolerated one another's company in their tub for untold nursery years, Suzanne Maintree, Kimberly Smith-Gordon, and Ramsey Hoth did not endure amicably for a single day. To begin, Ramsey was deflated by Kim's un-impressed dismissal of his tub. "Nice little boat," Kim observed casually as he strolled the teak decks of the sleek steamer. "Ever seen the Vanderbilt yacht?"

Her white linen skirt looped up over a chocolate and white pleated under petticoat, Suzanne strolled after the two men. She would not have missed Ramsey's tour with Kim for the world. To purchase his travel kit, Kim dawdled a week in Vera Cruz's best shops. He ordered a leatherbound set of Shakespeare, evening clothes with pearl studs, and a dozen white silk shirts—"no boilerplate bibs for me, thank you"; two pairs of white flannel pants, a brass-buttoned navy flannel coat, a gold-braided captain's cap, a pair of white leather deck shoes, and a set of grossly oversized, yellow foul weather gear. Three boxes of Brazilian chocolates, a hamper of tinned gourmet snacks, and a case of the best champagne were also trundled up the gangplank. Ramsey was livid when Kim sent him the bills on account. "Does that shyster think he's a seagoing clown?"

Athwart of Ramsey's offended nose, Kim shook hands with the crew, inspected the steam room—"Paint the engines white, do you?"—and joined the steward behind the bar in

58

the mahogany-sheathed main salon. "Oh, dear, no real scotch," he murmured, perusing twenty varieties of liquor sparkling under a bilious painting of *The Rape of Europa*. "I'll make do with that vodka, Toby," he told the beefy ex-pugilist who had the overscrubbed, falsely cheerful mien of a toby mug. "When my case of Inverness scotch comes aboard, please have it delivered to my stateroom." He turned to Ramsey's moody stare, "By the way, where is my berth, old man?"

Ramsey's red beard fanned around a maliciously sly smile. "The steward's name is Frock, he is my personal manservant, and you are in the bow."

Kim frowned. "The bow, hm? May I have a look?"

Suzanne had her turn to wince upon accompanying them below. Her stateroom door was ajar, her evening dress laid out upon the bed. All that was lacking was a sign stating, "This Way, Mr. Smith-Gordon." Kim's preference for the stateroom across from hers was no surprise.

"I really doubt if my digestion is up to a bow berth, old man," he informed Ramsey. "I'm an inexperienced sailor, you know. Why don't I just take this room?" He patted the door opposite Suzanne's.

For an inexperienced sailor, noted Suzanne, Smith-Gordon certainly knew the bow took the worst beating in a rough sea. She waited in vain for Ramsey to suggest another stateroom, but he did not mean to be the only one harassed by their unwanted guest. Without hesitation, he agreed to Kim's choice, then flashed a cynical grin at her abrupt retirement to her own room. As her key turned loudly in the lock, Smith-Gordon called, "I hope you like the roses, Mrs. Hoth. They're fresh from the florist's this morning."

Suzanne whirled. From the dressing table and bedside table four dozen creamy roses nodded in the breeze from the open portholes. Furiously, she crammed the stems through the ports until upon the *Spangled Lady*'s wake drifted a luxury of roses: except one. As Suzanne turned, nursing a thorn-stuck thumb, she saw it . . . lying delicately upon her pillow.

Kimberly Smith-Gordon must be put in his place. She would make him pant, then slap a muzzle on him.

* * *

Nursing a scotch at the salon bar, Kim was making an observation to Toby about Europa's many chins as Ramsey moodily studied the moonlit Mexican coastline sliding past the port windows. Kim heard the salon's heavy mahogany door open, then a whisper of silk against the lintel. The startled change in Ramsey's sour expression was the first suggestion that Suzanne looked different than usual. When Kim turned, all he saw in the dimly lit salon was the lambent glow of her skin. A tinder glow of high piled, titian hair, the long-lashed slant of sea-green eyes. Just as he could sense the sinuous, silent pad of a female panther in the steamy night of a Yucatan jungle, he could feel the way Suzanne moved. Smell her too-warm skin, muskily perfumed and touched with a trace of perspiration. She wore his white rose at the cleft of her décolletage. As he came to his feet, the soignee black dress registered. The severe, daring cut exposed the rise of her high, white breasts, the curve of her bare shoulders. The black glove on her left arm was slightly dropped with the provocation of a negligently donned negligee. The cling of midnight silk to her slim-waisted body was impersonal, a shaping of the quintessential female. Despite the severe elegance of her toilette, everything about her suggested sexual surrender . . . yet he suspected surrender was the farthest thing from her mind. Not only was she girded for a war between the sexes, she was afraid to lose it.

Her uneasiness stemmed not from naivete, but the lack of it. She knew how to lure a man too well. Her every gesture was planned, her every glance a seductively flung challenge.

Kim had known many beautiful women; bareskinned in a dozen shades, with faces clean and dirty, at their best and worst, they held few secrets for him, yet beguiled him still. He understood women, and had an instinct for making them comfortable. A comfortable woman was generous and patient. He had never seen a woman more beautiful and less comfortable than Suzanne Maintree costumed as a femme fatale. This one, Kim warned himself even as his senses screamed, *charge*! would be as easy to snare as the man-eating *gata* who tried to rip off his head in the Yucatan.

The rake of his hot blue eyes as she walked into the candlelit salon told Suzanne that Smith-Gordon assumed his place was in her bed no later than midnight. She did nothing to dispel his illusions and knew she had won the first skirmish when Ramsey moved forward to take her hand. "You look like a million, missy," he said with relish, then his voice dropped. "What are you up to?"

"I thought you might like to see what a million dollars buys, Mr. Hoth," she murmured in his ear, ". . . or rather what your son thought he bought."

Languidly, she turned to Kim. "Good evening, Mr. Smith-Gordon. I hope your new quarters are agreeable."

"Delicious," he said softly, his rapt gaze gliding over her lustrous skin. "I'm happy as a grig"—then, catching Ramsey's warning expression, added—"particularly with your father-in-law next door. Sleeping beside the ship's captain gives one a sense of reassurance. You don't happen to snore, sir?"

Ramsey's smile lay somewhere between cynical amusement and an urge to heave Kim overboard. "Suggesting I move to a more distant cabin, Mr. Smith-Gordon?"

"Heaven forbid, but if you have any sleeping pills . . ."

"As a matter of fact, I do. Would you care for warm milk as well?"

Kim appraised his glass of scotch. "Good idea. A drop of warm milk in a nightcap should put me out like a baby."

"How many nightcaps do you customarily drink, Mr. Smith-Gordon?" inquired Suzanne lightly, with the languourous, scented waft of a black ostrich fan grazing her décolletage.

"Oh, I don't know." He dreamily admired his rose nestled between her flawless breasts where the fan's fragile feathers left a fine tracery of shadows upon her white skin. "I either lose track after a time or drift on to something else."

"Something else" hung in the air like the scent of a roaming tomcat. Ramsey was enough of a practiced prowler himself to disembowel presumptuous rivals who sniffed his selected mate. Whether he chose to take her or not, he had seen this aloofly alluring she-cat first, and shying a moth-eaten stray out of his son's territory was a point of family pride. Besides, the interloper was two hairs from handsome in his evening clothes, as casually distinguished as a raffish earl turned out for a manorial evening. Despite Kim's evident dissipation and boneless posture, he had a slim, well-knit build, his long limbs adapting themselves to any position as if elegantly poured into space. His blonde hair was neatly combed into a sleek mane that rebelled at complete decorum by ruffling in a cowlick off his forehead. Despite Suzanne's pretence of disinterest, Ramsey noticed her glance at the Englishman from under the curve of her lashes with wary fascination.

In the blink of an artificial eye, Ramsey turned on the charm that had led more than one man . . . and woman to folly. "Why don't we have dinner now?" he suggested smoothly. "The junior cook shot a brace of doves this morning. Suzanne, you will sit on my right."

Not at the distant end of the table as I have since leaving New York? Suzanne refrained from retorting as Smith-Gordon escorted her to a gold-brocaded chair. When they were all seated at the long damask-covered table, she ironically surveyed the salon's lavish appointments. The heavy Beidermier table was laden with gleaming English silver and Chinese porcelain, with an ornate, crystal, hanging chandelier weighted to resist the roll of the sea. Money did seem to take one serenely through stormy seas. "Are you related to Colonel 'Chinese' Gordon, Mr. Smith-Gordon?" she asked offhandedly as Frock served the turtle soup.

"Afraid not. Is the colonel one of your heroes?"

"Indeed. Colonel Gordon is indomitable. Nothing stops him once he decides upon a course of action. Mr. Hoth . . . Ramsey"—she smiled distantly at her rough-hewn father-in-law—"is that sort of man. Are you that sort of man, Mr. Smith-Gordon?"

"Is your husband?" He sipped a spoonful of soup.

"I only know that Bradford was a persistent suitor, Mr. Smith-Gordon. We were married a very short time."

"Were?" Kim blotted his lips with his napkin.

"Bradford may be dead, Mr. Smith-Gordon. A telegram

sent from Colorado nearly a month ago informed me that he drowned in a mining camp flood.''

"Pity." Kim reapplied himself to his soup. "Is that why you wear widow's weeds, Mrs. Hoth?''

"Bradford liked black, Mr. Smith-Gordon,'' she drawled.

"As well he might,'' he murmured into his spoon. "You must have been very close.''

She distastefully recalled Bradford's relentless attention on their wedding night. "Inseparable.''

Kim laid down his spoon with the solemnity of a parson. "In view of this touching confession, shall we spare a moment of remembrance for the dear, departed weasel?''

She stiffened. "I beg your pardon?''

Ramsey, his temper rekindled, started to shove back his chair. "Mind how you talk about my boy!''

"Correction: your turd,'' Kim responded implacably. "I merely quote you both in the heat of the cantina battle. Gracious''—he smiled benignly at their flushing faces—"you've forgotten. I have been tactless''—he waved Frock to take the cooling soup away—"but then I have cause to resent your weasel turd somewhat.''

"Because he left you behind in Vera Cruz without a sou?'' rallied Suzanne sweetly as Frock removed Kim's soup with the caution of a man about to duck an attack. "That is, ah . . . one objectionable object calling another black.''

Frock darted in for Ramsey's plate.

"Forgive me.'' Kim lifted a mockingly deferential glass to Suzanne. "I had not realized myself in the company of turds nonpareil. Considering the customary glut floating in and out of Mexico, it's increasingly difficult to distinguish one from another.''

Just as Suzanne started to snatch his rose from her cleavage and smack it across his face, Ramsey curtly intervened. "Look, we won't get far insulting one another.'' With a spark of impatience, he handed his plate to the warily hovering Frock and shooed him away. "Shall we all say we have our private reasons for retrieving Brad and let it go at that?''

"No, Mr. Hoth,'' replied Kim, "I don't care to let it go at that. Despite appearances''—he held out an excess inch in his hastily tailored tuxedo jacket—"I am fastidious about my travelling companions. Not that I demand perfection"— he dismissed Ramsey's scoff of laughter with a negligent hand—"but if I happen to run short of ammunition while facing a charging lion, I like to understand the commitment of the hunter, or huntress, standing at my back."

"I'm a good shot when I like a man, Mr. Smith-Gordon," said Ramsey bluntly as Frock placed a glassily quivering jellied lamb upon the table with a wasted flourish. Meekly, the lamb knelt in a silver-bound pasture of parsley with radish flowers; Ramsey plunged carving implements into its haunch. "If I dislike a man, he may as well say his prayers."

"What if I prefer to step aside for this hypothetical lion," mused Kim, "and let you contrive the 'amen'?"

Ramsey sawed at the lamb. "My motive is simple. I want my boy back. I'm mad as hell at him, and he's due the thrashing of his life, but I don't want to see him end up in prison or on a hang rope."

"That would be heartrending as well as embarrassing, wouldn't it?" Ignoring Ramsey's glacial expression, Kim directed his attention to Suzanne. "And you, Mrs. Hoth?" His bold, disconcerting gaze dropped to the seductive rose at her breast. "Do you mean to welcome your errant husband back to your bosom?"

"Yes," she lied, her eyes cat-green with vengeful resentment. She might not enjoy turning mercenary, but what other choice had she? How could Kim understand loyalty? A need for dignity? She might have invited Kim's chamberpot jibe, but she had not forgotten it. No barroom scum was going to infer that a Maintree was ordure. "I love Bradford," she lied passionately over the sceptical glint in the whittled lamb's beady olive eyes. "And when I find him, I mean to show him just how much I love him."

"Weak tea that he is."

She raked the rose across Kim's mouth, leaving tiny claw marks of blood. When Suzanne's hand drew back for a second slash, he caught her wrist. "You've made your points, Mrs. Hoth. Let's not be redundant."

Over her whitening fist, Suzanne glared at him. With blood

trickling from his lips, he held her sulfurous gaze unflinchingly. And then, her wrist aching, she knew how to make him let her go. He would insult her no matter what she said or did. Why should she care a damn what he thought of her? Her eyes cooled as if her heart was frigid as a remote polar ice cap. "I want the money, Smith-Gordon," she said with slow, cold finality, "and I don't care how I get it."

He let her go then, his eyes going as chilly as hers. "Then we know where we stand." He appraised her a moment as if he had kicked a rock off a rattler, then shifted his gaze to Ramsey. "I don't suppose this is the right moment to mention that I plan to assume the name of Rafer Smith once we dock in New Orleans."

"Weak tea that you are," baited Suzanne.

"You show a lot of claw for a pretty woman," the soft note in his voice carried a subtle note of menace, "and you invite a trim."

"Try it," she hissed, "and I'll carve out your heart with a dull fingernail file."

"My," observed Ramsey in a pleased tone as he motioned Frock to distribute the lamb, "we are getting off to a good start."

Kim polished off a bottle of Rothschilde '56 champagne that night at dinner, wove with dignity to his stateroom with another bottle under his arm, and for most of the next day, showed not a fair hair of his head. Just after sundown, he emerged on deck with the glazed fixity of a mildewed vampire stowed in the hold. From a sling chair on the afterdeck, Suzanne contemptuously watched him retch over the port side for twenty minutes. Finally, his misery passed. "Lovely sunset," he announced in slurred admiration of the coppery, burnished colors lingering in the western sky. "That apricot's just the color of Malcolm's watered whiskey." Barefoot, his hair dishevelled, and his errant shirttail liquor-stained, he propped his elbows on the rail to meet her pitiless gaze. "What a starched girl you are"—he blearily regarded her white linen shirtwaist and veiled straw hat—"to be so greedy and wicked. Don't you know money is the root of all evil?"

"Only if one is penniless," she retorted coolly and went back to reading her dime Western.

The open navy coat over his misbuttoned silk shirt flapped in the wind as he carefully trod across the deck to her side. "*Trails of Blood*, that's a winsome title. Boning up on the boneyard of the West, are you?" He swayed in opposition to the rolling swells. "Well, that sort of book gives all answers to all questions about the West. A gunfight a day keeps the tourists away."

"Why don't you go away, Mr. Today It's Smith. You're standing in the last of my light."

"Being annoying is part of my charm," he retorted, sitting down abruptly on the deck. Folding his long legs Indian fashion, he leaned slightly forward. "For instance, you might be both annoyed and charmed if I said you walk like an Apache girl. They use a slightly pidgeon-toed side-swing. Very graceful. Very exciting."

"As I recall, you excite easily, Mr. Smith-Gordon," she replied dryly, flipping the windblown grosgrain hat streamers from her face. "Why not see if any Apache girls are creeping about the salon bar."

"Tsk. Now you're being patronizing. All the Apache girls I know are chewing bear hides around Taos."

"One has a tendency to patronize sots, Mr. Smith-Gordon." Snapping the book closed, she swung her feet down from the slatted lounge chair.

"Don't go," he coaxed. "Don't you want to know why I drink?"

In spite of herself, Suzanne was curious enough to postpone departure. "Why do you drink?"

"Because I am disillusioned and dismayed by the prospect of trekking through 100,000 square miles of Colorado Territory with such a beautiful, heartless woman as yourself."

She might have known. The amount of truth in his assessment stung and she regretted giving him such a whip for her sensibilities. He must be only too aware of her insidious vulnerability to him, but she would never lose hope of finding her father. Somewhere, Edward Maintree must be alive. But alone, she might as well seek a needle in a haystack. And how was she to care for him decently without income? Employment was scarce, rent rates in even the most squalid New York dwelling were astronomical, and neither she nor Edward were likely farmers. She wanted to do more than support him. She wanted him to keep the house where he had loved her mother, to keep the precious peace of Broadacre. She wanted him to have the life he was born to, had earned, and was due. Jay Gould had robbed him. Maintrees had not become Maintrees by accepting such assaults lying down! She started to rise again.

"Don't you want to know what I think of Ramsey Hoth, who is running steadily to type?"

Stoically, she waited.

"He's a treacherous pig." Kim's blue eyes were deceptively clear and boyishly earnest. "But I can bear up. By the time we reach New Orleans, I shall be a veritable Sampson between two pillars of Mammon." He extended his right palm out to port. "I shall place one hand against Ramsey Hoth's excuse for a heart, the other where yours has ceased to beat." His left palm levelled at Suzanne's breast. "Then I shall push." His arms forcefully extended, remained suspended, then acquired a martyred droop. "Unfortunately, I doubt if anyone will heed the crash."

"Mr. Smith-Gordon," she declared emphatically, "I have had quite enough of you. Either stay away from me or I shall not be responsible."

"My dear Mrs. Hoth," he muttered under his breath at her departing back, "I should sooner insert my pecker between a pair of hedge shears."

Despite a sodden effort, Kim did not bear up as quickly as usual when disappointed in a woman, particularly a woman he barely knew. Perhaps he had never before had two cases of liquor to delay his resurgence. Short of brooding in his stateroom for two sedate weeks of exploring his collection of Shakespeare and pickled squid tins, he could not ignore Suzanne. Her incredible looks were hypnotic, aphrodisiac. She was a bitch, but one hell of a beautiful bitch who padded with Circean relentlessness through his scotch-tinted dreams. Despite his instinctive aversion, Kim mentally removed her black dress from her perfect body a dozen different ways and made love to her in several more that would have sizzled her starch. Enough passion to melt a gold bar simmered under her smooth, velvet hide and Kim would have bet both his cases of hooch that Bradford Hoth had not aroused more than five degrees of it. Despite Bradford's sly appeal, he was weak, and vivid, tempestuous Suzanne was no fare for a weak man. She was more Ramsey's type. Suzanne in Ramsey's bed was a bitter prospect.

So why do I give a shit? Kim asked himself as he lay spreadeagled amid bottles and tins on his stateroom bed. What if she is a two-timing gold digger? I'm a sometime thief and an all-time lecher who's cheerfully boffed women who would steal the fillings from an old man's teeth. Why waste this much lovely liquor mooning about a mean-tempered, chiselling female I won't see again twenty minutes after we dock in New Orleans? Once the gangplank hits the quay, I'm off for Colorado Territory and the Hoths can whistle Dixie.

Growing sobriety increased his practicality. He would bed his tormentress and get her out of his system.

"Brace yourself, my dear," advised Ramsey the next morning at breakfast. "I think our Mr. Smith-Gordon is ready to rise from the dead. Frock tells me he took a bath this morning."

Suzanne stabbed a fork into her soft-boiled egg. "I don't care if the Colorado Territory is frozen solid and amok with savages, I say, drop the sotty beast overboard. Preferably into the maw of a shark."

"Beast? Mr. Smith-Gordon seems to have annoyed you unduly. Not much impressed by your pedigree, is he? To Mr. Smith-Gordon, all women are equal lying down."

Her forkful of egg poised in the air. "I haven't noticed his lying down under your broad boot, father dear."

"He will," replied Ramsey, his grin fading into a cold stare, "and don't call me father."

That afternoon, Ramsey spent four hours on the afterdeck playing gin rummy with the beast. He rose from the final game with a smug flip of the score pad. "That's two hundred points, Smith. Gin isn't your game."

"No," agreed Kim wistfully, "I usually drink the stuff. You must deduct my losses from my salary, sir. I am temporarily dependent upon your generosity."

Ramsey scrawled an entry on the pad. "I'll put the $100 on the tab . . . on one condition. There can be only one head of any organized venture, Smith: packing houses, ships, expeditions . . . whatever. I think you're beginning to see who has the cash . . . and the savvy to lead this trek into Colorado. You're the guide, but I'm the boss. *Comprendes?*"

Kim touched his hat. "Yes, boss."

"Good." His heavy stride resounding on the deck, Ramsey headed for the bridge. "See you at dinner."

Whistling an Irish carnival melody softly through his teeth, Kim rested his head back in the sling chair and tilted his ludicrous captain's cap down over his patient, ironic eyes.

Suzanne, playing shuffleboard across the foredeck with her hat streamers aflutter, was in a stew. She must be rid of Kimberly Smith-Gordon or whatever his name was. He was proving a damned nuisance.

That pseudo-sanctimonious bounder meant to cause trouble, either out of spite or sheer mischief, she predicted tensely, giving the disk a sharp crack of her cue. She could not be the only gold digger he ever met . . . why does he resent her so much?

Her misgivings were uneased when she caught a gleam of calculating, piratical blue under Kim's cap. Biding his time, he was watching her now as if he had a cutlass clamped in his teeth. She would not put it past him to try to whisk her off over his shoulder again like stolen booty. Her next shot wavered, skidded off into the Gulf. Her cue poised uncertainly, then she hurriedly snatched another disk from the rack. More than once, she had wondered what tumultuous adventure that mysterious cantina bedroom might have held. Kim was a renegade, as willful as any amoral freebooter, despite his pretense of disdaining filthy lucre . . . and yet, on that grubby cantina floor, he made her feel like a flesh and blood, sensual woman. Passion, real primitive passion opened up a whole realm of emotion that she never knew existed . . . but deeply feared. For all his barbarous dissolution, Kim held the power to cut a heedless, destructive swath through her hopes for herself and her father, but only if she granted it to him. Defensively hoisting the cue, she turned to confront him. The sling chair was vacant.

For days, Smith-Gordon behaved so beautifully that he might have been newspaper trained. He deferred to Ramsey on everything; called Frock, *Frock*; and smiled at Suzanne like a benign clam. I am not fooled, she wanted to yell at him. You're probably peeing in the closets!

The night was sultry as the yacht lay off the mouth of the Mississippi, awaiting daybreak. As she rose from dinner for a walk about the deck, Kim settled her cerise taffeta cape over her shoulders with the deliberate insinuation of an eel.

He followed her into the hazy darkness that closeted the deck. The candlelight through the salon windows carried only a few feet across the teak planking, the binnacle lights were a distant glow, and the southern latitude stars shone with the splendor of pinwheels. Like a little boy trying to watch his sister dally with her beau in a porch swing, the helmsman vainly peered through the wheel spokes. As Suzanne stalked irritably toward the bow, waiting for Kim to make an ardent attack, he strolled after her. She could almost feel his breath on her neck. The memory of his lips on hers in the cantina made her unsteady. With shaking hands, she caught the cape close, although the night was warm, like a caress . . . like a hot, close room above a cantina, where they were alone, with nothing between them. Where he could take her if he wanted, and no one would hear. She could almost hear herself crying out, in fear, and ignominious, shameful surrender . . . to a man who cared nothing for her. Nothing for Edward. Finally, her tension unbearable, she wheeled. "Touch me," she spat, "and you won't have enough teeth left to gum oatmeal."

"Whatever makes you think I'm having any difficulty restraining myself?" he tossed back. "A rather sordid kiss on a barroom floor seems to have gone to your head."

He blocked her wild slap before it landed. In the next second, her arms were pinned to her sides and he was kissing her again; hard this time, and not leaving any fairy tale illusions about passion between a man and a woman. Fire leaped between them, searing out all thought of resistance. Her head arched back under the fiery onslaught of his mouth, and even as she hated her helplessness in his rigid grip, she molded to it, shaped to it. Her hardened fists opened, her fingers trembling. His hands moved to her hair, pulling the coiled masses from their pins, raking through lush silk like a man finding the riches of Cibola.

His kiss deepened, pillaging her mouth until he became a victim of his own plunder, lost in her as she was in him . . . lost to treacherous, torching desire. His kiss held perfidy and unwelcome hunger, as if it were a collision of their differences and antagonisms. A reawakening. A threatened theft of their souls . . . but neither could tear away.

"You want me as I want you," Kim muttered hoarsely against her mouth. "Come below with me now. To hell with Ramsey Hoth and his brat. Come with me, Suzanne . . ."

Suzanne heard little more than the pounding of her heart, was aware of little more than her dazed surrender and terror. Her name would never sound the same again on any other lips but this gypsy swindler's, this electrifying cheat whose name and path shifted with the wind. He would take her to bed and the stars, then leave her alone to shiver among their empty echoes . . . echoes that recalled all her lonely childhood, her desperate longing to be loved by a father seen too rarely, and a mother gone forever. The years barely dulled the sharp edge of their loss. She could not risk loving anyone who would thrust her back into that void.

"Let go of me," she whispered wildly. "I cannot go with you. I can never go with you."

"Why?" His voice was hard again, his fingers knotting in her hair. "Is a stack of gold all that important? Do you want a lover like Ramsey Hoth?"

This had to stop. He must leave her alone. "Can't you understand?" she cried frantically. "You're everything I don't want! You're insanity, chaos. We don't live in the same world."

"Don't we?" He tilted her head back. "No woman satisfied with a corsetted existence in New York would try to scratch out my eyes over a mutton platter. She wouldn't kiss me as you just did. You want me to strip off that corset—along with everything else on your beautiful body."

"No!" This time, she thrust away and ran before he could lure her back into his mad world of spinning stars.

Kim started after Suzanne, but before he completed two steps, Ramsey Hoth's tolerant advice issued from the darkness. "You don't want to follow her, Mr. Smith-Gordon. My son had cause to bitterly regret his pursuit of that lady. Don't make the same mistake. Not only is she a lying, greedy cheat, I might have to kill you."

Kim turned to see the slope of Ramsey's broad shoulder faintly silhouetted against a dusky, blue white steam funnel. In shadow, Ramsey's face was as darkly ominous as an impassable mountain peak. "You'd better be holding a gun, Mr. Hoth," he replied tightly.

"Oh, I am. I am. The Colt .45 revolver Frock keeps under the bar. A .45 makes a hole you can shove a baseball through. Nobody aboard this boat'll say, 'boo,' if I blow you into the Gulf. A man with all your names, now, he'd be hard to trace."

"Why murder a man over so worthless a woman?" parried Kim, gaging the distance to the shield of the davited lifeboat. "You must have some reason to be barking in the manger."

"She owes me. She went after every rich Johnny in New York. After the last one dumped her, she hooked my son for cold cash, then cost him his reputation and maybe his life. She's a brass-bound whore, Smith; worse than that, she's a vulture out to pick the bones of every man to occupy her bed."

Now Kim measured the distance to Ramsey. "From your note of pique, one of those resentful fellows might be you,

Mr. Hoth.'' Now he saw the gun, the salon light glinting a
fine line along the ponderous barrel; it was levelled at his
head and at six paces, Ramsey was unlikely to miss. Having
his brain aired was a riveting possibility. He was pissing off
Mr. Hoth.

"I'd sooner court a crone with clap as Suzanne Maintree,"
snapped Ramsey. "My son ruined himself trying to afford
her. Did she care? Like hell. As soon as he ran off to Mexico,
she was at the bank quicker than a lizard after a missed fly.
When she heard Brad died trying to recoup his losses, did
she shed a tear? No, she told me cold that she'd make his
ruin public unless I paid her off.''

"Then why not turn that .45 on her?" Kim could not detach
his mind from the gun, also the dismal suspicion that Ramsey
Hoth was telling the truth. Bradford Hoth might not be so
virtuous as his father claimed, but the rest of the story had
a ring of authenticity, or at least of conviction.

"What I do with my daughter-in-law''—Ramsey's street-
honed voice came out with a grate of malevolence—"is my
business. You stay away from her. She's playing you like an
accordion.'' With that, Ramsey's broad, black-clad bulk lumbered off into the night.

Kim listened to the grind of steam engines below decks,
the rush of swiftly passing water. More than ever, he wanted
to see the last of the Hoths in New Orleans. He tugged a slim
cigarillo from his vest pocket, cupped his hands against the
wind, and lit it. The match was a brief flare in the blackness,
the tip of the cigar a tiny, steady afterglow. Leaning upon
the rail, he watched the cigarillo smoke drift down across the
soft pools of light from the portholes of Suzanne's stateroom.
In a few minutes, the water's rushing current went black again
as her light went out. She must be waiting in the darkness
of her wide bed, wondering if he would come to her.

His cigarillo struck the water with a dying hiss as he abandoned the rail for his own stateroom. Man-eater or not, the
seductive Suzanne spelled trouble. He already had trouble
enough waiting in the Colorado Territory.

SIX

Nuns and Brass Knuckles

Ten minutes after *Spangled Lady* docked in New Orleans off Jackson Square, Kim and his saddlebags were aboard a carriage rattling toward Gallatin Street. To call upon some old friends, he said. "That's the last we'll see of him," Suzanne observed expressionlessly as she stood with Ramsey at the head of the gangplank.

"I think not." He watched the carriage roll out of sight around the wrought iron wreathed Pontalba buildings, then turned to Frock, who was loading luggage into an open barouche. "Forget the trunks, Frock. Don't lose our guest."

Frock dropped the luggage and trotted off toward a hack.

"Why not just let Rafer Smith go?" Suzanne asked Ramsey wearily. "He doesn't know enough to cause us trouble, and I doubt if he knows enough to do us much good." The sickly sweet scent of tobacco warehouses lay heavy in the humid air, weighting her fatigue from a restless night. The least of her problems was learning to think of Kimberly Smith-Gordon as Rafer Smith, who was not going to hang around long enough to let his new identity tax anyone's memory.

"He's run up quite a tab with me. I didn't get to be where I am without collecting bills." Ramsey smiled grimly. "Besides, if that tramp's lying, I want his balls." He pinched her pale cheek. "Don't worry; you needn't lose any more sleep over Mr. Rafer Smith. Frock will bring him back safe and sound. Unconscious if necessary, but with that damned shit-eating smile on his face."

Having no wish to see Rafer again, Suzanne heartily wished him as far away as the Sahara. He was no answer to a maiden's prayer, but then, he did not precisely evoke her maidenly modesty, did he? She reacted to him like an Arab deprived of water, even when the waterhole was poisoned. That made her blindly desperate or plain stupid.

But Rafer wants me in the same way, and mistrusts me as much as I do him, she argued. Surely no man could kiss a woman so fiercely and not be in love with her.

But was he in love? Marcus Hampton's kisses had hidden ambitions for her money. Bradford Hoth kissed her with an eye on the envy of his peers. What did she lack that men only saw her as a trophy? Or was she easy prey because she was deluded by her own pride?

With a pounding head, she stared out at the hubbub of Jackson Square and prayed Rafer would not return to prove she was one of P.T. Barnum's suckers.

Aware Ramsey was mean minded enough to have him followed, if only to collect a gin rummy debt, Rafer directed the carriage driver back and forth through the heavily trafficked, narrow streets to lose undesirable company. After spotting Frock on Ursuline Street, he gave him the drift on Chartres. When finally certain he was safe, Rafer ordered the driver to the west levee, where he intended to buy a steamboat ticket for St. Louis with his last cash. At the levee, the steamboats were so tightly packed, their paint nearly scraped. Then, as the carriage threaded through boarding passengers and Negro roustabouts laboring under trunks, cotton bales, and cordwood, he abruptly changed his mind . . . which was still stubbornly entangled in Suzanne Hoth's glory of red hair. Forgetting a woman was a shell game; the quickest way to make a mark lose track of one shell was to shuffle attention to a couple of others. "Driver, take the shortest route to Coco La Tienne's on Bourbon Street."

Madame Coco was the last woman in the world to be shocked when Rafer took two girls upstairs to the Rose Room, but when an hour went by and he sent down for another two, she went upstairs herself. "Rafer, *mon cher*," she said huskily, an elbow propped on the brass bedrail, "every time you got a sheriff on your ass or a woman on your mind, you act like a kid in a candy store. You're not seventeen any more, and you try to stuff yourself with all the peppermint sticks like you did last time, you're going to make yourself sick. Besides, I bet you ain't got the price of a penny jaw-breaker.''

With an surfeited grin, Rafer crooked a beckoning finger. Coco might be a beehive of fat now, but she was a magnificent woman. Her flashing dark eyes, devilish strut, and honey skin had made her the most sought after quadroon in the Quarter in her heyday. She still had numerous bids for her favors, presently bestowed only upon men who could do her good, either physically or politically. If she disliked a man, he could drool until kingdom come; if she liked him, he had a friend for life and a lover of monumental skill. "*Viens à moi, ma belle mère*," Rafer purred in Cajun French. "Just one warm, beautiful mama to love me and I won't be so hungry." Teasingly, he fondled the rounded rumps of the luxuriating girls on either side of him. "How long has it been, Coco? Or haven't you missed me?"

"Five years. Before that, two. And before that, another two. I found myself a slew of seventeen-year-olds in all that time." Her sloe-lidded surveillance was shrewd. "You picked up some lines around those bad blue eyes, baby boy. Been living a hard life and chasing poon across the border again, I hear."

The smile lingered on his lips, but not in his eyes. "What else do you hear?"

She waved the girls out. Reluctantly, they pulled on their wrappers and ambled for the door. "Step it up, ladies," Coco ordered. "You ain't gonna have enough 'pluck, pluck' for the mayor tonight, you spend all day with this rooster."

When they were gone, she sat on the bed, which sagged alarmingly. "Sugar, you better keep your sassy ass out of the north. Now that the Union Pacific railroad's rolling into Denver this year, Colorado people are mighty ambitious. The territorial population's fixing to shoot up like new corn and shove statehood right through the U.S. Congress. That place is going to be too pious to piss. It's bad enough right now.

My stars and garters, you know there's a real opera house in Denver?''

Although Coco was more politically astute than most senators, little of her appraisal was news to Rafer. Her intensity suggested she knew more than she was telling. "What else have you heard, *ma belle*?" he persisted.

"A big time mine owner named Helmut Banner has supplied $50,000 to the territorial governor's administration; that kind of money would buy the whole Louisiana legislature." She watched Rafer's impassive eyes. "Banner doesn't appear to hanker after political office himself, but he swings a lot of weight behind closed doors. Some say he had plenty to do with diverting the railroad out of Golden, and if he keeps on the way he's going, he'll control the first state governor.''

"Why should I give a damn about Helmut Banner?" Rafer folded his arms under his head.

"You gave one hell of a damn one night when you were just a scrap-tailed kid with a man's share of girls and liquor." She leaned against the brass rail. "Expect Helmut Banner don't mean two cents now that you're all smart and grown up."

"Expect you're right." Helmut Banner meant more than two cents; he was worth $200,000 in gold, plus twelve years' interest. Twelve years ago, Banner made him run barefoot through nearly three hundred miles of cactus for his life. He hated him with the venom of a scorpion.

"I have something for you, *belle mère*." From beneath his pillow, Rafer drew out the last box of chocolates from Vera Cruz.

With a rueful smile, Coco shook her head. "You're trying to distract me; that means you're chasing trouble again. When you showed up last time, you were busted up so bad I thought you were going to die on me. The boss of that Mississippi chain gang near killed you for running so often . . .''

He leaned forward to nuzzle her cheek. "I finally got away, didn't I?''

"Darlin', when are you going to learn? Lady Luck don't hang around with nobody forever." Finally, Coco just gave up and kissed him. She had walked into his room knowing she was not going to leave without taking him to her breast again. He was the best lover she had ever had, and the biggest liar.

She first encountered Rafer Smith—alias Kimberly Smith-Gordon—when he was seventeen. He drew her notice when a little Cajun girl he approached at her old place on Gallatin Street refused to take him to her room. "Not that scarey limey," the Cajun whispered to Coco. "He's a stick of dynamite just lookin' to have his wick lit so he can blow half the Quarter to glory. I ain't about to find that fat-ass knife of his whittlin' on me in the middle of the night."

Coco summoned Rafer to her sitting room where she held solitary court at a Louis Quatorze tea table with a sawed off shotgun mounted under its Venetian embroidered cloth. She sympathized with her Cajun girl; despite his polite, softly clipped drawl, Kim was a savage. He was poised like a young lion encountering a hunter. A tall, sandy thatched string of rawhide in trapper's buckskins, his blue eyes an unnerving blaze in his deadly young face, he exuded such a sense of explosive danger that the air made a space about him. A skinning knife was strapped to his thigh and there was a thought in his head about killing the first fool who crossed him. He told her a Colorado plainsman named Jack Carlisle sent him, then continued to coolly study the concealed shotgun. "I'm Jack Carlisle's son . . . and he's dead."

Coco's face twisted with grief. Jack had lacked the ruthlessness for living long outside the law. She had met Jack at her old place in St. Louis before his wife died. When he came to St. Louis as he did yearly to sell a winter's supply of skins, he was still trying to make a go of the trap lines, but he had other ideas: damned fool ideas about turning bank robber that made her shake her head in dismay. Those guileless, mischievous blue eyes were telling her that Jack's death was violent. Those eyes were so changed in this boy that they were almost unrecognizable. "Sit down," she said wearily.

They talked for a time, or rather she talked until the boy finally accepted a drink. After the mickey hit him, she had him taken up the back stairs to a bedroom and handcuffed to a bed.

The next morning, he awoke ready to kill her. "Just you settle down," she advised him. "I got to do a little checking before I give you the run of the place. Now, how about some cornbread and molasses for breakfast?" Although his ribs were nearly protruding through his shirt, the boy would not eat. By nightfall, he was feverish, and by afternoon of the next day, delirious enough not to fight her when she stripped off his clothes to cool him. His body appeared to have taken the worst of a knife fight, until she noted the precise regularity of the narrow gashes and burns. Jack Carlisle's son had been tortured. His feet were such a mess that she wondered how he could walk. Months, perhaps even a year old, most of his wounds were healed, but several new ones on his back had reopened and festered, the infection causing his fever. The boy had travelled a hard path to New Orleans.

When he recovered consciousness and saw his bandages, his heart-stopping stare fixed her. "So, what do you mean to do with me? You ought to know by now that the reward business doesn't pay piddle even if I did have a price on my head."

"I had a newspaper friend roust up some back issues of the *Rocky Mountain News*." Coco nodded at the stack of yellowed newspapers in a nearby wooden chair. "That pile came out around the time you say your daddy died. Expect I know most of what I need to know now. You ought to be dead, boy. You go on toting the load of hate you've piled up, you might as well be dead. You can stay with me for a while and I'll call you Rafer Smith, but if you so much as belch at one of my girls, you'll be out on your mean ass."

Coco and young Rafer Smith fought regularly, but in the course of a summer that stretched into two years, grew on each other. They were a natural pair. He was ice to her fire, unwilling to let her provoke him into a flare-up that might yield her any degree of control or domination. With equal stubbornness, Coco tried to break him to the saddle, if not her own, then that of the world he must inevitably endure.

Coco usually hounded Rafer for hanging around the local gambling dens, but after a few months, Rafer learned enough to go into business for himself. In the currents and treacherous undertows of gilded swamps like Lou's and The Golden Palace, minnows and monsters who survived by camouflage and frightfulness came and went. Smith opted for camouflage. He began to resemble his father: raffishly charming, deceptively lazy, and careless of tomorrow. He learned to smile; wheel and deal, and lie. Failing to knock it out of him, Coco took him to bed. She had watched him, ready as an untried young stallion, sniffing at her girls. "Your mind is messed up enough," she sighed. "I ain't going to have you trashing what's left by going with tramps that don't care nothing about you."

Rafer knew little about women, but he learned with precocious mastery from the best. What Coco did not know and could not imagine, did not exist . . . until Rafer taught it to her. "My stars and garters, darlin', if you were a girl, I could make a fortune out of you," she purred one luxurious night, "but I wouldn't change a hair of your head for every dime I got. You sure know how to spoil a woman."

She spoiled Rafer, too. Coco had a warm heart and the stamina to keep it that way in a cold world. She made him care for her when he wanted to care for no one. She was the mother he never had, and his first love. In her bed, he lost his virginity, and when his heart was wounded, he always came home again.

This time, something bothered him besides Helmut Banner; when he left her exhausted at dawn, Coco knew the something was a woman. Danger sharpened his concentration in bed; during the night, his mind had been somewhere else.

Ramsey hovered longingly over his eggs and kippers. "Well, where's Smith?" he demanded of Frock. In his cheap bowler hat and checked suit, Frock was out of place in the elegant La Vielle Orleans Hotel suite. "I expected you back long before this."

"I lost him, boss," Frock admitted, but added hastily, "so I spent the rest of the time combing the levees and seamy side of the Quarter. I spotted him leaving a cathouse this morning. He looked a tad tuckered. Expect he spent the night."

With a grunt of laughter, he peered brightly at Suzanne's stony face over the table's bouquet of silk lilies. "Well, where did you think he'd be? Early mass at Saint Louis Cathedral?"

She precisely forked a bit of omelette. "The question is, where was he all day yesterday?"

"New Orleans is full of cathouses." A kipper disappeared into Ramsey's mouth. His cheek full, he poked his fork at Frock. "Where is the SOB now?"

"Hustling penny ante blackjack in a gambling place called The Wheel of Fortune on Gallatin. Appears to be building a stash so he can sit in on a high stakes game." Frock's bassett gaze followed another forkful of kipper into the great beyond of Ramsey's mouth.

"Had breakfast?" Ramsey pursued a slippery egg.

Frock perked up. "No, sir."

"You aren't going to. Get back to that gambling hall. Around four o'clock this afternoon, see Smith gets this." He handed Frock a note. "We pull out in the morning. I want him in evening clothes here at the hotel tonight by eight o'clock. If he tries to do a flit, change his mind but leave his face in one piece. I don't want him to be an embarrassment. If he gives you real trouble, break his legs and hang the embarrassment." He returned to his breakfast. "You lose him again and I'll toss you to the chef for jambalaya."

Frock spent a dismal afternoon observing Smith work his way up to a private poker game at Melisande's on Bourbon Street. The back room door closed at three-thirty. As eight o'clock approached and waned, Frock tried to buy into the game only to be rebuffed by his croupier. When the doors reopened at ten o'clock to expel the poker losers and suck in new blood, he tried again, his ulcer prodding him to desperate effort. When the burly, frock-coated, black door guard took one look at his cheap hat and thrust a massive arm across his path, Frock waved frantically at Smith, who was preoccupied in conversation with the blonde, faux-Parisienne lady proprietor. Frock let out a loud squeak as the guard's elbow aimed for his windpipe. "Mr. Smith, I gotta talk to you!"

Rafer glanced at him, and for a moment, Frock feared his

windpipe was a lost cause. Finally, Rafer nodded to the guard. "Let him through, George. I'll speak to him."

Frock scuttled past the stakes players who regarded him as if he were a roach. He bent quickly over Rafer's shoulder. "Mr. Hoth wants you."

"He undoubtedly also wants Texas and stands an equal chance of getting it just now."

"Mr. Smith," said Frock nervously, "he told me to have you at the La Vielle Orleans Hotel by eight o'clock. That's two hours ago. He's going to be real mad."

"Then he'll just have to bite his tail, won't he? Run along, Toby. I'm on a roll."

Frock fidgeted, then chucked the note over Rafer's shoulder. "Mr. Hoth says we're pulling out in the morning. You coming or not?"

The note lay on the table. "I'll think about it."

Madame Melisande waved a languid hand. "Remove this Toby gentleman, George. He's delaying the game." Frock was removed.

Rafer's concentration vanished with Frock. The note silently shrilled by his elbow as he played two hands, his mind unwillingly on Suzanne. If Coco had been unable to banish Suzanne from his thoughts, he had a problem. The last thing he needed in Colorado was distraction; on the other hand, Hoth's expedition provided a good cover. Too, while Suzanne might be trouble, she was also *in* trouble. Unpleasantries could happen to a woman alone with Ramsey Hoth in the empty wilds of the Colorado Territory. If Suzanne locked horns with Ramsey over that gold claim and his son, she might just find herself handed over to the Utes or tossed to the wolves. Ramsey hated her, and he was a man who went after what he hated with a hatchet.

Finally, Rafer reluctantly read Hoth's note: "$10,000 and expenses. The redhead misses you."

He wadded up the note, then tossed down his cards. "I'm out, gentlemen. A lady calls."

Suzanne was dancing with a handsome Creole when Rafer, suave despite his loosely hung dinner clothes, strolled into the hotel's cream and silver Empire ballroom. If she missed him, the quick, dismissive turn of her beautiful head advised him she was bearing up well. She was wearing a crystal embroidered, rose silk dress cut down to her exquisite essentials, and the Creole, whom he recognized as a rich lizard named Jacques de Laury, was murmuring seductive nothings in her ear.

Frock put a restraining hand on his arm when he started forward. "Mr. Hoth wants you," he reminded with the pedantry of a hammer, "and he's already waited three hours."

Rafer plucked his hand loose. "Just tell him to reel in the redhead, Toby. His trout has taken the bait."

When Rafer walked up behind her whispering Creole, Suzanne tried to ignore him. "Nice to see you again, Jacques," Rafer murmured into the Creole's ear. Jacques jumped.

"Rafer." The young Creole laughed awkwardly as he turned to face the casually elegant Englishman. "What are you doing back in New Orleans?"

"Actually, I've been assisting this young lady in replenishing her corset supply. I keep telling her she doesn't need a corset, but you know women." Rafer beamed at Suzanne's outraged face. "She's a good sort of girl despite her wicked temper. You'll like her. She'll like your money."

The tightness in her chest at seeing Rafer saunter into the room exploded into a scarlet flush that set her aglow like a lighted fuse. Bearing Rafer's impudence as well as his whoring in New Orleans was the last straw in a bad two days. When Rafer ducked, Jacques caught Suzanne's roundhouse swing on his ear. Ready to weep with pain, he clasped his ringing head as the surrounding dancers backed away like sheep startled by a she-wolf. "God in heaven, madame, you've injured me!"

In no mood for snivelling, Suzanne snapped, "I never saw this British bounder before in my life. Call him out!"

"Rafer Smith?" Jacques stammered, turning whiter than his pain merited. "Madame, I think you had better call him out. Your corsets are your business, no?" With a hasty jerk of a bow to Rafer, he fled through the buzzing ballroom crowd.

"Pity," mused Rafer, looking regretfully after him. "You

might have gotten on with Jacques. He owns an impressive amount of swamp northeast of town.''

"I'd like to shove an impressive swamp down your gullet!'' spat Suzanne, nearly dizzy with rage. "I'd like a froth of alligators to go north, east, west and south with your miserable skin and leave your entrails for the vultures!''

"'Guts for the buzzards' has a more authentic ring in this part of the country, but heaven forfend I should distract your train of thought when your eloquence has drawn such an admiring crowd. Do go on.''

Suzanne went white upon perceiving the number of people gaping at them. She had committed the ultimate social crime: a public scene. The waltz issuing from the string ensemble dwindled to a timid whine. Rafer Smith had gaged to perfection her lack of control when sufficiently provoked. "Dance with me until I can decently escape, you worm,'' she hissed under her breath, "or I'll tell them you're the one who enjoys wearing corsets. Why should I slink off into the night alone?''

"You shouldn't,'' he agreed sagely, taking her into his arms. "And I shouldn't think of letting you.''

She blasted a brilliant smile at the ensemble leader, willing him to begin.

Rafer's blue eyes danced with mischief as the orchestra hesitantly wheezed into Strauss's *Tauberwalzer*. "Why, Mrs. Hoth,'' he whispered into her ear, "you're not wearing a corset.''

She trod viciously on his toe.

Suzanne soon found Rafer had no intention of aiding her escape. Despite her efforts to steer him toward the main door, he propelled her elsewhere. He was such an adept dancer that no one guessed they were conducting a minor wrestling match. "Give up and enjoy the music,'' he soothed as she struggled. "You owe me at least one dance for rescuing you.''

"You humiliated me. Why?'' She was ready to weep with frustration. "Why insult me publicly!''

"When I saw Jacques oozing all over you, I was seized by uncontrollable jealousy,'' he confessed with a bland lack of remorse. With the aplomb of Louis XIV selecting a new courtesan, he appraised her approvingly. Crystal and pearl paillettes studding her bodice and capped sleeves were echoed by a pearl necklace which caught the unusual color of her hair. A single, thick, glossy ringlet caught by a creamy gardenia hung over her shoulder. "Besides, I didn't care to run a gauntlet of men to gain your attention. Now I have you all to myself."

"I behaved childishly tonight," she rejoined heatedly, "but you're worse. You're more of a spoiled baby than Ramsey."

"He thinks well of you, too. A 'brass-bound whore' he fondly calls you." His fingers tightened on hers as she tried to jerk away. "Are you certain you want to pursue this Colorado venture?" he went on more soberly. "The Territory is a rough place, and Ramsey Hoth is a rough man."

"I can take care of myself. After all, Colorado is practically a state; how wild can it be?" Her emerald eyes flashed with defiance. "I'm also aware of my father-in-law's capabilities. I can deal with him, too."

"Had plenty of practice quelling monsters and mountains in New York City, have you? I thought your expertise lay in seducing unwary young men and picking their pockets." His fingers clamped again. "Now, now, don't fly into another flurry. Yours is an old and honorable profession. You are perfectly vindicated for wishing to assure the security of your old age before you lose your looks."

"Stop it! You know nothing about me, and could care less. You want me like a glutted porker wants another bucket of slop. Where have you spent the last twenty-four hours, you saintly reprobate? Were you taking tea with the Ursuline nuns?" Her eyes grilled him. "No, you were wallowing in the muck of places like Coco La Tienne's and The Wheel of Fortune. Don't preach to me, you pillar of vim, vigor, and virtue."

"Now that you agree we have interests in common," he said agreeably, "why don't we go up to your hotel room and explore our mutual lack of character?"

She stared at him. "Your amorality is dumbfounding. Your mother should have slapped you from her breast and given you a bottle of gin."

"Mum and I never enjoyed the usual domestic joys," he replied quietly. "She wasn't up to the rigors of Colorado and bearing three sons. She died as I let out my first wail."

"Oh . . . I'm sorry," said Suzanne awkwardly. Her last sparks of anger sputtered. Her furious explosion at Rafer had released pent-up bitterness and cleared her mind. Suddenly, she began to think, and think hard.

She had attacked Rafer and Marcus Hampton, blindly striking at all the humiliations she had been unable to fight. Rafer Smith was teaching her how to fight, and not with a child's puny fists. Ramsey's transparent ruthlessness and blind temper were his greatest weaknesses, while Rafer had the scruples and flexibility of a chameleon.

Suzanne felt a grudging twinge of sympathy. Had they both struggled to fill the same need? Despite her father's indulgence and love, she missed terribly an underlying peace she never had: something Rafer missed, too. That tranquil security had nothing to do with money, yet they both pursued money with reckless single-mindedness as if it were an impossibly perfect love. The love she envisioned glittered as brightly as a priceless jewel, but its facets were devotion, loyalty, honesty. True love might be spent and wasted, but never hoarded. And enduring love of such depth was unimaginable with Rafer.

Still, as Rafer waltzed her along the line of gaslit windows, they shared a tenuous, fragile intimacy that ventured beyond their usual sexual tension. His arms warmed her like a golden circle of light that revolved the ballroom into a slow whirl of distant music and chatter. They might have been dancing within a chandelier lit by waxen candles tipped with rose gold teardrops of flame and crystal. A lullabye of prisms. When the music ended, she said softly, "I lost my mother when I was two years old. My father was involved in business, so I was reared by aunts and nannies—too many of them, I suppose." Her lovely green eyes held an unwitting trace of wistfulness. "Do you still have family?"

"No." Rafer's crooked profile was outlined by the wan gleam of streetlights in the misty street outside. "I was raised by my father and brothers. Like you, I assumed I had too many." His jaw tightened. "Then one day, there were none."

"What happened?"

He gestured ironically to the ballroom's glittering throng. "Like many in our society, they succumbed to a contagious illness: gold fever, and in their case, it was fatal."

"They all died in the gold fields, as Bradford is supposed to have done?" Scepticism tinged her voice. Was Rafer lying about his family, just as he lied about everything else?

"Are you so sure your husband is alive?" he countered. "Colorado claims a great many casualties."

Her eyes narrowed. "Are you, by any chance, trying to frighten me into staying in New Orleans?"

"Your father-in-law's trek is no journey for a woman, and New Orleans is no place for a woman alone. You'd be better off going back to New York."

"So you and Ramsey can divide my husband and his gold between you." She smiled sardonically. "Mr. Smith, I wouldn't think of returning to New York. If Bradford has gone as far as Tibet, I shall follow him and nothing you or Ramsey Hoth can do will stop me."

"So it's we three jolly cannibals for the road, and poor Bradford bound for the pot," came Ramsey's voice from behind her. As they drew apart, he gave them a missionary's smile, with the diamond blazing in the vast white shield of his boilerplate shirt front. His crow black, strikebreaker's shoulders appeared capable of snapping the slim, polished Creoles like kindling. "You appear to have reconciled, but I daresay my daughter-in-law wishes to welcome you back properly, Mr. Smith. As we've an early departure in the morning, I suggest we retire and you kiss Suzanne good night at her door."

With Frock in their van, Ramsey led the way from the ballroom up the broad, scarlet-carpeted stair to the top floor of the hotel. Pausing at Suzanne's door, he motioned benignly to Rafer. "Go ahead, don't mind Frock and me."

Suzanne had not taken Ramsey seriously, but when Rafer pulled her into his arms, she had no time for more than a startled gasp before he kissed her with a thoroughness that left her itching to murder him. Instead, when he finally let her go, she ignored Ramsey's malicious smile and calmly unlocked her door. "Thank you for a pleasant evening, Mr. Smith," she said sweetly as she swept into her room. The subtle click of the lock promised, "I'll poison you all in the morning."

Ramsey showed Rafer to the door of the room next to his own. "You should be comfortable in this suite, Mr. Smith-Gordon." He handed Frock the key. "The hotel only rocks in hurricanes."

Rafer sighted the distance back to Suzanne's room. "I'm sure I'll be fine."

"Good," Ramsey said genially. "Before we say good night, Mr. Smith-Gordon, I must ask you to do a couple of things for me."

"What do you have in mind, Mr. Hoth?" Rafer turned absently, his mind still on Suzanne's lips.

Ramsey bent him double with brass knuckles to the stomach, then slammed down a double-handed rabbit punch on the back of his neck that stretched his length on the scarlet hall runner. "Never embarrass my son's wife in public again." The toe of a polished evening shoe sheared into his ribs. "And never keep me waiting." Ramsey motioned Frock to help the barely conscious Rafer into his room. "Thank you for a pleasant evening, Mr. Smith-Gordon."

Rafer awoke to find his evening clothes neatly hanging from a wooden valet and his ribs solicitously strapped. The dresser clock indicated 3:00 A.M.; a rib that it was broken. Wincing with pain, he rolled over to see Frock placidly watching him. Leaving Ramsey's payroll presented a problem, but it was staying in his employ that worried him: suicide for a salary. He eased down on his pillow and closed his eyes.

With Frock as escort, Rafer met Ramsey in the lobby at

dawn. "How are you feeling this morning?" Ramsey purred. "You look a trifle pale."

"Oh, I feel splendid." Rafer directed a conspiratorial grin at Frock. "Toby and I had a race downstairs after breakfast, didn't we, Toby?" His smile altered subtly. "We didn't want to keep you waiting."

"That was considerate of you."

Ramsey shoved a roll of bills over the manager's desk. "Give me change. Your service stinks."

As the manager stoically counted out Ramsey's change, Suzanne descended the stairs. She wore a navy blue, braid-trimmed traveling outfit with a high, ruffled collar, and in the light from the lobby's Tiffany windows, her chignoned hair was strawberry gold. The navy ribbons of a white Neapolitan hat trimmed with silk tassels and white poppies curved along her flawless cheekbones. With the skirt flounce designed to show off her graceful, gliding walk, she looked vivacious and exceedingly feminine. Her eyes were bright with confidence and a hint of mischief.

Rafer had encountered other women who were as delicious as they were dangerous, but Suzanne had a spark of genuine warmth that drew a man more surely than her seductive heat. Despite her fiery temperament and imperious vanity, he suspected she might be more compassionate and sensitive than she cared to pretend. Had she been the naive, motherless child of yesteryear, her hair loosed to a nimbus of rosy gold, he would have taken care of her; as it was, she was a full-blown woman.

I could risk my neck for a lot less than this lady, estimated Rafer. I'd like to wrap around her like a mink.

"Good morning, gentlemen," Suzanne murmured in her melodious contralto as she joined them. "I hope I haven't kept you waiting."

"Oh, no," Rafer reassured her. "Ramsey would let you know if you did. Probably snap your parasol over his knee."

When Ramsey took his measure like a waiting billy club, she laughed. "Don't be silly. Ramsey is a perfect puss. We are all pusses with saber teeth and grand appetites."

"Exactly," Rafer agreed. "And if an occasional tiff leaves a few scratches, what group tour doesn't end by longing to feast upon itself?"

SEVEN

Falling for a No-Good Man

A day later, Rafer and Suzanne strolled the deck outside the dining salon on the steamboat, *Memphis Belle*, as she churned up the Mississippi River toward Natchez. On the main deck below them, crew and deck passengers dozed against walls stacked high with cotton bales to find relief from the heat in the cooling breeze lifting from the river. The *Belle*'s great paddlewheel spilled like a rushing waterfall in the dusky quiet of the broad, brown current laden with mud from the delta. The westering sun's last fire faded from a tawny violet sky, leaving the forested banks and bluffs to the grazing of the first fireflies. Cicadas chirred in the reeds, frogs croaked under the mud banks where long grass hung lank from yellow fields that rolled between the woodlands to the river. Suzanne gazed after a meadowlark kiting low to its nest. "The river is so peaceful here; it meanders as if looking for a place to sleep."

"Don't you miss New York?" queried Rafer, toying with his dice. His loose-jointed stance suggested he was mildly drunk, after spending the afternoon in the main lounge playing blackjack and roulette. Ramsey was still at the tables. Frock was spotting for Ramsey at poker, so Rafer could cheat with the professional cheats.

Suzanne smiled without her customary wariness. Like a bird let out of a cage, she had spent most of the time since leaving New Orleans on deck. She was relaxed, her color wonderful. "One doesn't hear cicadas in New York, Mr. Smith. And now, with the rise of so many buildings and ship masts, one has difficulty viewing unmarred sunsets."

"What do you do when you want to hear cicadas?" he asked softly, perusing the tender, heart-shaped curve of her jaw.

"I go to the family cottage in Connecticut where the trees and crickets are enormous. The frogs are enormous, too; dozens of them once lived in the garden reflecting pool. My nannies were very put out when I returned to the house with green skirts after wading barefoot in pursuit of the frogs."

He grinned. "Fie, what a wicked child."

Her lustrous green eyes danced impishly. "Not merely wicked. I was the horror of the gardeners, too. Once I cut every flower in the garden to cover the bed of a visiting actress who was occupying one of our guest rooms. She was very beautiful, but unfortunately allergic to pollen. She broke out with a rash and was unable to perform for a week."

His grin broadened. "Surely she realized the gesture was well meant?"

Suzanne's vibrant smile faded a little. "Unfortunately, no. When she stopped shrieking, my father gently informed me that actresses were a bit highstrung for mother substitutes, and that as he did not intend to remarry, I should probably get on with life."

"That was blunt," he observed soberly.

"But honest. My father was a good man who loved me dearly. I was difficult to dissuade when I wanted something. He had to be blunt." Noticing his involuntary wince as he shifted at the rail, she broke off. "Are you all right?"

At her unexpected note of concern at his grimace, Rafer almost told her the truth about his injury, but reconsidered. How could a woman respect a man who let another man kick in his ribs? "Indigestion." His rueful expression deepened the sun lines around his eyes. The lines were scarcely noticeable of late, lightened by the pallor beneath his tan induced by night owl hours and jabs in the ribs. Despite the well-cut finesse of his attire, he was tired, and looked it. "I didn't drink nearly enough this afternoon."

Sadness muted the reproach in her eyes. "Barring that lugubrious tale of disillusioned woe you delivered on the *Spangled Lady*, why do you drink so much?"

"Practice for the times I might want to appear sober. Being sober when one is not, is not only a social advantage, but a real necessity for an Englishman."

"Appearing drunk when one is not is also a social advantage," she suggested shrewdly. "Do you also practice for those occasions?"

He stroked her wrist above her pearl-buttoned kid glove. "Your father produced a cynical daughter."

She withdrew her wrist. "No, men like you did that."

He pursued her wrist. "Do I detect a note of experience?"

She gently slapped his hand. "Let us just say I am not the callow girl I was."

Half wondering why she had not tried to break his fingers, Rafer appreciated the magnificent curve of her breast beneath the close-fitted polonaise. She was quite right; nothing callow there.

He was enjoying this new Suzanne. On the *Memphis Belle*, she was pleasant, even sociable. If she bore a grudge over the New Orleans ballroom episode, she did not show it. Her composure might mean she was learning acceptance, which relieved him, or that she was learning, which intrigued him. He leaned casually on the rail to improve his view of her face, its tranquil mystery lent an air of ageless femininity by the veiling of her hat. He risked a probe. "Obviously, given your nannies, gardeners, and whatnot, you didn't claw your way up from the bottom of a frog pond to marry Bradford Hoth. From my experience of him, I might suppose your union was more the princess wedding a frog who continued to croak on the nuptial night."

"I never supposed Bradford was a prince, Mr. Smith: merely human."

"And rich."

She eyed him coolly. "In New York, being poor is equivalent to warty."

"And so you went through a wealth of princes to catch a frog."

"I'll tell you the sad, sordid story of my life if you tell me yours," she replied ironically.

"Of course. We have all night." As if baring the innocent face of his bride, he lifted the veil to smooth a tendril of her hair, lulled across her cheek by the breeze off the river.

Her dark lashes flicked down, veiling her reaction to his touch; when they lifted, her eyes had darkened as if a clear lagoon was disturbed by a fleeting, threatening shadow. "I don't think so. I'll wager you change life stories like pillow cases."

He laid a hand over his heart. "I don't lie about some things."

She laughed. "Rafer, you were boozily floating in Vera Cruz like a bass waiting for a minnow. A hook lurks in you somewhere that isn't merely set to snag passing women. At the heart of your devotion warms an inevitable frying pan; I have no intention of being devoured or burnt, thank you." She sobered again. "You are making a great mistake in baiting Ramsey. Sharks are nearly impossible to fit into frying pans."

"You don't think I could just whack him up and fry him a slice at a time?" he parried.

"If you care to continue a culinary career without arms." She touched his sleeve. "You really ought to cut the line on this one, Rafer."

He studied her sleepily beneath his tawny lashes. Tiny, evanescent, coppery lights from the setting sun played in the depths of his blue, impenetrable eyes. "If I could find Bradford and his gold claim," he drawled, "what would you give me?"

"Twenty percent of whatever I received from the claim."

"What if I wanted more than money?"

Her mind went blank, flailed for a bluff. Her grip tightening on her parasol, she forced herself to hold his steady, cobalt gaze. "We might come to some arrangement," she lied valiantly.

"Like you, I prefer guarantees," he said huskily.

"Would you accept my promise?"

"Would you accept mine?"

"We seem to be at an impasse." Her eyes turned sultry.

"Unless, of course, you give me more assurance of what you know about Bradford and his claim."

"You mean tell you where they are? Now? And you invite me to your cabin . . . now?"

She took a deep breath. "Something like that, yes."

"Of course, I'll talk," he said readily. "I'll chatter like a parrot."

"And lie like a blanket." She sighed. "We do seem to have a problem."

"If you're willing to seduce a man into a confession, you should be willing to believe him," he reproached mildly with a graceful, negligent gesture of water flowing over a rill . . . or the curve of a woman's body. "Even if he lies, what is one deliriously happy night, after all? I may be a rotten character, but dissipation calls for experience. Your husband was a rank beginner . . ."

"But promising," she amended slyly.

"Ah, judged by an expert, I see." The answering mischief in his eyes teased her into attempting an orderly retreat.

"I am not an expert," she retorted, "but a connoisseur, and fastidious. A cheap vintage may be had anywhere and is particularly distasteful saturated with scotch."

He eyed her flushed cheek. "Seasoned connoisseurs don't turn pink when comparing vintages. They sip, then discuss bouquet."

"You don't sip; you guzzle."

He moved closer, so much so that his breath shirred her veil. "I would drink deeply of you." His seductive gaze seared the curve of her throat and fragile, mutinous jaw. "Too deeply, perhaps, for either of us to forget"—he traced her earlobe—"but what is life without memories?"

She hastily edged away. "I want more than memories. I want my husband and his mine."

Rafer spread his hands helplessly. "If I give all you want now, you won't respect me in the morning. You might even leave me to appease Ramsey's patriarchal irritation while you chase off alone after your golden calf of a husband."

"We could both go . . . together," she pressed. "Once we found Bradford, I would give you . . . what you want."

"One night wouldn't be enough . . . even with you, beauty. I want tonight, and tomorrow night, and a good many nights thereafter."

She considered his suggestion with maddening concentration. She considered it through dinner that evening, and afterward as they danced in the *Belle*'s chandelier-hung salon. "Very well," she agreed finally. "We take on wood tomorrow at Natchez. Suppose I leave the boat first in pretense of shopping. You could meet me . . . do you know a decent hotel?"

"The Savoie; it's one of the finest in Natchez," he said quickly.

"Good. I'll check in for both of us as Mr. and Mrs. Madison." She was filled with triumph, amusement, and regret; baiting Rafer was going just the way she had hoped. The rascal really believed she would bed him just to pick his brains. By the time he realized his mistake, she would be long gone, with the both of them being better off. Once she found the claim, she would be bound to find Brad. She might miss Rafer more than she ought, but at least he would keep his skull in one piece.

Rafer must go, for his sake as well as her own. He ceaselessly wreaked havoc with her emotions and plans. He danced before Ramsey as if baiting the baleful Minotaur; inevitably, he would be gored. His drunken self-destruction also disturbed her, but then, arousing her sympathy was the most insidious of his seductive ploys. He was using every wile at his command to lure her into his bed, and they were all working. As she once overheard a dejected maid complain, "I'm a woman falling for a no-good man . . ." There was also her father's welfare to consider. She must be rid of Rafer!

With a conspiratorial air, she pressed closer to Rafer. "You mustn't come until the *Belle* has left at four o'clock in the afternoon. That way I shall know you are in earnest."

"I've never been more earnest in my life," he breathed. "I'll be there with castanets. But"—a knowledgeable glint appeared in his eyes—"how do I know my dance partner won't leave me performing a lonely fandango?"

Her eyes widened in half-real indignation. "You have my word."

"We have those all the time."

Her indignation became authentic. "You have the Maintree word."

"See you at the Savoie."

Upon entering his cabin after midnight, Ramsey was startled to find Suzanne rocking contemplatively in his Lincoln chair. "What the hell are you doing here?" he growled. "If you think I'll play footsie with my own son's wife . . ."

"I don't think we need Rafer Smith's escort into Colorado." The rocker did not alter a beat. "Would you be agreeable to being rid of him if we can discover all he knows?"

His eyes narrowed as he swayed against the bunk. His black cravat was askew beneath his coat, his flowered satin waistcoat stained. "Expect me to have Frock break his fingers?"

"Nothing so crude. I just want you to look the other way when I lure Rafer off the boat tomorrow, then not to raise a row if we aren't aboard when it departs. I'll meet the boat upriver in Vicksburg."

"Missy, I'm not dumb enough to let you run off with that bum after Brad's mine, and I'll break your fingers if you try." The erratic smash of his hand confirmed his drunkenness.

"I'm only going as far as the Savoie Hotel. You can have Frock follow me, so long as he remains out of sight."

Ramsey's suspicious expression turned ugly. "So I was right all along; you greedy tart. You'd bed a cactus to squeeze a drop out of it."

"Rafer Smith will get nothing from me, but whether he does or not is none of your business," she retorted coldly. "What he presumes he will get is the important thing. I plan to order quite a lot of champagne to lubricate Mr. Smith's memory at the Hotel Savoie; will you pay for it?"

"If you come back with the goods," he said slowly. "If not, you pick up the tab."

"That's businesslike." She pushed up from the rocker and headed past him for the door. "Your crude exterior hides a clerical mind, Ramsey. Just don't water the champagne."

He seized her by the arms. "Don't laugh at me, missy. You may think you can play Smith for a fool, but don't take me for one." Hard and hurtful, his mouth came down on hers in a short, brutal, bourbon-fumed kiss. "I get you in bed, you'll find out how much of a clerk I am."

Her eyes flaring with fury, she shoved against his chest. When he didn't let go, she slapped him with all her strength, leaving white marks on his face. He started to kiss her again and she hissed, "So you aren't too good to molest your son's wife!"

His liquor-flushed face darkening, he shoved her away so hard that she reeled back against the open door jamb with bruising force. She bolted from the cabin, and seconds later, slammed her own door and locked it. Shaking, she sagged against the door. Perhaps she should run away with Rafer . . . he was not the only one who should stay clear of Ramsey Hoth.

Upon leaving the *Belle* in Natchez the next day, Suzanne did some authentic shopping. After hiring out a leggy bay gelding with dynamite in its hindquarters, she bought a Colt derringer capable of making a nasty hole at close range. When the shopkeeper displayed a bizarre garter holster, she bought it, too, peeling off several bills from the small amount of pocket money she had pried out of Ramsey; he might pay for his own funeral as well if he grabbed her again. She devoutly hoped she would not have to shoot Rafer.

Rafer was at the door of her Savoie suite before the *Memphis Belle*'s farewell toot sounded around the Natchez Bluff. In his white linen suit and tilted straw hat, he was sober, suave, and rakishly attractive. "Good afternoon, ma'am." He swept off his hat and handed her an armload of red roses. "You look particularly charming; that's a wicked outfit."

Suzanne indeed looked wicked. She had purchased a canary satin peignoir ensemble trimmed in black ostrich from a disreputable shop near Under-the-Hill. The canary satin was in the worst possible taste, but she was suiting Rafer, not herself. This was not precisely her bridal night, and a man who spent his nights in places called Coco La Tienne's was not a man of cultivation.

She struck a pose that she assumed had lowbrow merit. "I enjoy dressing for a man who appreciates women, Rafer. Thank you for the lovely flowers." She delicately sniffed the bouquet of scarlet roses, then held them as far as possible from her peignoir; the colors clashed like a pair of cats. "Do come in." Retreating gracefully into the suite, she swiftly kicked back her limply dragging train.

As she put the roses in a gilt-handled vase, the door lock's click frisked butterflies through her stomach. She must keep Rafer in Natchez for six hours before she could escape. Six hours with no defenses except her brain, a sleazy outfit, and a two-shot gun. Sensing Rafer behind her, she gave the roses a last flick and turned quickly before he could settle upon her neck. "Rafer . . ." she began, but got no further before his arms went around her and his lips descended on hers. He kissed her for a long time that spun her imagination like a child's bright top. Scarlet on yellow, a spiralling, dervish flame. He was hungry for her, and while she might dislike his taste in negligees, she liked the taste of him. The sensuous skill of his mouth. The raw excitement, the hard possessiveness of his arms about her. The way his long body fitted to hers as he bent her back and sought the hollow of her throat. If he dizzied her the moment he touched her, she would be longer than six hours in Natchez. "Don't, Rafer," she protested faintly, "you make my head whirl . . . I'm losing my balance . . ."

"Good," he breathed, "I want you off balance. I want to make you crazy." His fingers slid beneath the peignoir to the satin-sheathed undercurve of her breast as he found her mouth again. Sheer electricity shuddered through her as he brushed the soft peak beneath the satin.

"No!" she gasped desperately against his lips as she tried to press away. "Rafer . . . please, not yet. This is too sudden . . . I need time to become used to you . . ."

"Why?" he murmured, still caressing her breast. "We're not here to take tea, but to make love. Hot and sweet." His lips grazed hers again. "You're trembling. You have trouble breathing when I touch you. Let me touch you, Su. Let me touch you all over. Let me make you shake like a leaf in a

hot summer storm . . ." The satin-covered peignoir buttons
were opening, his lips exploring her from bare throat to shoulders to the curve of her breasts. His murmured crooning was
like a wind, his touch like a searing lash of new rain on a
sultry Louisiana day.

I'm losing this fight, Suzanne thought dazedly. I'm going
down like a sapling in a hurricane, only to be left high and
dry when the storm's spent. My father isn't going to blame
the rest of his life because of one insane picnic in the rain!
Summoning her willpower, she gave Rafer a resolute shove
out of character with a swooning mistress. Later, she realized
she should have been warned his mind was not entirely on
romance when he did not lose his balance. "Rafer"—she
said breathlessly, her palm outstretched to ward him off—
"I see our time together as a sort of movable feast . . . with
courses . . . anticipation." Brushing a lock of hair from her
face, she backed toward the dressing screen. "I thought we
might begin with champagne, then dinner"—she hastily retreated behind the screen—"then perhaps take in a play . . ."

"A play?" He sounded bemused, if a bit breathless himself. "Are you serious?"

Well he might ask. Groping at her slipping peignoir,
Suzanne peeked over the screen. "Of course I'm serious.
The Lyceum Theatre is presenting a marvelous piece: *The
Drunkard's Daughter*. I've been wanting to see it."

"Been waiting with baited breath, have you?" He withdrew the champagne bottle from the bucket the room service
waiter had left on the table. He drew out the champagne and
expertly decanted the cork. "Anything else doing in town?"

"No," she muttered lamely as she repinned her hair, "*The
Drunkard's Daughter* appears to be about it." Trudging eight
blocks in a frantic effort to discover a way to occupy Rafer
had taught her one thing: in late June, Natchez was dead of
heat prostration. Hearing the champagne bubble into the
glasses, she squirmed hurriedly out of her ostrich feathers.
The more quickly she was into her black evening dress, the
safer she would be. Thirty-six buttons should daunt any man.
Kicking away the ostrich pile on the floor, she jerked up the
black dress with a rustle of silk.

"Actually, darling"—Rafer drifted with the champagne glasses toward the screen—"I was looking forward to another sort of show tonight. Wouldn't you prefer to spend the evening in?"

"Humor me, darling"—her fingers flew at the buttons—"I shouldn't want our first tryst to be rushed . . . and well, you see how . . . rushed we become after one kiss."

He offered her a sip of champagne, then ignoring his own glass, folded his arms over the screen top and intently watched the pale dart of skin exposed midway to her waist slowly narrow and deepen the cleavage of her full breasts. "Oh, don't mind me," he reassured as she fumbled at the buttons. "I wouldn't hurry you now for the world."

"You aren't angry, are you, Rafer?" She willed the stubborn buttons to shrink tamely into their loops. She could still view herself down to Hades and Rafer must be ready to vault the screen.

"Ever seen me angry?" His chin rested on his arms; from her low angle, she could only see his eyes: blue and disturbingly serene.

"No, but that simply means you conceal your emotions." Then something disturbed her more than his tranquility. "Could you make love to a woman you didn't desire?"

"Sure." He grinned lazily. "I'd just think about you."

The last button crept into its hole. "You sound as if you've said that before . . . to other women."

"I'm no virgin, Su. Was Brad?"

The question caught her off guard. "I . . . don't know. I don't think so."

His eyes became gentle. "You can't have been a brass-bound whore long if you don't know."

She went scarlet. "Ramsey assumed I seduced Brad. I didn't seduce him"—then her chin lifted—"but that doesn't mean I couldn't have."

"Darlin'," he murmured, "you could lure a man into hell even if he heard the howl of the devil. Come, finish your champagne and we'll go see your little morality play before we're very, very immoral."

Relieved, she emerged from behind the screen and accepted the champagne: halfway through it, he said casually, "Where's your luggage?"

"At the livery stable where I rented a carriage for us," she lied evenly, bolstered by champagne and foresight. "Levenson's Livery, near the river. I supposed we might spend the night here, then catch a packet boat in Ferriday. Ramsey will look for big boats coming from Natchez." She finished the champagne. "He didn't see you disembark, did he?"

"Oh, no," Rafer replied softly, his eyes enigmatic beneath the shadows of his thick lashes. "He was in the middle of a poker game. Wild horses couldn't tear him away. Old Toby, now, wasn't around and that's a bit odd."

"When his stomach ulcer troubles him badly enough, he keeps to his cabin."

Rafer drew her wrap about her pale shoulders. "How well do you know Ramsey?"

She ignored his subtle inference. "Well enough not to underestimate him."

He held the door open. "Clever girl."

They dined in the rococco splendor of Maximilian's. Candlelight, crystal, and a second bottle of champagne as the evening wore on made conversation easy. Suzanne almost felt as if she were in New York, but a New York where no one knew her, and she could do as she pleased. She could openly flirt, have fun. She could pretend she was going to make decadent love at midnight with a dangerous riverboat gambler whose blue eyes were luring her to blissful, if tragic ruin. Around his irises, the candlelight made golden circlets like the haunting underwater rings of the Nibelungs. Rafer was good at playing this sort of imaginary game. He looked the part of the seductive stranger, and his mysterious mood complemented hers. He kissed her fingers at the table and murmured pretty things, but part of him was restrained like a tethered hawk. She supposed he was either constraining his desire or mistrust, although he was in no hurry to finish dinner. He was satisfied to play her game for now. His British accent readily extended into a Southern drawl. He had an actor's melodious, effortlessly flexible voice; listening to him talk was like being stroked.

"Are you really from Colorado?" she asked finally. "You might have gone to school at Oxford."

"Would you believe that I could find your husband in the wilds of Colorado if I weren't a native?" He toyed with her fingertips. "Actually, I was born in a gardener's cottage on one of my grandfather's estates in Sussex, England. My father was the youngest of five sons of a baronet, which left him without even a cabbage patch, but with a yearning for the cabbage keeper's daughter. My grandfather raised quite a row when she produced my eldest brother. After exacting father's promise not to marry the lady, grandfather banished her and her father to a family game preserve outside London. Father adored the old baronet, but adored his rustic Chloe more. When he got her with a second son, grandfather insisted he choose between exile and respectability. Father moved to the game preserve. Four months later, the lady fair was blooming with me. Afraid she and dad would keep rabbiting until they were banished to the Isle of Man, grandfather gave up. He allowed them to marry and gave dad a stipend. Dad resented living on the dole, and as much as he hated leaving the old man, he finally packed up his rabbit tribe and moved to Colorado."

"Where your mother died."

"Yes."

"In New Orleans, you implied your mother bore you and your brothers in Colorado . . . that she was not up to the winters and bearing three sons." She arched an eyebrow. "You also inferred she breathed her last bearing you."

"That's right. You mentioned losing your mother and I assumed you would feel better if I had lost mine, too. Sorry to have confused you."

Suzanne stared at him. "That's despicable, but why should I be surprised?"

"Oh, don't worry. The belle of the cabbage patch left me in England when I was six months old. I never saw her again. She died when I was four and I didn't ship out for Colorado until I was ten years old. I stayed in Sussex with Grandfather. He didn't think I ought to toddle about in snowdrifts over my head."

"Why don't you ever call your mother, *mother*?"

There, she had him off guard. The golden rings radiated outward as if a stone had been thrown into still water, then retracted again about their dark, impenetrable pupils. His response was not as quick as usual.

"She wasn't; not really. Until I was six, I was convinced I sprouted from a cabbage patch. My grandfather made a magical flourish with a hoe, and lo, there I was, round and green."

She was undiverted. "You mean your grandfather, the baronet."

"God, no. I never saw him with a hoe in his life."

"Then you stayed with your grandfather, the gardener."

"Off and on."

"Then you were mostly at the manor."

"Mostly, I was in Ireland."

"What, pray," she asked patiently, "were you doing in Ireland?"

"Trying to figure out how little boys came from cabbage patches."

She sighed. "So Ireland's the source of this round of blarney, is it? Rafer, me darlin', or whatever your name is, you're a sad, funny man."

His riveting blue eyes held hers intently. "Why do you say that?"

"Because a man without a self is a sad thing, entirely. I don't say that, but my Irish great-grandmother always did."

He kissed her palm. "Did you really have an Irish great-grandmother?"

"Redheaded as meself. She had a black temper, too, and she married a ne'er-do-well named Tom from New Jersey."

"Who left you a Connecticut estate stuffed with nannies and gardeners."

"No, his brother, Kevin, did that. Great-granny's Tom broke his neck falling down a brothel stair. She buried him with a broomstick sticking out of his grave. She said the stick was his unmentionable and the only part of him that stayed upright in his life. The morning after the funeral, the broomstick was gone. A neighbor claimed great-granny had whittled the thing away with a bread knife at midnight. Incensed, great-granny went after the neighbor with the alleged weapon. In the midst of the fray, she fell dead of an apoplexy. Great-uncle Kevin buried her next to her departed husband under a gravestone as big as a buggy; he declared it was the only thing that would keep the old witch down.''

He grinned. ''You made that up.''

''God's truth. I have the broomstick chips in a mother-of-pearl chest at home to prove it.''

This time he laughed and she fell in love with him. She did not know she was in love, but later, much later, marked the moment . . . and understood why her redheaded grandmother loved a black sheep, set up a phallic monument to him, then whittled it to a splinter out of grief and spite.

The Drunkard's Daughter began at 8:00, then ran on and on. Rafer bent his fair head to Suzanne's glossy curls as the heroine of *The Drunkard's Daughter* bleated her woes to the gray, unfeeling canvas skies outside the pasteboard saloon where her father guzzled up the family's last dime. ''Do you know,'' he whispered, ''I think it's going to snow on the maudlin little twit's head, too.''

At Suzanne's stifled giggle, everyone within three seats' radius peered at her. ''Stop it, Rafer,'' she whispered. ''These people take temperance seriously.''

''I take it seriously, too, but you don't hear me groaning for a drink in execrable verse.''

Reassaulted by the urge to laugh, Suzanne coughed. Several people shushed her. Resolutely, she fixed her attention on the ragged waif onstage, only to hear Rafer's sigh of boredom. ''God, if the poor imbecile would only sing 'Dixie' and liven things up.'' When the heroine failed to oblige, Rafer began to whistle ''The Battle Hymn of the Republic.'' Soft and tuneless at first, the Northern battle song soon became recognizable to a predominantly Southern audience. Suzanne clutched his arm. Heads began to turn, indignant mutters to rise.

''Rafer,'' she pleaded under her breath, ''Appomattox was only five years ago. Don't start the war again.''

"Sorry." With a contrite squeeze of her hand, he switched to "Marching Through Georgia."

The theatre shortly exploded. "Shut ups," turned to, "why the hell should he's?" until *The Drunkard's Daughter* feebly squeaked into cowed silence. Shirt cuffs were rolled up, threats compiled, and the fracas began.

By that time, Rafer and Suzanne were climbing into their rented carriage. For two blocks, she did not speak to him, then questioned tightly, "Rafer, did your cheating start that fight in Mexico?"

"Which one?"

"The one where I rode you to ground before you raped me."

"I wasn't going to rape you; I just didn't sweep you off your feet with enough alacrity." He gave her a tender smile, rendered incongruous by the rakish buccaneer slant of his hat. "Instead of blithering after a bed, I should have made love to you on the barroom floor; you seemed quite content there." At her flush of remembrance, he clucked to the horse. "Get up, Nellie. The lady and I intend to view a lantern show of romantic Mexico tonight."

Suzanne assumed he was joking; he was not. Upon reaching their Savoie suite, he produced from his valise a lantern projector and twenty views of lovely Mexico; all naked and voluptuous with eyes of doelike submission.

Suzanne dropped the one he handed her like a hot potato on the scarlet rug, where it regarded her glassily. "How dare you show me this . . . this . . . ." She almost lost her temper and hit him again.

"Erotic art." He traced the Mexican lady's ample posterior with his polished boot toe. "She's a trifle Rubenesque, but aren't those plump elbows perversely fascinating?"

"I don't care to look at her elbows . . . or any other part of her!" Suzanne kicked the lantern slide across the room; it hid under the bed.

"Oh?" drawled Rafer. "I thought you wanted to kill time."

A warning bell clanged in Suzanne's mind, stopping her

in mid-contemplation of the sizzling epithet she was going to yell at him next. "Why should I want to do that?" she demanded warily.

"Because we're trying to outwait one another . . . I don't tell you anything until you tell me something . . . and vice versa." His bright blue eyes held a less than angelic glint. "That is why you're putting off going to bed, isn't it?"

Virtually leaping at the excuse, she flung her lace stole toward a chair as if impatient to lapse into abandonment. "Yes, that's it! Why not take care of business first, so we can relax?"

"Why not take turns? A little business, a little relaxation?"

"I'm . . . not sure i like that idea." With a provocative gesture, she invited him to open the new champagne bottle chilling in the ornate silver bucket. "I fear we should accomplish far more relaxation than business."

With a lazy smile, he unwired the champagne cork. "Our business can be dispatched in five seconds; that gives us tonight and every night on the way to Colorado to relax."

"What a wonderful prospect," she replied distractedly, her attention on the champagne. Room service would not have expected them to return so soon. If the champagne were insufficiently chilled, it might not cover the taste of the laudanum.

He handed her a glass of champagne with a suave smile of invitation. "To us."

Her crystal glass delicately clicked against his. "And to all those marvelous nights under the Western stars . . ." that you, dear boy, are going to spend alone with your Mexican art collection.

Her eyes seductively on his, Suzanne sipped her champagne. "Now, why don't we just spend our little seconds discussing my husband and his gold before I slip into a negligee?"

"Oh, there's no need to change . . . and I'm not in the mood for business just yet. Do you play poker?"

"A little . . ." She was bewildered. He wanted a round of cards?

"We'll keep the game simple . . . suppose we make it

blackjack. The winner asks a question and requests some trifling love token; the loser answers the question and surrenders the token.'' The twinkle in his eyes teased her. "Don't you think that might be amusing?''

"For you, perhaps. Frock says you're a very competent hustler at blackjack.''

He chuckled. "Good old Toby. He doesn't miss much, does he?'' He considered for a moment. "Why not have the hotel desk send up a new deck of cards to assure they're unmarked? I'll roll back my cuffs so I won't be able to palm anything, and you do all the dealing. I'll never touch the cards. What could be more to your advantage? Certainly, the proposal is more fair than my flashing my gold claim in innocent hope of some future reward.''

"It sounds fair,'' she agreed reluctantly. She smelled a rat somewhere, but if they debated protocol all night, she would miss the *Belle* at Vicksburg and Rafer might grow suspicious. Besides, if they played blackjack, they could not play what Ramsey Hoth so inadequately called, "footsie.''

The cards arrived by the time they had finished another glass of champagne. Suzanne reminded herself to ration her liquor; the idea was to snocker Rafer, not herself. Rafer smoothly pulled out a chair for her at the suite's bridge table. After placing the champagne stand closer to the table, he sat down and rolled back his cuffs. She dealt. He lost. "Where is the mining claim?'' she asked quickly.

"In Colorado.''

"I know that!''

"No, you don't.''

He was right; the mine might have been in California and he had lied about it being in Colorado. She began to deal again.

He eased his hand over hers. "Aren't you forgetting something?''

She had forgotten. "I'm supposed to ask you for . . . a love token.'' She hesitated, feeling as if she were a child fearing to put roses on the wrong bed again. "I'm sure I don't know what to request. Have you a handkerchief or well, whatever?''

He picked up a discarded cufflink, dropped it in her palm, and closed her fingers over it. Suddenly, she envisioned a bed of roses. She was sinking into them . . . sinking . . . and Rafer was making love to her, his touch igniting all the petals. As if the metal were scorching, she quickly put the cufflink aside and forced her vividly wandering imagination back to the game. He lost.

"Presuming I find my husband with his gold, where in Colorado is the claim?"

"Outside Denver."

"This is going to take all night, Rafer."

"In a hurry?"

"Well . . . naturally, I don't want to play cards until dawn." She managed a come-hither smile. "Why don't you toss me your other cufflink." He tossed.

She dealt. He won.

"Tell me one of your favorite ways of making love."

Was there more than one? She toyed with her necklace. "I like to have my earlobes kissed."

"Is that the wildest thing you can think of?"

"You didn't ask me for wild," she retorted uneasily, knowing he might next time. "Now, what token would you like?"

"Your necklace . . . but I want to remove it."

"That isn't in the rules."

"But it's more fun." He rose, came around to her chair back and delicately unfastened her paste emerald and pearl pendant . . . then let it drop into her cleavage. When her hands flew to retrieve the necklace, he gently caught her wrists. "Let it be. I'll have it another time."

"It's cold," she protested.

"Not for long," he murmured in her ear. "The cleft between a woman's breasts is as warm as summer on the Nile."

"I don't think so," she said weakly. "I feel like summer in Norway."

"Let's experiment. If the stones are still cold when I remove them, I'll kiss your pretty earlobes."

She swallowed. "Do sit down. You're affecting my concentration."

"Ah, yes, we must keep our heads, mustn't we?" He resumed his chair, and stretching out his long legs, lazily waited for the next hand; he won it.

"The necklace?" she said faintly.

"I haven't had my question yet. Do you like having your nipples kissed?"

She flushed crimson. "Must you keep being so personal?"

"Yes, intimate intrusive questions give your skin a delicious tint of vin rose." He quaffed his champagne. "I can almost taste you."

His bold blue gaze challenged her as she tried to shield her burning cheeks with her own glass. "If you don't answer a question," he reminded when she continued to evade the discussion of her breasts, "you forfeit your next one and I win an extra token."

"You're making up the rules as we go . . ."

"It's a fair rule, isn't it?"

She stared at the table. "I suppose I like . . . the area of kissing you mentioned."

"Your nipples . . . you suppose." He watched her turn a deeper shade of crimson. "Another experiment is wanted, I perceive." He lounged back in his chair. "Give me one of your slippers."

In five minutes, he won both slippers and knew she had been first kissed at the age of twelve. In seven minutes, he had a glove and knew the kiss was delivered by a fifteen-year-old boy in her father's library. In fifteen minutes, she had his jacket and knew the gold claim was not in Cripple Creek. By the hour's end, she was bare armed, with her combs lost, her hair tumbled about her shoulders. She had also lost twenty buttons down to her waist; Rafer insisted on cutting them off one by one with his penknife. The weight of the necklace in her bodice was pulling her décolletage dangerously low. Rafer was barefoot and minus vest and shirt studs. His tan did not stop at his neckline and the gold fur on his chest shimmered to his belt. Beyond that, Suzanne hesitated to imagine. She was playing for blood and honor now. She had narrowed the claim's location to a 50,000 square mile area, while Rafer knew, or presumed he knew, practically every detail of her personal life. When he started on Brad, she started lying . . . and prayed he was not. The card game was fair; he lost as often as he won, but the psychological edge ran against her. She was in a hurry; he was not. He could think clearly with his clothes falling off; she could not. Having to drink enough champagne to keep him pouring did not help. She was tight, and while not precisely sober, he held his liquor better than she.

Now she began to realize why Rafer did not have to cheat to win. They were not playing a game of cards, but of wills. Why not employ his own weapons? When he next claimed a silk stocking, she took it off slowly and deliberately. Watching his eyes go almost sulfurous with desire as he followed the trail of sheer silk, she saw she had discovered the flaming sword of victory.

After he lost the next hand, she waved negligently to his suspenders and with a supple gesture, he started to strip them off his shoulders. "Wait . . . why not make this more interesting, Rafer?" she suggested huskily, leaning across the table. "I'd like to take off your suspenders."

He gazed raptly at the jewels winking from the shadows between her breasts. "Shall I throw in everything attached? I do want to hold your interest."

"You're in no danger of losing it. I'm just warming to the game." She sauntered around the table and slid her palms down his chest to the suspender catches. The straps came off like a stripper's boa. She flipped the suspenders around her neck, and giving him an unimpeded silhouette of her breast in her half-buttoned dress, strolled back to her chair.

Inspired, he won the dress. She steeled herself for a stubborn seige.

On the next hand, she eliminated southeastern Colorado and claimed his pocket watch, but dared no more. He had three garments left to her three: her silk petticoat, wisp of a black lace merry widow, and a wispier stocking. Besides, his open shirt had the same effect on her as her exposed flesh had on him. They were staring at one another like smitten owls.

He won her petticoat on the next round and forgot his

question. She won the next round, scratched northeastern Colorado, and kissed the back of his neck. He won the next round, swung his chair around so she could put her foot on it, then slowly peeled down her stocking. She caught her breath when he bent to kiss the inside of her thigh.

"That equals two tokens, Rafer," she protested uncertainly as his head lifted. "I . . . want another glass of champagne. We're getting ahead of the game."

"I'll owe you a token," he murmured. "Care to unfasten my breeches? Without suspenders, they're sagging frightfully."

Involuntarily, her eyes dropped to the trail of fur below his navel where his breeches sagged precariously about his narrow hips; an assertive projection strained the linen. "I . . . I'd rather have the champagne first. This room is so hot I'm perspiring."

He trailed a finger down her bare, moisture-sheened shoulder. "So you are. So am I. This is a hot climate, isn't it? Almost as hot as Mexico."

At mention of Mexico, she snatched the champagne and glasses, then traced a hurried, if slightly erratic retreat to the comparative safety of the mantel. The mantel clock indicated a quarter until eleven. She must find out what Rafer knew now or never. She would be stone drunk if she had much more champagne. And if he inveigled past her merry widow he would find the vial of laudanum. "My father always insisted liquor made one overly warm, but I suppose you would know about that . . ." Her back to him, she babbled steadily as she placed the glasses on the mantel and poured the champagne. With trembling, awkward fingers, she fished for the vial, and emptied it into his drink. She turned, extending the doctored glass. "Let's have a final drink, Rafer, and a final game. After all, I'm wearing only one garment and you're down to three . . ."

"Two," he corrected amiably as he accepted the glass. "I forgot to buy underdrawers in Mexico."

"And you were too busy in New Orleans," she amended less amiably. She tossed down her champagne glass to reinforce her courage. "Rafer, I'm not conceding this game until you tell me what I want to know"—she struggled to frame the ultimatum coherently—". . . precisely what I want to know."

He saluted with a slight lift of his drugged glass. "You have been patient . . . and I might add, enchanting. You've very nearly earned your gold claim, so far be it from me to deny you any longer. Undoubtedly, you'll find your husband digging like a prairie dog at approximately 106 degrees latitude, 39 degrees longitude. Site number 43. There. Happy?"

She was and she was not. If Rafer was telling the truth, she had what she wanted, but his trust would be ill repaid. She suspected that Rafer bestowed his trust as sparingly as winter filtered snow over Georgia. She would not know whether he was lying until she reached mythical site number 43.

"You still don't believe me, do you?" he probed softly when she hesitated, her lovely green eyes perplexed.

"I suppose I have to believe you," she conceded faintly. "I've little choice."

"You always have a choice." He walked forward and took her into his arms. With her hands full of glassware, she could offer little resistance. "String along with me, Su. Even if I don't take you where you want to go, I'll give you a hell of a ride."

Something new underlay the passion in his kiss; she might have called it yearning, had her mind not been reeling with champagne and the sheer sensual sensation of his mouth. Warmth rushed through her, made her melt against him, her wrists locked behind his neck. She felt his readiness, luxuriant, against her body. The heat of his lips shifting to the arch of her throat. Her own treacherous willingness to surrender . . .

Then his head lifted as if he had been startled. He laughed. "*Carita*, those cold champagne glasses are dripping on my neck. Why not put them back on the mantel and finish the rest of this game in bed?"

Suzanne felt as if ice water had dripped on her neck. If she surrendered the glasses, she surrendered the game. She would wake up in another hotel where she could not pay the bill, with another man as reliable as Jesse James in an unguarded bank. Her senses still reeling, she forced herself to ease away and slip Rafer's drink into his hand. "I should like to offer one last toast to us." Blindly, she tried to think of one, then said the first thing that popped into her head. "To the gold and good times we shall share."

"Gold and good times; that's an interesting phrase coming from a lady like you," he mused, his blue eyes studying her with both desire and irony. "You wouldn't be leading on a poor, naive plowboy, would you now?"

"Come to bed and see for yourself, plowboy." She clicked his glass, and with a sultry stare, invited him to drink.

Wrapping his fingers around the curve of his glass as if it were her body, he swiftly complied, then firmly set the glass down on the mantel, took hers away from her, and placed it beside his. His arms went around her again. "And now, my fair seductress, it's time to pay the piper . . . or plowboy, if you will." With that, he gave her a kiss that obliterated any notions she might ever have had about his naivete. The next thing she knew, he was carrying her to the bed.

Frantically, Suzanne peered back over his shoulder to see how much he had drunk of the doctored champagne, but she was too giddy to tell. Not two, but six glasses seemed to dance across the mantel. "Rafer," she protested as he lowered her to the bed, "you wouldn't take advantage of an inebriated lady, would you?"

"Only with the most considerate devotion," he breathed as his lips grazed her neck and shoulders.

She shivered with mingled fright and anticipation. The apothecary said the laudanum took over a quarter of an hour to take effect. How much could Rafer do to her in that short a time?

She soon found out. Rafer could do little things with his teeth and tongue that made her senses sing. His hands shaped her, gentled her, distracted her from everything but his touch—and the quick, uneven sound of her own breathing. Rafer buried his face against her open bodice, his voice husky. "I like warm places, warm women. I guess that comes from freezing in so many Colorado winters. Your skin is like the sunlit snow on the Rockies: all golden fire and promise . . .'' Slowly, he lifted his head. ''I wonder if that necklace I dropped in the snow is still cold, *carita*.'' His fingertips slipped into the black lace, and her breath stopped as he withdrew the emeralds, one by one from their hiding place over her hammering heart. The smooth caress of his fingers, the minute rake of the hot, little jewels darted fire into her limbs and lower belly, as he undid the minute hooks, his lips tracing the path of the emeralds. He was finding softness, more softness, discovering a mysterious need in her that was becoming immediate. When he kissed her again, she kissed him back with a growing heat that made his hands quicken upon her body until she whimpered, wanting something more from him. His tongue had gone from teasing to erotic plunder, his fingers sliding up her thigh past the garter beneath the silk of her underthings. His lips found the crest of her breast at the same moment, his fingers slipped into her, finding a startlingly liquid heat. The delicate petals hidden between her thighs began to bloom, burn, blaze. Now she was beginning to understand the meaning of desire and the desperation to have it assuaged.

She forgot about winning the game.

Until she cried out his name and felt him go limp. Rafer did not fade out all at once, just slowly enough for her stark disappointment to register . . . and his realization of what she had done to creep into his eyes. He tried to say something, then gave it up. ''Damn . . .'' he finally whispered faintly. ''Damn . . . cold snow . . .'' His head dropped laxly upon her shoulder.

She could have screamed with frustration and disappointment. To be brought so close . . . Closing her eyes, she swore vehemently under her breath. Justice had served her exactly as she deserved by cutting her off in the prime of her passion. Rafer had gotten some of his own back. She would have given nearly anything to have him alert and ardent: anything but her father's future.

With a sigh from the bottom of her soul, she eased from under him, then sadly ruffled his hair. As tranquil as a child, he lay sprawled on his face, his long body taking up most of the bed. One bare foot hung over the end. She kissed the back of his neck. "Sorry to have missed that hell of a ride, cowboy. I wish we could have been going in the same direction."

Reluctantly, she rifled his pockets, but all that spilled out were a few coins and a curious, wadded up, long strip of cotton. Had he planned to tie her to the bed? Perplexed, she stuffed everything back.

Suzanne changed to riding clothes from the saddlebags concealed behind the screen, then caught up her discarded clothing from the floor. As she scooped up the last shoe, her attention was drawn by Rafer's bare foot. Level with her eyes, his sole was a single mass of scars as precise as if they had been calibrated. His other foot was a cruel match. She felt suddenly cold as if evil had crept into the room. Nowhere in Rafer's laughing eyes had been this horror. Who . . . what had done this to him? Fury filled her, then mixed with the champagne, making her want to retch.

Go, go! her mind screamed. His scars are old; you are young and cannot help him. God knows what scars lie inside his soul, why he drinks, and lies, and cheats. To stay with him is to venture into a hell you cannot conquer because you are not strong enough. You are not woman enough. To desire him is not enough. The delight in him you refuse to admit is not enough.

With a stinging sense of loss, Suzanne looked down at Rafer lying on the bed. You made me laugh, she reflected dejectedly, and did even that with a lie, because something inside you must twist in torment. With you, I never knew what was true . . . and in time I might not have cared. But you are the proof that no one can dwell in a carnival hall of mirrors; scars or no, you have been walking on shattered glass. Goodbye, Rafer Smith; I shall miss you very, very badly. With tears stinging her eyes, she started to touch his hair again, then did not. Swinging the saddlebags over her shoulder, she headed for the door, then just before closing it, stuck her head back into the room and yelled unevenly, "Don't drink yourself to death, dammit!"

EIGHT

Copper and Smoke

Suzanne's ride to Vicksburg was a long, unsteady one, particularly aboard a crazed antelope like the rented gelding. The gelding knew only how to run; to achieve any other gait was a battle of physical intimidation. Being drunk, Suzanne was not up to intimidating any creature weighing over a hundred pounds. The gelding had its way for more than a mile until she could control it long enough to manage a stumbling dismount and throw up. Woozily, she rode on at a jarring, sickening jog until dawn, when dispirited remorse got the better of her. In a black depression, she slid off the horse, slumped on a log, and held her head between her knees. Half of her wanted to return to Natchez before Rafer awakened; the other half recognized the disaster of that choice, also her incapacity to manage it. She must be nearly halfway to Vicksburg; but by the time she returned to Natchez, Rafer would be awake and furious. Even if he said nothing, his eyes had been markedly disillusioned before he lost consciousness. Her meager ration of the farm boy's trust was used up. If she failed to intercept the *Belle* when the steamboat took on wood midway to Vicksburg, she would also forfeit Ramsey's fickle allegiance and be stranded. She retched emptily and climbed back on her horse.

When the gelding wrenched a tendon in a rut three miles from the fuel landing, Suzanne tried not to give way to despair; barely two hours remained to intercept the *Memphis Belle*. She patted the gelding's sweaty neck. "Come on, Flutterbrain, we still have a steamboat to catch."

Suzanne led the gelding nearly half an hour before spotting

a white-framed farmhouse on a river bluff. Below the farmhouse was a dock with a fishing boat drowsing in the midday
sun. Haggling over boat rental would take time she no longer
had; also, the farmer might refuse. She tied Flutterbrain to a
scraggly farmyard pine, stuffed a reasonable price for the
boat under the saddle blanket, then scrambled down to the
dock. Flutterbrain's rump clearly bore the insignia of his
Natchez livery stable. If the farmer neglected to return the
gelding, she would be an accessory to horse stealing.

"Papa," she muttered, swinging the boat out into the current,
"I have tried to be respectable; to manage it, I have resorted
to the sale of my flesh, blackmail, saloon brawling, near
adultery, and maritime piracy. Being wanted as a horse thief
may not be a step up in life, but it proves I'm no shirker!"

Perhaps as a comment from some higher justice, the boat
leaked.

And when she caught the *Memphis Belle* by the skin of
her teeth, Ramsey was in one of his best moods. Suzanne
particularly loathed him when he was jovial; it invariably
boded ill. With a broadening smile, he looked her up and
down after she wearily rapped at his door. "You look terrible.
Had a hard night?"

Her hair straggling about her shoulders, Suzanne wiped
mud splatters off her face. Her hands were chafed, her back
ached, and she was starkly sober. "Natchez is a long ride,"
she rasped, "and a longer row. My horse gave out just before
noon. Your bill will be presented in the morning; it should
wipe that smirk off your face."

His smile turned flat-edged. "The bill bounces until I hear
what you pried out of Smith."

"Then it can bounce all the way to Colorado. Rafer Smith
is more talkative than I. I know what you want to know, so
mind your manners, Mr. Hoth, because I should like nothing
better than to stew you in your own arrogance."

He roughly caught her shoulder as she turned to leave.

"Wait a minute. Don't get smart with me just because you
screwed Smith out of some tall tale." A sharp prod in his
stomach registered the snub black nose of her derringer.
"What the hell . . ." At a sharper prod, he wisely silenced.

His horny-knuckled hand floated off her shoulder to hover like a battle-axe waiting for an opening.

"I'm in no mood for your insults just now, Ramsey," Suzanne said coldly, "so don't push me . . . and don't ever touch me again. I didn't 'screw' Rafer Smith, as you urbanely put it, and I am most certainly not going to screw you. Just now, I could cheerfully rerifle your pecker bore with a bullet. With you for a father, no wonder Bradford is warped. You're a disgusting sonofabitch."

His anger mixed with growing fascination, Ramsey watched her stride away down the narrow top deck. He was beginning to see why his son summoned nerve enough to marry Suzanne Maintree. She was one beautiful fistful of heat lightning. But she had given him the perfect way to snuff her out . . . with a little help from Rafer Smith.

Suzanne locked her stateroom door, and with a sigh of exhaustion and regret, sagged against it. The bittersweet mystery of Rafer lingered in her mind like the distant, out of tune piano music that drifted from the scarlet glow of Bourbon Street on a steamy night. Now sad, now gay, always haunting, the music came from a dark, forbidden region that beguiled the passerby with hopelessness, allure, and defiance. She remembered Rafer's deceptively guileless blue eyes, his ready smile, his scars . . . The splendor of his hands upon her. Gone.

Like that jellied lamb aboard the *Spangled Lady*, respectability awaited her: respectability in the meek shape of a dead, jellied sheep with glassy eyes.

Despite the heat, Suzanne did not open her stateroom shutters. She wanted the shelter of the cabin's shadows and musky copper light, its distance from reality and an empty dawn. Wearily, she tossed her hat and gloves on the dresser, then sat on the bed and pulled off her muddy boots. Lax with fatigue, her fingers slowly worked at the buttons of her riding habit. A few minutes later, her clothes hit the floor. With a kind of dull, inner rage, she stripped naked, then sponge bathed at the washbowl. As if it were a burning brand, she let the sponge linger on her skin, obliterate the memory of

Rafer . . . but in the dusk air, the sponge was cool, the water delicious as it trickled between her breasts and down her skin to fall unheeded to the floor. Her profile bronzed by the slits of sunset coming through the window shutters, she bathed her neck, then shook down her hair to cling damply to her shoulders and back. When her skin dried, her heavy, luxuriant hair would weigh hotly. She fanned the shadowy skein out and let it drop. One day, my hair will be white, yet I will remember a man who made me take it down for him at the turn of the cards.

Suzanne threw herself face down onto the bed and tried to sleep, but the heat wrapped about her like a restless lover. Fitfully, she tossed and kicked the bedclothes to the floor. At last, she dozed, to dream of Bradford in her bed, pressing her down, making her want to scream. She fought him this time, not giving in like a startled, frightened child. Then subtly, his clumsy, hurting hands turned into Rafer's hands that soothed her and lulled the fear into a waiting languor. She was floating, her heartache and fatigue easing away. I could sleep now, she thought, sleep . . . and forget.

Rafer's hands could always make her forget anything. Rafer's hypnotic . . . treacherous . . . hands . . .

Her eyes flying open, she screamed, but the sound did not carry beyond the cabin door, beyond the skilled mouth covering hers, already beginning its insidious enchantment. Rafer had never touched the laudanum for he had never touched that last champagne glass, she realized wildly. He let her think he was drinking the champagne just as he let her think she was winning, while she had been losing to a stacked deck. He held the high cards, and his ace in the hole was seduction. He had made her want him past reason, then denied her. She wanted to kill him, she wanted . . . Wanted.

Rafer's hands were pinning hers behind her head now, giving her no chance to fight him, fight the rosy glow of temptation that he was spinning about her. He was naked, the long heat of his body against hers a searing flame in the smoke-shaded shadows. Belying the soft, luxurious heat of his mouth, his sex was rigid, poised like an unsheathed weapon against her belly. She was afraid of his domination, yet relished the fear, embraced it. She had no chance against his superior strength, but refused to make his taking her into his world of mirrors easy for him. She bucked, bit at him until he fought her down with a skill that took her breath, her sanity.

When his head lowered to her breasts and he found their taut peaks, she cried out and arched against him, defying him, begging him. His shoulder muscles corded as he moved over her, sliding his nakedness against her, his sex seeking the entrance she struggled to defend. Their perspiring bodies writhed in growing darkness as if the last bars of sunlight were a lash, whipping them to desperate urgency. Rafer forced his knee between her thighs and opened her. Then, in a single thrust, he buried his sex deep. Her body stiffened at the shock, her lips parting in a single, muted cry of defeat that his own lips swiftly sealed with triumph. And yet, in his ragged breathing and the taut demand of his body as he began to move inside her, Suzanne knew the victory was not his alone. Rafer wanted her as badly as she wanted him. Their passion was a trap that caught hunter and hunted alike . . . tormented and exalted and maddened them. He was beyond teasing her . . . they both sought release and tore away any distraction, any barrier to it. Perspiration soaked the sheets as their bodies tangled, their wanting a blind, animal thing.

The hard-muscled drive of Rafer's body quickened and Suzanne clung to him, her body and mind no longer her own, but melded to his in chaotic need. Then he buried his face in her neck and took them both to a hidden, primeval place where they were inseparable. Where a piano played out of tune until its song became a high storm wind in the dark forest of their desire. A red glow wove through that darkness like a scarlet serpent that entwined about their mating bodies; it pulsed and twisted, then tightened unbearably to break into fiery stars. The stars blazed until the shivering forest bent low, blasted with an unearthly light. When that light faded, Rafer held Suzanne close and still, no longer fighting him. For better or worse, they were mated for life; deep within themselves, they both knew it, welcomed it as much as dreaded the hell it must bring them.

And yet . . . when she touched him, he found himself whispering, "Let me love you, Su. It's all so simple . . ." He kissed her until her head slipped back against his arm and her body went liquid against his. To Suzanne, his naked flesh was warm, like fawn velvet; the glide of his fingers across her shoulders irresistible seduction. He seemed to be carrying her into the garden at Broadacre. Green was the place where he lay her down, lush and silken the vale, like his touch upon her breast, his lips upon her eyelids and hair . . . her red gold hair, that she wove about him like an airy web. All sweet witchery was in their lovemaking, a spell that shivered in the rich silence.

In Rafer's touch was both ageless wisdom and the joy of newborn discovery. Dazzled by the sweet, Alexandrian splendor of his consort, his saturnine features were softened by the luminous light, making him younger than the Rafer she knew, unmarred, without mockery that slighted the world's injustices and obsessions. Like Druid's pools, the azure clarity of his eyes might have been painful, had she not seen herself reflected in them with such serene acceptance. He saw her flaws, saw her human soul beneath the fair, deceptive trappings the gods saw fit to give, yet loved her still.

In the lush spring of their unfurling desire sprang honeysuckle, its fragile coils slight serpent vines, young and green with quick, heated tongues. Bloomed fragile, trumpet honeysuckle from whose fragrant hearts slipped honey in pensive, pendant drops. With the soft whiteness of a swan, she lay innocent, her fingers winding in wonder through the silk of his hair, finding threads of gold, silver, and tawny russet; tracing the slant of his brows and feline curve of his lips. His lashes were like fine wires wrought by a gifted artisan who loved the effect of gold against lapis, but were so soft to her fingertips that they vibrated like tiny chimes through her skin. He let her touch him, explore him minutely, sensitively: each long, relaxed curve of muscle, the golden pelt thick as Jason's fleece across his chest . . . his subtly powerful shoulders. All that she had once touched in quick passion's heat, she enjoyed in abandoned languor, her exploration trickling down to his flat belly and below . . . to there. To that fair, curling thicket where his sex lay like a springing thorn grazed by a passing, heedless hand. Her imagination snagged, caught . . . became ensnared by smooth, pagan, swelling heat.

His body bent like a golden bow to play upon her ivory set with emeralds and rubies, as a bard from whose lips so purely spilled ancient, wondrous songs of misted legend, of ruined stones upon a plain at nightfall, and viridian dragons enwreathed with seductive smoke, of priest and priestess, witch and warlock, sinuously mating by equinoctial moon. Of torchlight weaving above a chanting in strange tongues by swaying figures with naked bodies painted in changing hieroglyphs. The lush ivy, the pale-berried mistletoe wrapped their glistening bodies in joining, the restless phallus seeking, distracted by the rise and fall of her lush breasts, her lustrous, lax thighs pressing swelled, scarlet fruit. Blue-fired, that fierce gilded shaft blindly split her, the berried juice spilling high to swarming bees of Eros. About their bodies' ripe, wanton scent came the sweetly repeated sting. The flaring in his eyes gave lie to his patience, warning that she tarried too carelessly. His arms tightened, his deceptively languid kiss slow, sweet retribution. She bloomed beneath his caresses, the rosy peaks of her breasts grazing his fingers. Catching desire in virginity's fragile snare, her body opened again to him, unfolded before the thorned prick of his manhood with the passion of a flower unfolding to embrace its sting. The fierce, gilt-sheathed shaft pressed deep, inflamed at her sweet yielding. His caresses wound about her like garlands of clarion lilies. She embraced him, celebrated him, and spring's starry night became a summer of suns. The zenith centered, splintered, flowered across the sky in slowly fading arcs until descending night left only a memory of their patterns.

Rafer's arms tightened with involuntary possessiveness about Suzanne as her head rested upon his shoulder. He had been virtually ready to rape her in Natchez. To let her walk out of that Savoie Hotel room had taken his last mangled shred of willpower, and now his desire was merely whetted. She was an unpredictable young lioness who might easily turn on him in mid-purr, yet he could no more shed his fascination with her than cease, breathing. He had wanted many women; schemed and fought to possess them, but Suzanne awakened a primal obsession. She was all claws and lush velvet, sophistication and vulnerability, tempestuousness and surrender. No female had ever resisted him so fiercely, only to yield with such entrancing complexity.

How could a woman with Suzanne's slight sexual experience of men know so unerringly how to ignite them? She feared men, and him most of all, yet when she gave herself to him, she held nothing back. Although unable to see her face clearly, he knew she must be weary, her lips bruised from his demanding kisses. He stroked her, and beneath his fingertips her breasts were full and beckoning, while the slope of her slim belly was a soft, mesmerizing plain that dropped to the lush, coppery pelt between her thighs. She stirred beneath his caresses, touched his face in mute appeal. Silently, he moved over her again and kissed her eyelids as he slowly pressed himself within her. Like sleep, he drifted upon her, lulling her into an erotic dream, letting her wind about him, taking him deep within the heart of her. Rafer made love to her as if he were night upon the river, swirling, easing, quickening until the night birds called low over the water's sigh. Then the river spilled in a pure, silver, moon-spun waterfall that welled serenely outward toward sleep.

A sleep that Rafer could not share. As soon as Suzanne's breathing evened, Rafer rose from the bed. Soundlessly, he dressed, then brushed a kiss against the spill of her hair and left her before dawn.

Suzanne did not awaken until noon. Drowsily, she lay with her eyes closed, hoping to drop off to sleep again. Her body protested any effort to move, yet the ache was soothing, almost pleasant. Slowly, the reality dawned that she ached inside as much as out, with Rafer to thank for it. At that vivid recollection, she abruptly sat up, all vestiges of sleep departed.

How could I have let him! she railed, perfectly well aware how, and just how deliciously. Rafer had been as wonderful a lover as she hoped he would be; if truth be told, he was unnervingly better. If she had known upon meeting him in Vera Cruz what she knew this morning, she would have throttled him on the spot with her parasol.

Then throttled herself out of remorse.

Rafer must be gleeful as a grig this morning, and why not, when he only needed to look at her to make her go soft in the knees . . . and the head. They had both known last night was inevitable; it was also disastrous. The hard light of day shone on several immutable unpleasantries; Rafer was more in lust than in love. Mining claim number 43 that he described during their blackjack game in Natchez must be nonexistent; a sop to put her off guard so he could seduce her. Whatever his emotional involvement, he would try to use her now. Rafer was as manipulative as Ramsey, and far more skilled as a cheat than either Marcus Hampton or Bradford. If she let him outmaneuver her, whatever hope she, and her father, had for the future would be wrecked. She might go to hell in a red satin-lined reticule, but she had no right to let her father down. What was she going to do now?

Finally, she thought of something, and it made her cringe.

NINE

Duplicity and Second-Hand Doxies

Just after dawn, Ramsey rapped on Rafer's cabin door. Receiving no answer, he glanced speculatively toward Suzanne's nearby cabin. He started to knock, but changing his mind, went directly to breakfast. Suzanne's losing Rafer in Natchez was as likely as a watermelon scampering away from a hungry urchin. En route to the lounge, he spotted Rafer's rangy figure lounging at the bow. An ironic smile twitching his lips, he strode forward. "You're up bright and early for a gambling man."

A trace of fatigue blended Rafer's husky reply into the lulling rush of the paddlewheel. "I like the quiet after the rattle of the roulette wheels." Low-lying mist threaded across the water. A heron minced along a fallen tree trunk partly submerged in shallows turning platinum in the low, hazy sun. Ramsey noticed a stillness about Rafer, a serenity beyond his customary laziness. Ramsey attributed Rafer's serenity to the complacency of a presumed victory. Either Suzanne had gotten her bustle dusted, or she and Rafer were up to something. A secret alliance might present some trouble, but he was not much worried; having fed less trouble to the Chicago River fish.

In reality, Rafer was merely observing the heron reflected in the flickering, satin glow of light on the water. Suzanne's beauty was as luminous as that light, her mind as intriguing as that inquisitive, hunting heron. Perhaps, one quality without the other would not have appealed to him . . . and without her underlying vulnerability, all the beauty and brain in the world would not have drawn him. She lingered in his mind like a soft, lambent flame: sunrise on a still river.

"Considering you haven't been near the *Belle*'s gaming tables for two nights, I'd almost believe you've exchanged roulette balls for monk's beads. Did you enjoy your retreat in Natchez?" His eyes were bright and sharp beneath his bushy brows.

"I always enjoy myself in Natchez," drawled Rafer with a wicked grin, "but I expect Toby told you just how much."

Ramsey pulled out his fob watch and flipped up the cover. "You were alone with my son's wife for three hours and forty-six minutes total." The watch case snapped shut. "Frock's an accurate man . . . knows I'm a bear about details. Sooner or later, I exact an accounting."

"Yes, expectation salves the spirit, doesn't it? And so few people like to disappoint a bear." Watching the heron snatch a bullfrog, Rafer meditatively stroked the stubble of new mustache begun in New Orleans. "Were you disappointed in your daughter-in-law?"

Ramsey laughed shortly. "Cats go after rats." With a flash of monogrammed cufflinks as he gripped the rail, he leaned toward him. "Suzanne says you told her where to find the gold claim. Is that right?"

"One must never underestimate that lady's elusive charm. I practically invented fillings just so I could surrender them. In the mad excitement of those three hours and forty-six minutes we were alone together playing blackjack at the Savoie, we talked of nothing but drill bits"—Rafer yawned—"but I daresay she doesn't believe me this morning."

Ramsey's blunt hands tightened on the rail. "Don't lie to me about shuffling cards at the Savoie, you sonofabitch . . . did you lie to her about that gold?"

"A man is never responsible for anything he tells a woman before breakfast." Rafer winked and strolled off to breakfast.

He was less laissez faire when Suzanne drifted languidly into the dining salon at dinner. A cream panné dress was caught at her shoulder by a peach gold lily embroidered in seed pearls. Despite the slight weariness in her posture, she looked particularly beautiful, like a full bloomed rose before it drops its first petal. She kissed Ramsey's cheek as he rose to greet her. "Forgive me for napping so long, dear," she murmured conspiratorially. "I slept so little last night." Her arm linked in the bemused Ramsey's, she glanced at the table she had bribed the waiter to set for two, then offhandedly at Rafer. "Do take your chair, Mr. Smith. Ramsey will order another place setting for me. We really didn't expect to see you this evening."

"Where did you think I would be?" Gallantly, Rafer offered her his seat and took an extra chair.

"In Natchez," she replied evenly as she picked up her water glass. "Where else?"

Rafer was puzzled. What was her game? "A man can play blackjack only so long," he replied softly.

He expected her to flush; she did not. Her attention was all on Ramsey, who was ordering the extra place setting from the maître d'. Rafer Smith might have been in Natchez. "You lost at blackjack, Mr. Smith, and I won," she lied baldly, when the maître d' was dismissed. "Twenty-two hands to twenty. Remember?"

"If you say so." Rafer smiled into Ramsey's hard stare. If Suzanne hoped to quell the old man's suspicions, that was fine with him, but she had not a prayer in hell of succeeding.

As the evening wore on, Rafer knew Suzanne was bent on convincing someone of something. Her behavior subtly suggested she was Ramsey's mistress rather than his daughter-in-law. She laughed at his jokes, lit his cigar, and when the tables were cleared aside for dancing, lured him out onto the floor for the first waltz. Ramsey was not a difficult man to lure. He considered a beautiful woman on his arm his due, and enjoyed that prerogative to the hilt. While he had no illusions about Suzanne's motives, he displayed her like a king his queen. Having always suspected Ramsey's interest in Suzanne was less than paternal, Rafer now began to wonder whether her interest in Ramsey was less than filial. When Ramsey drew her too close, she always evaded him with a laugh, and yet . . .

Pricked by jealousy, Rafer cut in. After Ramsey reluctantly surrendered Suzanne and forged through the crowd to the mirror bar off the salon, Suzanne immediately preferred to discontinue dancing. "Good," agreed Rafer swiftly. "We'll stroll on the deck." His voice lowered as she started to demur, "We can either talk here or in private, but you're not wriggling out of it. You slipped me a mickey last night, remember?"

"Don't blame me because you drank too much," she retorted, futilely trying to pry his grip loose from her wrist, but he inexorably drew her toward the door.

"I do blame you. I've been doctored with laudanum in my time; you put enough in my last glass to drop an elephant." He whisked her out onto the deck. "That wasn't sporting, darling."

"If you prefer sporting, darling," she muttered with a rising note of anxiety, "try cricket. Now, let go!" Nodding politely to the deck passersby, Suzanne tried to jerk away without being obvious; the ballroom battle in New Orleans had been sufficient embarrassment for a lifetime . . . and the last thing she wanted was to be alone with Rafer. She had to end any idea he might have of their sleeping together again. Once he assumed she was involved with Ramsey, he would leave her alone. Their relationship could not possibly continue if she hoped to find her father. Rafer was much too unreliable, untrustworthy . . . and distracting to risk her father's welfare by pursuing a doomed love affair. If he began to make love to her, she would never be able to sustain the farce of preferring another man.

"Oh, come on, Su, don't be prickly," Rafer soothed, sterring her away from the salon lights. "I gave you what you wanted, and you gave me what we both wanted; that wasn't so bad, was it?" he whispered. When they were in the dark shadows of the aft deck, he drew her, still struggling, into his arms.

Aware that they promised her ruin, she evaded his lips. "What do you mean? You had nothing from me but a less than fond farewell at the Savoie." Her tone barely managed the conviction of a martyred saint.

He nibbled her ear. "As I recall, your farewell was rather reluctant, and last night . . . in your cabin, we were deliriously fond of one another."

Pushing against his chest, Suzanne fought to keep her voice steady. "Spare me your ambitious imagination, Rafer. You were not in my cabin last night."

He laughed softly. "If I wasn't, who was?"

In the darkness, he must have been unable to tell whether she was flustered or confused. Finally, she croaked, "Can you not guess?"

Rafer started to throw back his head and laugh, but then the laughter stuck in his throat. "Come on, you don't seriously think . . . that I think . . . you didn't know . . . good God, you expect me to believe you believed you were . . ." He looked as if he wanted to be sick. "Have you been sleeping with Ramsey?"

She forced herself to meet his eyes. "He came to my cabin for the first time last night."

"You thought that rotten old boar came to your bed?" The words came out like jagged glass as his hands bit into her arms. "You're lying."

"Why should I lie?" Suzanne whispered miserably. She expected jealousy, but not this strong a reaction. Lying about an affair with Ramsey was bad enough, but surely she had little power to hurt Rafer. Last night could never mean as much to him as it did to her. She tried to soften the blow. "In his own way, Ramsey has a strong character . . . and can protect me. Can I ever really count on a tree spirit like you for that?"

"What are you trying to do, play us against each other?" he gritted. "The old boar's rich; that's it, isn't it? Nothing will ever mean as much to you as money."

His stinging insult roused her flagging resolve into hurt, defensive anger. "You're out of the game, Rafer . . . even if you're sitting on all the gold in Colorado."

"Well, you'll never find your unlamented husband's claim without me, and if you think you anticipate a repetition of last night with Ramsey, you're in for a dreary surprise." He pushed her away.

"What makes you think you're the best lover in the world?" she cried softly. "There is more to love than expertise on a playing field. What is sporting about a man who sees love as a game and a woman as an opponent? I'm tired of playing games and competing for everything, Rafer. I don't want to fight anymore."

He started to turn away, then abruptly changed his mind and caught her to him. "If this is your idea of fighting, you'd better arm for war." He kissed her then as if he would crush her, beat her down into the earth, and never let her rise. "We're not done yet, Mrs. Hoth. If you spent last night with another man, you still owe me a night. When you have the most to lose, I'm damned well going to collect." His mouth covered hers again, his kiss both a threat and a promise.

Rafer did not return to the salon, but to the roulette wheels where a buxom French girl copped shills for a croupier. The gleam in her black eyes matched the croupier's knife, which suited Rafer just fine.

Suzanne went to her cabin and took a cold bath, which turned lukewarm. Sitting in hip deep, tepid water like a forgotten baby, she bawled.

Rafer avoided Suzanne for the next three days, while Ramsey's persistent company sorely tried her patience. At length, she became accustomed to Ramsey; despite his rough manner, he was a shrewd and interesting man. Born in an alley, the idea of living in one was even more repellent to him than her, with one difference; he did not fear poverty. In his climb to financial and political power in Chicago, he had been beaten down more than once, only to rise from his defeats.

"You know, Ramsey," Suzanne observed late one morning as they promenaded the deck, "you and Rafer are exact opposites; you're inflexible as iron, while he bends with every current, yet you both seem indestructible."

"We're different, all right. I'm a winner and he's a loser. As for indestructible, I can swat him like a fly." Ramsey tilted his gray stovepipe hat down against the bright sun. "I'm a lot meaner than Rafer Smith; had to be, to claw my way out of the gutter. He likes the gutter; rolls in it like a pleased pig." He fixed her with a sly eye. "Night before last, he had a penny ante knife fight with a croupier pimp who floats a floosie past the suckers. She's not talking, but the pimp left the boat somewhere between the wood stop and Vicksburg."

"The boat doesn't stop between the wood stop and Vicksburg," Suzanne replied between set teeth, then caught herself, realizing what he meant. "Will Rafer be in trouble when we dock in St. Louis?"

"Not if I say he was with me when the departed party went over the side. You worried about him?"

"Only until he leads us to Bradford," she retorted. She was worried, but also seething.

After the noon sun emptied the upper decks, she beelined alone for Rafer's cabin. Taking his time to answer her angry knock, he opened the door six inches. Unshaven, his shaggy hair dishevelled, he wore only breeches, a worn bandage around his ribs, and another bloodstained bandage carelessly wound about his upper arm. The cabin was hot, his brown body sweat sheened. For an easy living man, he had a whip-cord torso and the shoulders of a stevedore. "You rang, madame?" A note of irony tinged his easy drawl.

Clang! A brassy bell at her back made her start. A small boy dragging a toy fire engine along the rail, clang, clanged toward the bow. Suzanne gave a sigh of relief; she did not need to be seen conversing with a half-naked man at his bedroom door. "Did you kill that . . . that . . ."

"Pimn? No, indeed; unfortunately, he could swim like an otter."

"Well, he might have killed you," she reminded sharply. "Can't you behave for three days running?"

"You mean grow plump and boring? A fit reprobate generally endures to a ripe old age."

"Unless he has his throat cut."

Sliding his hand up the door jamb, he leaned toward her. "Do you give a damn?" he murmured.

She hesitated, then heard an impatient stir of sheets. He must be fornicating with the departed croupier's floosie! Pain and sheer, green jealousy swept through her. "No . . . I don't give one blithering damn! And I hope your second-hand doxie bites off your head!"

His undomesticated grin flared wickedly. "Oh, she loves to bite, but it's not my head I'm worried about."

She was too angry to know what he meant, then abruptly, her confused eyes widened. "You . . . are . . . disgusting!"

"Oh, I don't know," he murmured. "She is my age and has all her teeth; that's more than you can say for your latest lover."

Too hurt to snap back, Suzanne was surrounded by dry desolation. Rafer owed her nothing. To him, she was one more woman in a long line of them, and whatever loyalty she might have won from him was forfeited. "That's fair," she replied expressionlessly, "but if you become involved in a criminal case or scandal, we'll leave you flat. Do you understand me?"

"If I understood you, you'd be in my bed with Ramsey for a bearskin rug." He smiled quizzically. "You've caught a grizzly by the tail there, my sweet. A grizzly has no tail to speak of, and less patience. When the fur starts to fly, it's likely to be the shade of your pretty hair."

"Don't count on it . . . but do stay for the show; vultures thrive on that sort of thing." She left him to his impatient sheets.

The next day, most of which Rafer spent in the gambling salon with the French whore, they left the boat at St. Louis to catch the Kansas Pacific train for Kansas City. The train station where they waited for four miserably hot hours, was bedlam. With St. Louis both the wagon train jump-off and the railhead for points west, no one who could afford a train ticket cared to spend months trekking by wagon to California. The West was the promised land with the lure of gold still singing its waning siren song in California and the Pike's Peak region of Colorado. New opportunities and dreams daily sucked pioneers and adventurers from the overcrowded East and war-battered South into St. Louis. Where once the city was crowded in spring, emigrants now arrived year-round to jam the train station and compete for seats. With heads full of illusions and pockets nearly barren of money, they crammed dusty cars, where men perched like scrap-tailed crows on rail car tops heaped by luggage.

Standing with her back to Rafer on the train platform behind a barrier of streamer trunks, Suzanne viewed the hubbub with a New Yorker's wary interest, while Rafer, with his planter's hat tilted low over his eyes, appeared half asleep. Her own hair sodden with perspiration in the July heat, Suzanne gathered with asperity that his poker game and tart were demanding. Ramsey was shouting orders to Frock and three Irish redcaps ferrying luggage to his private rail car. The outsized rail car stood out from the dusty train like a peacock on a line of sparrows, the shine of its polished green and gold as bright as new money in the prairie sun.

Finally, Ramsey beckoned. With Rafer drifting behind her, Suzanne passed slat-seated cars overcrowded with flushed, tired adults cramming baggage beneath seats, and tugging overexcited children away from open windows. Suzanne and Rafer boarded Ramsey's car in the wake of her luggage to enter a serene, luxurious world.

The rail car was fitted out like Ramsey's yacht, with mahogany panelling, green plush upholstery and swagged, gold-fringed curtains. Etched crystal kerosene lights were mounted on the walls between paintings of hunting scenes. Along the dining table was a fixed Collcutt sideboard with crystal liquor decanters, a silver tea service, a tooled cigar box, and all the trappings of a travelling potentate. Lining the side walls were two green plush banquettes with folding snack tables. A redcap disappeared through a sliding door into the rear of the car containing the galley and bedchambers. Despite the car's grandeur, the windows were closed and the staggering heat slammed into Suzanne. Faint, she tugged hard at an unyielding window, then started to summon the redcap. Rafer moved her aside. "Go to your room and loosen your stays. On the open prairie, the dust will be as bad as the heat."

She started for the back of the car, but unable to catch her breath, leaned against the sideboard. No air came to her stifled lungs. "Where is my room?" she asked vaguely as a redcap hurried back past her. Spotting her pale, dazed face, Rafer pushed around the redcap, caught her up, and disregarding her fallen hat, carried her back into one of the sleeping compartments. "Is this the right one?" she whispered faintly, her head lax against his shoulder.

"Does it matter?" He dumped her on the bed and unfastened her buttons. Halfheartedly, she fought his fast-working fingers, then her stays gave, and with her eyes closed, she inhaled a deep, grateful breath of stale air.

After a few moments, her temples ceased to pound. Her head clearing, her eyelids flickered open as she stirred. Rafer was staring down at her, his blue eyes hard and intent; in them was a feral, even ruthless gleam of resolve that made her start in apprehension. Suddenly aware of her open garments, she defensively caught at her bodice and reared up, ready to fight him. "Relax," his clipped drawl was mocking. "Give me credit for a sense of timing. I could rape you in a matter of minutes, but haste makes waste, doesn't it? Besides"—his face neared hers—"your aged lover should have his due; he's paid for it, just as you'll pay for him. Is the luxury of this plush-lined coffin worth being groped by his greedy hands every night?''

"Stay away from me, Rafer," she flung back tersely. "Keep to your cards, and your bottle, and your tarts. You're a bounder and you'll never be anything but a bounder; at least Ramsey goes after what he wants.''

His narrowed eyes burning into hers, he placed his hands on either side of her. "You want me to go after what I want?''

"You don't want anything . . . not badly enough to hold on to it." She challenged his lynxlike glare. "You don't want me that much.''

He shielded his intensity. "Probably not. A woman for sale is rarely worth the price, particularly when a man has to stand in line. On the other hand, a complacent woman is a sitting duck.'' He touched his hat rim in a mocking salute as he eased open the door and stepped into the aisle. "You are in my room. If you care to stay, I prefer the left side of the bed.''

In less than a minute, Suzanne was installed in her own room.

Missouri was flat; according to Ramsey, Kansas was flatter. Suzanne had never seen so much sere, monotonous country. The rare breaks in the vast, treeless landscapes were occasional, meandering cows and rivers. Rusty water towers and windmills stood like spindle-legged storks above the simmering prairie. Along the railway, raw-boned towns were laid out in sparse lines as relentlessly straight as the track. Behind gimcrack facades, the buildings looked as temporary as unpainted cardboard. Despite the heat and blowing buffets of dust, the streets streamed with people. When the train wheezed into a stop, they squeezed down the metal steps to stand tired and bewildered with their bundles on the train platform; more passengers boarded, their clothes and faces worn, their children apathetic. Waiting for the eastbound train was an even poorer, paler lot, bound back to the dead hopes left on the far side of the Mississippi River.

Was this the golden West, the new land of milk and honey glowingly described in the St. Louis newspapers? wondered Suzanne, gazing with glazed boredom from the rail car window. Her ennui was tinted with uneasiness. This country might be newly settled, but its towns resembled skeletons picked clean by ants. The landscape was as lonely as a sigh.

When the air cooled at dusk, Rafer followed Suzanne out onto the rail car's rear platform. Against a red and purple dusk, the setting sun was turning the prairie to a golden sea, where long waves of grass rippled southward with the Canadian winds. Although the rustling lullabye of the prarie was overwhelmed by the train's noisy passage toward the huge, blazing ball of the sun, the land held an undisturbed sense of peace. Arching her head back, Suzanne leaned against the platform's vibrating rail. The breeze felt wonderful, drifting her perspiration-dampened hair, whipping the strands escaping her chignon like long sparks of fire in the lilac light. Suzanne leaned against the rail, and arching her head back, took a deep breath of cool air. "I wonder what makes the Western sunsets so red."

"Tomorrow's dust." Rafer joined her at the rail, his loosened cravat winging like a sailor's scarf. "Depending on the geography, the sun's light alters in shade as it filters through the horizon haze. I don't know precisely why." He cocked his head. "I also don't know precisely why you became involved with Ramsey."

Brushing back her hair from her forehead, she considered. "His business and family concerns aside, I think he takes me seriously; he would not have come this far with me if he did not."

"And Bradford?"

She had almost forgotten Bradford existed. "Bradford has always done what he liked," she replied evasively. "He's quite independent in some ways."

"But not much of a man."

I wasn't looking for much of a man, she reflected with a twinge of guilt. I just wanted a husband. Why keep trying to hide the obvious truth? Rafer must already believe the worst.

"Bradford was man enough for me," she said quietly. "Insensitive immaturity is unpleasant to admit, but at the time we married, I didn't deserve more of a man, and perhaps if I had been more understanding, he might not have run so cravenly.'' She caught Rafer's dubious expression. ''I never tried to understand Bradford until I feared him dead. He was simply there, like the sign on Fifth Avenue. Go this way to Park and Forty-fifth for a secure life.''

''What if his father gets you pregnant?'' Rafer countered expressionlessly.

''He won't.''

His lips curved sardonically. ''Why not? Because he's old? Ever read your Bible? Abraham began Isaac, and Isaac begat Jacob, and so on through Aminadab, Slathiel, and the rest of their earthy host. How many of those randy old sheep-herders were under fifty?''

She returned to the subject of age. ''Ramsey's age really bothers you, doesn't it? If you were my lover, what would you do if I were pregnant? Take off for Tucson or wherever?'' She patted his arm with jaded affection. ''Save your concern, Rafer. Virtue fits you like a five-fingered glove fits a bobcat.''

His lips crooked. ''What nannie taught you that well-bred phrase?''

She laughed. ''A nannie named Ivan Imagination, who writes well-bred articles for *Godey's Lady's Book*. Thanks to you, I am developing an ear for colloquial dialect . . . which reminds me, you never said whether or not you were really English.''

''Perhaps a wee bit more Welsh.''

She laughed. ''Even more than Irish? And what about ever having been married?''

''God, no.''

''Pregnant?''

''Beg pardon?''

''Have you never been a father?'' she expanded helpfully.

''Possibly.'' With an unsettling lack of remorse, he nuzzled her ear. ''I never lingered long enough to find out. Always headed to Tucson or wherever.''

She oozed away from his diverting exploration. ''Aren't you concerned that some poor girl might have been left in the family way?''

''Oh, my poor girls always had some poor fellow to take

over the family end. He'd invariably merited every wet dia-
per." His lips grazed her nape. Despite the treacherously
delightful tickle down her neck, her wary recollection of his
lecture on maternity left her undeterred. After Natchez, he
had begun to grow a mustache; it tickled.

"Do you mean to say you've never made love to a virgin?"

"That," he retorted mischievously, "would be like mating
a Stradivarius to a cigar box banjo."

Turning, she chucked him lightly under the chin. "I didn't
know you played banjo." With an impish lilt to her walk,
she drifted back into the rail car. "Kansas City should be in
for one pip of a minstrel show."

TEN

The Queens Meet

The next morning, Suzanne entered the blue and yellow
"Chinobethan" hotel dining room to meet Ramsey. Nearly
every padded Jacobean chair was full, the conversational buzz
at high hum, with black-coated, white-aproned waiters zoom-
ing like bees through a mélange of tasselled lanterns, Roman
statues, and oak tables. Ramsey was not yet at their table,
but unexpectedly, Rafer was halfway through a plate of ham
and eggs. "You're up early," she observed like a blithe
mother inspecting a usually grubby child.

Rafer rose with a grin. As he seated her, he lingered to
admire her profile against her piquant, daisy-smothered chip
hat with yellow velvet ribbons secured in a gay bow beneath
her left ear. Her yellow-dotted swiss frock and fluffy parasol
reflected her sunny mood.

The waiter returned. She requested a second pot of tea,
"and the blintzes with applesauce." Prying a cracker from

a red tea tin, she confessed cheerfully, "I could devour half the menu."

"I like that old black dress."

Her own smile curved more gently, the cracker hovering over the tin. "Only you would call a Worth original an old black dress." Making sure the other diners were beyond earshot, she leaned toward him conspiratorially. "Before Ramsey arrives, tell me, was he really a war profiteer?"

"He was in partnership with a New England senator whose family woolen mill needed financial shoring. The two of them supplied Union soldiers with blankets and uniforms that fell apart in a month. The senator was put out of office after the war, but Ramsey turned a tidy profit." He polished off his last morsel of ham as Suzanne nibbled her cracker, a pensive furrow between her brows.

"How do you know all this?" she asked dubiously. "You only met Ramsey a few weeks ago."

"I rode with the Union army in Georgia. A man badly supplied in the field likes to know why." He applied his napkin. "Still, the Union army had an easier time than Southern civilians." His face sobered as he poured a second cup of tea. "After helping General Sherman make war hell for a lot of scared, half-starved women, children, and old men, I switched sides."

"You what!" she gasped.

"Why not? The North had already won. The Yankees upheld the Union; the South held my friends."

"But you could have been shot as a spy and deserter by both sides!"

"I nearly was, except the Rebs were too short of ammunition after Vicksburg to waste it on firing squads." Leaning back in his chair, he stretched out his long legs alongside her skirt. "I spent the last two months of the war waiting to hang in Andersonville. After the surrender, former Yankees and Rebels turned nostalgic about who was who and what was what. After a few unpleasantries, I drifted down to Mexico."

"Wafting feathers from the tar on your backside."

"Something like that." His rueful smile broadened into a

mischievously sensual grin. "You have to know me to love
me."

Her eyes quickly averted to the waiter bringing the blintzes.
"If that's true, every tart from here to Vera Cruz must adore
you . . . except you're not precisely looking for love, are
you?"

"Are you?" Seeing her taken aback, he waited until the
waiter finished serving and hastened to another customer.
"Well?" he pursued. "You don't strike me as sentimental.
Of course," he continued as she fiddled with her fork, "you
might be the sort of girl who presumes making love with the
man she loves isn't *comme il faut*. To her, sex is earthbound
bestiality and love exalted to wishful thinking."

"Actually," she retorted distractedly, "all I wish at the
moment is sugar for my tea . . ."

"And elusion of the question." Leaning over to the next
vacant table, he purloined its silver sugar bowl.

She plunged the sugar tongs into the bowl. "I have been
in love; there's nothing exalted about it. Frankly, I prefer to
be out of love, particularly as I have deplorable taste in men."

"Good," he said softly. "Then you're bound to fall for
me."

Heaven help me, she beseeched. He's probably right.

While conversation shifted to safer topics, Ramsey never
showed for breakfast. Involved with his bankers, realty bro-
kers, and expedition suppliers, he nearly missed the Denver
train's 11:00 departure. Once aboard, he busied himself with
stacks of correspondence, business files, and account ledgers.
Suzanne grudgingly admired his shrewdness and industry.
Ramsey might be a bull, but he had his merits.

When I am solvent again, I shall handle money as Ramsey
does, she decided. I shan't live off my good luck, but shep-
herd it.

Denver, Colorado, Queen City of the Rockies, dumped
Suzanne back into the doldrums. Craning from the rear rail-
car platform to catch sight of the city, she was glumly disappointed. The Queen was a drab regent, the only relief a
narrow ditch leading from the Platte River spreading a net-

work of green. A monotonous array of unimpressive cabins, frame houses and dun brick buildings spread across a dismayingly brown plain. Every fifth construction appeared to be embellished with a garish saloon sign. On the near side of town was an intimidatingly large graveyard, and by the Platte River huddled a cluster of flimsy tepees.

The most gifted designer could not improve on the glory of the Rockies. Stretched to the north and west, their pristine magnificence was breathtaking. If Denverites had a dream, Suzanne saw why they clung to it. Those distant snowcaps defying the summer sun were a realm of dreams. Against the cobalt sky, their rusty purple crags ranged on endlessly, summoning the spirit, promising adventure and fabulous beauty. The eye was distracted from the city blighting the discouraging plain to that splendid ocean of timber-couched stone. A blue-gray summer storm ranged to the west like the cloud of an escaped genie, its trailing rainbow arcing the hazy sky.

Beneath his natty bowler hat, Ramsey wore the expression of a pleased, if jaded tourist. "Quite a town, isn't it?"

"If one doesn't mind overdone toast," returned Suzanne, her brows knitted dubiously.

"That'll change," asserted Ramsey. "Ten years ago, Denver was a patch of shacks and big ideas. She not only pulled herself up by the bootstraps, she wove the whole, damn thing from tall tales of gold and glory." He gripped the platform railing with evangelical excitement. "Four years ago, when the transcontinental Union Pacific bypassed Denver, everybody predicted Denver's funeral, but Coloradans wouldn't sing *amen*. Denverites raised money and rousted labor for a spur connection to the Kansas Pacific and another one to Cheyenne and the Union Pacific Transcontinental. General Palmer, down in Colorado Springs, means to lay track for the Denver and Rio Grande Railway to connect with El Paso, Texas. Know what that'll do for the price of beef? This is the start of an era for the cattle kings . . . and Denver. One day, Denver will be the capital of a new state. Ten years from today, you won't know this place."

Ramsey's enthusiasm was contagious. He was like a boy

revelling in a splendid, new toy train. Why not? He and Denver shared the same rough, hardy beginning and hard-won success.

His brigand's profile made spare as the rugged plain by the noon sun's harsh glare, Rafer had the same light in his eyes as Ramsey, but like Joshua seeing the promised land, was intent on the mountains. Suzanne wondered how long Rafer had been away from Colorado, but did not ask. While Ramsey was uncharacteristically pleasant, he was increasingly watchful.

They disembarked at the month-old Denver train station, where three soberly suited men, alert as roosters after corn, awaited them. Pumping Ramsey's hand in turn, they introduced themselves as Gerald Chapin of the First National Bank, Luther Bolls of the Colorado National Bank, and Horace Calber of Bela Hughes law office. Calber discreetly added that the first two gentlemen represented incorporators of the Denver Pacific Railroad and Telegraph Company. Assuming Rafer to be an associate of Ramsey's, they were equally cordial to him, and went into a beatific trance at the sight of Suzanne in her snappy black and white boleroed traveling dress. The bearded Chapin apologized for their informality. "You must forgive our hasty preparations, Mr. Hoth, but your Kansas City telegram just arrived this morning. As we've been having a host of railroad celebrations this summer, Judge Roe Maxwell and his wife would like to invite you and your party to a reception tonight in honor of the opening of the Kansas Pacific spur line. Tomorrow morning, Mr. Hugh Hamilton of Texas is hosting a coyote hunt." He turned to Suzanne. "I hope you ride, Mrs. Hoth."

"Well, I've never ridden after coyotes," Suzanne hedged. "I'm not really sure . . ."

"Oh, you'll like it," overrode Ramsey briskly. "Just as lively as a fox hunt."

Clapping Chapin's broad shoulder, he steered him toward the street with the others flanking him. "I appreciate your hospitality, gentlemen, but I'm in a hurry. I have five days to examine your financial presentations and pull a mountain expedition together . . ."—his attention flicked ironically to Rafer—"we are going into the mountains, Mr. Smith?"

Rafer nodded. "I can start expedition arrangements this morning."

Ramsey's expression said that no man who boarded a yacht with three boxes of chocolates and a toy captain's uniform was outfitting his expedition. "I'd as soon handle logistics myself, while you run along and enjoy Denver's fine drinking establishments. This promises to be a dry trip." Ignoring Rafer's patient shrug, he crooked a finger at Frock. "See Mrs. Hoth to the Colorado Hotel, Frock. I'll be there about sunset."

The lawyer, Horace Calber, craned anxiously forward. "Please reconsider the hotel, Mr. Hoth. You can all stay with me and Mrs. Calber. Not that the Colorado Hotel isn't a very comfortable accommodation at most times, but Larimer Street is likely to be a little noisy for the next few weeks with the railroad anniversary and all." He gestured as they walked toward the street where awninged hotels, stores, and tawdry saloons sandwiched throngs of weathered, bushy-bearded miners in cracked Wellington boots, uneasy looking immigrants, buckskin-clad trappers, and copper-faced Indians in grimy calico shirts. Calber led them past piles of fur, shipping crates, and lumber piled with the morning's sagging inebriates near the saloons. The dry, wagon track gouted ground was as hard as many of the faces that streamed by them with unvarnished appreciation of Suzanne. The buzz of saws and whack of hammers drowned out any rude observations, if they were not discouraged by Rafer's discreet display of the .38 Colt revolver beneath his coat. Buildings were being erected in virtually every lot.

Despite mounting annoyance at Ramsey's habit of depositing her with Frock as if shelving a sack of flour, Suzanne hoped he would accept the Calbers' invitation for she would have welcomed the hospitality of a home.

He refused. "Too many things to do, Mr. Calber, to operate out of a house. And Mrs. Calber isn't going to want a bunch of mules and horses crapping on her flower garden." The last flattered Denver's brave young grass and tree plant-ings. "Now, Mr. Chapin, we'll begin with your bank's proposition . . ."

Suzanne sighed as Ramsey departed with the welcoming party. "Where is the Colorado Hotel, Frock?"

With Rafer bringing up the rear, Frock directed them to a three-story unpainted building. Echoing construction all along the street, half a dozen carpenters sawed and banged on the upper floor. While a few rooms were complete, a haze of sawdust hung in the air through several unglassed windows. The hair of a blunt-faced Arapaho squaw selling tobacco on the hotel's corner was dusted tan. Breathing heavily in the heat, three pigs sprawled on the hotel steps. The pigs were altogether too reminiscent of the squalid regions of New York where Edward Maintree was exiled.

Tapping her trim parasol against her skirt, Suzanne fixed Rafer with a jaundiced eye. "Why do I feel we're beginning a venture we're going to regret, Rafer?"

"Beats me, what with Ramsey setting up the expedition and all. He's liable to buy you a pink satin tent."

"Bother the tent. Isn't there a better hotel in town?

"Well, now, the last time I was in Denver"—his ruminating drawl implied he had sprouted as one of the original weeds—"the hotels were shacks. You might find one without pigs . . . then again, pigs go pretty much anywhere they please. Doesn't do to boot 'em out of the way too hard; they bite."

"I can deal with the pork." Her parasol clicked open. "Just now, the only element as disagreeable as an aggravated pig around here is your evolving pseudo-Western accent. Save it for the natives."

He touched his hat. "Yes, ma'am. You want I should swear at the swine in French?"

She stalked across the dusty street, to hear a pig's resentful, surly belch as she mounted the hotel steps. Her parasol snapped closed, and flattened against a pig's backside. Shrieking, the pig fled. The next pig, catching a whack between the ears, shrilled in protest, but hastily retreated before Suzanne's next swing. Enraged, the third pig turned on her. She levelled her parasol like a baseball bat, ready to smack the shrilling creature in the chops. At the unsettling instant when the 300 pounds of enraged pork charged her and she realized what big, wicked, yellow teeth piggy had, Rafer shot it dead.

Followed by Frock, he crossed the street, prodded the flaccid beast with his boot toe, then slipped his revolver back under his jacket. "Told you not to kick the pigs," he rebuked mildly.

Although a trifle shaken, Suzanne ignored him. "Mr. Frock, please advise the hotel manager that if he serves ham for breakfast, I don't care to meet it on his front steps. And I want a quiet, clean room; otherwise, I shall write the Eastern newspapers about the barnyard accommodations in this God-forsaken place."

"You don't want to do that," said Rafer soberly. "These folks may want to attract business, but they don't cotton to being ordered around. The West is no place to forget your manners."

Her retort was halted by the dead pig's red, accusing eye. "Very well. How do you suggest I receive proper service from such exquisitely polite people?"

"If you want something, ask for it yourself. Say please, thank-you, and smile." He grinned. "Didn't your nannies teach you anything?"

She brandished her parasol like a mallet. "How to play croquet. I just never tried whacking a pig through a wicket." Tucking the parasol under her arm, she headed into the hotel to say please and thank-you. Five minutes later, she had a room at the rear and the manager came through the main door to check his stoop for pigs; spotting only the dead one, he dragged it into the street, then returned to his desk.

Under the shade of the hotel's striped awning, Frock solemnly regarded the pig. "Where there's a woman, there's progress."

ELEVEN

Cat in the Sack

That afternoon, Rafer left beers virtually untouched on the bars of seven saloons. Although there was no news of Bradford Hoth, he learned Helmut had financed part of the new railroad spur line. Growth-bent Denverites and mining operations desperate for supplies and ore transport, considered him a hero. The only discouraging words issued from smallfry prospectors and settlers who decried his usurious freight rates.

After another drink, the men drifted to gossip of a live puma captured by a rancher named Henderson, who lived a few miles outside of Denver *en route* to Boulder.

Half listening, Rafer gazed from a saloon window at the distant, jagged red rocks of the foothills that capped Boulder. The last time he slept under a sky full of fresh Rocky Mountain air with a few million stars in it, he had been a kid: a starved, hunted savage for whom even starlight was an enemy. After ten years, that strangling terror still grazed his neck with ghostly fingers. Now he was a man, accustomed to terror. He also felt playful and the puma gave him an idea. Visiting the puma was less risky than attending Judge Maxwell's reception. The gathering would be full of Banner's cronies, Hamilton's hunt more so.

He changed clothes, rented a horse, and rode to Henderson's to see the puma. He arrived about an hour before sunset. Henderson was shoeing horses in a lean-to behind his two-room house. He glanced up at Rafer's alert face, then over his wiry build and worn chaps. "If you're wanting a winter job, I ain't got any. I only use spring help."

"Thanks, but I'm not looking for work, Mr. Henderson." Rafer scanned the ponies moving restlessly in Henderson's pine log corral. "I'm out to buy a good cow pony. You have some likely ones."

"Yep, and I need all I got." The wizened Henderson gave a horseshoe nail a whack.

"I guess you do," Rafer said agreeably. "This must be a nice sized spread."

"Runs nigh all the way to Bear Canyon." Finishing off the nail, Henderson dropped the horse's hoof.

"You don't say." Rafer laughed ruefully. "With a spread that size, I guess you don't need forty dollars for a green mustang like that paint pony in the corral."

Henderson adjudged the paint. "That's a good horse; pick of the corral, but you're looking at seven already broke and near as sound in there. Why bother with a green mustang?"

"I like to break and train my own horses." Rafer grinned with an engaging trace of sheepishness. "A man who spends a lot of time talking to his horse, kind of likes to know it ain't going to complain about its last owner."

Henderson's windburned face creased in an economical smile. "Yeah, know what you mean. I break all my own. Last time I cottoned to another man's horse, it spooked at a wolf pack, and dumped me in a blizzard. Ran out of ammunition on the wolves and near froze my feet off trying to get home. When that damned horse showed up, I sold it first chance I got."

"Tell you what," responded Rafer. "You let me buy the paint mustang and I'll shoe the rest of that string for you. Free you up to break those new ponies before winter comes on."

More dickering, and Rafer walked into the corral to have his first conversation with his new mustang. "Don't you want to throw a rope on him?" called Henderson.

"Nope," said Rafer. "Just finding out how he likes his pancakes."

At that point, Henderson saw the strangest way of breaking a horse a white man might imagine. Rafer stood silently in the middle of the corral, letting the wild horses scatter and bunch in alarm. Sometimes they ran at him, but never touched him.

Finally, they began to stay away and settle. Then he began to call softly to the paint pony in a string of sounds that were not words, but more like the groan of trees and the sigh of wind mixed with bird and horse sounds. Directly, the paint listened, and after a time, sniffed at Rafer. Rafer slowly feathered his fingertips over him. The horse shied, but was lured back; this went on until the sun set and night fell, and the paint and the man kept sidling up to one another. Fascinated, Henderson leaned on the corral fence and watched. In time, the mustang accepted Rafer's hand on his withers, his back, his flanks trembled as Rafer stroked his legs, then at last, accepted a rope bridle and brush of a blanket over his back. At that point, Rafer stopped. "That's enough for now. I'll be back tomorrow and finish up, if it's all right with you, Mr. Henderson."

"All right? Hell, I wouldn't miss this show for the world. Indian, ain't it?"

Rafer ducked under the corral rail. "Guess so. An uncle taught it to me."

"Your uncle wouldn't happen to be Uncompahgre Apache, would he?"

Rafer's clear blue eyes fixed him. "Do I look Apache?"

"Nope, but you sound it," replied Henderson coolly. "Heard enough Taos Apaches to know."

Rafer smiled easily. "Guess my uncle knew some Apaches, too."

"Guess so." Henderson's gray eyes glinted, then he shifted the subject. "Like to see somethin' interestin' before you tackle the shoes on those ponies?"

"Sure it ain't an Apache trap?" parried Rafer, guessing what Henderson had in mind.

Henderson chuckled. "Sure, now, and I guess it might be." He led Rafer around the side of the house. The scent spooking the horses strengthened. Although he expected it, the sudden, chilling snarl that issued from the darkness raised the hairs on Rafer's spine. A chain rattled, then a mind-numbing roar of frustrated rage vented as the chain snapped short a few yards away from him and Henderson.

"Some barn cat you keep," he said quietly.

"Treed him a couple of weeks ago and creased his skull

so's I decided to keep him for a spell. Expect I'll have to shoot him in a few days. He's et up a whole deer this week."

Rafer nodded and the two men talked for a while longer.

That night when Suzanne and Ramsey left the Hotel Colorado to attend the reception, the outline of their waiting carriage was barely defined in the faint light streaming from the hotel and noisy saloon. Stepping into the street, she tripped, and except for Ramsey's support, would have fallen on her face. Catching up her skirts, she recoiled. The New York streets were often garbage strewn, but usually the line was drawn at corpses. "It's my dead pig!" she blurted in disgust. "When do they clean the streets here?"

"Oh, 1875 is my guess." Unruffled, Ramsey steered her around the pig. "Coyotes'll drift into town after the saloons settle down. There'll be a lot less pig left tomorrow." At her groan, he chuckled. "Cheer up, Judge Maxwell is bound to serve up a nice side of ham at the reception."

Boredom soon drove Suzanne to explore Denver. Rafer had seemed to disappear of late. Had he decided to end their mythical gold hunt and resume his solitary rambling? From his elation at first sight of the Rocky Mountains, he was where he wanted to be. Why should he care what happened to her and Ramsey?

In the two weeks that passed while awaiting delivery of Ramsey's expedition supplies, Suzanne's consternation grew. Rafer must be gone. She was puzzled by his indifferent farewell, but if he suffered no regret, why should she? Nothing mattered to Rafer but his own amusement. Her fierce, angry hurt contended with sad confusion. Finally, she sought out the company of the Denver women to find distraction. Her own problems and responsibilities forbade mooning about like an abandoned cat.

As the days drifted by, she became increasingly anxious to set out after Bradford and the gold. Over four months had elapsed since news of Brad's death; he might have penetrated the Amazon. Every wagon and horseman who left town and headed west added to her impatience. Frustration led her to notice things that she might otherwise have missed.

The saloons celebrated a lively anniversary business that promised livelier nights. A printing press thumped-thumped over the cry of street vendors hawking pretzels, Indian jewelry, fob watches, souvenirs. Steady streams of customers moved through the general stores where they loaded buckboard wagons with purchases. Outside the S.B. Williams assay office was a short line of miners waiting for inspection of their samples. Most of the emerging men headed forlornly for the Palace saloon next door.

There were nearly two men for every woman; the men were young, and many of the women hardened. Children roamed the street. Some looked as hungry and neglected as the multitude of stray dogs underfoot. When a grocer chased a seven-year-old pilferer from an apple carton beneath a sign originally pricing them at one dollar each, many attributes of frontier life fell into perspective. The price was now seventy cents due to the new availability of railroad transport. Fruit was a handsome luxury in a country new to farming. Before the coming of the railroad, every stick of furniture and lumber had to be imported by wagon. Denver's building site was as unlikely as Leningrad's perch upon a swamp, but its air of raw, determined energy was untainted.

Most disconcerting were the drawn, faded women who wandered the streets as beggars. Ragged children huddled in alleys to plead for food. Such refugees saddened her greatly. In New York, vagrants were a single element in the panoply of misery until Edward Maintree joined their ranks. One day, she might be one of them. Now she was perpetually aware of the poor wherever she went. "Who are all these women and children, Millie?" she asked one afternoon as Mrs. Maxwell showed her the town.

"The families of men who never returned from the gold diggings. The town is full of them. Elizabeth Byers started a shelter, but it isn't enough; every spring, there are more indigents. They keep waiting for so long . . . until their money runs out. Few people come here with much money; if they had it, they would probably stay back East. With only so many positions for laundresses and domestics, the women usually end up working the saloons if they have any looks;

the children manage however they can. A few orphans are adopted by locals, but not many families can afford more mouths to feed, and in the worst cases, the children are employed as drudges.''

''What happens to the ones unable to find help?'' queried Suzanne softly.

''They seem to disappear, perhaps because no one looks that closely at their faces. They may just grow older, but I expect most of them end up in the graveyard.''

''Where is Mrs. Byers's shelter? If you don't mind, I should like to see it.''

She spent the next two days assisting in the shelter, mostly by scrubbing children, as she was unable to cook. Her darning was no better than her cooking, but improved with enforced practice.

Meanwhile Ramsey persuaded the marshal to show him the wanted files on pretext of not wanting to hire any known felons for his expedition. At the marshal's house, he flipped through every wanted poster issued in the territory, but nothing surfaced on Brad, and the only detail that bore the slightest resemblance to Rafer Smith was a terse description of an English boy named James Carlisle who was involved in a freight robbery in the territory's early days when it was still dominated by fur trappers. Organized law was rare, wanted posters more so, and the Rockies full of English immigrants. Quelling his angry impatience, Ramsey dropped the poster back into the pile. *Rafer flaunted the law too often not to have run into trouble. And if I don't find anything on him,* vowed Ramsey, *I'll invent enough trouble to jail him until hell freezes.*

The next morning, the train station was bedlam. Twenty locally purchased mules brayed and kicked as ten panicky thoroughbred geldings were wrestled off the train by cursing hostlers. Following bags of Kansas City feed, crate after crate marked Abercrombie and Fitch, and Portnoy's of London were shoved down the rail-car ways as Ramsey bellowed orders and complaints. Camp stoves, fine English linens and silverware, wine casks, crocks and cans, mapcases, and photographic equipment were piled atop campaign chests, trunks,

and mountains of harnessing. There was even a commode
with a porcelain chamber pot, and enough ammunition and
weaponry to raze the wildlife of Tanganyika. Most of the
kerosene lanterns were broken, and two crates were smashed,
their bottles of cognac invaded somewhere *en route* from
New York. Skittish mares and saddle broncs plunged among
a gathering melee of cattle and stolid draft horses, while a
scarlet and gold Arabian tent unfurled for Ramsey's inspection stunned all of the bystanders. Rafer, sitting crosslegged
on a crate, gave a resigned sigh. Despite a hardy effort,
Ramsey's perception of essentials was more erratic than he
imagined. To label the ponderous shipment impractical was
an understatement; better to rechalk it with a skull and cross-
bones.

Death on delivery.

TWELVE

Cities of Gold

Like King Solomon displaying his splendid court to Sheba,
Ramsey presented Suzanne the assembled expedition two
days later. Rafer had reappeared the night before looking
tanner than ever for having spent time under the brilliant sun.
But now it was Suzanne who rode by his side as they passed
along the light-wheeled carts, baggage carts, twenty pack
mules, Conestoga and supply wagons: in all, thirty horse-
drawn conveyances stretched nearly three blocks. Headed by
Frock as steward-valet-chef, his crew included fifty hostlers
and wagon drivers. Seven Maryland-bred hunting hounds
capered about the edgy livestock. The only crew member
missing was the man who knew where the whole parade was
going. As dawn brightened into mid-morning, Ramsey's face

flushed like the noon-bound sun. "Where the hell is that lazy sonofabitch?" he stormed. "Fifty thousand dollars in equipment and overpriced freight is held up by a bum who won't even pay for his own boot soles!"

Her velvet habit stuck to her ribs, Suzanne was impatient as well. Her leggy chestnut was listless in the heat. Sifting street dust now dulled the teams' bright harnesses and the wagons where drivers slumped apathetically over their reins as the mules and horses dozed. The spectators gathered since dawn were now as much amused as bored.

Finally, a lone horseman ambled into view. Trailing his paint mustang mount were four mules with canvas tarped packs. "Where have you been?" demanded Ramsey. "We've been waiting all morning!"

"Considering that we've yawned around town nearly two weeks, I presumed you weren't in a hurry," replied Rafer lightly. He touched his wide-brimmed hat to Suzanne, then scanned the assembled men, equipment, and animals. "You appear to have bought out the store. Guess you won't need this gear." He handed Ramsey a weathered notebook.

Expecting an account of Rafer's usual "necessities," the glowering Ramsey flipped through the book. "Hell, you not only want a windlass, but carpentry, smithy, and wheelwright equipment. If I run down all of these supplies, we won't get out of Denver until tomorrow."

"Well, the next place West you'll be able to find them is a fair piece." Rafer eyed him sleepily. "Of course, that's up to you."

With a sour grunt, Ramsey handed Frock the notebook. "Take three men and two buckboards to collect this stuff. Be back in two hours."

As Frock hurried off, Ramsey settled irritably in his saddle. Rafer continued to peruse the train. "Now what?" Ramsey demanded.

"How long do you propose to use these pack mules?"

"As long as it takes. Why?"

Rafer slid off his horse. "Because this lot will be cankered by sundown." Going along the line, he methodically checked each set of packs as well as the wagon harnessing, then walked back to Ramsey. "Where did you find your hostlers?" he inquired quietly.

"I put up notices for experienced men in the saloons," returned Ramsey with mounting sharpness. "Where do you think I got them?"

"Abercrombie and Fitch. No man worth his salt would volunteer to take this sultanic mess into the Rockies for an extended trip into cold weather. You need oxen, not plow horses, and certainly not mares. Besides, only four mules are packed properly. The packs are unevenly weighted and overloaded, the harness is too light. After you unload tonight, these beasts will be unfit for weeks."

"Are you suggesting I unload all this muck, buy new teams, and hire new men?" gritted Ramsey.

Rafer shrugged. "Cankered mules don't grin and bear it; they become unmanageable. They also won't eat anything that grows above the tree line. Horses now"—he waved toward the flat plain—"you're looking at what they'll eat. As for hiring new men, you'd be wasting your time. You're better off training the ones you have."

Ramsey's voice lowered. "I'll be a laughing stock if I start dismantling this expedition!"

Rafer's answering silence intimated Ramsey could either look like a fool or be one.

Ramsey shot a look at Suzanne, tactfully focused the other way. "All right," he roared. "Unload the damned mess!"

Revamping the expedition took nearly three days. Rafer either supervised each hostler or repacked the mules himself, and handpicked new oxen. He also checked the thoroughbred horses' shoes. "Too light. Have them reshod in a week or so." When he suggested dumping their luxury goods, Ramsey balked. Rafer did not press, but the ironic look in his eyes bewildered Suzanne. Why not be well equipped? she wondered. When the weather grew colder, they would be glad of comforts.

Finally, at two o'clock in the afternoon of July 18, the Hoth expedition moved out of Denver toward the front range of the Rockies. At six o'clock, Rafer, who ranged ahead as scout, signalled a halt to make camp. Due to the slow oxen,

they were still within sight of Denver. Ramsey's exasperation
drew her sympathy. Not only did she enjoy the open plain's
silver carpet of sage and spiny cactus, Rafer's predictions
about winter and Ramsey's lack of preparation were disconcerting. The Maxwells had warned of catastrophes befalling
mountain travellers. Despite their invitation to winter with
them in Denver, she dared not leave Brad and the claim to
Ramsey. The greatest danger was impending cold weather.
"Perhaps I can change Rafer's mind about stopping," she
ventured.

"Don't bother. We're pushing on. I've taken enough from
that tin cowboy today." He signalled the drivers to continue.

Suzanne urged the mare ahead to intercept Rafer on his
way back to the train.

"Why stop so early?" she protested when they met near
a clump of scrub oak. "We can be on the trail another two
hours before dark."

"Ever pitch camp by starlight?" he responded. "One of
these greenhorn hostlers may pound a tent peg through his
toe."

She glanced back at the apathetic drivers atop the wagons.
"Surely these men cannot be entirely inexperienced if they
managed to reach Denver."

"They're tinhorn clerks, laborers, schoolteachers, pan-
handlers; you name it." Rafer hooked a knee around his
saddlehorn with professorial patience. "Ramsey's collected
amateur prospectors are either bound for the gold field or out
to earn enough money to return East. After collecting their
first wages, most of them will disappear. Some of these fellows probably arrived on foot pushing a wheelbarrow with a
few supplies. The bones of their kind are spread all over the
Pike's Peak trails."

"You mean they starved?"

"Froze, starved, died of thirst, disease, ran into Indians . . ."

She scoffed. "Indians like those poor, downtrodden red
men in Denver?"

"Considered the Platte River Arapaho a tame lot, did
you?" His lips curved ironically. "Well, if we meet any

misanthropic red men along the trail, just remember that gorgeous red hair is a wildly inviting scalp."

Catching the calculating glint in his eyes, she straightened, her epauletted Eugenie habit giving her the air of a resolute military cadet. "Forget scaring me with scalping stories, Rafer. I've no intention of knitting for weeks in Denver while you and Ramsey pursue Brad and the gold."

"Weeks?" He gave a sardonic laugh. "We're unlikely to see Denver again until next spring, my sweet. You're not in for a pleasant afternoon of sledding and cocoa."

"I can endure whatever lies ahead as well as you and Ramsey. I come of sturdy stock." The gray tissue veil of her ostrich-plumed hat moulding her regal features, she cantered back to join Ramsey.

Rafer appraised her straight back, her ease of horsemanship as the thoroughbred settled in alongside Ramsey's big bay stallion. Suzanne had grit and competence, but the gold claim was trail's end for her and Ramsey. Once worried that Ramsey meant Suzanne harm, he had accompanied them to Colorado, but Ramsey was now infatuated with her. Given time, she would wrap the headstrong tycoon around her little finger. While he longed to wrest her from Ramsey, he could not take her with him after Helmut Banner.

His plan was simple: whet their interest at the Black Hawk smelter, then take the expedition directly to the claim before the full onslaught of winter; whether or not Bradford Hoth was there, pursuit would undoubtedly end after the first snows. Once preoccupied with the claim, they would winter in a nearby mining town, freeing him to go after Helmut Banner. Most of Colorado's hard rock gold passed through the Black Hawk smelter; with gold streamed news. He might find Banner.

His current task was to keep Suzanne and Ramsey safe, but miserably eager to return home.

Hardship seemed faraway, denied by the magnificent splash of Ramsey's scarlet and gold tent in the firelight, the silver plate and porcelain, the assurance of indomitable civilization. A gold-fringed miniature of Ramsey's, Suzanne's tent was pegged between Ramsey's tent and Rafer's bedroll.

Rafer preferred to sleep in the open while weather permitted
. . . also to make certain the gaping hostlers remembered
Suzanne was off limits. No indication remained of the effort
required to set up the tents and dining arrangements, circle
the wagons and unhitch draft animals, pasture less valuable
stock and secure the best horses in camp. Twice the normal
time was necessary to clumsily accomplish what might have
been smoothly done by daylight. Ramsey wore evening
clothes Frock ironed by lanternlight, while Suzanne, in her
black dress with an aigrette crowning her hair, might have
been dining on Fifth Avenue.

Ramsey leaned forward. "Rafer, suppose you be less mysterious about our destination. It's damned difficult to outfit
an expedition as easily bound for the desert as the snow-
fields."

"I apologize, but the secrecy couldn't be helped." Rafer
blotted his lips, then his lace-trimmed napkin resettled on his
denimed thigh. "Trustworthiness is a virtue lacking in all
three of us. The moment I revealed where we were bound,
I should have been rudely deposited by the wayside. As it
is, we anticipate a pleasant trip to Black Hawk."

Suzanne straightened. "Is the mining claim at Black
Hawk?"

"No, Black Hawk offers a sort of educational tour . . ."

"We have no time for tours . . ."

"Oh, you mustn't miss this one. Every prospective mining
magnate should visit Black Hawk."

Ramsey interrupted Suzanne's next objection. "Rafer's
saying Brad's claim isn't worth a plug nickel without running
its ore through a smelter." His voice was hard. "That right,
Rafer? You trying to peddle off a hard rock mine?"

"If the ore were easily accessible, do you suppose I'd
bother with partners? My father staked that claim in the '50s,
years too early to employ the new Black Hawk smelting
processes. If he had registered his claim today, he would be
rich in five years."

"I don't know any such thing. You may have salted the
claim, rigged the assay. A shyster like you knows every trick
in the crooked book." Ramsey tipped a cigar with his pen-

knife. "How come you're admitting the claim is hard rock just two hours out of Denver? I might trot this show back to town." His eyes narrowed as he lit the cigar. "That what you want me to do, Rafer? Go back to town?"

The faded blue bandanna looped about his throat as neatly as an embassy cravat, Rafer smiled with the geniality of a professional diplomat facing a truculent Turk about to dramatically tear up and eat a treaty. "Why should I do that, when you've come so far and gone to so much trouble?"

"Maybe because you've picked up another buyer with a better price in Denver. Maybe because you'd as soon cut me out because I turned out to be more of a grizzly than Brad." Ramsey jerked his shaggy head at Suzanne. "Maybe because you want her. If you don't find Brad, you can both kiss him off as dead, and ride into the sunset."

Suzanne regarded Ramsey coldly. "I'm not riding anywhere with Rafer . . . and forget my returning to Denver. You may go back to town, but I mean to find my husband and his claim if I go alone."

Rafer and Ramsey exchanged knowing looks. "Oh, you're not worried about going off alone," corrected Ramsey. "As long as you've got your looks, you'll always have a hand up into the saddle." He took a long pull at his cigar, then peered through curling smoke at Rafer. "All right, we go to Black Hawk; then what?"

"Then we have a look at $5 million in gold."

Ramsey grunted. "Spouting from the fountain of youth, no doubt. You ought to bottle yourself and go into business with P.T. Barnum."

Much later, after the camp settled for the night and Rafer slid into his bedroll, a yelp issued from Suzanne's tent. Heads appeared in a flurry of tent flaps and bedrolls under the wagons as her kerosene lantern flared and Ramsey scurried to the rescue with his rifle cocked. Rafer peacefully burrowed into his blankets. Suzanne's bare feet had encountered the cactus he had scattered beneath her canvas tent floor. Shortly, she would be as eager as a singed rabbit to leave Colorado.

Would she be just as eager to leave him?

He still wanted her. Badly. The ache of desire filled his

whole body and brain like potent, simmering tequila. The copper light from their lovemaking in her cabin on the steam-boat flickered across his mind. He could smell her musky, impassioned woman smell, imagine the caress of her hair. The memory of her lovemaking was as ever-present and real as his own skin. He had tried to imagine a dozen women in her place; dark eyed, fiery senoritas as quick with a knife as a kiss; ambitious, inventive Bourbon Street wenches; long-stemmed *criollas* who forgot their disdain on satin sheets; the war's manless belles. Their shades of hair, their passion-darkened eyes and parted lips all distilled into an emerald-eyed enchantress with the rose gold translucence of Suzanne.

But he'd be damned if he would share her with a greedy old man.

Rafer watched Suzanne's tent for some time, but once back in his own tent, Ramsey did not reappear. Rafer counted the few steps separating Suzanne's softness from his stirring de-sire. More than one man on this black, still prairie must be lying awake with imaginings of her. To have made love to her, to have known the excitement of her passionate response transformed the pallor of those imaginings into a needling torment. The cool prairie breeze carried the silkiness of her hair, her breasts, slipping across the restless heat of his own body.

Angrily, he kicked off his blanket, stripped off his shirt, and pulled on his rawhide Apache boots. He crept past the unwary sentry out into the sagebrush, then without a sound, began to run. No sage, no pinon did he brush; no rock impeded his swift path. As he had done every night for the past three weeks, he ran as if the night were noon. After eight lung-tearing miles, he halted, trembling and drenched with perspiration. Physically, he was out of condition from a white man's life, but his mind still retained Apache teachings from his year with them. He did not have to see the desert im-mediately about him to be precisely aware of its contents. A coyote paralleled his trail a few hundred yards to the south. A rabbit family was unaware of a stalking owl upwind of a patch of yucca just ahead.

Rafer even knew where Bradford Hoth was . . . or rather,

where he was not. After the loss of his family, Rafer had gone south to Taos . . . to the Apache. Long before Jack Carlisle's death, he realized his father and hellbent-for-leather brothers, reckless and brave as they were, could not teach him to be a man, any more than could his grandfather, by restraining him with centuries-tested stern discipline. Rafer had not gone looking for the Apache, but knew they would find him. Had he still been smooth skinned and clear eyed, they would have killed him something the torturers had lacked time to do; instead, he had been saved for last, and allowed to watch the others die. Those hellish hours had given him the strength to escape when night had fallen and the others became too drunk with liquor and killing to guard him closely. His back torn, he had crawled on all fours into the darkness, then run on bloody feet to the river, and drifting with a fallen log, reached Uncompaghre country. The boy the Apaches found was spiritually maimed, lambent with hate. The hate drew them as surely as a magnet; because of that hate, they had let him live. To them, he was already dead, his consuming hostility giving him great spiritual force.

The Apaches taught him to be a man, but could not teach him to be an Apache. An Apache would know where to find Helmut Banner by pondering everything known about him and deciding where he was. This prescience was incomprehensible to a white man. Rafer had learned to be aware only of immediate surroundings. Distant sensitivity required great concentration. Even when he focused all his mind, he was less aware than an Apache child, but sometimes that infant perception kept him alive; it also made him a peerless card player. When he was ready, the Apaches let him go, perhaps thinking him a weapon against his own kind.

Rafer gazed into the desert blackness toward the craggy front range. Bradford Hoth was farther away than he ought to be; when Rafer directed his mind to him and the claim, he received only dark, empty silence. Bradford might be dead.

Considering Bradford's appealing widow, a cynic would have termed that possibility wishful thinking.

At seven o'clock the next morning, Frock found his master still asleep. After putting a kettle on the fire and laying a Brussel's carpet, he set up Ramsey's copper tub. Then he went to Suzanne's tent through the bustle of camp breaking. Dressed in her broadcloth habit, she was finishing her toilette. "I gather you won't be wanting a bath, ma'am."

"I assumed there wouldn't be time," she replied, her hairbrush poised. "Doesn't Mr. Hoth plan to leave soon?"

"Well"—he hesitated—"I suppose so . . . if he rises for his bath in the next twenty minutes. By the time he dresses and has breakfast, we should be away by nine o'clock, provided the hostlers have everything square." He caught the hint of exasperation upon her face. "Guess Mr. Hoth sees no need to hurry. Mr. Smith says the oxen can only make sixteen or so miles a day.

"Sixteen miles a day? We won't reach Black Hawk for a week!"

"Got a lot of gear, ma'am." His stoic tone refrained the knell of overpacking. "Will you want a morning bath in future?"

"I shall let you know directly." Nearly an hour after Frock left, Suzanne impatiently poked her head from the tent flap. Frock was idling by a three-foot-tall coffee pot on the campfire. Rafer was nowhere in sight, but hostlers were ready to go, the teams hitched. She strode to Ramsey's tent.

Ramsey was vigorously scrubbing himself in his bath, his chest a furry mat of lather, his ruddy skin ruddier from the steam. With a firm series of raps on his tent pole, Suzanne stepped just far enough inside the tent to preserve his modesty. The long-handled brush ceased sawing just long enough for him to appraise her exasperated stare. "I don't deal with business and complaints before breakfast," he said flatly. The brush resumed its industry.

Dismissing his modesty, she went to the coffee pot on the iron camp stove, poured coffee into a waiting Heidelberg mug, then thrust it under his nose. "Here's the start of breakfast. We aren't on holiday, Ramsey. We must make the best speed possible."

He settled in the suds. "You want the gold, not Brad; and it's not going anywhere. I'm running this show, remember?"

"Perhaps you should leave the show to Rafer, considering our race with bad weather," she retorted tartly. "He seems to know what he's doing."

"You're saying I don't?" Ramsey truculently ignored the extended mug.

Stoicly, she surveyed his shelves of leather-bound books, his silver shaving mirror, his sheepskin covered chaise longue. Open steamer trunks were lined up beside his huge brass bed, over which hung a Stubbs painting. Her tent was scarcely less elaborate. "I'm saying Rafer's suggestions are practical. He is right about our being overloaded. Three people do not need thirty wagons of trappings that must be hauled at a snail's pace. If we could be rid of the oxen, this trek might be finished in a fraction of the time."

With a scornful grunt intimating he would not travel like a peasant, Ramsey aggressively reapplied the brush to his callused foot. She tried to mitigate his intractability. "Rafer grew up in this country; you grew up in Chicago. Would you expect him to know his way around your neighborhood? Don't you want to find Bradford?"

"Rafer Smith could be a native of Poughkeepsie for all you know . . . and don't you fret, I'll find Brad. He'll poke his head up sooner or later; if he doesn't, he's either dead or buried alive in some slime pit that serves him damned right." He snatched the mug. "Gimme that coffee, stop meddling, and get out of here, you impertinent hussy."

Suzanne retreated in exasperation, regretting her blunt tactics. She should have coddled Ramsey's pride, but considering his bald proposition that they sleep together in her tent last night, she was wary of displaying much warmth. Ramsey had asserted that she owed no faith to a wife deserter; besides, such clandestine familial arrangements were not unknown. Henry II of England had enjoyed his son Richard's fiancée for years.

His arguments were casually delivered, but the patient

gleam in his eyes made her uneasy. Was she the reason Ramsey was suddenly in no hurry to find Bradford? Did he merely think she was playing hard to get?

Rafer's drawl cut through her preoccupation. "Why the long face, Su?"

She looked up from her campaign chair by the guttering campfire. Making him blonder than he was, the sun at Rafer's back hazed his edges, but chameleonic Rafer was always a blurred figure. He seemed like a complete stranger, his chaps, calico shirt and hightops replaced by a worn, open-throated gray flannel shirt and deerhide boots. Beneath his weathered buckskin hat, his faded blue cotton scarf was tied Apache style about his head. A heavy Spanish silver belt buckle glinted against his ancient jeans. Except for his fair hair and blue eyes, he looked as much Indian as white.

"We're not moving fast enough," Suzanne replied curtly. "Ramsey might as well transport an elephant herd across the Alps."

"And you've been reminding him that he's no Hannibal."

"Guilty." She grimaced ruefully.

"Old Ram may surprise you"—he tipped back his hat—"but I wouldn't egg him into it. The surprise might be unpleasant." He paused. "Why is Ramsey taking his time? He's usually a dawn riser raring to go."

"I don't know. He seems as healthy as ever." She evaded his eyes.

"You don't suppose he's reconsidered returning his prodigal son to your bosom?"

"Possibly. He dislikes me."

"That hasn't kept him out of your bed . . . or has it? You two sounded prickly last night."

Her eyes narrowed. "Did you select my tent site?"

"I may have . . . unless I was preoccupied; I think about women a great deal, even when directing mule drovers. Sleeping with mule drovers arouses all my vileness." His gaze caressed her from head to toe. "Can you imagine what I imagined about you last night?"

"Was I stitching your leer in place?"

"Ouch. You are a pet this morning."

"No, prickly, as in catcus spines under my tent."

"An oversight, which will never happen again . . . although"—his eyes turned mischievous—"cactus warns against intruders, particularly if they wear slippers."

"Thank you, I'll remember that." She slid a sardonic glance at his footwear. "I daresay deerskin boots manage very well in cactus."

"Slick as a rabbit." He continued to peruse the cling of her habit

"Well, Mr. Rabbit had better be careful where he hops, because I keep a pistol under my pillow. What a pity to blow his charming arse to smithereens."

He touched his hat with mocking deference. "If it soothes your disposition, I'll send the ox carts ahead this morning. I've already sent the heavy wagons ahead. We'll pass them sometime around noon, and let them catch up to us by the time we make camp."

"Thank you, Rafer," she replied, relieved but wondering how Ramsey would accept being set aside.

Ramsey took the insubordination rather well, wrapped in Rafer's guile. Noticing the missing ox carts when he emerged from his tent, Ramsey immediately charged Rafer, lounging by the one fire left burning to accommodate Ramsey's breakfast. Suzanne, twiddling with cold coffee at the nearby campaign table, flinched at Ramsey's roar. "Where the hell are my ox carts?"

"About a mile ahead, just as you ordered," Rafer replied in a carrying tone, then murmured, "and lower your voice. Leapfrogging is standard practice. I figured you might have forgotten; you can't be expected to remember everything at first. Bossing a train is a hell of a job. I was sure you'd want to reassure these drovers that you know what's what; if they get too nervous, they skip out." He soberly rose to his feet. "I don't envy your responsibilities, but I admire your nerve. Any man willing to attempt the Rockies with an expedition this size in the dead of winter has real balls."

"Save the blather, Rafer; I'm on to you," growled Ramsey. "You're not conning me into letting you take over."

"Farthest thing from my mind; to prove it, I'll stay the

hell out of your way. Good luck to you.'' Rafer strolled to his horse and mounted.

"Where do you think you're going?" demanded Ramsey, pursuing him to catch his bridle. "You're supposed to ride scout."

"I will; probably see you every few days or so. You won't need the compass; just cut up Cold Creek Canyon Pass and look out for falling rock, Utes, and whatnot. If you have a serious problem, send up a flare.''

"What do you consider serious?" gritted Ramsey.

Rafer looked thoughtful. "Well, dropping a wagon down a canyon isn't serious. What's one more hand on a burial detail? But if you meet a Ute war party, let me know so I can ride for help." He smiled sweetly. "May I have my bridle now?"

"Stay close, you sonofabitch. I want to see your ass every three hours." Ramsey snapped loose the bridle.

"Yes, boss." Rafer rode off across the prairie.

The day's hot trek was boring; the next day as much so. Ramsey and Suzanne passed the ox carts after lunch. They had a long way to go, with little to enliven their journey, but Suzanne remained solid in her resolve to achieve her goal.

THIRTEEN

The Dastard

The Cold Creek Canyon passage was steep, arduous and lengthy. A single wagon's width in span, the trail was fairly well marked. But the oxen slowed considerably on the rugged, rutted upgrade, their muscles straining as they attempted to avoid the deep, uneven ruts of previous wagons. Occasionally, heavy planks were laid to guide the wagon wheels over trail edges gouted by rock slides and rain. Sometimes, the drovers walked, leading the animals. The hounds ran underfoot, making nuisances of themselves, until banished to their cages in two wagons at the rear of the train, where they howled pitifully for nearly two days.

Despite the hounds' racket, Suzanne delighted in the winding canyon trek through tall blue spruce, white barked aspens and ponderosa pines alive with red squirrels and camp robber birds. Periodically, the canyon walls turned to sheer plates of ruddy rock, the pines thinning to disappear entirely. The lush, long grass at the canyon base was scattered with flattened, silver patches where deer and elk herds passed the night. The nights were starry and clear, the wind sighing an ever varying song through the pines and rocks.

While rarely with the train, Rafer always seemed to be around for serious emergencies, even if he offered no advice on how to handle them. All in all, stung by his early mistakes, Ramsey managed reasonably well. He knew how to make the men step lively, his orders leaving no room for argument. Rafer never inserted his subtle influence unless lives were at stake. He had no regard for equipment, appearing to need nothing more than his horse and the clothes on his back. He never used the .38 Colt at his hip or the Remington rifle in his saddle scabbard, and while he unloaded his pack animals nightly, he never opened the packs. He usually showed up for dinner, but not for breakfast. Before dawn, he was on the trail, sometimes spotting back at noon camp, but just as often he was gone for two days at a time. Not only did Suzanne miss him, she felt safer with him nearby, having gained respect for his judgment. Sometimes, she caught him regarding her with cynicism, regret, and calculation. When she expected a taunt, he would be almost tender. Desire lay between them like a waiting snare, yet he made no move to touch her.

A mass of smelter towers, Black Hawk was a fledgling sparrow of a town perched high in the fork of two narrow canyons. The smelter foreman, D. O. Burkette, was a dark-haired, middle-aged man with a neat, short beard, and penetrating eyes. Burkette rose from his cluttered desk to shake

Ramsey's hand, then Rafer's. He nodded to Suzanne, then offered them all chairs. "My clerk tells me you're interested in a smelter tour for a feasibility study, Mr. Hoth."

"Actually, Mr. Burkette, I am the current claimant's widow and Mr. Smith is my partner," Suzanne intervened swiftly. "My father-in-law is acting in my interest." She was not about to let Ramsey gain a reputation as claim owner. On the other hand, if Rafer ever decided to yell "theft," Bradford would still be held accountable, not her.

Ramsey angrily started to countermand her statement, then abruptly changed his mind. Rafer let out a sound of muffled laughter as Burkette reassessed her. "My apologies for the mistake, Mrs. Hoth. Which claim do you propose to develop?"

"I prefer not to say for the moment, Mr. Burkette. Extensive exploration must be done, and while I am confident of your discretion, news invariably travels."

The foreman nodded. "I understand completely. Most speculators wish to keep their interest secret."

"Thank you, Mr. Burkette." Suzanne unbuckled a satchel at her feet. "I can show you an ore sample." Hoisting up Rafer's ore, she handed it to Burkette. Rafer stiffened slightly.

Quizzically, Burkette shifted the ore in his palm. "You mean to transport your ore quite a way, Mrs. Hoth, if you smelt it here."

"Then you know its origin?" she asked breathlessly.

"Mr. Burkette can guess," intervened Rafer, "but only by the rock type surrounding the gold. Rock strata often covers hundreds of miles. Isn't that right, Mr. Burkette?"

"Well, yes, specific identification is impossible." Burkette smiled up at Suzanne's tense face. "So your secret is fairly safe, Mrs. Hoth." He returned the sample. "Now, would you all care to join me in the smelter?"

The smelter interior was noisy, smelly, and dirty. A huge, thudding stamp mill crushed ore brought by freight wagons and pack mules, then a bumping table shook free the waste rock from the ore. Depending on the ore, the gold and silver was amalgamated with mercury, roasted to remove the sulfur, chlorinated to precipitate the gold, or treated with cyanide to remove the gold by electrolysis. The smelting cost would probably run half the ore value. Rafer assumed Suzanne would soon lose interest in the processing technicalities, but her face lit with intensity, her hair reflecting the furnace glow like a bright, copper flame as her hands locked about the railing that separated the processing area from the catwalk. To Rafer, she resembled Vulcan's Venus: beauty bound to a dark, coarse god. "Nothing connected with money bores you, does it?" he murmured into her ear.

"You spend enough time chasing money; it certainly doesn't seem to bore you."

"Rafer!" yelled Ramsey from the smelter floor. "Come down here. You need to see these mattes!"

With a parting glance at Suzanne, Rafer headed down the metal steps. For a few minutes, he conferred with Ramsey and Burkette, then Burkette went to fetch account notes from his office. Suzanne silently followed Burkette. She sidled into his office as he scooped up his note pad. "Mr. Burkette, I'm sorry to trouble you again, but I am fascinated by your geological sleuthing. Did you really recognize my ore sample?"

"Well, yes," he answered, flattered, "I believe I did."

She laughed teasingly. "Please don't keep me in suspense. Where does it originate?"

"Somewhere in northern California."

Her throat closed. "Not Colorado?"

"No ore that color around here." He cocked his head like a pup expecting a head scratch. "Well, am I right?"

He received no answer. She had already gone to strangle Rafer.

Unable to commit mayhem on Rafer in front of Ramsey, and not daring to test her self-control, she went out to the buckboard, then began to pace like a trapped, ravening tigress. I'll kill him! she vowed wrathfully. Inch by despicable inch! This time, that rotten cheat will get exactly what he deserves!

Ten minutes later, the men emerged from the smelter. Rafer warily regarded her flushed face. "Too hot around the furnaces?"

"I'm afraid so"—her tone suggested the delicacy of a bruised rose—"but, it was all so exciting. I can scarcely wait to visit the claim." She gazed up at him with false innocence. "You did say we would go there after visiting the smelter?"

He gave her a virtuous smile. "You know me. A promise is a promise."

Like a pile of penguin droppings in Algiers. Suzanne mentally trod on the urge to attack. Why carve out a heart the conscienceless no-good would never miss? She could wait. Rafer deserved to roast over a slow fire. And she knew just where to drive the skewer.

After bidding Burkette farewell, Suzanne and Ramsey returned to camp, but Rafer lingered in town most of the afternoon. He went to Banner's freight office, and on pretext of needing transportation for a shipment of food supplies to Breckenridge, asked a number of subtle questions as to the whereabouts of Helmut Banner, should he have compliments about the service. Unfortunately, Banner's close-mouthed freight manager gave him a wary stare, then firmly changed the subject. Rafer waited across the street until after the clerk tucked the "Closed" sign in the window, then picked the rear door lock and let himself into the office. Intent on finding Banner's mailing address, he rifled the records in the file cabinets, but found only financial accounts. Burkette's files were more productive. Several letters of inquiry about smelting had come from the mining town of Breckenridge during the past three months; one sounded as if it might have issued from Brad. Burkette's file on Banner reflected a string of successful mining investments. The most recent letter was from San Francisco; the rest came from freight depot sites. Burkette's return letters were all mailed to a Grand Junction address.

That night over dinner, Suzanne doggedly pretended enthusiasm for discussion of the smelter's production capabilities, all the while wondering how and when to inform Ramsey the expedition was a goose chase. Was this really the end of the trail? She could blackmail Ramsey into supporting her father and herself, but the prospect was repellent. Ramsey had so far held up his end of their bargain. Brad's desertion was not his fault, and he had lost a son.

She sighed inwardly. What tangled webs we weave: I should love to wrap Rafer in one and leave him for a nubile Mexican tarantula.

Full of brandy and plans, Ramsey went to bed early. Suzanne retired to her own tent, changed to a nightgown, snuffed the lantern, and waited. Around midnight, she took out a revolver filched from Ramsey's collection, then draped a long, cashmere shawl about herself to conceal the gun. She eased back the tent flap to survey the sleeping camp. A guard paced idly on the dark rim of the camp. One was across the clearing near the remuda, another by the ammunition wagon. While their backs were turned, their stances were fairly alert. The other two guards' footsteps stirred twigs beyond Ramsey's tent.

Stealthily, she crept to Rafer's bedroll. He slept on his back, hat covering his face. She knelt down and put her lips next to his ear. "Rafer . . . darling," she whispered seductively. "Wake up, please."

His hat flipped back with such startling alacrity that she almost lost her balance, hastily grabbing her shawl to keep from revealing the gun. He was oblivious, intent on the curves beneath her nightgown. "Rafer," she whispered unsteadily. "I have to see you . . . alone."

In one easy motion, he was on his way to her tent. She caught his arm. "Not there! They'll hear us!"

He turned, an impish grin flaring in the moonlight. "Inclined to be noisy, are we?"

Scarcely able to hear him, she jerked her head toward the forest.

He took her hand. In seconds, they were enveloped in the dark shelter of the wood. Before she could protest, he picked her up and strode swiftly through the trees. "You don't have to carry me," she whispered.

"I do if we don't want to wake every dog in Christendom."

She had forgotten the dogs. His soft shod feet made no

sound on ground strewn with loose rock and timber debris. In a few minutes, he started to put her down. "No, further," she protested as his lips hovered over hers, then at his muffled laughter, added lamely, "remember those dogs."

He carried her another quarter mile, then let her slip down against him, his lips hungrily claiming hers before she could struggle. His arms wound about her, holding her immovable. She hated him, hated him, but somehow his kiss was wrapping that hatred about her until it was turning into something else: a scarlet haze of heat quickening like a heartbeat that throbbed unbearably throughout her brain, her body, making her strain for air, for sanity. She must fight him, must . . . A whirlpool of confusion and desperation swirled about her as the gun hung from her lax fingers. As he kissed her slowly, repeatedly, dizzy desire made her unable to think . . . remember how much she despised him. His kisses deepened, their liquid, pulsating fire playing over her, binding her to him with a growing, primeval passion that seemed to throb in the velvet silence of the forest about them. His eyes beneath their shadowing lashes held a dark mystery that she found increasingly irresistible, as if they held an irrevocable promise, a lure to expore all the reaches of desire where only he could lead her. She could not trust him, must not . . . for if she did, he would cast her from some high precipice of love and she would be lost forever, aching for the sound of his voice . . . for his touch that was dazing her even now. Oh, God, she thought weakly, how can I shoot a man who makes me feel like this . . . His lean body was hard against hers, the thin gown no barrier. His hand caught in her hair, tugging her head back to expose her throat to his lips. She tried to pull away, but her struggle was of no use for he clasped her more closely than before.

"Su, Su, I thought you'd never come," he breathed huskily. "I've been going crazy . . ." His hands moved quickly, surely. This time there was no anger in his touch, nothing but the same relentless hunger that tormented her. He slid the linen from her shoulders, his mind and hers one, knowing where, how to caress her until she was torn between the fading need to escape and wanting to beg him to assuage

the desire mounting within her. The linen pressed taut against
her breasts, molding them beneath his adroit, heated mouth
until the peaks of her breasts became hard little points of
longing that filled her with increasing, delicious torment. She
still wanted to fend him off, only somehow she was losing
her will, her strength, for it seemed to be pouring into the
ground as if she were as parched as the dry earth and he were
a burning, obliterating rain. Whatever happened, whatever
he was there was this between them . . . like a shameless
obsession. The gown parted, making her shiver against him
until his urgent hands slipped beneath to seek her, find her
so quickly wanting him. "I've never known a woman like
you," he whispered huskily against her soft, fevered flesh.
"I thought I might have to cut through your damned tent
tonight and hang at sunrise."

When he kissed her again, she knew all reason and shame
had fled her, leaving only her need for him, and his for her.
His fingers drew hers to the heavy swell between his hard
thighs, let her tentatively stroke him beneath the denim, open
him, touch him. She was shaking now. He lifted her, let her
slide down on him until he filled her, and in the first, deep
gliding stroke, the gun dropped unheard to the ground. Her
arms wound helplessly about his neck, her face pressed
against his as he surged again and again. His hands shifted
to grip her, move her until she moaned with the tremors
tearing through her body. A moan of sheer distraught disappointment welled from her throat as he suddenly stilled
. . . only to bear her to the bracken and drive to that secret
depth that welcomed him, revelled in him. The muscles moving in his lean back, the urgent thrust of his hips, his ragged
breathing against her bare shoulder as if she could never hold
him closely enough. Now, now, let him, she pleaded in silent
desperation, oh, please, now! His back arched, his hips curling under so strongly that he gasped, his own desperate release
exploding with hers. Let me have enough of him, so besot-
tedly much that I never need him again. I don't want to want
him . . . don't need . . . need . . . oh, please. For a long
time, he clung to her as if like her, he could never have
enough of the lightning that sulfurously played between them

each time they touched. A suble tension rippled through his body as if he were both repelled by his desire for her as much as inexorably drawn.

"Forget Ramsey and his damned expedition," he breathed. "Wait for me in Denver until he's had his fill of playing Hannibal and I'll come back for you. You don't need him. You sure as hell don't need that amateur swindler you married."

His words probed like needles, stinging away her languor, the haze of lingering desire upon her mind. His loose shirt cast a shadow across his bare chest, the deep vee of his breeches where his temporarily appeased sex was half hidden. He meant to have her again . . . tonight . . . any night he wanted. He meant to use her, and go on using her, not only as an object of his lust, but in any manner that suited his tawdry ambition. She must stop him, if it required the resolution of a cobra. No wonder Rafer wanted her to forget the expedition; it was going nowhere. Sitting up, she fastened her gown with leaden fingers. "Why should I be any better off with a professional swindler like you, Rafer?" she countered with ominous quietness. "You tell nothing but lies. You cheat everyone, even yourself. Why treat me any differently?"

He was silent for a moment. "Because I would like to treat you differently."

Her eyes flinched closed for a moment, then her fingers closed on the gun in the bracken. Rafer rose even as she did. She backed away, but while the aiming gun registered in his eyes in the slanting moonlight through the aspens, he appeared unsurprised, undisturbed. She wrapped the shawl around the gun muzzle to muffle the sound. "You don't believe I'll use this gun, do you?" she questioned softly.

"Why should you?" The shawl silencer imparted resolution on her part, because his nonchalant stance was growing a trifle wary.

"Because you deserve to be shot," she replied vehemently. "Because there is no gold claim. No reason for us to be here at all. You picked up that ore sample in California."

"I picked it up in a Baton Rouge card game. Nobody carts a chunk of rock that size from California, much less Colorado, then carries it around for ten years."

In reply, the revolver trigger cocked.

Rafer decided to employ reason. "You aren't going to shoot me with that thing, Su. You probably can't hit the side of a . . ." A bullet nicked his ear, leaving the shawl smoking. His fingers came away bloody. "What the hell do you think you're doing?" he demanded furiously "You could have killed me!"

In reply, the gun went off again, her accuracy a product of Connecticut skeet shooting. This time he grabbed at his upper arm with an oath, a neat, scarlet groove oozing through his rent shirt. He started toward Suzanne, then hearing the trigger recock, abruptly changed his mind. "Are you going to kill me?" he asked huskily.

"How could I? You said I couldn't hit the side of a barn." Although her voice and the gun were still carefully levelled, her fingers shook slightly as she fastened her nightgown, which was tangling her legs in the rising wind.

"Look, Su—" he watched her sharply—"I can explain about the ore . . ."

"With prologue and epilogue, no doubt. You're always Johnny-on-the-spot with a story . . . but I need my rest; it's a long ride back to Denver." The next bullet creased his thigh.

He grabbed his leg, the words coming out in a rush. "Look, as you're in a hurry, I'll make it short. The ore didn't come from my mine . . . don't shoot me for that, there's more. I left Colorado when I was a kid, for Chrissakes, and I haven't been back until now. If the mine's real, what the hell difference does it make where the sample comes from? How many people know quartz from granite. Do you?"

"I know a liar when I see one." The trigger cocked.

"Christ, we just made love!" he yelled. "What are you, some kind of black widow spider?"

"Hush, you'll wake everybody up." The gun spat through the shawl again, grazing his inner thigh.

He worriedly inspected his wound. "I'm not lying!" he hissed angrily. "The claim is real, but if you blow one more stinking hole in me, you'll never see it!"

"What? Crankiness? Don't you like being the butt of a bad joke for once, Rafer? I can assure you, I immensely enjoyed the one you played on Ramsey and me. Would you like to know why?" Her voice tightened. "The '69 gold crash ruined my father. He's on the streets and I haven't seen him in nearly a year. This expedition meant everything to me . . . but to you, it was merely amusing." The trigger cocked again.

"Wait," cautioned Rafer, the anger gone from his voice. "I can prove there's a claim. You've come this far; a little farther can't make much difference. Stick with me two more weeks; that's all I ask."

She surveyed him. He looked genuinely regretful, even sympathetic; given his mercurial nature, he probably was, but compassion rarely hindered his selfishness. "Sorry, request denied," she replied tiredly. "I'd really like to kill you, Rafer, but it would be like killing a child for stealing candy. You haven't the morals of a baby and you've turned a fine mind into an elaborate toy." She lowered the gun. "Run along back to camp now. Not that you will be so inclined after tonight, but if you ever touch me again, I'll shoot you. I don't deny you excite me, but I want a man, not a boy."

Without a word, he started up the trail. At six paces distance, she followed him. They had not gone far, when he halted. She readied the gun. Placing his hands behind his head, he turned. Although his body was poised warily, his eyes were level with a sobriety unlike him. "The claim is outside of Breckenridge. You don't need me to get there. Unless he runs into Arapaho, Ramsey should be able to reach Breckenridge before the first snow."

"Taking the usual flit now that the cat's out of the bag, are you?" she observed tonelessly. "Why not? Ramsey will probably kill you if you stay." She felt sick, and hideously lonely, as if the forest emptiness filled her heart. She had feared their attraction must eventually come to this mean, denigrating end, laying bare all of his petty, larcenous soul . . . and her foolish weaknesses. She would never be so weak again . . . for any man. "I won't tell Ramsey what you've done; he'll discover that himself in Breckenridge. You should be able to go a considerable distance in a fortnight, but you had better leave tonight." She lowered the gun.

He lowered his hands. "If you'll accept one piece of advice. When you come out of the Breckenridge claims office, quit while you're ahead. If Brad isn't in Breckenridge, sit tight for the winter. Don't keep trekking with Ramsey: his inexperience is deadly."

"But he learns fast, doesn't he? And he doesn't take flits. Whatever else he is, he's a man, and that's more than you'll ever be." She headed up the trail before he could see the tears starting to pour down her face. "Goodbye, Rafer."

Momentarily, Rafer considered kidnapping her for her own good, but held back. She had just scratched him; he could travel easily enough. She had to do what she had to do, just as he did, and she was not going to change her mind about him. He could make love to her until they both saw pink, but she would still come off her back trying to escape him. By her standards, he was flamingly irresponsible. What sort of life could he promise her? Now that he was closing on Banner, the last thing he needed was a woman who mattered. Suzanne mattered. He no longer cared who she was or what she was, only that he might lose her. Now he was irrevocably losing her to contempt, removing her as far as death.

He silently followed her at a distance to see her safely through the pine shadows into her tent. The flap fell, then all was still, the sleeping camp unwary as an animal sprawled lax on its back. A guard dozed, while two of them stared with dull boredom into space. The only one alert was edgy because he feared some horror would leap from the shadows. If he stayed with the caravan beyond Breckenridge, he would meet horror.

But that's not your worry now, is it, Mr. Smith? Rafer reminded himself. You've been given your walking papers. So walk.

And he did.

FOURTEEN

Boom!

Ramsey's roar split the dawn air of the camp. "Where the hell is that sonofabitch? We're supposed to leave this morning and we could be headed for China for all I know!"

"Calm down, Ramsey," Suzanne said quietly. "We're going to Breckenridge."

Ramsey whipped around to see Suzanne already dressed in her riding habit, her hands wrapped about an untouched mug of coffee as she sat on a log by the campfire. His eyes narrowed at the suspicious smudges under her eyes. "Oh, Rafer just up and told you, eh?"

"He just up and told me," she responded flatly, dashing the cold coffee out. "He made an early start to check the passes ahead."

Ramsey strode back to his tent after ordering Frock to check for the tracks of Rafer's unshod mustang beyond camp. He turned back to Suzanne, who had followed him into his tent. "We'll see quick enough whether Mr. Smith's on the job or skipping out. If Rafer's headed anywhere but Breckenridge, I'm going to smell a rat . . . maybe two rats."

With an ironic laugh, Suzanne moved past him. "Why not have Frock serve cheese for breakfast?"

He caught her arm. "You're not leaving this tent until you tell me what you were up to with Rafer last night. And don't lie. You've got circles cut to your teeth."

"Perhaps I had a toothache," she shot back defiantly. "Do you still think I would bed Rafer just to pry information from him? What would be the point? He'd lie, wouldn't he? Did

a woman ever get anything out of you, just by bedding you?"
Her green eyes flared suppressed torment that approached
hysteria. "No, sir. With you, a lady pays her way because
the only thing you love is profits. Well, I'll pay! You want
to be rid of me, don't you? After Breckenridge, you'll never
see me again!"

When she tried to jerk away, Ramsey's grip tightened
painfully on her wrist. Suddenly, his face twisting, he jerked
her to him. Then he kissed her, hard and hurtfully, but with
an inner pain in himself she could dimly feel. Share. And
so, she did not fight him.

When he let her go, his voice was roughened with anger
and desire. "You're not cutting out just yet, missy. If you're
playing with me, I'll make you wish you were dead . . . but
if you're straight, you won't be sorry. I can treat the right
woman like a queen."

Her face filled with bleak frustration. How could she make
him see she was grateful that he cared for her when she
desperately needed tenderness, but that she could never belong to him? "I'm married to your son, Ramsey. As long as
Bradford is my husband, I will not be your mistress. Even
if Bradford and I were to be divorced, even if he were dead,
you could never marry me. The world would view our living
together as incest. I couldn't face that vilification; I've already
endured enough to last a lifetime."

"I'll take you away," he argued. "We'll go to Mexico or
Brazil . . . the South Pacific, anywhere you want. "I'm older
than you. When I die, you'll be a rich woman . . ."

"Stop it!" Her hands clasped over her ears. "Stop talking
about the money! All I want now is . . . affection. Simple,
decent, human affection. Without grasping, without deceit."

Frock's voice cut in mildly from the tent door. "Sorry to
interrupt, Mr. Hoth, but Mr. Smith is headed southwest. Told
the guards he was going scouting."

Ramsey's eyes held Suzanne's. "Which way is Breckenridge, Frock?"

"Southwest." At the relief in Ramsey's face, Frock smiled
faintly. "I take it, we don't shoot him yet, sir."

"Be patient: the necessity will undoubtedly arise." Ramsey's gaze shifted to possessively appraise Suzanne. "Won't it?"

For three days, the wagons threaded along Durango Creek toward the Continental Divide without sign of Rafer. Wherever he was bound, he must be miles ahead of their slow-moving train. Now that Rafer was gone, Suzanne's sense of adventure was gone, as well as her laughter; something else was missing too, that she dared not name. Ramsey must guess what was going through her mind, but despite his anger at Rafer's disappearance, he was also considerate, making no jibes, no recriminations, no physical assaults. They almost became friends. Indeed, from the watchful puzzlement and uncertain, reluctant tenderness in his eyes, he gave every sign of a man on the verge of falling in love.

The approaching September weather was cool at night, leaving the sunny days brisk. While afternoons sometimes spilled rain showers from gray skies, mornings were invariably bright with the silvery trunks of vast colonies of green-aspens, boldly striped across the mountains. Spangled with wildflowers, the thick bracken resembled a tropical forest due to the rain. "Hope all this rain don't mean more snow than usual this winter," Frock moodily observed one wet afternoon as their wagon lumbered over muddy ruts.

"With any luck, we'll be back in Denver by Christmas," blithely responded Ramsey, pulling up his slicker collar. He glanced back into the wagon, where Suzanne was curled up with the journal she had purchased in Black Hawk, her skirt tucked against the drizzling damp. "What do you want for Christmas, Suzie? An ermine coat?"

With a rueful smile, she paused in her scrawling. "I'd settle for a turkey for Thanksgiving. Do you really think we'll reach Breckenridge that soon?"

"Ought to, if the weather holds."

Under his dripping bowler hat brim, Frock uneasily peered up at the wet, red canyon walls with their tailings of loose rock traced like gigantic flakes of rust. Gray-green Durango Creek rushed over shallow lichened boulders and fallen logs a few feet from their wagon wheels. The bank was fallen away in muddy chunks from networks of tree roots. "When do you expect Smith to show, Mr. Hoth? He's never stayed away this long."

"He may not show up at all," was Ramsey's rough response. "He could complicate things if he tosses a horseshoe into this mine deal."

"If there is a mine deal." Ramsey's blunt chin settled into his limp, rain-spangled beard. "If there isn't, he may just find himself run headfirst through an ore crusher." He slid another speculative glance at Suzanne. "That prospect doesn't appear to worry you. You know something I don't?"

"If Rafer lied about the claim, I shall hold your coat while you crank," she replied evenly. "I stand to lose as much as you, don't I?"

His hard gaze lingered. "Sometimes I wonder."

They reached Georgetown in midafternoon. Along the valley floor lining Clear Creek in a cottonwood grove banked between mountain walls thick with ponderosa pines and blue spruce was a small community of mining shacks, modest bungalows and prosperous, gingerbread houses. Bred on silver, Georgetown was the most appealing town they had encountered in the territory. With mounting nostalgia, Suzanne shifted on the wagon seat to crane at passing windowboxes of petunias and marigolds; the frail rose-bushes set in a few scattered lawns with neat, brick walks along Brownell and Alpine streets. Housewives in crocheted shawls plied brooms to porches and called to playing children. Cats reclined on windowsills, while well-fed dogs trotted the wide, dirt streets. Georgetown even had a solid, little jail-house across from the courthouse down Argentine Street. Rafer would be as alien to this world as a unicorn.

Beside her, Ramsey reined in the mule team slightly to avoid a boy darting after a cocker spaniel, then leaned from the driver's box to call to a man crossing the street. "You there, sir. Where's the best hotel in town?"

"The Hotel de France," the man called back. "Down the street a bit."

Mr. Perdoux's establishment, styled after a comfortable Normandy inn, was a pleasant surprise, to say the least.

George Perdoux, a sharp-eyed, sandy-haired man with military mustaches, met them at the front desk register. He went to the door to calmly survey the long caravan waiting in the street. "I regret my three remaining rooms will not possibly accommodate your entire party, but there are a number of smaller establishments about town."

Ramsey summoned Frock, waiting in the street. "Post a guard around the train; give our crew a blowout in the nearest saloon, then cart their carcasses into the wagons. Skunk drunk, they won't care where they spend the night."

"Yes, sir." Frock departed on his errand.

Ramsey turned back to the hotel proprietor. "I want your best room, Mr. Perdoux, with a hot bath and stiff toddy before dinner."

Realizing Ramsey intended Perdoux to assume they were married, Suzanne quickly added, "And I should like a room with a town view, if possible . . . as well as a bath."

"*Certainement*," replied Perdoux, positioning the register for Ramsey's signature. "Dinner is served at 8:00." He rang for the chambermaid. "Show Mr. and Mrs. Hoth to numbers nine and six, *s'il vous plaît*, Sarah." He accompanied them to the steps, then retired into the parlor. From the upper landing, Suzanne heard a lively murmur of voices drift up the stair from behind the half-closed parlor door.

"I gather you have a full house, Sarah," she commented.

"Oh, yes, ma'am." Sarah grinned. "But then we always do. Mr. Perdoux is what you'd call famous in these parts."

"Famous for what?" queried Ramsey, his wariness cut by curiosity.

"Oh, *Troot Foomie* and such like!"

"I see," murmured Suzanne, becoming discouraged. "Sarah, may I have a hot toddy during my bath? When I've finished the first glass, I shall want another. The road to Monsieur Perdoux's *Troot Foomie* has been a lengthy one."

An hour later, with the warmth of the second toddy seeping into her spine, Suzanne lay her head back on the walnut-encased rim of the steaming tub. The bathroom window's colored glass was fogged, her mind cushioned on ethereal fumes of rum. She was drifting like an unanchored vessel

. . . slowly, inevitably drifting toward the rocks. She was an officially fallen woman who contrived to be deserted as often as others of her sex spring cleaned. Her game was up and Rafer departed with half the cards protruding from his sleeves. Neither would win now, far less her father. Since Rafer's departure, she had been assailed by anger, hurt and guilt . . . although the guilt was beginning to fade. She might as well have attempted to resist a force of nature as Rafer. He was too outrageously wily, too scruffily appealing   too endearing. He was an unabashed rat, yet she liked him: his resilience, his wit, his acceptance of life. She missed his arms about her, his reassuring voice . . . even when he was lying through his teeth. She cared about him, but he cared nothing for her; otherwise, he could not cheat her so coldbloodedly. She had not believed any man could hurt her as much as Marcus, yet Brad's cowardly duplicity made Marcus's disloyalty seem insignificant. Of them all, only Rafer could strike at her heart. Now her breast felt as if it were cracked glass encasing dull fear and defeat. Morosely sinking deeper into the tub, she took a moody, reckless gulp at the toddy.

The door creaked open. Sarah must be bringing extra towels and the third toddy. Opening her eyes a fraction, she halfheartedly addressed the towel stack progressing to the heated rack. "What sort of salary does Monsieur Perdoux pay a beginning chambermaid, Sarah?"

"Your talents were never designed for honest employment, sweet," murmured the towels. "You could make a fortune simply by posing as Bathsheba for the local Masonic Lodge."

Her eyes widened in shock as the towels lowered to reveal Rafer's wolfish grin in a three-day growth of beard. The impish arch to his brows mimicked her astonishment as he surveyed her luminous form beneath the lilac-scented water. "Lo, what charms I see before me, and in what a lot of light."

Abruptly, she sat up, her heart pounding. "Rafer! What are you doing here!" Then just as abruptly slithered down again. The subtle change in his expression at her nudity and his wet yellow poncho made him resemble a reckless *bandito*. He must have come from further south where the thunderheads had been lurking all afternoon. "Are you crazy? You should be headed for Mexico!"

He dropped the towels neatly on the brass rack, then flipped back his poncho and hunkered down by the tub. "Mexico would welcome me like a rabid Chihuahua." His bold blue eyes appraising her cornered expression, he dabbled his fingers in the water, then trailed them to her bare arm. "When I really thought about it, I knew no one would be as glad to see me as you."

Quickly, she pulled her arm away. The bullet holes in his shirt and jeans were neatly darned, his expression innocent. "Me? In all modesty, why me?"

His fingertips pursued her. "Because you covet my claim shares . . . among other things."

"What claim shares?" In nervous exasperation, she slapped his hand away. "There is no claim."

He stood up, tossed his wet hat on a wall hook, then pulled off his poncho and began to unbutton his shirt. "Oh, there's a claim . . . and Ramsey's going to slide it right out from under you. If he leans hard enough on his son, you'll find yourself quite literally out in the cold; it gets down to thirty degrees around here."

"Hard enough to freeze your ever enterprising balls"— her tartness edged a desperate urge to flight—"so put your shirt back on. Bathsheba isn't selling tickets today."

His shirt open to the waist, he flicked loose his belt buckle. "But she might tomorrow if the going gets rough, mightn't she? Bathsheba's three ways tight and feeling sorry for herself."

She threw the soap at him, but he ducked almost without looking. "Get out of here, Rafer! I'll scream!"

"No, you won't," he said calmly. "You can't afford to involve Ramsey." He pulled off his boots, then his shirt.

Suzanne stopped in mid-grab for the toddy glass when she saw the scars. A single faded white streak marred the smooth brown skin beneath each collar bone. Like a delicate, wicked web, a fine network of smaller scars traced his right shoulder and side as if an indolent, virulent spider had casually preyed upon him. Only the pattern's sadistic artistry revealed it had been created by a human . . . or inhuman. "My God," she whispered in horror, "who did that to you?"

"A gentleman who threatened to peel my skin scrap by scrap if I withheld certain information from him." Calmly, he peeled off his pants. The scars might have belonged to someone else.

"Obviously, you told the gentleman what he wanted to know," she said unevenly, her shock unleavened by his careless nudity.

"Hardly. He would have killed me. What's a little skin compared to a permanently punctured throat?" He warily eased into the water. His caution was warranted, for she immediately tried to kick him in the crotch and bolt from the tub. He grabbed her foot and wrist, then dragged her atop him. Water splashed the black and white marble floor as they struggled. Desperate, she almost squirmed out of his grasp as she surged toward the side of the tub, but quick as she was, he was quicker. Because he was accustomed to Apache style wrestling, she was no match for him, but this time she refused to let him have his way so easily. Thrashing, writhing, she fought him doggedly . . . to no avail. Minute after wet, splashing minute passed, until Suzanne began to tire and his old mesmeric sway over her began to take hold. His lips soft as his hands were hard, his kisses trailed down her mutinous jaw, the arch of her throat, the corners of her mouth until the storm in her eyes began to darken into conflicting emotions that mixed with the fury: entreaty turned into frustration, flared into unwilling passion. His lithe body was slippery beneath hers, his sex hardened, taunting, exciting. Wherever he touched her, her body reacted, roused. Hearing her angry, frantic breathing alter, Rafer laughed softly, then his hand locked behind her neck, forcing her face slowly, inexorably down to his. "These scars taught me there's a time to fight and a time to surrender, *carita*. This is your time to surrender."

"Let go of me, Rafer!" she railed, her hands cording on his wet shoulders in resistance. "This is rape!"

"No," he corrected gently, "it's anything but rape. And after that round of shells you let fly in the woods the other night, we both know you wouldn't use a gun if you had it. You might shoot me up a little, but you haven't the heart to finish me off.'' His lips brushed hers, teasing, tender. Then he kissed her fully, taking his time, making her tremble even as she struggled to pull away . . . but his mouth was warm, so warm and he was too strong for her . . . too determined . . . too ready and skilled and sure of how to make her desire him. His hands clamping her shoulders, his tongue daringly probed hers, then his hands tangled in her flaming hair. Their lips took fire, kindling their need to be joined together, inseparable and lost to all the differences that separated them. Their bodies entwined, met in struggle that was gradually giving way to passion as his mouth devoured hers. Suzanne hated herself for needing Rafer so much. Hated him. And he saw it. Saw the cloudy rage and hunger in her eyes when his lips left hers.

"I'm the only one packing a weapon now, *querida mia*," he breathed huskily, his hands relaxing on her shoulders. "Use it. Use me. Fight me if you want . . . and you do want, hm? Rape me . . . show me how strong you are . . .'' When she hesitated, he murmured something liquid and taunting in Spanish she could not understand, but it detonated the anger in her into recklessness. She mounted him, thrust her hips down upon his. She began to move swiftly, caring only to end the burning ache he had so perversely roused within her. The wet riot of her hair streaking across her breasts, she used him, with little skill and no concern for his pleasure, but with the pent up violence and resentment her soul had begun to harbor for all men. He gripped her hips, not in constraint, but in challenge, as if urging her to claim her revenge. His own eyes were incandescent with desire, but defiance, too. He wanted something from her, more than her body, and that, she would not give him. I'll never yield my heart to you! I belong to myself, her stubborn mind stormed. I won't be ruled by you, by anyone! I'm the one in control!

She kissed him then, testing her skill, daring his retaliation, and got it with an intensity she had not before encountered in him. The battle locked, their wet bodies strained. Their hunger mounted, the need for defeat and victory becoming as intertwined as their battling spirits. Suzanne's body shuddered as her passion found its answer again and again, until hatred became craving, erotic oblivion. Sensation. Rafer's mouth, his flesh, his sex, his hunger mingled with her own.

Neither one of them could win, and neither cared. When the last shreds of Rafer's control finally ripped away, they were of one body and mind. "How soon can we do it again?" murmured Suzanne as she lay draped in exhaustion upon his shoulder.

"As soon as my pecker cools off," he muttered, his head lax against the tub rim. "Then *querida mia*, we are going to soar the time-honored practice of fucking one's brains out to a dizzy height."

She grinned ruefully through the dripping hair sticking to her face. "At least until someone else wants the tub."

"Let them have it. Where's your room?"

Noticing twilight dimming outside the window, she hesitated, then shook her head. "Ramsey expects me downstairs for dinner. He'll look for me if I'm not there." Reluctantly, she began to braid up her burnished hair.

"Plead a headache." Rafer's blue eyes slitted with a steely glint of jealousy beneath his thick lashes. "Keeping my hands off you for over a month was an unwelcome test of character. Don't I deserve a little time off for good behavior?"

"You don't deserve anything," she replied softly, her hands poising in her hair, then evaded his trap, "and if you mistake a few days for a month, your restraint couldn't be too overtaxed."

Letting out a sigh, he captured a wet strand of her hair and began to toy with it. "You're a hard lady, but as a demonstration of my devotion, I've a proposition. Leave with me tonight and I'll sell your husband's claim shares to you."

"What difference does that make if they're not legitimate?"

"What if, as sole owner of the mine, I swear to the claims recorder that they are?"

Knowing where he was headed, she played along. "You'd create confusion, a court fight with Ramsey. Quite frankly, I cannot afford a lawyer."

"You wouldn't need one, if the case stayed out of court. Ramsey has led a checkered career; perhaps, with a touch of encouragement, he might do something foolish . . ."

"Are you suggesting we blackmail him into not contesting Brad's interest?"

He tapped her nose with the curved tip of his captured hair strand. "You're due for a nasty fight with him no matter how you maneuver in Breckenridge. You need an ally."

She rested an elbow on the tub rim. "What's in it for you, Rafer?"

"You," he said calmly.

"And when you've had enough of me?" she countered coolly. "What happens when the bath water turns cold?"

He pulled her to him. "It's cold now." Then his mouth and body covered hers and he slid her down, down, until only her fingertips showed above the tub rim. She shivered once, then her arms went around him, seeking his heat, guiding him to hers.

Out in the hall, Sarah shook her head at the trail of water seeping beneath the closed door. "That redhead must be drunk or dead," she muttered, then tossed down the twice-warmed toddy on her tray. "Some folks just got no sense of time when they get into a bathroom."

Ramsey's eyes narrowed as Rafer followed Suzanne into the hotel parlor. Her braided coronet was wet and Rafer's sandy thatch was suspiciously damp. "Well, if you aren't Johnny-Jump-Up," he observed caustically, reaching for the cigar humidor on the mantel. "I was beginning to think you weren't going to show." The muted buzz of conversation in the parlor faded as Ramsey selected a cigar and lit it.

"Don't I always follow the money?" Rafer eyed the other guests, several of whom were edging away with expressions ranging from affront to horror. To smoke before one of George Perdoux's famous dinners was a cardinal sin. Nearly everyone was well dressed, some in suits and silks, some formally as were Ramsey, Suzanne, and a few others. Of the twelve guests, only three were women, the youngest a blonde with the eager, untested look of a bride. She murmured something to her husband, who glanced at Ramsey and shook his head, apparently uneager to correct Ramsey's manners.

Ramsey drew on his cigar, then leaned against the mantel and studied Suzanne in her black dress. She was white skinned, her high breasts made more provocative by the lack of a corset she had dressed too hurriedly to don. Having lost weight on the trail, she seemed taller, more slender. Her color was high, her eyes bright and defiant. A high-mettled thoroughbred, nothing about her suggested a new bride. "Yep, you're one reliable man, Rafer," Ramsey said with a grate to his tone. "You'll always trail the smell of money . . . and women; be the death of you, one day."

"You've a sharp enough nose yourself," returned Rafer mildly, "yet reached a ripe old age. Perhaps I should simply trail you, Ramsey."

At Rafer's inference, hatred glimmered like heated, rusty iron in Ramsey's jealous eyes and for the first time, Suzanne feared him. Rafer might more safely prod an asp than provoke him now. Quickly, she diverted the subject. "Monsieur Perdoux enjoys some local renown as a chef, Rafer, but Ramsey and I are puzzled by his cuisine . . . *Troot Foomie*, for instance, is particularly mysterious."

"Knowing the resiliance of local palates, *Troot* could be anything from Beef Wellington to steer testicles." A steely tint entered Rafer's clear blue eyes. "The buffalo variety are considered by some to be intriguing due to their inflated size, but aside from a brief novelty, ultimately prove disappointing."

Suzanne's socialite smile congealed. Rafer was out for blood, and likely to get it: his own, from a flattened nose. Ramsey's face was nearly purple. Ready to duck, she stepped between the two men, desperately snatched Ramsey's cigar and stuck it between her teeth. "Do you know, I've always been tempted to try one of these . . . they really are utterly foul, aren't they?" Coughing, she wove to block Ramsey's advance. As he thrust out a hand to move her aside, she withdrew the cigar to stab its hot end down on the first fist that flew. Fortunately, the impending brawl was forestalled by the appearance of Monsieur Perdoux.

"Good evening, ladies"—Perdoux's eye caught the cigar in Suzanne's poised hand—"and gentlemen. Dinner is served."

Dinner was a delightful surprise. Rafer and Ramsey refrained from murdering one another; the dinner conversation exchanged by several mining engineers, a woman botanist, a geographic journal writer, and a New England philosopher, was cultivated and lively. *Troot* turned out to be smoked trout, beautifully prepared and served with clear venison consommé, salad, ptarmigan, roast pheasant and peach Charlotte. At ten o'clock, Rafer departed to make his rounds of the saloons. Suzanne almost relaxed.

Until she retired to her bedroom. Scarcely had she undressed when a knock came at the door. She caught up a wrapper. "Who is it?"

"Ramsey. Let me in." The roughness in his voice put her on guard.

"I'm going to bed now, Ramsey," she replied firmly. "We'll talk in the morning."

He rattled the brass knob. "Now."

"No. I won't be treated as a bone between you and Rafer. Good night, Ramsey."

After a long silence, he grudgingly retreated. "All right, but we have to settle some things."

"I know," she murmured. After his footsteps faded down the hallway, she slipped off her lawn wrapper, then slid under the white down coverlet, blew out the fluted kerosene light, and stared up at the moon-cast shadows on the ceiling from the cottonwoods outside the window. From the hall came the murmurs of bed-bound guests. Her eyes closed tiredly. How was she to keep Rafer and Ramsey from each other's throats? Not that there was a claim, but if by the slimmest chance it did exist, she must play her cards carefully. If she bet on the wrong man, she was out.

How could any woman with a shred of sanity bet on Rafer?

She stirred restlessly, then pommeled her pillow and sought a warmer spot; there was none.

She went rigid at a brush of lips on her neck, a seductive

hand massaging the small of her back. When she started to
rear up and scream, the hand on her back pressed down.
"Relax, darling; you're all tense," murmured Rafer.

She flung herself over, darted a bewildered glance at the
closed window, then glared up at him. "Where did you come
from?"

"Under the bed." He sat beside her as if preparing to
deliver a bedtime tale. "I read part of your journal while I
waited, then took a dive when Ramsey escorted you upstairs.
Sneaky devil, pussyfooting back like that, wasn't he?"

She sat up abruptly, her hair tumbling about her shoulders.
"You complain about sneaks when you read my journal!"

"Considering there was no Bible next to the bed, and none
of us can afford to fight fairly, I snatched it up with the ardor
of an achaeologist unearthing Helen of Troy's memoirs.
Sadly, but predictably, the journal revealed only a few dusty
inscriptions; you and Helen being too discreet to put girlish
confessions on paper." His voice lowered. "That nightshift,
now, is most revealing and indiscreet. You've really exquisite
breasts."

"Why not trot out a magnifying glass to examine them?"
she gritted, heading for the far side of the bed. "You cannot
even be civilized for three hours running! First you creep into
my bath . . ."

He caught her about the waist and pulled her back on the
pillows. "Whereupon we both discovered that neither of us
is very much civilized."

She pushed at his chest. "And you nearly provoked a fight
with Ramsey, who has forty men on call to beat you to a
pulp!"

"I'm moved by your concern, but Ramsey's forty minions
are all pie-eyed. It's just you, me, and your naughty nightshift, darling." He firmly pushed her hands above her head
and kissed her. She squirmed, but indignation was a difficult
emotion to sustain, when his lips were so distracting.

"I really hate you sometimes, Rafer," she breathed when
he stopped kissing her.

"Yes, I know. I'm vile"—he kissed her neck—"repre-

hensible''—her shift strap descended—''depraved''—the
minute buttons at her cleavage parted—''but I make your
heart sing.''

''Something like that,'' she whispered as he buried his face
between her breasts.

Sometime well after midnight, Rafer rose silently from
Suzanne's bed and went to his own. As his door closed, the
door across the hall opened slightly. Moments later, Frock
scratched at Ramsey's door, which almost instantly opened.
''You were right,'' Frock informed his superior with private
pleasure. ''He just left her room.''

Ramsey's face twisted as if jabbed by a splinter, then
resumed its usual harshness. ''I have another errand for you,
Frock . . . to the local marshal.''

Rafer flung his arm across his pillow, caught it close, and
burrowed into it. Gunfire rattled across his mind, cheers
sounded as heavy freight sacks were ripped open. All the
deadly, desirable gold of Midas lay beneath his fingertips . . .
only to sear the flesh from his bones like acid. Assailed by
an evil dream he long ago thought vanquished, he twisted
onto his back, his fingers tightening in his hair. Banner was
a vast, dark specter that faded before his blows, to enfold
him like a malevolent, suffocating serpent. With Banner returned the cloudless sky, the merciless heat, the hideous pain
. . . the dying screams.

Perspiration drenched, he jerked upright to meet a gun at
his throat. For a moment, the pain was so intense he thought
the gun muzzle might have cracked his trachea. Coughing,
he fell back against the pillow. The gun muzzle followed
him. His clearing vision revealed the glint of a metal star
pinned to the frock coat of the hard-eyed gentleman holding
the gun.

''Sorry to wake you so sudden like, Mr. Smith,'' murmured the marshal, ''but you're under arrest for robbery.''

Ten years. Despite ten years, a new identity, and a home-
baked law system that kept few formal officials and fewer
records, he still had been snapped up like a yearling trout.

Gripping the bars of his dark, clammy jail cell, Rafer tried not to panic. The territorial judiciary was little changed since the old days. Communities had better things to do with their funds than feed felons. The tiny, free-standing stone jail had two small rooms, one contained the marshal's desk the other was a cell, which presently contained four snoring drunks rousted from the saloons last night, and Rafer. As the drunks would be released when they sobered, the lack of contenders promised a pristinely clear court docket. The local magistrate would hold miners' court, then hang him from a cottonwood before dinner time, if nostalgia about the Carlisle gang did not wheeze on too long.

He had no doubt of the verdict. The marshal must have the goods on him, and considering he had not been wandering the streets abusing women and otherwise drawing attention, he had an excellent suspicion of the source of those goods. His perspicacity was soon rewarded.

At midmorning, Ramsey popped in to see him after three of the drunks had been booted back into the streets. The remaining drunk was still dead to the world, his stockinged feet curled under him on his chain-suspended cot. From Ramsey's angle, he resembled a pile of blankets. His thumbs jammed into his vest pockets, Ramsey smiled grimly. "Finally got caught with your fingers in the jam pot, eh?"

"I can guess who slammed the lid down," Rafer retorted. "All good things come to an end, eh?"

"Not necessarily. You have a week or so until the serial numbers are confirmed in Denver. Frock may have miscopied one of them, which will practically guarantee a trial delay."

"What serial numbers?" queried Rafer blankly.

"The ones on the currency you stole when you cut out on us at Black Hawk. Five thousand dollars worth of payroll money"—Ramsey's lips quirked with a genuine hint of amusement—"enough to constitute grand theft and ship you to prison."

Rafer felt a surge of relief. He was in trouble, but not hanging trouble, unless Ramsey kept him in jail long enough for the marshal to paw around for old warrants. In tattered hope that his drunken cellmate was reasonably alert, he leaned against the bars, his lips moving in a stage whisper. "What if you were to find that $5,000?"

"What if you were to sell me your claim stock and hit the high road?" broadly whispered back Ramsey.

"Leaving you the whole pot, so to speak."

"The whole pot. With no fond farewells."

"Done."

Ramsey grimaced sardonically at Rafer's lack of hesitation. "So you'd leave Suzanne without a backward glance. She's better off without you, you damned jellyfish."

Rafer thought fast. He might be in the soup, but Suzanne need not be. Ramsey's vindictive mood might predict a vengeful jab at her as well. "Of course she's better off without me. She needs a horseshoe crab like you: an antediluvian prick with a brain like a spoonful of spoiled caviar." Rafer laughed shortly as Ramsey's flush glowed to his collarline. "Oh, you needn't glare, you sod. You're mean, old, and selfish and you want to spike her on a pin like a chloroformed butterfly." Then he shrugged. "But if she wants you, she wants you."

"If she wants me," hissed Ramsey, "what the hell were you doing in her room last night?"

"I was lolling in the lint under her bed. She didn't know I was there until it was too late. Fought like a tigress. I've got scratches I could never show me mum, I can tell you."

"Bullshit."

"Oh, she likes the cut of my jib, mind you; she just questions where the rest of the ship is bound. Prod Suzanne and you prod a Puritan."

Ramsey seized the metal bars. "I ought to break your neck for that crack, you scummy . . ."

"Ah, ah"—Rafer wagged an admonitory finger—"better get me out of jail first. You don't want to damage your manicure on the bars."

"I'll get you out when I see those claim shares!" hissed Ramsey. "Frock's been through your gear. Where the hell are they?"

"You've made me so flustered, I can hardly think."

"Look, they're not too formal around here," Ramsey gritted. "I can always have the sheriff let me beat it out of you."

Rafer's face turned cold. "Try it, and you'll freeze in hell before I tell you shit. We both know that if I sign over those shares before you 'find' your stolen money, I'm going to end up in prison. That money will stay gone and so will I: so you've a stalemate, old man, because I'm not signing anything."

Ramsey's brow puckered, then he jutted his face close to the bars. "You know what I think? I think if you rot in here long enough, that marshal's going to find something on you, whether I press charges or not. You've led too wild a life, boy, not to have left skeletons around." He cocked his head like a crow spying a bright, shiny bauble. "Besides, if that gold claim's in Breckenridge, I don't need you to track it down. Half of the shares are in my boy's name, and if you end up in prison, you can't work what's left. In a few years, mining law will decree your unworked share is up for grabs. You can take it to court, but nobody will listen to a con. You've reached the end of the trail, Mr. Smith; try not to get too flustered." Cocking his hat at a jaunty angle, he sauntered down the sunny street.

"Smart fella, but I wouldn't cart him home to mother," woozily muttered the drunk from the top bunk. Clad in dirty buckskins, with a full bush of gray beard, he unsteadily sat up and peered down at Rafer. His faded blue eyes narrowed with unnerving clarity. "You're the youngest Carlisle boy, ain't you?"

His blood running cold, Rafer stood quite still, not breathing. "If I were," he said softly, his hand linking through the bars with apparent casualness—"it wouldn't be very clever of you to tell me so, would it?"

Scratching at a flea, the grizzled mountain man smiled quizzically. "Jack Carlisle never spawned any killers, less'n you picked up some bad habits, son."

"Everybody picks up bad habits," replied Rafer coolly. "I'm only human."

"Simmer down," drawled the mountaineer. "I ain't a

snitch like yer frame-minded friend, but it wouldn't matter if I was. He's right, y'know; nobody listens to jail bait.'' He leaned forward at a precarious angle. ''So don't get your hopes up. I ain't going to testify for you, either. That antedi—whatever sounds like a whole mess of trouble this old turtle don't need.''

''Now you're being clever . . . despite your confusion. Why suppose I'm a Carlisle? By all accounts, they left the territory years ago. Even if they're still alive, none of them would be foolish enough to come back here.''

''Well, I tell you''—the older man eased down from his bunk and lowered his rheumy voice—''my eyes ain't what they used to be and you not bein' a ringer for Jack, him being a big, Borstal-style redhead, I didn't catch on for quite a while. 'Twas the listenin' without lookin' that clued me, and mind, I didn't start listenin' until you mentioned rollin' under some female's bed. After a time, I got the weirdlike feelin' of hearin' Jack. He used big words in that limey clip that sounded as if he was laughin' at the world . . . like he could be a judge if he wanted, but had more fun bein' up to no good.'' The mountain man studied Rafer for a moment. ''Your face I don't recognize, but you've got your mother's eyes and your father's style. You might want to tone down a mite; I ain't the only one around here likely to remember Jack Carlisle.''

''I don't know you,'' said Rafer softly. ''Why do you think you know me?''

''Never laid eyes on you. Knew your ma and pa, though, when they first came to this country. Expect you were born some years after the last time I saw 'em. Jody would've been six or so, and the other one, what's his name . . .'' When Rafer offered no assistance, the older man rambled nostalgically. ''William . . . Billy, was a scrappy two year old . . .''

Rafer listened to the man run on as if every word were a knife in his heart. Carving out memories. Death. Finally, he curtly cut the mountaineer off. ''You're wasting your time. My name is Rafer Smith, and I never knew any Carlisles.''

The mountain man nodded. ''Fair enough. My name's Joe

Cousins. I'm a fur trapper, and I never knew any beaver. Some other greedy sonofabitches trapped 'em all.'' A gold tooth gleamed as he stretched. ''Appears we'll be in here a while. Stowed a bottle?''

''The marshal didn't give me time to decant my brandy,'' replied Rafer tiredly. Then lest his tension whet Cousins's suspicions, added idly, ''Why are you in the pokey, besides breaking up a bar?''

''Killed a man. Caught him robbin' my cabin supplies, but he had friends and they said different. One of 'em whacked me on the head, stirred things around a bit . . .'' Cousins shrugged. ''I only been around here a season. Should have stayed up to Wyoming where I could have got some witnesses of my own.''

''Why come back? The trapping's nearly played out in this region.''

''Well, I developed a whiskey habit. Travoising whiskey cases into the high country for winter got to be a pain, and I stayed so drunk, I nearly killed myself. Figured I'd better set up shop near a saloon and ration out the booze.'' He sighed. ''Trouble is, I hate towns so bad, I drink worse'n ever.''

Rafer drifted dejectedly to the tiny, thickset window. ''Considering our present circumstances, Wyoming does have its appeal. I sure as hell should have kept riding.''

Joe chuckled. ''Except you hung around under a bed. Guess the view was good.''

Rafer suddenly brightened. ''It's even better from here.'' He pulled off his blue bandanna and waved it from the window.

Joe joined him to see a lovely redhead stroll down the empty street toward the courthouse. Her parasol tilted, she paused by a wrought-iron fence to graze her hand across a rose hedge, then continued down the walk. Rafer's bandanna assumed a frantic speed. Just as the redhead passed the courthouse, the bandanna's flurry snared her notice. She stared in puzzlement, then her parasol abruptly sagged. Catching up her skirts, she hurried toward them. Joe whistled wistfully. ''Don't tell me that's the Puritan.''

Suzanne's flushed face appeared at the bars. "Rafer, what are you doing in here?" she whispered wildly. "What have you done this time!"

His head and shoulders blocking her view of Joe, Rafer kissed her hands through the window bars. "Nothing, for once." Briefly, he explained.

Suzanne's face went scarlet with fury. "That old tyrant won't get away with it! I'll blow the whistle on him!"

"I appreciate your loyalty, Red, but when it comes to that claim, you're in Ramsey's way as much as I am. Make him mad enough, and he may accuse you of being my accomplice." He nuzzled her palm. "There's another way out of this mess that's much more fun."

"Fun!" she echoed upon hearing his plan. "It's a felony! We could all end up as chopped suet!"

"Not if you do as I say." He gave her a tranquil smile. "Have faith."

"God is going to fry you like salt pork, you heathen." Turning on her heel, Suzanne left.

Joe peered after her angry, departing back. "She's awful het up to be reliable."

"She's as dependable as a clock."

Suzanne was back in twenty minutes. With an unfriendly scowl, she drew from her closed parasol a cylindrical object.

Rafer frowned. "What's that?"

"Dynamite; it's new."

"I know," he answered tightly. "What I don't know is how to use it. I sent you for black powder."

"The store was out of black powder. This is better."

"Who says?"

"The clerk."

"Fine. Good. Go to another store."

"Look," she explained with grim patience, "I don't live here, so I cannot pretend I'm trying to blow a stump out of my garden. I certainly cannot go all over town buying explosives to celebrate my husband's birthday. You may not mind arousing suspicion, but I don't care to be chased halfway to Sacramento. Besides, I know how to use dynamite; the clerk showed me." Her fingers shaking, she whacked off some fusing with the embroidery scissors from her reticule, then awkwardly lashed it to the tail of the dynamite with embroidery thread. Finally, she bored a hole into the dynamite with the scissors, then stuffed the detonator into the hole. "See, there's nothing to it."

"Just any old amount of fuse, eh?" observed Rafer dryly.

"Why don't I just forget about you and use it to floss my horse's teeth?"

With a martyred sigh, he held out his hand. "Give me the dynamite."

Starting to hand it to him, she snapped her fingers in exasperation. "Drat, I forgot matches. Stay here." She scurried off again.

Joe sagged down on the bunk. At his dismal face, Rafer urged weakly, "Oh, come now. You know how to sing 'Happy Birthday.' "

Nearly an hour passed before Suzanne returned. Rafer snatched the matches she poked between the bars. "What took you so long?" he hissed, beginning to stuff the dynamite into a crack.

"You need your horse, don't you? Patch is hitched behind the building. I also had to pack your things." She shot him a fierce look. "Must you carry those Mexican postcards everywhere!"

"They're rather like a portfolio." He grinned. "Samples of my expertise, if you will."

"Well, I won't." Scanning the street for passersby, she twisted the reticule cord in agitation. "Creeping under my bedsprings shows a want of manners."

Joe poked his head around Rafer's shoulder. "How do, ma'am. Expect sleepin' on the ground might solve your problem."

Suzanne's cheeks flamed. "Who's he?"

"An old man who talks too much when he drinks."

"Surely, you're not bringing him along after the jail blows!"

"If I can recover most of his pieces . . . not to mention mine."

She swallowed hard, her face colorless. "I'm going back after that black powder."

"No, you aren't; it's too risky. At best, Joe and I will be lucky to scramble out of here before the marshal drills us," he advised firmly. "Kiss me and go back to the hotel. I want you out of the way."

For a moment, Suzanne didn't move. Rafer might be killed. Even if he survived the blast, he would have to run for his life. The best she could do was delay the chase. Her green eyes filled with blurry rebellion. "Don't give me orders . . . and if you want a kiss, come after it . . . only you'd better not wait until I'm married to some rich, old man, because you damned well don't look like anyone I could hire as a gardener." Catching up her skirts, she took off down the alley.

Rafer waited ten minutes, lit the fuse, then crawled under the bunk with Joe.

Suzanne's voice rose outside the cell. She sounded distraught, but he was unable to understand what she was saying, not only because of the closed door, but the fizz of the dynamite fuse. Adrenalin surging, Rafer rolled from under the bed to smack his hand down on the fuse; it burnt and he swore.

Joe peered from under the bunk. "Think she's turnin' you in?"

"For all I know, she could be selling me into Egypt to be castrated." Rafer distractedly rubbed his forehead. "Why, just once, won't she stop being a challenge?"

Suddenly, Suzanne's voice carried in a tragedienne's rising clarion of pain. "I hope my information on that vile thief will be of some help, Marshal Dewitt, but I'm afraid my stumble on the walk has fearfully twisted my ankle. Would you assist me back to the hotel?"

"It's worse than castration; she's still being helpful." Rafer lifted his face to heaven. "I don't mean to be ungrateful, Lord, but please snatch your ministering angel the hell out of here."

In reply, the metal guardroom door slammed.

Joe shifted his tobacco. "Sure hope that weren't The Almighty's last word on the subject. That's a short fuse we got there now.''

"Then we'd better light it before The Almighty remembers exactly who we are, eh, Joe?''

"Amen.''

The blast shivered the leaves off the cottonwood trees outside the jail. Suzanne's knees sagged as smoke scattered with bits of debris billowed high above the alley. "Oh, God''— she grasped the marshal's shoulder—"everyone in that jail must be dead . . .''

He flicked out his gun. "I'll soon find out.''

Scarcely listening, Suzanne stumbled toward him, dazedly wondering if she were going to faint. Deciding to apply her collapse to good use, she sagged heavily into the marshal's arms.

Whereupon he dropped her like a hot potato and raced for the jail. Rafer's unclaimed paint mustang still reared at his hitching post, confirming her fear. Rafer must be still in the jail! When the marshal reached the guardroom door, he whirled, red faced and yelling. His pistol firing into the air, he ran through people pouring from the buildings . . . and a bay stallion carrying Rafer and Joe raced for the river bridge leading out of town. Stifling the urge to cheer, Suzanne fought to her feet. As the bay disappeared, men vaulted into their saddles. With a Mona Lisa smile on her face, Suzanne rubbed her bottom, then limped through the melee to the hotel.

Amid curious guests, Ramsey met her in front of the hotel with his lunch napkin still tucked into his collar. "What's going on over there? Somebody have an accident?''

"No,'' she responded breezily. "Somebody broke jail.''

Ramsey ripped the napkin from his collar. "That damned sneak! He'll be off to Breckenridge!''

"Like the proverbial bat.''

"Frock!'' Ramsey collared his manservant. "Get a telegraph off to the Breckenridge marshal.''

Suzanne peacefully watched Frock forge down the steps. Prosperity had not yet brought the telegraph to Georgetown. Noting her tranquility, Ramsey swept her back into the hotel parlor away from the guests goggling at the dust cloud still hanging over the town. Thrusting her down into one of the mastiff-headed chairs, he glared at her. "You didn't have anything to do with this, did you?"

"I wouldn't have been so reckless and impatient. Nailing Rafer in Breckenridge would have given him less time to retaliate."

"But better ground to counter the accusation." Ramsey's iron grip dug into her arm. "You're coldblooded about your would-be lover . . . or is he a has-been now? What was he doing in your room last night?"

"Gathering lint." She shook off his hand. "Like you, he doesn't know when to accept no for an answer. Now, do we argue or reach Breckenridge in time to recoup our losses?"

"We go to Breckenridge," he asserted flatly. "You figure to have both me and Rafer sniffing after you, so whichever man wins, you're safe. But if you keep trying to play both ends against the middle, you'll be squeezed flat." He stalked off to round up his crew.

Three hours later, Ramsey and Suzanne in the lead wagon drove at a rattling pace across an uneven trail winding toward the Argentine Pass. The ride was jarring, with two prospective days of Ramsey's suspicious silence ahead. Frock was dourly installed in the wagon behind them.

Suzanne pulled her cloak closely about herself. The rustling aspens were beginning to turn yellow among occasional orange broadleafs. The morning sun was taking longer to burn off the growing chill of the nights. The weather was overcast, making the valley's verdant undergrowth a dark, lush blue-green among rotting, lustrous aspen logs in the forest gloom beneath the firs.

Her elation at Rafer's escape dulled by the harsh reality of his loss, Suzanne listlessly attempted to regather her defenses. She would be relieved to end the journey in Breckenridge. She wanted distance from Ramsey's resentful disappointment, from Rafer's persuasive seductiveness. She wanted to settle with Brad so she might return to the peace of Broadacre . . . yet adventures happened only to children there. At Broadacre, she would live as a lady and never lie in its deep

green garden with a lover. Never again know a lover like
Rafer, who made her senses sing, her heart and soul exalt in
the unpredictability of life. Rafer lived and loved with abandon, and for a time, swept her up in the mad magic of his
feckless existence.

Like all the other women he had known, she loved him.
A woman might love Rafer only a little, but that little was
inevitable . . . and she loved him more than a little. Her fear
at the jail explosion obliterated all doubt. Loving Rafer terrified her, so much so, that for a long time, she had denied
it . . . but bit by bit, she knew. Also that she would lose
him, for Rafer was not one who mated for life. He had merely
made love to her. Not only was her citadel fallen, but he
might enter the gates as he pleased. Whatever the future held,
the wind past the citadel towers would one day carry a fresh
scent of adventure, perhaps in the perfumed allure of a new
woman, and he would be gone forever.

Better that he was gone now, before he took her whole
heart, before . . . She stiffened at a familiar, "Halooo!"
behind them on the trail. The voice belonged not to Rafer,
but to Marshal Dewitt. Her heart hammered in her breast.
Had he caught Rafer?

Ramsey reined in the wagon and the train ground to a halt.
Suzanne heard the posse's oncoming hooves stir the trail
undergrowth, then a sudden, muffled sound from Ramsey.
His face was suffused with startled anger. The cause of his
perturbation was Rafer, three inches from his back. With a
blanket swathed over his head and shoulders, he had a rifle
pressed into Ramsey's spine. "What the hell do you think
you're doing?" Ramsey gritted. "You're surrounded by forty
men and a posse!"

"Numbers are irrevelant when only one man and one gun
count. Do precisely as I tell you, or you will gum gruel from
a wheelchair for the rest of your life"—Rafer's voice was
quick and icy—"provided this rifle spares a shred of your
spine, which you will agree is dizzily optimistic."

Seeing Ramsey start to wrench around, Suzanne grabbed
his shoulder with real panic as Rafer's gun rammed into his
back. "For God's sake, Ramsey, he means it! Don't move!"

Ramsey's jaw muscles bunched. "What do you want, dammit?"

"Tell the marshal you found your money."

"What!"

"Cross your heart as well, you miserable sneak; you're as close to dying as a twitch." Rafer eased back into the wagon; the gun stayed put.

Seconds later, Marshal Dewitt reined in beside the driver's seat. Five tired, exasperated men were with him. "Afternoon, Mr. Hoth," said the marshal. "Appears you're making pretty good time."

"Time is money, marshal," grated Ramsey. "This expedition runs about $200 a day."

"Runs a good bit more than my pay. So far, we're not having much luck running down Mr. Smith, which puzzles me a mite, considering he was carrying double."

"Double?" stalled Ramsey. Frock had descended his own wagon to stand by the driver's box.

"Yep. The other man was a trapper who busted into a cabin after whiskey and killed a prospector around The Seven Falls."

"Looks like your work is cut out for you." Ramsey waited. Suzanne realized that, unwilling to let Rafer off the hook, he was going to play possum until the marshal left. With his gun on Ramsey, Rafer's back would be exposed.

Rafer was equally perceptive. Carefully keeping Ramsey's bulk as a shield, he drew back the wagon curtain to peer drowsily at the startled marshal and his men, whose revolvers sprang from their holsters like jack in the boxes. "Oh, good," he drawled sleepily. "Glad you fellows finally caught up. Come on, Ramsey, don't be embarrassed. Tell 'em the truth, there's a good boy."

Ramsey's jaw set. The rifle dug. "Mr. Smith means to say that Mr. Hoth found his money," Suzanne blurted. "It was an accounting mistake."

Catching Ramsey's basilisk eye, Frock melted behind the wagon as the marshal leaned angrily forward in his saddle. "You had me throw a man in jail, then chase him all over the countryside, not to mention have my jail busted all to bits and lose a murderer sentenced to hang? All because you can't add?''

Having a hideous suspicion of Frock's intent, Suzanne held her breath. As the marshal continued to vent his annoyance, she flicked a fearful glance back into the wagon to see Frock staring uneasily into the barrel of Ramsey's English shotgun held by the murderous Joe, lying on the wagon floor.

''Well,'' demanded Marshal Dewitt, ''you'd better say somethin' fast, Hoth, or I'm going to pack you into the pokey so long your fancy expedition will grow cobwebs.''

''On what charge?'' snapped the infuriated Ramsey.

''I'll think of somethin'. Gross negligence leadin' to false arrest, vandalism . . .''—his dark, hunter's eyes narrowed —''you blow up my jail, Smith?''

''Not me, marshal,'' lied Rafer blandly. ''Someone apparently slipped my cellmate some dynamite. Scared me silly, I can tell you. Talked him into dropping me near town, so I could rejoin the expedition to straighten things out.'' With a rueful chuckle, he slipped an arm about Ramsey's shoulder. ''I admit holding a gun on Ramsey to make him check his books, but he found the error quickly enough . . . didn't you, Ramsey?'' Not waiting for an answer, he continued smoothly, ''The mistake was Frock's. Frock keeps the books. So you mustn't be too hard on Mr. Hoth, marshal. You were unfortunately unavailable when the error was discovered, but Mr. Hoth left a $3,000 bank draft at the courthouse to cover the jail damage and your inconvenience.'' He sighed. ''Unfortunately, there's not much we can do about Joe Cousins. The last I saw of him, he was headed for Mexico.''

Dewitt stared grimly at Ramsey, who was glaring straight ahead like a general interrupted in mid-charge. ''I want an affidavit that confirms your clerk's mistake, Mr. Hoth, and you can forget that draft at the courthouse, because I want a new one signed here and now. I'm not having any black marks on my record. You're lucky me and Mr. Smith are forgivin' souls, because I'd like nothin' better now than to haul you back to face the town council.''

"The check ledgers and writing materials are in the back of the wagon," volunteered Suzanne quickly. "I'll get them."

The deed was shortly done after a replacement of the pen broken by Ramsey's forceful pressure.

That night, Joe shaved off his beard and let Suzanne cut his hair, while the shotgun rested across his lap. As intended, he looked entirely different; few people would have recognized him in a change of clothes. While hard drinking had aged his face, he was about forty years old, much younger than she realized. Although they were alone with Rafer in the wagon, Joe's bloodshot eyes were wary.

"You neglected to tell me you killed a man in the wrong cabin, Joe," remarked Rafer idly. "You must have been drunk, indeed."

"I was drunk, all right. Hell, I was there two days before he caught me. I'd have left sooner, only I was too pie-eyed to walk. He came in yellin' with a gun. I just shot him afore he shot me." He squinted into the mirror Suzanne warily offered. "Still don't see how I hit him."

Rafer kept an eye on the armed guards loitering conspicuously outside the wagon. "Well, much as I enjoy your company, you can't stay with the expedition. Wouldn't like to see you backshot before Breckenridge."

"That's a fact, but how about you? Hoth'd like to put one in your gizzard."

"I have insurance . . . and if Ramsey tries to put me in the pokey again, I have the best character reference in the world: the Georgetown marshal. Actually, Hoth's done me something of a favor."

"Huh," grunted Joe. "With friends that generous, you're liable to end up cut and dried for jerky." Clapping on his battered hat, he pumped Suzanne's hand. "Thankee, ma'am. To look at me now, I could be some fancy gamblin' man 'stead of an old mule."

"You're welcome, Joe," Suzanne responded uncertainly. Cutting the hair of an admitted killer made her distinctly uncomfortable. After all, she had procured the dynamite that freed him.

Joe sensed her uneasiness. "Don't fret, ma'am. You ain't likely to see me again, but, if you run into any trouble, I'll be down around Breckenridge myself for a while. Just ask for Sally at the Placer Saloon; she'll know how to find me."

Joe looked as bashful and contrite as a boy caught operating on the family cat. No sadism was apparent; he did not seem to understand how the cat died. "It's all right, Joe," she replied lamely. "I'm sure you'll try to do better, and I appreciate your offer. Good luck."

Joe solemnly shook Rafer's hand. A few moments later, he touched his hat to the guards outside the wagon, then, with Ramsey's cradled shotgun, disappeared to the black forest.

Two guards followed him. Leaning over Rafer's shoulder, Suzanne watched tensely from the wagon. "He doesn't stand a chance, Rafer. Those rifles have more range than his shotgun."

"Nobody's going to shoot anybody, Red," said Rafer softly.

He was right. In the morning, the guards were found with their throats cut.

FIFTEEN

The Shell Game

The expedition arrived in Breckenridge on September 17. Situated in a spacious valley along the Blue River banked with gold dredging barges, Breckenridge was as appealing as Georgetown, its long main street lined with thriving businesses and tidy gingerbread houses. While Suzanne should have been elated, she was not. Not only was Ramsey in a foul mood and her time with Rafer at an end, she was contracting a nasty cold . . . probably from that woodland romp with Rafer the night she should have shot him, she brooded, resentfully mopping her sticky nose as Ramsey assisted her from the wagon in front of the Breckenridge claims registry office. She stuffed her handkerchief into her sleeve.

Still, as she accompanied Ramsey into the claim's office, she was unable to help wondering at Rafer's precipitate generosity. Last night, he had signed over his mine shares without her needing to beg, cajole, or bargain. He simply stepped into her tent while she was asleep, slipped the signed shares under her blanket, and departed. This morning, when she approached him while saddling his mustang and asked him why, he replied, "You could have made the claim shares your price for getting me out of jail; you didn't." He tightened the saddle girth. "You also remembered to fetch my horse."

"But surely you expect payment," she said in bewilderment.

"Of course"—he smiled faintly at her apprehensive blush—"and in currency of the realm, if you please. I shouldn't care to tarnish our relationship with an unbusinesslike arrangement. I can afford to be patient. Ramsey or someone like him will pay the tab."

Her cheeks flamed at the unexpected insult. "That's crude, Rafer."

"But practical. If nothing else on this trip, you've learned practicality."

Angry tears sprang to her eyes. "Perhaps I deserve that assessment, but somehow I expected less hypocrisy from you. You've never let fine sensibilities stand in the way of your having what you wanted. Well, you can keep your damned shares; I doubt if they're worth the price!"

Catching her shoulder as she spun away, he gave her a shake, sending her shawl half spilling to her waist. "Don't be stupid. If you don't take control of the claim, Ramsey will. You don't have the nerve to be poor."

She started to wrench his hand away, then wariness overshadowed her hurt anger. "Why are you being this rotten now? You're up to something again, aren't you?"

"Let's just say I'm separating pleasure from business."

Reluctantly, he released her. "When you reach the claims office, register your shares immediately and don't let Ramsey talk you out of anything. In fact, don't let him know you have them until the last minute. Then hire a lawyer: a good one." He pulled $500 from of his pocket and gave it to her. "This ought to cover the initial legal fees until Ramsey stops thrashing and kicks in for a partnership. Just remember to keep the controlling interest."

Catching up her shawl, she regarded him in dismay. "Aren't you coming?"

"I'll see you at the claim site." He swung onto his horse and without a backward look, headed down the trail.

After twenty minutes in the Breckenridge claims office, Suzanne discovered why Rafer left so quickly; he meant to evade being strangled in the legal spaghetti resulting from nearly a decade of swindling. Matters began calmly enough. When she placed her mining shares in front of the claims clerk, Ramsey merely gave her a cool stare. "I figured to lose this hand after that jail stunt, but then maybe I should have had a tart soften up our mutual friend like you did."

"Our mutual friend is less sentimental than you might suppose," Suzanne said expressionlessly. "These shares are costing me $50,000."

"That you don't have."

"I will. As Rafer says, if I don't deal with you, I can deal with someone else. And if the claim isn't worth a plug nickel, I lose nothing." More worried than she sounded, Suzanne watched George Harmon, the balding clerk, examine the documents.

As meticulously as a jeweler appraising diamonds, he sorted them out in order by numbers one through twenty-four along his counter, and reviewed them again. "Well," he said at last, "this is a new twist on the old Coco claim."

"I'll bet," observed Ramsey dryly.

Suzanne's hands tightened on the counter edge. "Aren't the shares authentic?"

"Well," intoned the clerk, "yes and no . . . some, maybe. I think."

Her heart sinking, she and Ramsey exchanged world weary looks. "Would you mind elaborating, Mr. Harmon?"

"Well"—Harmon pulled a fat ledger from his desk— "let's see. Here it is. Back in 1858, a fellow named Jack Carlisle laid claim to the Coco, which at that time, he called the Blarney, because all he could do was brag about it, being a hard rock mine he couldn't afford to develop." He peered over his spectacles. "You do know it's a hard rock mine, don't you?"

"We know," said Ramsey flatly. "Get on with it."

"Well, Carlisle made his sons shareholders and registered the Erin Mining Company in Denver. There was Jody, Will and Jamie. In '61, Carlisle and his boys struck it rich by holding up a freight shipment worth $200,000 and disappeared from the territory." He nodded in agreement when Ramsey whistled under his breath. "For a long while, that mine just sat there until it was nearly liable for reclaim, since the law invalidates an idle claim. A New Orleans lawyer showed up with a power of attorney for a fellow name of Rafer Smith, who'd bought the whole claim from the Carlisles down in Mexico and renamed it the Coco. Every signature was right as rain with the Carlisles safe as bugs in a banana. This lawyer puts an advertisement in the *Rocky Mountain News* for men to work the Coco. Well, at fifty cents a day, nobody showed but a couple of Chinese. They dug on the Coco for a couple of months or so, just long enough to reestablish the claim, then took off."

"Standard practice," Ramsey elaborated for Suzanne. "The advertisement was merely for documentation of legal proof of intent."

"That's right," assented the clerk, checking his ledger again. "So, six months later, this Rafer Smith sells 48 percent of the claim to a fella name of Kimberly Smith-Gordon, and Kimberly Smith-Gordon turns around and sells 30 percent to a man named Rowland. Rowland actually came out here and worked the claim for a summer, but had a hell of a time. He brought up some quality ore, but couldn't make a profit because of the smelting expense. He gave up and left. Next spring, another fellow shows: same thing. Next two years, two more people tried and failed to work the claim, only the claims started overlapping, because this Kimberly Smith-Gordon kept selling his same shares over and over. A fellow named Brad Dillon was the last, early this summer.''

Suzanne was getting the swindling swing of it. "And Rafer Smith?''

"Never saw his name on any more shares until now. So far as I know, your Smith shares are genuine, and free and clear of claims, but the other 18 percent'' he held up the Smith-Gordon series—"represent about fifteen different partners . . .''

"And enough counterclaims to choke a horse if that mine ever shows a profit,'' finished Ramsey. "Once the Coco is developed, you'll be up to your pretty scheming neck in lawsuits.'' Ramsey benignly smiled at the desolate expression on her face. "It couldn't happen to a more deserving soul.''

"I still have the controlling, and legitimate, claim to the mine,'' retorted Suzanne, trying to cover her dismay.

"You have no mine, dear; Mr. Harmon just said so,'' replied Ramsey blandly. "It's been divided far more effectively than Gaul.''

She could not bear his smug expression. "What about this Brad Dillon?'' she demanded of Harmon. "What did he look like?''

"Auburn haired, brown eyed . . . if I remember correctly,'' mused the clerk. "He was a young city fellow. Felt sorry for him. He looked lower than a bassett hound when he found he'd been had.''

Brad Dillon had to be Bradford.

"Where is Dillon now?'' coaxed Ramsey with frayed patience.

"Last I heard, he'd quit working the mine like all the others and headed off toward Crested Butte.''

Ramsey forcefully led Suzanne from the claims office. Once on the sidewalk, she promptly swore. "Those two sons of bitches!''

"You still have me, dear,'' benignly soothed Ramsey.

The color drained from her face. "I want to see that claim.''

She and Ramsey went out to the site and walked it for half

an hour: ample time considering the extent of its progress. The Coco was a hole in the ground; more exactly, as many holes as a prairie dog town. Someone had sunk money into its development. Timbers, sledges, picks, and shovels rotted alongside a rusting steam pump and the remains of an iron stamp mill intended to crush the ore. The equipment morosely adorned the craters and nibbled dents, ditches, and dirt dumps scarring the forested mountain, but altogether, Ramsey was accurate; there was no mine.

"Rafer Smith!" Suzanne howled across the valley. "Where are you so I can kill you."

"I'm here," called back a soft voice twenty yards behind her. "You needn't be blatant."

She whirled to see Rafer lead his horse from the forest, his face as tranquil as a summer meadow. "How dare you show your face again!" she screeched and went for him with a rusting shovel.

Ducking, he grabbed her so that she and the shovel swung in an impotent arc. "There, there. Let's not throw a tantrum."

"Tantrum! I'll show you a tantrum!" She flailed wildly, her bell-sleeved garibaldi blouse blurring like a battle flag. "You rotten, miserable liar! You ruin everything you touch!" Her feathered hat lay in the dust. She was coughing now, the insults refusing to come out fast enough. "You're as weak and corrupt as Brad! I wish to God you were both in prison where you belong! Cheap, cheating . . ." Coughing overcame her at the same moment as tears of frustration. Careless of her gray woolen skirt, she sagged to her knees. "I hate you!" she sobbed, then sneezed violently.

Hunkering down, he offered his bandanna. "For what?"

Oblivious to the bandanna, she stared at him, then went at him again. He simply toppled her into the dust and tossed her the bandanna. "Wipe your nose. Indignity doesn't become you."

She caught up the bandanna, applied it fiercely to her nose, then threw it at him. He caught the soiled cloth daintily and tossed it down one of the Coco's aborted holes. "For the past ten years, Mr. Smith or whoever you are," she gritted, "you knew there was nothing on this blasted land to sell, but you sold it anyway, to fifteen different claimants. You posed as two different owners."

"Maybe three," mused Ramsey, leaning against a piling.

Rafer glanced at him, then crossing his legs, sat down Indian style as if to patiently await Suzanne's continued vilification.

She obliged readily. "Mr. Smith has probably assumed a horde of identities in his scummy career. In time, all he had to do to regain complete 100 percent ownership of the Coco was to discount Kimberly Smith-Gordon's existence. His New Orleans lawyer would simply show up in court with Rafer Smith's affidavit that he never sold any portion of the claim to one Kimberly Smith-Gordon. And as Kimberly Smith-Gordon doesn't exist, he could not contest the case . . . and neither could any of the other claimants. Am I right, you rat?"

Rafer nodded.

"So you made money off an unworkable claim for years until it promised to show a real profit by being developed. You didn't even have to meet the legal requirements for working the Coco. Your deluded purchasers did that. All the while, you were careful not to sell the shares to anyone with enough money to sit on the mine until its development became feasible. Now, it is feasible. Now, some rich, unscrupulous investor will move on the claim if you don't. Considering the Coco's colorful record"—her green eyes flashed— "Coco theoretically referring to a New Orleans madam, said investor's lawyers will ferret through your schemes so industriously that you'll not only lose the claim, but end up doing ninety-nine years for fraud. You had to sell the whole shebang!"

"I thought Brad Dillon owned it," Rafer said innocently.

"You know perfectly well Brad doesn't own a damned thing," she cried, "and I can't claim what he doesn't own because he isn't who he says he is!"

"This gets better and better," sighed Ramsey, fishing for his penknife.

"Oh, shut up," Suzanne snapped. "You taught that wretched Ivy League sneak everything he knows."

"Well, now . . . to echo our methodical Mr. Harmon," observed the unoffended Ramsey, beginning to pare his nails, "I do know that if Rafer here is triplets instead of twins, you have 52 percent of a workable mine and one-fifteenth of the other 48 percent." His penknife pausing, he caught up a sprig of grass, and peered speculatively down at Rafer. "If you're not only Rafer Smith, but Kimberly Smith-Gordon, you might be Jamie Carlisle, too, mightn't you?"

"Jamie Carlisle is dead along with the rest of the clan. Mexico didn't agree with them," Rafer informed him unsentimentally. "As Kimberly Smith-Gordon is non-existent in this country, you and Suzanne need only deal with Rafer Smith as the sole legitimate owner of the Coco. Brad Dillon can ill afford to take the matter to court, considering his past."

"You're in the same boat, Mr. Smith," retorted Suzanne, heedlessly wiping her nose on her sleeve. "Particularly if Ramsey's right and Jamie Carlisle isn't as dead as you say."

"Oh, he's dead," said Rafer in a matter-of-fact tone that chilled her like a wind blowing over a grave.

"So now what?" queried Suzanne wearily, her temples pounding. She was exhausted, fed up, and miserable. Thanks to the cold settling firmly in her chest, her temperature promised to soar.

"Tomorrow, I'll sign an affidavit at the claims office, stating that Rafer Smith never sold any shares to Smith-Gordon. Brad and all the other claimants are out of the action, leaving you in clear control of 52 percent of the mine and in a strong negotiable position to assume the rest, provided you take a partner willing to pay legal fees in the event of contesting claimants." He looked up at Ramsey. "You deal with Suzanne or you don't deal, *comprendes*?"

Ramsey grimly nodded.

Suzanne was stunned. In his convoluted, devious fashion, Rafer had fought her battle. The mine was hers. He deserved her every vile epithet, but he meant well . . . more or less. She rose unsteadily to her feet. "If you think you're due an apology, Mr. Smith, you're not going to get it . . . because I'm too ill to . . . separate your immorality from your generosity." The ground was heaving, dissolving into liquid, her strength pouring into it. In her vision, Rafer's and Ramsey's faces were turning into a sea.

"So . . . thank you, one and all," she croaked, "but I intend to pay back all . . . those poor fools who hoped to find the end of the rainbow here. That 48 percent you kept selling, Rafer Smith"—her finger jabbed out shakily—"I'm going to give away. I won't let greed make me . . . like you two." She wavered as the fish began to indifferently swim away. "How do you like that?"

Rafer came quickly to his feet and caught her as she dropped.

Ramsey hastily crammed his penknife into his pocket. "She's out of her mind."

Rafer's grip tightened imperceptibly as he looked down at Suzanne's unconscious face. His eyes filled with ineffable tenderness, triumph . . . and fear. "No, just out of her element."

Suzanne awoke in a mammoth brass bed in a rose-papered hotel room to find Rafer and Ramsey worriedly hovering over her. Buried in pink blankets to the neck, she still felt damp and chilly. Her lusterless hair stuck to her face, she had difficulty breathing, with most of her body seeming to have departed elsewhere, leaving only her clogged chest and head behind. Rafer and Ramsey were as rumpled and exhausted as she felt. "What's wrong this time?" she murmured vaguely. "Is another marshal outside the door?"

Ramsey let out an expletive of relief, while Rafer's eyes never left her face. "The fever has broken." His fingertips gently brushed the damp, curling hair from her wan face. "You're going to live, *carita*."

"Of course," she agreed faintly, "what did you think?" Her hand hanging slack over the bed edge, she tried to push upward on the pillows. Why did they look so perturbed? Everyone caught cold once in a while. She struggled against the blankets' weight, then gave up the effort. She must be sick if she could not summon the strength to lift her head.

Ramsey sat on the rumpled bed beside her. "Just rest, Suzanne. You've had a bad week. In a few days, you'll feel much better."

"A week? I've been in bed a week?" Suzanne was taken aback, then upset. "We cannot stay here a week. We must locate Bradford." The high-necked linen nightgown sticking clammily to her damp body, she tried to get up again. "I need to straighten out the claim affairs . . . with a lawyer, so we can leave . . ."

Ramsey pressed her down. "We'll leave when you're well enough to travel. If you rush recovery, you may provoke a relapse. According to the doctor, you've both altitude sickness and mountain lung fever. With rest, you'll be right as rain."

"But Brad may not be far . . ."

He squeezed her agitated hand. "Don't worry. We'll find Brad."

"If we don't linger here until snow closes the passes," she protested. "Why not just bundle me up and pack me in one of the wagons? . . ."

"We're not packing you anywhere," Rafer said softly. "You nearly died."

Proximity to the grave took a moment to register. Death happened to old people, weak people. She was young, vigorous . . . "Really died?"

"Rafer and I had a row about whether to put roses or lilies on your coffin," quipped Ramsey. "Thanks to a frost last night, we expected to settle for juniper."

She fell silent. Despite his easy tone, in his soiled shirt-sleeves with his collar open, Ramsey looked older than he had a week ago. He might have seized the opportunity of her illness to go on alone after Brad, somehow devise a means to wrest the mine from her: but he had not. And Rafer . . . Rafer looked like a man who had been fighting off death. From the exhaustion and subtle pain in his eyes, Rafer might have been struggling for his own life. While he and Ramsey were unrepentant, irredeemable rascals, she felt a stubborn surge of affection for them both. Her fingers tightened on Ramsey's hand, as she held out her other hand to Rafer.

"Juniper would have been a good choice; it's prickly." A glimmer of mischief entered her green eyes. "Thank you for not leaving me to strangers."

Ramsey made a bluff show of indignation. "You're our heller, aren't you? Think we'd miss dancing on your grave?" He kissed her cheek. "Now get some sleep. The quicker you're well, the quicker we leave."

Rafer said nothing. Seeming preoccupied, he gave her hand a slight pressure, then let it slip, and moved away toward the dormer windows, rimed with white, crystalline frost, as were the Breckenridge rooftops and rutted streets. Winter's first warning glazed the town and valley beyond like Swedish pastry. To the west, snow was sifting across the White River Range.

During the next week, Suzanne did her utmost to cooperate with the doctor and her self-appointed guardians. She ate beef barley soup by the tureen, endured mustard plasters and steam pots of boiled sage, as well as muttered arguments as to who should brush her hair. In the mood or not, she slept eighteen hours out of twenty-four. Her only visitors were a pair of lawyers from the Breckenridge firm which handled the town council affairs. Rafer allowed them a daily half hour with her after lunch, so that she might thread through the Coco's entanglements without undue fatigue.

She was learning to accept Rafer, with an odd sort of blind trust as if he were taking her by the hand to teach her flexibility and sensitivity. She might be slow to learn, but she was learning, perhaps to be a real woman. Why did she feel so much like a child as well? Her thick hair spilling across the pillows seemed too heavy for her head, her body small, but cosily safe beneath the high-piled comforter. Her journal lay on the bedside as it might have done at home. Rafer made her feel both secure and certain, but fearful of being left again to stumble about on her own: lost in a world whose seasons of cold threatened to freeze her into a transparent pillar of ice. Even now Rafer registered a perplexing ambiguity.

"I could do without legal matters. They cost time, money, and concentration I prefer to spend elsewhere," he told her once after he had ruthlessly ushered out the lawyers.

"I'm beginning to suspect that Rafer Smith is no more real than Kimberly Gordon-Smith," she countered softly. "That's why Rafer Smith stays out of court."

His smile was enigmatic. "I hope Ramsey doesn't press that theory. He'd whisk that claim from under you like a slippery rug."

"I've been swept off my feet before"—her voice lowered—"you have made love to me. I need to know, Rafer. Who are you?"

"A man who has pressing business elsewhere," he replied gently. "As soon as you're well again, I'm leaving you in Ramsey's care."

At her effort to hide her startled dismay, he rose, swung the chair from his path, and sat on the bed. His fingers entwined hers. "You'll be all right."

"Will I see you again?" she asked faintly. She felt cold, frightened, as if a window had been suddenly thrown wide.

"Will you wait here for me?"

"I cannot dismiss Brad, Rafer. I've crossed half a continent to find him."

"Why?"

"Because I'm his wife. Because certain private matters must be settled between us. Because . . . I am partly to blame for what he's become." Beneath the silken fringe of her dark, russet-touched lashes, sadness crept into her eyes. Her hand slipped from his to lie with the other, opaque as ivory on the papers in her lap. "More than that, I cannot tell you . . ."

"Because I'm an untrustworthy cad." An ironic smile creased his freshly shaven face. "Don't blame yourself too much for your husband. People are what they are when opportunity knocks; I've made a living from that proclivity."

Her sadness deepened with a tinge of defeat. "You cannot cheat an honest man."

"Something like that." He brushed back the silky spill of hair from the lace ruffle at her throat, then as if reluctant to stop touching her, retucked her white angora shawl about her shoulders. "I've never given you much advice, have I?"

"No. You've been singularly unintrusive in that area . . . if only in that area."

"Then perhaps you'll yield me a little patience now." His hands covered hers. "Whatever you do, don't let Ramsey talk you into searching for Brad until spring. You both have business here, and if Brad is in the Rockies, once it snows, he'll keep for months. I'll send you word, if I hear anything of him. When the passes clear, you and Ramsey can resume the chase."

She eyed him dubiously. "Do you want me to find Brad, Rafer?"

"You'll fret about him until you do." He kissed her fingertips. "I prefer to be your sole annoyance."

She laughed softly. "I must apply a rusty shovel to you more often."

"So long as you don't let Ramsey shovel any manure about wifely duty toward your errant spouse. His neck is his own concern, but I have a vested interest in yours." He rose from the bed. "Now for the lawyers . . ."

The lawyers proved to be no problem; Ramsey, on the other hand, was uncooperative. He welcomed the possibility of Suzanne's remaining in Breckenridge like plague; he would not consider it himself and adeptly defended his decision to press on to Crested Butte, if not with hard logic, then with fatherly emotion. "I want my boy back," he argued vehemently. "I don't want him running scared for the rest of his life. If he reached Crested Butte two months ago, he might have gone on toward the Sierras. We might never catch up to him." He turned on Suzanne, out of bed for the first time in two weeks. "We're in this together, aren't we? Or were you just after the claim?"

Stung, Suzanne retorted, "You were the one hesitant to leave New York until you saw that gold ore."

"Well, now we're going to be partners, aren't we? Show me the papers and I'll sign, but I want more than that damned gold. I mean to find my boy."

Sensing that Suzanne was weakening, Rafer sharply intervened. "Find him when the passes aren't seventy feet deep in snow. When the Donner party ran out of food in the Sierras, they began dining on each other. Nothing lies west of Breckenridge but Grand Junction and a few tiny settlements until you reach California. You'd be alone, miles from help . . .''

"I've gotten the hang of bossing a train," argued Ramsey. "I can manage."

"Not without winter experience. Not without a crew."

"I can learn. And I have a crew."

"No, you don't. I paid them off this morning. Every mother's son is off to the gold digs or headed back to Denver."

"I ought to blow your brains out!" yelled Ramsey, the blood vessels in his neck bulging. "Where the hell did you get the money?"

"I didn't need any. I told them you had run out of money, whereupon they applied an axe to your cash box and paid themselves."

Ramsey advanced on him. Hastily, Suzanne stepped between them. "You would have had to disband for winter, Ramsey . . . wait! I want to find Bradford as much as you do, but Rafer may be right."

"Rafer wants to duck out now that he's peddled his claim," Ramsey grated in angry contempt. "Eh, am I right, Mr. Confidance Man? Got other fish to fry?"

Increasingly distraught, Suzanne looked at Rafer. He shrugged. "Sticks and stones." His blue eyes turned cold. "Look, Ramsey, if you care to be suicidal, fine. I'm not precisely sentimental about a man who tried to frame me so he could practice extortion . . . and I don't buy your tale about longing for your fair-haired boy."

"Well, I'm going after Brad whether anybody goes with me or not," rejoined Ramsey. "Crested Butte is only a few days away, and it's only October." He looked at Suzanne. "Are you coming?"

Suzanne hesitated. "Yes, I'm coming." She winced at Rafer's expression. "I must go, Rafer. I talked Ramsey into this whole idea. I cannot let him go alone."

Rafer stalked out of the door. "Heaven help you then. Whoever said God helps madmen and little children was never in a public institution."

When Suzanne and Ramsey emerged from the hotel the

next morning to leave for Crested Butte, six pack mules were hitched to the rail beside their own horses. Three battered-looking mounted men waited on the far side of a single wagon with a half-breed driver; one of the men was Joe Cousins. "I had Sally look him up," briefly explained Rafer as he mounted his own horse. "He rounded up the others."

"But Joe's . . ." Suzanne's protest dwindled off as Joe doffed his pheasant-feathered hat with a broad grin. His beard was growing back. "Are you coming after all, Rafer?" Her voice held an ill-concealed note of hope.

"I preferred that option to shooting you like a doomed horse."

He looked grimly down at Ramsey. "I told these men you'd pay triple wages. Do you agree or do they go back to the bar and drink to your demise?"

"Agreed," asserted Ramsey gruffly.

"I also want another $10,000 for overtime. Joe's in for half."

"The hell you say!"

"Either I get it, or we drop the whole deal. The boys won't go around the block with you."

"They're likely to kill us all in our sleep," grumbled Ramsey.

"So say your prayers every night. Where we're going, the eccentricities of our escort will be the least of our problems."

SIXTEEN

Home Is Where The Heart Is

Journal Entry: October 21, 1870.
Autumn has nearly passed during my illness. The breeze-blurred, golden leaves of September have dropped, scattering

across gilded grassland fretted by silver, pungent sage. Like great prickle-back boars, increasingly barren aspen stands curl black and white spines across the spice-scented pine forests where spruces blaze blue and rivers run low over sun-yellowed boulders. Often the air is still and mellow as the drowsing, summer-wearied land, but when it stirs the last aspen leaves, the trees sway with a rustling shiver of spangles that spill upon our heads and horses.

While Ramsey and I still have tents, we carry no luxuries, but despite our frequent want of them, travel much faster than before. Like young deer discovering their strength, we rejoice in our expanded freedom. Ramsey gave away five of the seven hounds in Breckenridge, but insisted upon keeping Belle and Forester. Free of the wagons, the dogs are nearly hysterical with abandon. The nights, and sometimes days, are cold now.

Ramsey believes we will make the journey without mishap if the weather remains clear, but Rafer and Joe make no predictions. Mac is a humorless Mormon with the disposition of a clock. Although as stoically pessimistic as if his mechanism were running down, he is reliable. Certain of disaster, Frock constantly nibbled soda crackers to ease his stomach, and then what he most feared happened. We are all shaken, not only at the tragedy, but its abrupt issuance from the direction least suspected.

Ramsey, having tired of bird shooting, insisted upon taking Frock and Carl, the half-breed, after a cougar whose spoor Joe reported from his foray ahead into Fremont Pass. I was much surprised to see Rafer accompany their party as he cares nothing for sport hunting. Perhaps, knowing Ramsey better than the others, he feared what might occur. The dogs cornered the cougar in a pine. Merely grazed by Ramsey's bullet, the cougar leaped from the pine, knocking Ramsey to the ground. Fortunately, the cat wasted no time in trying to maul him, but instead, attempted to escape. Cut off by the dogs and men, it turned as Ramsey caught up his gun and coming to his knees, whirled and fired. Instead of hitting the cougar, mixed in a tangling blur with the dogs, the bullet struck Frock.

Frock is to be buried this afternoon, little more than two

*hours after his death. The sky is clear, the slow-moving clouds
leaving tranquil shadows upon the rusty bluffs. The camp
robber birds still quarrel with chattering squirrels who comb
the forest floors for pine cones like a puny, scavenging army
fleeing before the oncoming cold. The sun streams through
towering pines to lull the last hillside wildflower. How can
a man die on a day like this . . . in a place that makes him
feel, if not like a god, then richly and confidently human?*

With dazed truculence, Ramsey stood looking down at
Frock's body laid out on a blanket as if he would order the
corpse onto its feet if no one were around. Her heart aching
for him, Suzanne saw he still could not believe what he had
done. He hugged himself, his blocky hands doubled into fists
to control their unsteadiness. Shadowed by his crushed hat
brim, his eyes met those of the other men in brief glares of
defiance, only to avert in shame and fury. Rafer's contemptuous silence exuded no mercy. Ramsey snatched up a
hatchet, headed to the ammunition wagon, and started to
break into a trade keg. Rafer was on his heels. Before the
others realized what Ramsey was after, Rafer caught him by
the belt band and collar and threw him from the wagon.
Ramsey came to his feet like a snarling dog. "Leave me
alone or I'll kill you, you sonofabitch!"

"Then you'll have had a busy day, won't you?" said Rafer
curtly.

Ramsey started for Rafer, then hesitated as Suzanne bolted
forward to restrain him. "Don't, Ramsey!" she hissed in his
ear. "The expedition will fall apart if the others learn about
that liquor!"

"Come on, big man," Rafer baited, "either have a try for
me or go home." His eyes were icy, and Suzanne knew he
ached to kick Ramsey to blazes.

"Stop provoking him, Rafer! Don't you see he's upset? A
fight isn't going to bring Frock back."

Rafer swung down from the wagon. "Oh, Ramsey can
always pick up another Frock. That isn't what bothers you,
is it, Ramsey? You just discovered you might be mortal. It's
a long fall from Olympus and the ground is hard." His hand

swept up at the craggy ranges. "This country isn't going to soften up for you and the devil put together. It jumps you when you aren't looking. It freezes you into gray cordwood, then feeds you to the wolves. It swats fools like annoying flies." His voice was hard and relentless. "Go home, you vainglorious old man, and spend your last greedy days among the devils you know."

"I want my boy," grated Ramsey, his eyes fierce. His head lowered, his armed curved outward, hands taloned like a grizzly tensing to attack. "I'll have him!"

"Like a cannibal his feast," snarled back Rafer. Ignoring Ramsey's combative stance as if he were a wooden cigar store Indian, he strode back to Joe, abruptly motioned him to wrap Frock in the blanket. They carried Frock down to the river, where Joe swept off his hat, and awkwardly by-passing forgotten verses, began to mutter the Twenty-first Psalm. No one carried a shovel.

"What are they doing?" whispered Suzanne distractedly. "Surely, they don't mean to throw the body in the river!"

With a guttural oath, Ramsey started for the burial party. His steps quickened into a run as Carl and Mac picked up the blanketed corpse and started to swing it over the water. "Stop it, you hyenas!" he yelled. "That's my man! I want him buried right!"

For a moment, Suzanne feared they would ignore him, then Rafer gave a curt order in Ute to Carl. The body stopped its swing and lowered to the bank.

"What are you, a bunch of damned heathens?" demanded Ramsey, red-faced with rage.

"No man, or woman, rates a cold weather marker in this country, Mr. Hoth," drawled Joe, his feathered hat tucked beneath his arm. "The ground's too hard for digging and the Utes too interested in what's dug. My turn comes, I expect to end up in the river just like every other trapper come this way." He jerked his head at the other men. "My buddies feel the same . . . except Carl, who figures on being wrapped in skins and stuck up in a tree. We ain't un-Christian, Mr. Hoth; just practical."

"Well, Frock was a city man who wouldn't understand,"

returned Ramsey tightly. "I want him buried comfortable. If you boys won't help, I'll do it myself."

"Be our guest," Rafer replied coolly, handing him Frock's bowler hat. "The shovel's in the ammunition wagon."

Ramsey needed three hours to dig the grave. He grew so flushed and out of breath in the high altitude, Suzanne feared he might have a stroke. Ignoring him, the others stretched out on the riverbank. Rafer had gone downstream, away from the others. After helping Ramsey labor doggedly for some time, Suzanne went after Rafer. He was sitting with his back against a pine in a quiet bend of the river where leaves silently coasted its eddies. Flushed from carrying rocks, she unbuttoned her sheepskin jacket, and gathering her woolen skirts, sat down beside him. "Aren't you being too hard on Ramsey? His shooting Frock was accidental, wasn't it?"

"He shot Frock because he lost his nerve," replied Rafer flatly as he weighed a flat, riverbank stone in his hand. "Three hundred pounds of ripping cat with a screeching face out of hell has that effect on some men." His jaw set, he gave the stone a hard, long skip across the water. "Any man who works as hard as Ramsey to prove himself has something to prove."

"I don't believe he's a coward, Rafer."

"He's not. He won't allow it. That's why he's dangerous." Rafer skipped another stone across the water.

"So you're trying to force him to back out of the expedition by tormenting him about Frock."

He swivelled slightly, the shoulder of his worn jacket brushing hers. "That body in the blanket could have been you, Su. Any one of us. We could all die because of Ramsey's insecurity about his virility."

"He's not just here to prove his virility. He loves his son."

"Do you think so?" Rafer rested his head against the rough tree bark, his lashes shielding his gaze. Above his upturned collar, his lips were grimly ironic. "Frankly, I doubt it."

"Rafer," she said softly, "haven't you ever loved, been afraid?"

His sandy lashes lifting, he looked at her. "I'm afraid now."

The bitter irony in his lean face was gone, leaving a piercing intensity, an urgency that shivered into her troubled spirit like a swiftly loosed arrow. There came a loosening flow of blood as if she herself had died this day, only to be reborn in Rafer's eyes. Somehow, he had become intermingled with the slow, warm beat of her battered heart.

The moment she touched his face, he pulled her into his arms. In his kisses were all his frustration, anger, and need. And when he swiftly opened her clothing and made love to her, she did not fight him. Their bodies met urgently, starved after long weeks apart. Quickly, the climax came, hot and impassioned, and afterward, he held her tightly, so that breathing was difficult. A man was dead. Their blood pounded, sounded in their veins in primitive fear and defiance.

Joe's shout cut across their taut faces like an icy wind. "Come on, Rafer, he's going in the ground!"

The hole by the river was shortly refilled. Atop a crude cross of lashed wood, Ramsey tilted Frock's bowler hat. Black, brave, and ridiculous, the hat hung loosely, inviting the wind to carry it away. Already, the first flakes of patient snow were settling upon the brim.

October 24:
It snowed again last night. Joe dug me out of my tent, the drifts were so packed. The men dug a well in the snow to build our cook fire. I am wearing all my clothes, as the wagon shapes are scarcely definable in the snow. The flakes fall in soft, wet clusters that stick to everything. We eat oatmeal mush this morning, as cooking is difficult. The snow keeps trying to put the fire out and falls into the food so that it quickly grows cold. We do manage salt pork, which tastes delicious.

October 31:
Misfortune has struck again. While skirting a canyon wall along the Divide, the mules and wagon were dragged by a

*melting mud slide over a cliff to plummet over a thousand
feet to the canyon floor. As we were below the tree line, the
wagon and most of its breakable supplies were destroyed,
along with the dogs within the wagon: we were unable to dig
them from the snow quickly enough to prevent their suffo-
cation. The driver, Mac, miraculously survived with only a
broken arm, but a mule suffered a broken leg and had to be
shot. Rafer, Joe, and I reburied the dogs in the snow. Although Rafer does not say so, I suspect the dead animals will
surface after a few sunny days to be devoured by predators.
I could not help weeping. Those poor, foolish, friendly hounds
have become great pets of us all, particularly Joe, who
spoiled them with extra game. He wept, although he took
great care to hide it, cradling Belle, with her long silky ears,
like a woman. Rafer showed no emotion. Carl says he is
growing more like an Indian every day. I wonder. Carl, as
fond of the dogs as anyone, wanted to eat them, but out of
respect to Joe, did not insist. Ramsey would not touch the
dead dogs.*

November 1:

*It is snowing again. Rafer has ridden alone ahead of us
and although he has often done so, I am concerned. He wants
no part of this expedition now, and I suspect that if I were
not part of it, he would be gone. Although he does not complain, his impatience lies between us like a restive wolf. I do
not think he will desert the expedition, but I now distrust
these heartless mountains. While Rafer seems at home here,
I fear for him . . . and Ramsey. Ramsey's hair shows more
gray, and he has lost weight. I make a point of playing
backgammon with him every night, but now he and the other
men include me in their poker games as well. At first, Joe
considered my participation an indignity, but now helps to
polish my skill. He has an extraordinary poker face, for he
laughs at the worst luck.*

Morning brought Suzanne harsh, new awareness of her
surroundings. Snow blowing through the cabin walls covered
the rope-slung bed. She could hardly move for cold, and to

touch the disintegrating, mouse-eaten mattress was to recoil as if caressed by frost. The cabin had been deserted for years, but used by travellers for shelter and a postal depot; tattered notices, messages and letters, some dating back seven years, were nailed to the log walls. In a corner, a blackened mirror lay in shards, along with rotted clothing which included a wedding dress, a few bottles, and a syrup tin gnawed by animals. Outside, the snow lay higher than the windowsills.

Wistfully, she rubbed at her unwashed face, then went into the main room to find Rafer rebuilding the fire in the tumbledown stone fireplace. The erratic draft and damp wood posed difficulties. At Rafer's muttered epithet, Carl stirred under his buffalo hide, then resettled into a steady snore. Joe and Mac were asleep in the other bedroom, but Ramsey's blanket was empty. "Where's Ramsey?" Suzanne whispered, her mittened hands hugged beneath her armpits.

"Cutting wood. He's restless." Rafer blew on the fire. The reluctant kindling hissed, then exuded a feeble trickle of smoke.

Tucking her skirts about her cold feet, she sat on the splintered, rotting floor; the dirt beneath showed through. "You were lucky to find this place." When he made no reply, she glanced at him curiously. "Did you know it was here?"

"I knew the people who lived here." His monotone held an uncharacteristic note of preoccupied impatience, even anger.

Sensing that neither she nor the recalcitrant fire were the cause of his irritation, she prodded gently, "Who were they?"

"Dumb, green settlers."

"I gather they didn't fare well."

"The woman went mad after three winters and died during the ninth one; her husband and sons disappeared two years afterward."

"How sad." How many such tragedies were buried in these mountains?

With the sharp motions of a tactician placing tin soldiers on a campaign map to demonstrate fatal mistakes, Rafer readjusted the kindling. "They never should have come here in the first place. They weren't suitable. The woman wasn't strong. She wandered into the snow one night and froze on her knees in the dead flower garden she tried to start every spring. The family went adrift and wolves took their cattle. They might have fed themselves by sticking to traplines and hunting, but the father wanted something to show for his life. His mind ran to a quick fortune, so he turned petty outlaw with his sons. They had poor luck and barely escaped hanging. The last anyone heard, they finally pulled off one big robbery and left the country.''

''Still, the old man finally had something to show for his life after all,'' she added, hoping to cheer him. ''He's a local legend.''

''Local legends are a dime a dozen around here.'' Rafer sat back on his heels as the logs caught the tinder's blaze . . . only to sputter and die again. Swearing under his breath, Rafer headed for her bedroom. Seconds later, she heard him tearing up floorboards.

The noise had scant effect on Carl, but Joe emerged from their adjoining bedroom scratching his head. ''Damnation, it's cold as a witch's . . . sorry, ma'am. Didn't realize you was awake''—with an envious grimace, he viewed the inert Carl—''but, I guess it takes a heap of doing to sleep through Rafer and Ramsey rippin' the house down.''

She laughed. ''Just the floorboards. Rafer's trying to start a fire. Ramsey's outside cutting wood.''

''Good. I'm freezing.'' Rubbing his hands, he crossed the room to examine the remains of the recalcitrant fire. ''Um, um''—he shook his head—''that's fit to drip.''

She shivered in agreement. ''I'm not complaining, mind you, but this whole place is depressing. Rafer told me a madwoman once lived here.''

He looked startled. ''Anne Carlisle?''

''You knew the family, too?''

''Everybody who goes back to the old days knows about the Carlisles.''

For a moment, Joe's eyes were evasive; she wondered why. Then remembered the name, Carlisle, from the Breckenridge claims office. ''Was this Carlisle the same outlaw who ran off to Mexico after a big robbery?''

"Well"—he scratched at his new beard growth—"I couldn't say where old Jack Carlisle went, but he did live here for a time."

So that's how Rafer knew about this cabin, Suzanne thought. He bought Jack Carlisle's gold claim.

Joe was studying her pensive face. "Rafer mention the youngest Carlisle kid, Jamie?"

"No, just that the family was unprepared and Mrs. Carlisle lost her reason."

"Yeah. Anne was a real sweet woman. She'd have followed Jack anywhere, and him and the boys doted on her, but she couldn't take the winters up here. Went barmier and barmier. Got so they had to leave twelve-year-old Jamie with her when Jack, Will and Jody were off on the traplines. Went off for a week one February in '57. When they got back, the kid had been holed up with his dead mother for four days."

"How horrible!" she whispered.

"None of 'em could stay on the place after that." He patted her shoulder. "Think I'll give Rafer a hand with that firewood."

Suzanne stared into the empty fireplace. Jamie Carlisle's name was on the gold claim and he would be about Rafer's age. She remembered Ramsey's suspicion: if Rafer could be two men, why not three? If Rafer was Jamie Carlisle, what happened to all the other Carlisles? Were they still in Mexico . . . or his reason for being in a hurry to leave Breckenridge alone after selling the claim? Did they plan to rendezvous after all these years? Was that why Rafer came to this cabin?

No, the puzzle did not completely fit. The claims clerk, not Rafer, had sent her and Ramsey on this route. Rafer must have brought them here simply because the cabin offered shelter. He might have had only a passing acquaintance with the Carlisles. Still, why had he not mentioned this was the Carlisle cabin? He might expect her to be interested in the originators of her claim.

And then Jamie again. Keeper of a madwoman. Locked away with her dead body. Rafer, who never told the same story twice about his parentage. Who never called his mother, *mother*. Who was eternally restless as if he had once been intolerably confined. Although the puzzle pieces barely touched, they suggested an unspeakable fit. Joe had seen to that. She wondered why.

As the days passed, Suzanne was inclined to believe she was right about Rafer. He was withdrawn, edgy, as if the cabin walls pressed in on him and he anticipated some terrible event. Ramsey exhausted his energies by alternately cutting wood and floundering through the drifts after small game, then lapsing into apathy. He had little to do with the men. Each man seemed to have locked himself into a private hell which no human sympathy or contact could alleviate. She could not go to Rafer, for in coming to pity the child who might be Jamie Carlisle, she must also hate the man who had callously used her from their first meeting.

Rafer pressed his forehead against the whitened window pane, examining each falling snowflake as if it were a face: innocent, cold, relentless. The recurrent blizzard was like a rising, icy sea trapping . . . submerging . . . drowning him. He would have given his right hand never to return to the dark heart of horror that still beat within these Godforsaken walls.

In his mind, a dead woman and a living child embraced upon the bed. The child meant to give the woman warmth but in time, shrank shivering from the corpse. That night, filled with dread, he locked the bedroom door. By morning, a faint, sweet odor of death drove him from the cabin. He cut wood all day until his hands were torn, and when returning night's bitter cold drove him indoors, the odor was a horrid perfume; this was only in his mind, for the body still had no odor in the cold, but that scent sucked at his mind, his heart. After his mother's death, he suffered a sense of stifling, irrevocable failure compounded by tragedy to come. For ten guilt-ridden years, he had been neither able to save nor escape his mother . . . any more than his brothers . . . his father. And now he had brought Suzanne to this hellish place of ill omen.

Rafer alternately paced, then settled tensely against the wall by the fire. Suzanne twice noticed him looking at the bedroom door.

"You're getting as fidgety as that Frock," Carl teased him amiably. "That's what you get for hanging out with Apaches."

Rafer's head came up. "Why do you say that?"

"I've watched you track."

"You Utes get better results?" Rafer retorted.

"Hey, don't be mad. When Mr. Hoth gets back from chasing showshoe rabbits, we'll do a ghost dance and make peace with the spooks around here."

Rafer made an ironic sound, then relenting, slapped Carl on the shoulder. "Sorry, I just dislike being cooped up."

"Yep," drawled Joe, casting a glance at Suzanne as he rolled a cigarillo, "you ain't the cooped up type, and that's a fact. Where're you headed at trail's end, Rafer?"

"Oh, I don't know"—Rafer did not look at Suzanne—"California, maybe."

"Lot of pretty *senoritas* out there. Still a lot of gold, too." Joe lit his cigarillo with a long wood splinter from the fire. "You could do worse."

Suzanne felt like an insect stabbed onto a pin. Joe was reminding her and Rafer that there had to be a resolution. If Rafer was Jamie Carlisle, that resolution must be disastrous. Her gaze settled on Rafer, her voice emerging as if it were disembodied. "Did the Carlisles kill anyone?"

Rafer's head lifted slowly. "I expect they did."

She sat immobile for a long while, then quietly rose and went to the bedroom. Rafer did not follow. The icy room was full of silence . . . and Carl's spooks.

November 18:

After a week, the snow finally has begun to melt. Like a clock, the tedious drip from the roof monotonously spatters the snow.

We resume the trail. Snow and mud are mixed on the canyon's sunny side; in the shade, the snow is still deep. Carl says that if the spirits are willing, the snow will be gone in three days.

SEVENTEEN

The Mouse Catcher

Journal Entry: November 22.

The snow is gone. Against Rafer's better judgement, we have stopped to replenish supplies at a small trading post. The trader, a sly ruffian named Tysdale, speaks roughly to Carl and scarcely less well to a woman. Ramsey, Joe, and Rafer have corrected his manners until he is now punctilious, his resentful hypocrisy more distasteful than his crudeness. I see why Rafer did not wish to stop. Tysdale is not only unreliable, but he keeps a large liquor stock, which Joe and Carl refused to bypass. Rafer conceded only because he considered letting them have a ''blowout'' more prudent than risking their desertion. Joe and Carl are drinking heavily and playing dice with two Ute squaws and a skeletal old brave who hangs about the trading post like a cowed cur. The old man is the father of one of the squaws, who sell themselves to passersby. Although Carl pays the women little attention, Joe has gone twice into the woods with the squaws. Rafer is too wary and fastidious to drink trade liquor, and the Mormon, Mac Puckett, is a teetotaller. Drinking more than usual, Ramsey dices with the squaws. He seems grimly preoccupied with the old Ute as if he does not relish reaching that age.

To avoid the lecherous Tysdale and the drunken debauch in the trading post late that afternoon, Suzanne joined Rafer who was making a circuit around the post, rifle across his shoulder. "Carl said you spent time with the Apache. Is that another Rafer Smith myth?"

He scanned the forest before he answered. "I spent nearly a year with two retired Apache scouts who once worked out of Taos. They taught me a little about tracking, horses . . . being white, I was a limited pupil, of course."

"But you learned to see this country from another point of view . . . in a sense, as your mother."

"Something like that." Starting into the boulder-strewn wood, he assisted her over a log.

"Rafer"—she hesitated, then caught his hand when he would have let hers go—"your real mother was Anne Carlisle, wasn't she? You're Jamie Carlisle."

"With a slightly more florid reach of your imagination, I could be Father Christmas," he replied lightly, "although that's no fault of yours. I haven't been much of a rock to lean upon, have I?"

"Particularly when you're evasive." She restrained him. "Rafer, it all fits. You're wanted for robbery; that's why you couldn't sell the Coco directly. That's why you won't go into court. You're the third man, the only real owner of the claim."

"Feminine logic is incomparable," he replied imperturbably.

"There's more. Not only did you know how to find the Carlisle cabin, you couldn't bear to stay in it. You're that boy who was his insane mother's caretaker."

His eyes searched hers with a shadow of weary pain that allowed her to glimpse something of the disillusionment and frightfulness that splintered through his childhood.

Her heart ached for him, even as her grip tightened on his arm. "You knew once I saw that claim, I would put everything together," she said softly, "but to keep control, I could afford to say nothing. You became my lover to insure my silence. You intended to sell the whole claim before meeting us because you had no choice; the Black Hawk smelter made it too valuable to keep. Ramsey and I were ideal marks. You gained revenge by seducing Brad's wife and could use Brad as a skeleton in our closet; one even I used on Ramsey. While Ramsey had the development money, he would have exposed you, so you must have meant to sell me the claim as far back as Mexico. You used me. Now you want to put as much distance as possible between yourself and Colorado.'' She stood stiffly as a porcelain doll in danger of being knocked off a shelf. "Well, doesn't that cover it?"

"With one error. I didn't become your lover to assure your silence,'' said Rafer quietly. "I wanted you more than I've ever wanted any woman . . . and that about covers it.''

The mounting pain inside her lessened, eased its intolerable pressure. His wanting her was not the same as loving her, but to expect more from Rafer was like trying to grasp one of the sunbeams dancing elusively about the forest floor. Her eyes were vulnerable, her voice gravely earnest. "Rafer, you're still my silent partner. I need to know who you are; the kind of man you are, who and what I'm fighting for. Forget the myths and mad tales. I must know the truth.''

"The truth is comparatively dull," he teased gently. The sunlight filtering through the trees crossed his face in an evanescent play of shadows, subtly altering the shape of his features from moment to moment as though diverting her, warning her away . . . suggesting nothing about him would stay the same long enough to ever give her peace.

His face impassive, he studied the sunlight's flicker through the pine branches, then met her eyes levelly. "All right. You're right. I'm Jamie Carlisle, wanted dead or alive at age sixteen for armed robbery of a freight shipment out of Breckenridge in 1858. No doubt you can probably learn the details from one of your penny dreadfuls."

"Were you guilty?"

"As hell. So were my father and brothers. We got away with the whole kit and kaboodle."

"Did you kill anyone?"

His careless tone sobered. "Not during the robbery. None of us did. We weren't hardened, but only two men out of the eight-man posse returned alive."

She felt sick. "Then you're also wanted for murder."

"Technically. That posse wasn't out to take prisoners, Su," he said gravely. "They meant to either shoot or hang us."

The truth was worse than she had imagined. Her balance

uncertain, she sat carefully on a log. "Your upbringing seems to have taken quite a leap from a baronetcy in England."

"My paternal grandfather was a Kensington vicar; my father, Jack, a roisterous rebel who ran off to America with Anne Glynn, a local shopkeeper's daughter. Anne left me, the baby, with her parents until I grew old enough to withstand the wilds of Colorado. When my grandparents died, I was farmed out to the resentful vicar, who resolved to correct his laxity with my father. Until I was twelve, my strict upbringing included visits to our 'betters.' I learned to keep my elbows off the table and kowtow. I also accidentally set fire to the vicarage by running a flock of sheep through a tea with the visiting archbishop. The tea brazier was knocked over."

Suzanne was unable to help smiling. "Your life was not as dull as you predicted. You must have been a confused little boy."

His lips curved wryly. "Also a difficult one. As I couldn't suit anyone else, I suited myself. Seeing cowboys and Indians was more appealing than running away to sea, so when my father wrote for me, I came to America. The Colorado wilderness made England seem puny; my brothers made fun of my accent and clothes, and my mother was already insane.

"Anne Carlisle was a gentle creature and rarely violent, but she never knew me. To her, Jamie was the baby left in England." He looked out over the valley, his voice husky. "I longed for her, but she would rock by the hour and sing lullabyes to that baby. She believed I was some cousin sent to visit in place of Jamie. When would it be time for me to go home so Jamie would come, she would ask my father." He took an uneven breath. "That's why I made up the cabbage patch story. I was a 'made up' child from the cabbage patch of everyone's mind . . . except for my father's."

His eyes softened. "Jack Carlisle was a democrat of the first order. He had ambitions for us all, and my having been away mattered to him not at all; he gave me the same gargantuan share of love as the others. He hadn't the morality of a coyote, but I never saw him demean anyone. He had great respect for fair play, but a rather dreamy concept of the straight and narrow. He hated real evil, and he hated his father.'' Rafer glanced at the lowering sun. "The point of this maundering tale being that the Carlisles were not calculating murderers, but foolish, fallible people.''

"But in the end, you all got away scot free to Mexico,'' mused Suzanne. "For you, crime paid well, so you went on with it.'' She looked up at him sadly. "You are a confused little boy.''

"Perhaps,'' he said softly, "but on one matter, I am quite clear. I know your husband's precise whereabouts.''

Taken completely by surprise, she whirled on him, woolen skirts flying. "What? Where is he?'' Then suspicion dimmed the excited light in her eyes. Her temper rising, she snatched him by the sleeve. "Have you known since Breckenridge?!''

"No, since this morning, when I described Brad to Tysdale. He has a sharp eye for a well padded poke. Brad visited the post in mid-September on his way to Mi Vida, a large cattle spread Tysdale says was started by a Wyoming man, eight years ago. Brad's working as an accountant there, possibly for a grubstake to last until he can either sell the Coco or find a developer.''

"But you said Tysdale had an eye for a well-padded poke.'' She frowned. "You don't mean . . .''

"Brad was carrying a comfortable sum. I suspect Tysdale might have tried to steal it, if Brad hadn't been accompanied by three Mi Vida ranch hands.''

"I wonder how he acquired that money,'' she puzzled.

"Advance wages, perhaps; on the other hand, you might do well to find out whether he pulled any fast ones in Breckenridge when you return in spring.''

"Spring?! I'm not staying in these woods all winter!''

"You'll have no choice. In the mountains, snow stops everything but the revolving of the world; it shuts things down, shuts people in.''

His inference troubled her as much as the prospect of wintering in the mountains. "You're leaving us at Mi Vida, aren't you?''

He cupped her chin. "I have unfinished business, *carita*, and you have a husband. When the fates allow, we may meet again.''

The elusiveness in his eyes shocked her with sudden, painful realization. For a moment, she was unable to catch her breath. He had made her believe him again . . . after so many lies, he was still stringing her along. This time, she must cut the cord before she choked on her own everlasting, humiliating gullibility. "You don't have to let me down easily, Rafer," she said too quietly. "Once you're paid for the Coco, you don't plan to see me again."

"I have to see you to collect, don't I?"

"Having your lawyer call upon me in New York should eliminate that necessity and smooth the transaction for both of us."

He frowned at her forced, cold tone. "Transaction? We've been making more than business deals together in bed . . ."

"Stop it, Rafer. In your charming, selfish way, you've used me, in bed and out of it, all the way from Vera Cruz. You didn't come so far because you cared about me. I'm your front in a deal that promises considerable profit. You wanted me, yes, but what has lust to do with anything personal?"

At the stifled pain in her voice, he started to pull her to him, but she pushed free, her navy woolen cap falling to the ground. "Don't worry," she assured him unevenly, scooping up the cap like a shamed schoolgirl caught at her first attempt at hooky. "I won't renege. After all, I have more to gain than you and I've enjoyed you as a lover; I must simply remember priorities when encountering a new one." She ran back to the post.

"You take a lover while I'm around," he curtly advised her departing back, "and I'll feed him a live rattlesnake."

That night, the forest seemed unnaturally quiet beyond the racket issuing from the dimly lit windows of the post. Most animals now must be in hibernation, Suzanne reflected, brushing her hair in her tent before retiring in the wagon, but still she felt uneasy. The only sober heads in their expedition were Mac, Rafer, and herself. Carl had relieved Rafer and Mac from guard duty. Ramsey and Joe still caroused with Tysdale and the squaws, and the old brave disappeared in midafternoon. "I hunt mice," he declared with a broken-toothed grin as he tucked snares inside his calico shirt. He stayed gone; Tysdale said he did this to keep from sharing his catch with the squaws. Rafer sent Mac to be certain the old man was not up to mischief, but Mac soon returned to report the old man was setting snares in an upland meadow.

And Rafer? Rafer was cold sober. She had not seen him touch liquor since the expedition began. Dulled wits and reflexes might cost his life if someone recognized him. Was being a drunkard merely one of his many poses, designed to lull his marks and enemies into overconfidence?

He certainly snared her like a silly city pigeon. From bitter experience, she knew trusting Rafer was foolhardy, yet followed him into one endless escapade after another, out of ill-conceived love for him.

The canvas tent rustled; her brush poised. Breathless, she waited, only to hear the northerly wind rising in the pines. Shivering, she crept beneath the covers in anticipation of another bitterly cold night.

But not a lonely one.

She had no more than settled down when a shadow crossed her restless form. The dark silhouette of Rafer's face hovered over her wide, frightened eyes. "Don't make any noise," he whispered. "The guards are jumpy, and one of them is me." Quickly, he eased into the wagon, then peered through the flap at the trading post and dark, encircling pine forest, his expression tense as if he perceived some danger.

Suzanne pushed up to crane past his shoulder. "What's wrong? Did you hear something?"

"No," he murmured, still sharply scanning the darkness, "but I smell it; so does Carl."

"I know what you mean," she breathed. "There's something rotten about this place. Tysdale looks as if he would murder his own mother." Beneath the shadows of her heavy lashes, her emerald eyes narrowed. "How do you know Tysdale hasn't some Carlisles hidden away somewhere ready to murder us all somewhere?"

His eyes glinted. "The Carlisles weren't murderers . . . and that isn't the only wrong idea in your head." He pulled her to him and kissed her hard, his fingers knotting in her hair. The fierce, elemental fire of his lips against hers seared through her like a leap of heat lightning. In all the troubled night of her soul, he spread light as if he were a dark angel loosed to pursue and possess her.

She struggled, pushing at his chest, trying to keep at bay his near demonic skill, the turbulent passion he was already arousing so easily. She tore her lips from his, desperately arching away from him. "Leave me alone, Rafer!" she whispered harshly. "I won't be your whore any more, so leave me alone!"

Anger flickering across his desire-taut face, his fingers tightened in her hair. "If I wanted a whore, one of those squaws would be a hell of a lot less trouble than you. You're vain, arrogant, and selfish. Under that beautiful, deceptive hide, you're all pirate."

"Who's talking, you . . . Bluebeard!" she hissed.

"Two of a kind, aren't we?" he mocked harshly. His mouth plummeted remorselessly down on hers, ravishing its softness with a ruthlessness that gave the final lie to his usual mask of carelessness. In the hard, bow-taut body pressing her down ran a will as strong as hers, a hidden passion as quick to take fire. He did not have to talk anymore; his body was showing her what he wanted from her, craved from her. Suddenly, she knew he had come tonight not just to protect her, not even to pretend that his purpose was to steal a casual tryst. Like her, he had miscalculated; like her, he was too involved. He kissed her now as if he wished he had never seen her, but could not have enough of her. All her heart cried out in bittersweet triumph. Go on, sail away, you damnable pirate. Burn me to the waterline and leave me to sink, but I'll make you remember every blazing moment. For a thousand nights to come, you'll watch for my distant flames on a black horizon and your victory will recall the taste of ashes.

So she yielded, bent to him, let him have his will of her. Her lips were honey, her body fire. She revelled at his elated, quickened breathing, his racing heartbeat at her breast and his fevered fingers at her loosened clothing, then on her bare skin. This, this was destruction: in his searing lips across her flesh, the cold and heat upon her skin; her taut, straining thighs where he had pushed up her skirts, his first hungering thrust inside her. She took him, wound her long legs about him, enflamed him until she felt the perspiration upon his skin beneath his open shirt, the intensity of his moving muscles, the near desperation of his desire. Her own. She pinnacled with him in that final moment of unbearable, licking flame that left them both at last in breathless, silent darkness. For a long time, he stayed within her until the cold crept upon them, bringing with it bitter return to reality. His fingertips traced her face, abruptly stilled as he encountered her tears. Her body had gone rigid beneath him like a frozen, despairing mockery of their passion. "Dammit, Su, you don't have to pretend you want me!" he swore harshly, pulling away. "Don't ever lie to me like that again!"

"Why not?" she baited halfheartedly. "What is one more lie in a thicket of deceptions? You're a far grander liar than I am, Rafer, and surely women have lied to you before . . ."

His blue eyes blazed in the rising moonlight and for a split second, she thought he would strike her. Instead, he slowly fastened his breeches. "So, now we go for the jugular . . . or shall I crudely suggest a more vulnerable area." He flicked his belt through the buckle, then thrust his revolver back into his breeches band. "Fair's fair, I suppose. You're an accomplished actress"—he caught her up by her open bodice—"but not that good." He kissed her again until she caught at his shoulders. "And not that experienced. You didn't have a husband, my sweet; you had a sugar tit."

Just as she started to slap him, Ramsey's cold, slurred voice rasped over her shoulder. "Well, what have we here? A lovers' squabble?" Dismayed, Suzanne whirled as Rafer stiffened. Her white blouse had slipped off her shoulder, her tangled hair spilling down the exposed cleft of her breasts as she swiftly caught closed the unbuttoned linen camisole. Ramsey's smile was dangerously pleasant. "What's the matter, Mr. Smith? Has my son's wife withdrawn her adulterous favors now that she has your mining claim?"

Rafer pushed Suzanne aside to forestall her blistering retort.

"We'll discuss Suzanne when you're sober and I'm in a better mood." His blue eyes held Ramsey's with the lethal imperturbability of a cobra.

"We'll have a bash now, dammit!" snarled Ramsey. "I'm not too drunk to knock your shyster teeth out!" He jabbed an unsteady finger at Suzanne. "Then I'll feed that greedy Jezebel to my damned dogs!"

As Ramsey was armed with only a liquor bottle, Rafer let out an exasperated sigh, then warily shoved back the tent flap. No sooner had he stepped from the tent than the forest about them exploded with shooting stars that dimmed the real stars overhead. In a rattle of gunfire, whoops and screeches, a band of Utes poured into the clearing. Ramsey reeled around, mouth agog, when five riders, intent on his tethered thoroughbreds, cut between him and the remuda. He started forward with a roar of fury. Rafer hooked his feet with a fierce shove between the shoulder blades that knocked him flat, then dragged him struggling, into the tent. The Utes, using their horses as shields, were virtually invisible, so Rafer fired in front of the Indians' horses to shy them from the remuda. Carl ran from the woods with his rifle ablaze, while Joe stumbled from the trading post into the churn of riders, his pistol aimlessly firing at nothing. When Mac began to fire accurately from the post roof, the Utes fled. The thoroughbreds went with them. "Well, drat," said Joe as he sat down hard.

"I'll kill 'em!" screamed Ramsey, scrambling from the tent. Even more irritated by the cease-fire, he headed for a mule, tore its tether from the remuda line and vaulted aboard. In no mood for more nonsense, the mule bucked him off. Suzanne peeked from the tent. With the wary curiosity of children watching a dull-witted but intrepid fellow, Rafer and the rest of the men, except befuddled Joe, gathered around Ramsey. With a roar, he fought to his feet, knocked the mule between the ears with his fist, and started to board again. This time, the mule dumped him twice as fast, and twice as slowly he rose, grabbed Carl's gun, and staggered toward the mule again, aiming at its skull. Rafer sharply tapped him over the head with the butt end of his revolver.

Joe smiled benignly as Ramsey dropped. "I'd a given a week's worth of whiskey to see him catch them Utes."

EIGHTEEN

The Barter

In the morning, Ramsey awoke loaded for bear. Clutching his aching head, Ramsey crawled from the trading post fur pile where Carl and Mac had deposited him, and announced his grim intention of thrashing Rafer, then pursuing his prized horses. He was the last man up; the rest waited patiently by the fireplace. Suzanne placed a coffee mug in his hand, and when he started to fling it away, caught his wrist with maternal firmness. "You'll accomplish much more today without a hangover, so drink up." At his failure to cooperate, she added mildly, "Mr. Tysdale will lead us to the Utes, providing you wish to negotiate with them over only three horses."

"Negotiate?" Ramsey's bloodshot eyes pinned the nervous, hogtied Tysdale. "You expect to talk those thieving bastards into giving back my horses? With this sonofabitch taking us to the party? He probably sent that decrepit old mouse-catcher to fetch the Utes in the first place!"

"Mr. Tysdale pleads guilty," said Rafer calmly, his loose-limbed frame relaxed. His back was braced against the window frame, his rifle resting across a drawn-up knee as he kept an eye on the clearing.

Joe waggled his skinning knife. "Mr. Tysdale figured owning up was better than havin' a drunk lift his hide, I keep tellin' him a potful of Mrs. Hoth's coffee done give me a rock-steady hand, but he just swears losing weight so fast ain't healthy. He knows he can talk some sense into them Ute friends of his, don't you Mr. Tysdale?"

With a frantic nod, Tysdale began to babble tidings of good will until Ramsey disgustedly cut him off. "Oh, shut up; you're aggravating my headache."

During the hour-long ride to the Ute camp, Ramsey had to be convinced that, while the tribe was more enterprising than bloodthirsty, four men and a woman were no match for two hundred and fifty Utes. They were to barter for the horses. Also, Rafer warned Ramsey might expect to pay an exorbitant price for his own property, and that if he valued his scalp, he would be well advised to keep his temper. "If you don't," added Rafer flatly, "I'll kill you myself."

When Tysdale reluctantly escorted them into the Ute camp, Ramsey's control was sorely tested at the sight of one of his thoroughbreds grilling over a pit of coals.

Suzanne might have pitied Ramsey as much as the unfortunate horse, had she not feared they might all share an equally unpleasant fate. They were met on the village outskirts by fifteen hard-faced, mounted warriors trailed by snarling dogs who warily circled the strange horses and single wagon. Garbed in quill and beadwork-trimmed buckskins and bits of white man's clothing, they still wore the red, black, and yellow warpaint from the raid. Suzanne was certain the Utes noticed her nervousness; Mac and even Carl were as ill at ease, but Rafer and Joe might have been attending a garden luncheon with Tysdale as their contribution to the delicacies. Tysdale had a false, scared-rabbit smile the breadth of Texas pasted on his face. Beyond the forest fringe, nearly a hundred elkskin teepees were lined in parallel rows along the riverbank. Escorted by the braves, they approached a central clearing dominated by a large teepee of red-painted buffalo skins marked with tribal medicine insignia; to the right was the chief's dwelling heralded by a tripod of spears, weapons, and shields bearing scalps. While Joe claimed Utes rarely killed on raids, the scalps hung from similar tripods outside virtually every teepee in the village; Suzanne was only slightly relieved to note most of the scalps were Indian.

Attired in a stovepipe hat sporting an eagle feather, and a United States cavalryman's jacket rakishly scarfed by a series of quillery and beadwork-trimmed sashes, Chief Nine Claws strolled from his teepee with a muskrat-hatted son behind him. He surveyed his falsely benevolent guests with a deprecating grunt. His hooded dark eyes returned to Suzanne, then Joe, and narrowed a fraction. At a slight sign of the old man's hand, Joe straightened abruptly in his saddle, his smile giving an uncertain twitch. His right hand flicked from his rein, then poised as if he had changed his mind about something. In the next instant, he pitched from his saddle, four arrows in his back. A shiver ran through his body as his fingers raked the dirt. He died, surprise and self-disgust still shadowing his face.

The blood drained so suddenly from Suzanne's head that she grabbed vaguely at her saddlehorn to keep from slipping to the ground. Ramsey caught her arm with an iron grip, and for a moment, Suzanne dimly wondered if they would all be killed. Rafer and Carl had not twitched a muscle, while Mac muttered a heartfelt oath, his hands spearing into the air. In shocked horror, they gaped at Joe's grotesquely sprawled body, the death in the air as palpable as the scent of a chicken yard chopping block.

"We had trouble with this one in the old days," calmly observed the chief. "He shot a Ute who was hunting Rough Creek."

Rafer fought hard to control his anger. Joe was no longer in a position to refute the chief's story, but the fact that the rest of them were still alive asserted the chief had a precise bone to pick, but whatever his past crimes, Joe was dead because of three stolen horses. He might have gotten them all killed, had he not reconsidered going for his gun. "Nine Claws," Rafer said gravely, "we did not know of our friend's quarrel with your people. We grieve for him, but also for the man he killed. Because you have been clever enough to take horses from us, we respect you, but we do not fear you. You see we are strong and do not come out of weakness. We wish to travel to the White River country. Will you allow us to go freely, or must we fight you again? We will die; but so will many Utes."

The chief's eyes flicked over Suzanne, then glittered slyly. "You do not wish to trade?"

"Do you prefer whiskey to horses?"

A slight smile creased the chief's seamed face. "I like both. I can take both, also all your animals, your guns . . . and the woman. I can flay you all alive."

"Your warriors may do these things," countered Rafer softly, "but you will watch from the realm of spirits: without horses and whiskey, without guns, the woman, and scalps."

Nine Claws digested his implication. "I like whiskey. We talk."

The next few hours were the most frightening Suzanne had ever spent. She understood nothing of what had passed between Rafer and Nine Claws before they retired into the chief's teepee, and being uninvited to the council, was not further enlightened. Instead, surrounded by grim warriors and shawled squaws restraining peeping children, she was left outside with Mac, her tension drawn to the snapping point by Rafer's final order to Mac. "If there's trouble, shoot her."

Rafer finally emerged with Nine Claws from the teepee. Rafer's face was enigmatic, but the chief looked pleased, while Ramsey was furious. Red faced, he vaulted onto his horse while Rafer and Carl bid the chief adieu. The niceties ended, Rafer nodded for her and Mac to mount. With the back of her neck prickling, she obliged.

"You come back in spring?" queried Nine Claws as Rafer climbed on his horse.

"I doubt it," replied Rafer, "but if so, we must talk again."

Nine Claws nodded. "You come back; I want another horse."

Rafer pulled a long face. "You are a good trader. If I come back, you will be a rich man."

The chief laughed. "Come back. I will wait."

"What happened back there?" Suzanne asked breathlessly of Rafer as soon as they were out of camp.

"I'll tell you what happened!" Ramsey pounced in angrily. "This sonofabitch gave those dirty savages the whole show! They kept the horses, Tysdale, and the whiskey!"

"We kept our lives. Did you want them to follow us?"

retorted Rafer. "Now we have nothing worth their losing casualties."

"We've got her." Mac gestured toward Suzanne.

Carl shook his head. "No woman is worth a warrior." His philosophical gaze slid away as Suzanne snapped him a hard look.

"Well," said Mac, "I ain't chancin' another raid." He reined in the wagon team. "I've had enough of this hard luck junket. Two men got killed because this Sunday strutter had to have a moth-eaten cat and a few overbred nags. I know a jinx when I smell it." He regarded Ramsey stonily. "You best give me my pay now; I'm leavin'."

"You go off alone," snapped Ramsey, "and those Utes will barbecue you."

"They aren't cannibals, Mr. Hoth," corrected Carl mildly. "They just like horse."

"Along with the occasional dog," added Mac dryly.

"Actually, only Arapaho eat dog," observed Carl imperturbably. "Northern Utes prefer skunk."

"Whatever," summated Mac impatiently. "I want my pay."

"You'd better include mine, Mr. Hoth," added Carl. "Guess I've lost my appetite for this trip, too."

"Do something," Ramsey snarled at Rafer. "You hired these chickenshits."

"Pay them; otherwise, they'll collect when you're asleep or dead."

After swearing for a full five minutes, Ramsey foraged into his pockets and hurled a roll of bank notes at the pair. "All right, you welshers, get out of here! I hope those Utes skin you until your eyeballs pop!"

Unruffled, Mac slid down from the wagon seat to count the money; while there was clearly too much, he quickly pocketed most of the bills and grudgingly handed Carl the rest. Carl counted his money. "Well"—he smiled wryly at Rafer—"that's about it." He touched his fur hat. "Ma'am."

Mac mounted, then made an ironic pass with his own beaver cap. "Good luck to you."

Uneasy to her toes, Suzanne nodded curtly.

Seeming to expect Carl and Mac's desertion, Rafer bid both men an amiable farewell.

"Well, what do we do now?" demanded Ramsey as the two rode out of sight. "Those Utes are likely to track us all the way through their territory. Once they see we're down to two men and a woman, they'll have at us."

"Only if the risk is worthwhile," replied Rafer. He slid off his horse, and peered into the wagon. "I suggest we abandon the wagon and take only what we need to reach Mi Vida. The whiskey we gave the Utes should give us a decent headstart. With hard riding, we could be well away by the time they find the wagon." He let the wagon's drop gate fall with a bang. "Pretty as she is, they won't pursue Suzanne too diligently, given a more immediate distraction." He heaved out a flour sack. "Empty our small coffee bags, Suzanne. We'll use them for flour and cornmeal."

Ramsey's face went nearly black with frustration as she dismounted. "You're giving those Utes the rest of the whole damned store? Not to mention letting that bible-thumping cash register and half-breed just ride off the job!"

"Well now"—Rafer pitched another bag from the wagon—"what did you want me to do, shoot them?"

Suzanne feared a fight. Despite his deceptively calm voice, Rafer's jaw was tight with the urge to tear into Ramsey. They needed Mac and Carl badly, and despite Joe's unpredictability, Rafer had liked him as much as she did. Joe was always courteous, often trying to ease the journey for her. As soon as her nose poked from the tent in the morning, Joe presented her with a mug of steaming tea. He lined her boots with rabbit skin and contrived fur mittens and a scarf. He could even make Ramsey laugh at himself, but Ramsey was not laughing now, and neither was Joe.

Ramsey sourly helped with unloading, and they abandoned the wagon within the half hour, leaving behind all the trade goods, the tools, and four mules unhitched to be recovered by the Utes. With Ramsey leading a draft mule, they took their bedding, and three weeks of supplies and fodder.

Journal Entry: November 6.

I have salvaged my journal, and although I am exhausted tonight after making camp, recounting the day's terrible events affords my mind some relief. For the past twenty-eight miles, no one has spoken. The long festering antagonism between Rafer and Ramsey promises to erupt at the slightest pressure. The deaths of Joe and Frock, and Ramsey's rash arrogance are merely layers upon the opposition between himself and Rafer. Ramsey is the East; industry, competition, acquisition, while Rafer belongs to the West of the Indian and the trapper. Ramsey tries to remake the earth in his own image. While Ramsey is rock, Rafer is wind. One can find anchorage with a rock, but never with the elusive wind, yet rock wears away; wind is forever.

Ramsey eyes me with the hurt, sullen intensity of a rejected grizzly bear. He is accustomed to rule; now his prowess and right to rule has been denigrated, not only by a younger competitor, but the female he desires. The sackcloth of humiliation and self-doubt does not rest lightly upon the monarch.

Ramsey watched Suzanne write in her journal. She was uncertain now, worn by the journey, shaken by Joe's death, anxious about the Utes. She was also concerned for the old man; he hated her pity. At first, he consoled himself she had sold herself to the most profitable bidder, but no, she was in love and the ever perceptive, clever Rafer was unaware of it.

Suzanne had intelligence, breeding, stamina, and beauty. Also, he loved her. Thumbscrews would not have made him confess he had gone after his aristocratic thoroughbreds simply because they were beautiful, but he had a similar attachment to Suzanne. He did not love her as he had his wife, Elizabeth, but he valued far more than her looks. Like him, she was a fighter; she had heart and deserved respect. With her, he would not repeat his mistake with Elizabeth. She would have as much of him as she needed and live in all the comfort he could give her, while Rafer would give her only infidelity and heartache.

Rafer was not a monster, but neither was Ramsey a Gala-had. He would win Suzanne fairly if possible, but if not . . .

Suzanne started beneath her blankets as a shadow sheared across her face. Her eyes flaring open in alarm, she flailed for her derringer, only to see Ramsey hunkered down by her bedroll. The moon was too low on the horizon for his guard shift to have ended.

"We've been swoggled, you know." Not troubling to keep his voice low, he nodded toward Rafer's unmoving form. "He's played us both like brook trout."

"Ramsey," Suzanne said wearily, "I'm tired. I assure you my illusions look no brighter now than in the daylight."

"He used you as a blind for that claim deal," Ramsey went on relentlessly. "Once those conflicting claims hit the courts, we'll have a can of worms on our hands. Jamie Carlisle is gallows bait. I saw a wanted notice back in Denver; the Carlisles are wanted for grand theft and larceny."

She sat up, masking her uneasiness. "Jamie Carlisle ought to be safe enough in Mexico."

"If he's in Mexico." Ramsey glanced at Rafer again. "If he's in Colorado, he's run his neck into a noose."

Silent for a moment, she brushed her windblown hair from her face. "You're suggesting that I decide upon which side my bread is buttered."

"Stick with me and you'll live like a queen. You are a queen, and you know damned well what Rafer Smith is."

"Whatever Rafer is, what makes you think I'm any better than him? That you're any better?" Her green eyes were level, her voice unaccusing. "None of us is particularly virtuous. We're accustomed to fighting for what we want."

"All right, we'll play by our rules," he replied roughly. "I know you better than you think. You'll let nothing come between you and money. I didn't send all my Pinkertons to Colorado. Your father's rotting in the New York gutters. He's not a well man these days." His voice had taken on the unswerving cadence of a sledgehammer. "He's underweight, he coughs, and his color's bad; that was last spring. Whether he survives until next spring is anybody's guess. In a few months, winter rolls around again."

He grabbed her shoulders as she started to bolt upward. "There's nothing you can do now. You're in the middle of the Rockies until winter's done, girl. The point is, time's not on Edward Maintree's side. I can help you, and him, more quickly than any other man living. You may find a developer for that claim, but when? Next summer, next winter? The year after that? Rafer's giving you a quick screw and pie in the sky.

"When the Coco turns profitable, some gargoyle like me will declare your claim to the Coco invalid and instigate a court fight. You lack the cash to contest. You'll lose everything, including your two-bit lover"—he glanced over her shoulder at Rafer, who now lay on his side, his open eyes cynically appraising. "When the going gets tough, Rafer Smith will run. He always has; he always will."

"He hasn't this time," she flung back distractedly.

"But he wants to, doesn't he?" Ramsey's flinty gaze held Rafer's. "He's counting the minutes."

"Leave her alone," warned Rafer, the words soft as the shear of a hawk's talons.

"Just so she knows which side of her bread is buttered."

"The side that lands face down."

Ramsey snorted. "Choose, girl, if you don't want your mind made up for you." He stalked back to his guard post.

Suzanne passed a tortured, sleepless night. A merciless vision of Edward Maintree's pinched, desolate figure was irrevocably before her. Ramsey was right; she never really had a choice.

At twilight of the third day, they reached a broad curve of the river surrounded by high rolling hills. The forest lay behind them, the sun settling over snow-scraped mounds huddled like sleeping animals on the wasted grassland. Rafer dumped the packs, took an axe, and began to chop off branches for firewood from a dead tree whose silver, twisted length angled high on the riverbank. With a relieved sigh, Suzanne slid off her horse and stretched. If Rafer meant to build a fire, they must be safe from the Utes.

By the time Ramsey unsaddled his mount, Rafer was lighting a fire while Suzanne dug out the frying pan and coffee pot. Rafer hauled his saddle near the meager blaze. "Where does the White River Ute territory begin?" he demanded of Rafer.

"Where the forest played out."

Ramsey squinted at the empty hills. "What if they don't cotton to us any more than Tysdale's Utes?"

"The Yampas and White River Utes are fairly used to whites." Rafer adjusted the fire tinder. "We're small game, and in winter, they don't venture this far down river."

"So"—Ramsey's eyes narrowed speculatively after Suzanne as she took the coffee pot to the river—"looks like we have the place to ourselves."

Rafer's gaze followed his. "Looks like."

The oatcakes and remainder of a rabbit Rafer snared the previous night was brief and unsatisfying, but better than their fare for the past few days. Still hungry, Suzanne wistfully studied the rabbit's clean-picked carcass as Ramsey stoically washed down another dry oatcake with coffee.

Rafer, on the other hand, seemed to have lost his appetite. Sitting crosslegged and motionless, he was silent, thoughtful. Covered with buffalo grass, the barren hills surrounded them like the tiers of a ruined arena, the stars' ancient canopy shivering in the bitter, fitful wind. His eyes on Rafer, Ramsey sucked the marrow of his rabbit bones. Since time's birth, men and animals have fought over females and power; Ramsey knew precisely how to go about it. He tossed the rabbit bones away.

"Well, let's get to it, Mr. Smith." His grating voice was baiting, a little amused.

Beneath his wind-stirred bandanna, Rafer's blue eyes held the patient ferocity of a wolf's. The sun creases on his face seemed to have been carved in stone.

"A fight is unnecessary, Ramsey," intervened Suzanne quietly. "You've won everything you wanted. We'll find Brad and you'll manage the mine. I'll never see Rafer again."

The firelight glinting on his beard, his lips curved in a harsh line. "That isn't everything I want."

Her voice softened. "I'm sorry, Ramsey. My father would

not sell himself, and neither will I. I care for you, but not in a way that could lead to happiness for either of us.''

He turned on her coldly, without anger. "How long have you been 'happy' with Rafer?''

"Since Natchez,'' Rafer interposed flatly when she hesitated. Her gaze swiftly averted.

Ramsey snorted. "I figured. She never gave me the pleasure.''

Rafer mercilessly studied Suzanne's flush. "No? She assured me you were quite intimate.''

Ramsey was startled, then started to laugh. "Playing both ends against the middle again, were you, Suzie?'' His laughter altered subtly. "Who's to say you aren't doing it again? Eh?'' He shook his head with mock, chilling paternalism. "Guess it's time you learned what's what and who's who. I'm not as old and fumble fingered as you may think, girl.'' He shifted back to the fire, and to her horror, dug into the embers and extracted a coal with his bare hand. The red coal glowed through his flesh, but although sweat pocked his brow, his grasp was firm. "That's who I am.'' The coal neared Rafer's set face until its virulent light lent a violet, eerie glow to Rafer's cold blue eyes.

When Rafer made no effort to retreat, Suzanne flung herself at Ramsey. "Don't, Ramsey! This is insane!''

He shoved her off. "Stay out of this, missy. You've had your turn at the game; now it's between Rafer and me.'' He tossed the coal at Rafer's face. Rafer smashed it back to sear past Ramsey's jaw. The smell of burnt flesh hung sickeningly in the air.

"You want to play games, old man? Find a kid to impress with fierce faces and loud noises''—Rafer gestured sharply, then his voice lowered—"but don't waste your time fighting over Suzanne. Her choice is made.''

"Suzanne's a practical woman. Mi Vida can't be far now. Joe said we just need to follow this river, so your services are dispensable. We can borrow a scout from the ranch to steer back to civilization. So . . .'' Ramsey rose heavily to his feet with a taunting smile of undiluted hatred. "I am now about to indulge in the pleasure I have anticipated for 2,000 miles. I am going to break every bone in your body with my bare hands, then the lady and I will make the best use of our privacy. I promise you, she'll change her mind about a number of things.''

Suzanne recoiled in shocked anger. Good God, Ramsey had gone over the edge! She leapt to her feet, but before she could vent her outrage, Ramsey's left hand shot out to grab her breast. In mid-screech of fury, Suzanne sensed a blur as Rafer surged upward, but he was not as quick as the punch she slammed into Ramsey's nose. Frock's brass knuckles glinted in the firelight, but her nose shot had wrecked the timing of Ramsey's intended sucker punch. Rafer's left hand veered aside Ramsey's steel capped fist just as his other bored into Ramsey's stomach. Ramsey let out a whoof and Rafer shoved Suzanne out of the way so hard that she fell sprawling.

The two men went at one another with a gleeful ferocity that was horrifying. Rafer was quick, young, accurate as a rattler; Ramsey was ruthless, vicious, unyielding as granite. With heads down, bodies close, they slammed at one another until Rafer grabbed Ramsey's neck, hooked a foot behind his heel and dragged him down. Their faces bloodied, they rolled in the dirt. In a thrash of eye gouging, ear biting, kicking, they landed in the freezing creek.

Suzanne stopped yelling frantically and went for the rifle in Rafer's scabbard. They would kill each other! Snatching the Remington, she ran down to the creek. Sullen clouds overcast the pitch-dark river, revealing only a white froth of water kicked up by two black, frenzied shapes. "Stop, or I'll put a bullet in one of your stubborn hides!'' she shouted. She fired over their heads, but they ignored her bluff. Ramsey rolled atop Rafer and forced him under the surface. Gritting her teeth, she waded into the icy river to brain him with the rifle stock, only to lose her footing and go down, grimly holding the rifle. Wedged between a pair of boulders, the rifle stock snapped off. With a heartfelt oath, she struggled up and went after Ramsey with the gun barrel . . . but was unable to find him. Hard, uneven breathing betrayed desperate, murderous strain, then an enfeebled splash sounded a few yards upstream. Somebody was being killed.

Her heart in her throat, Suzanne floundered toward the sound, her wet wool skirts tangling heavily about her legs in the quick, icy current. She nearly fell over the combatants. A man's dark head and shoulders reared above the water, his muscles straining to keep his opponent's head beneath the water. The submerged man's hands were locked about the victor's throat, but even as she closed in, were going slack. She slammed the rifle barrel down on the head sticking above the water. With a curse of pain, Rafer turned to rip the rifle from her hands. Jerking Ramsey's head above the water, he slammed the barrel down on his skull. "No!" she screamed, dragging at his shoulders. "Don't kill him!"

Rafer came to his knees, then moving with painful slowness, dragged Ramsey's heavy bulk from the river. She scrambled after him. After dropping Ramsey's body on the bank, he staggered toward the fire. She ran after him. "You murdered him!" she cried, sick at heart. "You didn't need to kill him!"

"Oh, yes, I did," he gritted, balefully turning on her. She flinched from his gory face in the firelight. Ramsey must have used a rock. Rafer's nose was broken over his torn lips. Blood welled from a split eyebrow, his nose, and the rowel of Ramsey's fingernails down his cheek. Shaking with cold, he grabbed her by her blouse front. "That bastard doesn't understand half measures. He's lucky I didn't kill him. He may look like a beached whale, but his heart's pounding like a steam engine. At least, until he . . . just once, looks at me cross-eyed, or touches you again." Inexorably drawing her toward him, he swept his mouth down on hers. The cloth tore with a shocking lash of cold abruptly banished by the ruthless fire of his hand on her bare breast. His naked passion unnerved her. She tasted blood. Seduction was past; this was domination. There were no soft words; he had dispensed with charming lures. "You're mine," he said harshly when she tried to struggle free. "I know it; Ramsey knows it, and it's time you know it."

Her wet hair streaked across her face, she pushed fiercely against his chest. "No! I won't be claimed like some prize of combat! Let go, Rafer!"

"Not now, *carita*." His eyes narrowed with resolution, his breath coming raggedly from the strain of his battle with Ramsey. "Ramsey was right; you pitted us against each other from the start. The lure was winner take all; it's too late to change the stakes."

His mouth closed over hers again, filling her with fear and treacherous, primitive excitement. Rafer was dangerous. He could kill. He was a criminal, but she desired him. He was wild and uncivilized, and she could taste his blood on her mouth, but she hungered for him as if her soul were parched desert both threatened and exalted by the onslaught of a raging river. Only fear of immersion, obliteration, made her fight him as if he were death itself. So easily, she could surrender to him, but not this way. She had seen hardship, brutality and death at close range. This was a primordial, unforgiving wilderness that scraped the soul down to the marrow, then spat out whatever did not hook into its craw.

The unyielding strength of Rafer's arms, the wild fire of his kisses, her own passion promised certain defeat, but she fought long after her defenses were rubble. Her body craved him, but he wanted more than her body this time. He desired many women and stayed with none of them. She might endure abandonment, but not being discarded. If he took her spirit with him, she would be better off dead.

Rafer's embrace tightened. "You love me," he whispered, his face taut with desire. "Say it, Su. You don't care what I am. Yesterday and tomorrow don't matter! Only this matters!"

"It isn't enough!" Her desperate denial was edged with despair. "Tomorrow always comes, and you leave every yesterday a ruin!" She sensed his confusion at her continued resistance, but no lessening of his determination. His will was as strong as hers, his body forcing her down with a frightening, wildly challenging implacability. She scratched his face, tore his hair until he swore softly and shook her hard, spilling her hair across her face. Her teeth sank into his shoulder as he tore at her clothing. And in that black night, he took her while the wolves howled on the distant hills. A dark burning came into her, a primitive mating that sealed an unseverable bond. She might be forever his, but he was also hers. In pursuit of her soul, he irretrievably lost his own; becoming one with that which he sought and would have conquered. Her spilled hair, her ragged breathing, the pulse of her blood beating with his own, united in a basal, abandoned spirit, a mysterious magic old as the land itself. Surrounded by silent drums, a high-pitched rasp of bone, was a licking flame, bare sinuosity coiling and uncoiling into the potent strike, the languid drifting into a deeper darkness of ancient knowledge as enduring as painted figures upon the rocks.

Sifted by the wind, Suzanne's hair drifted across Rafer's cheek. She was still now, soft and pliant beneath him. He exalted in her shape, her firm, living flesh against the earth. His sex within hers. In her heat, her female power. In his own maleness and opposition . . . their melding until there was no ending between them. The brevity of their joining, their lives, paled before their timelessness. In this woman's eyes was his eternity, its magnificence already fading as she lost her somnolence, slipping from the peyote life dream of their mating. Her face unnaturally still in the firelight, she had gone inside herself again, her green eyes becoming as distant as those of a priestess, a desert Cassandra, sorrowing, defiant, and doomed.

Rafer smoothed the hair from her damp, pale brow. You have no need to fear me, he wanted to reassure her, but she had reason to fear. He knew the lesson that must be taught. If he did not claim her, Ramsey would. She would fight Ramsey as she had him, only to lose in the end. Suzanne would not see her father die for her own pride, and while entirely capable of rape, Ramsey would not have to go so far. The proud, intractable spitfire who dazzled and defied New York was no more; she was stronger, more resiliant; she had learned to make bargains, to survive. Ramsey's respect for her would not interfere with what he wanted. He could wear her down. In time, she would adjust from lack of choice; therefore, for once and always, Ramsey must learn that she was beyond his reach; Suzanne must learn that irrevocable lesson as well.

Rafer waited until Ramsey stirred. Unaware of Ramsey's returning consciousness, Suzanne half lifted her head. When she attempted to rise, Rafer thrust her down again, then, determined to destroy all possibility of return to the old pack order, he took her again, before Ramsey's dazed, increasingly aware, enraged, hate-filled eyes. He took his time, knowing that anything less than a bludgeon would fail to draw Ramsey's attention. Ramsey would have to know he'd lost, or one of them would end up killing the other. Ramsey fought to his hands and knees, but clawed his way no more than a few inches before he collapsed again. Prostrate, he had to watch, tears of murderous, fruitless rage squeezing from his eyes. After Rafer finally rose from Suzanne, thinking sleep unlikely, he took Ramsey's rifle from its saddle scabbard and ejected the shells into the dust, then resuming his seat by the fire, he waited for Ramsey to retrieve his strength. After a time, Ramsey stumbled toward the river to bathe his face.

Moments later, a bloodcurdling snarl from the river rent the air along with Ramsey's answering yell of, "Goddamn you!" Heavy growls mounted into a roar, partly Ramsey's. Rafer shot to his feet and started for his saddle scabbard to see it empty; the smashed gun was still in the river. Swiftly, he caught up Ramsey's rifle and brushed over the firelight-flickered dust in search of its ejected bullets.

Grabbing a piece of greasewood, Suzanne jumped up and started for the river. "Stay where you are, dammit!" snapped Rafer, cramming a retrieved bullet into the rifle chamber.

"But Ramsey's in trouble!"

"So is the bloody bear if he tries to digest that sonofabitch." Shoving another bullet into the chamber, he ran for the river.

"Bear!" echoed Suzanne in dazed horror. Gripping her greasewood, she scrambled after him. Two bullets wouldn't stop a bear!

The firelight silhouetted Rafer's back as he fired into the

shadows shrouding the bank and detonated the bear's ear-splitting roar. Sparks flew from the scrape of huge claws on rock as a huge shape hurtled toward them. Her heart slamming in her breast, Suzanne's involuntary gasp was drowned out by the second report of Rafer's rifle. Rocks scattered as a vast, terrible bulk loomed from out of the night. Rafer spun to shove her back even as she screamed in terror. He clamped his arms and legs around her and rolled, slamming her body against the rocks until her ribs threatened to break. There was a rush of air and heat as though a train's deafening roar were bearing down on them. She heard a heavy thud, then their hearts beating back stark silence. Only after a full minute, did they risk breathing. Rafer tensely lifted his head to peer into the blackness. Nothing stirred.

"For heaven's sake," she whispered, "is he dead?"

A faint moan issued twenty feet down the bank. "Not yet," affirmed Rafer laconically.

"I can hear Ramsey! What about the bear!" she hissed in growing desperation.

Gingerly, Rafer disentangled himself and crept over the rocks, then after a few minutes there came another hard thud, his verdict pronounced virtually at her feet. "Now the bear's dead."

"How do you know!"

"Because I just brained it with a forty-pound rock."

With a wince at her bruises she groped toward Ramsey's moan; Rafer was there first. "Ugh," he muttered, staring downward. "Sticky."

"Don't you have any heart at all?"

"I shot the bear before it made *fois gras* out of his conniving brain, didn't I?" At his prod, Ramsey groaned again. Rafer swore in an exasperated release of pent-up nerves. "I say we saw off whatever doesn't work, and cart the remains to Mi Vida before it snows again."

He exploded at her incensed glare as she cradled Ramsey's head. "You and your damned in-laws are more trouble than a pack of spoiled babies, so don't expect me to drool with sympathy because this black-minded old fart was chewed by precisely what he bit off. If he'd held the rifle, I'd add no more to the future course of history than a few inches of middle-aged spread on that bear!'' As if fighting the urge to leave Ramsey in the mire, Rafer grimly caught him under the armpits, heaved him over his shoulders and staggered off to the fire. After he dumped his burden, he and Suzanne spent most of the night repairing it. Ramsey's collarbone and arm were broken; his shoulder and back were mauled, and an ear hung in tatters; otherwise, he was intact.

Under slate-gray, ominous clouds, Ramsey opened a bloodshot eye to find Suzanne hovering over him. Rafer was cleaning the wet revolver. "God," Ramsey croaked, groping weakly at his bandaged head. "I feel horrible."

"You look like bat crap," returned Rafer unsympathetically. Ignoring Suzanne's reproachful scowl, he sighted through the revolver barrel. "Can you ride? We're two days from Mi Vida with promise of snow by tonight."

Tied to his saddle, Ramsey was slumped with pain, and generally half-unconscious, but he made no complaint. By midafternoon, snow began. Before dusk, Rafer called a halt. That night, shelter was a canvas tarp supported by a scrub oak and weighted by rocks around the edge. When they burrowed under the tarp, Rafer ordered her into his blankets, two bodies packed together being warmer than one; Ramsey would have to settle for whiskey-laced coffee and Rubenesque imaginings. After a dinner of jerky and gruel, they settled down for the night. As Rafer clasped her beneath his blankets, Suzanne saw his blue eyes implacably meet Ramsey's and by the guttering fire's dim glow, bitter, futile rage and shame filled Ramsey's face. He refused to look at her. Rafer was right; Ramsey might one day try to kill him, but he would never touch her again. Exhaustion made her sag against Rafer without protest as he opened her clothing and his own to increase their shared heat.

At dawn, they mounted in blustering snow-laden wind that buffeted the horses. Ramsey was less strong, less aware as miles passed in a monotonous rhythm of white-blanketed, wind-swept hummocks. Night descended without sign of Mi Vida. In a blinding blizzard, while Ramsey lay unconscious along his horse's neck, they dug a hut in the snow with thick-packed walls shelved for sleeping space above gathering snowmelt from body heat. Rafer bundled Ramsey into the hut and packed him in beneath his buffalo robe, then built a small fire to boil snow water, while with freezing fingers, Suzanne fed the horses. Out of coffee, they drank the hot water to warm themselves and wash down their jerky, then poured some into Ramsey. Unable to concentrate on the jerky, he fell asleep halfway through his cup of water.

Dazed from the cold, her mind drowsy and limbs leaden, Suzanne stared vaguely at her fallen cup. Rafer drew her down with him into his blankets, where he made love to her until she stopped shivering. Making love on a bed of ice was strange . . . particularly with another man inches away. Unable to stop Rafer, she did not try, letting the rhythmic sensations sweep over her as if drifting in a dream. He was loving her, taking her into a safe haven where she could sleep. Sleep. He was melting into her like sweet, rose-tinted honey: luxurious, delicious. Then came the sweet, probing sting that made her gasp softly, bloom, and enfold him again. To sleep, sleep until another spring . . .

By morning the hut entrance was sealed with snow. They were slow to rise from the warm blankets. Ramsey stirred restlessly in his sleep, while Suzanne lay still, her head on Rafer's chest. "Do you think we missed Mi Vida in the snowstorm?" she murmured with a trace of anxiety.

"No chance." He toyed with a silken strand of her hair. "We've been on Mi Vida land since noon yesterday."

Her head lifted. "Aren't there any fences?"

He laughed. "This isn't Connecticut, yet. I doubt if Mi Vida has any neighbors except Yampas and wild animals; fences don't keep them out."

"But surely there's a ranch house, some sort of shelter . . ."

He jabbed his thumb westward. "That way . . . maybe."

She reared up in alarm. "Don't you know?"

"I haven't been here for ten years"—he gently pressed her back down—"and I had other things on my mind." His lips grazed hers, teased down her throat. She tried to evade him. "Ramsey needs medical attention and decent food. We could wander for days if . . ."

He wound his hand into her hair and kissed her again, lingeringly, deeply. "He also needs rest. What difference will another hour make?"

What difference, indeed? her quickening pulse argued. Why not just lie back and rest?

Ramsey's eyes opened. "Give me . . . a drink," he mumbled.

Rafer sighed. "Give him water, Red."

"Whiskey," corrected Ramsey with a shadow of his old impatience. "I feel like hell."

His mood was little improved by two drinks neat and a three-hour ride through a blizzard that swept down on them. He insisted they were going in circles. In fevered delirium, he plunged off on his own route. Before he had gone a dozen feet, Rafer brought him back, cursing. Ramsey's imprecations had a hollow, feeble ring, but Suzanne, feeling like a frozen block in the saddle, had her own doubts.

Not quite half an hour later, they floundered upon the Mi Vida ranch house, a tumbledown, three-room shack that collected snow in its ruins. Feeling a sickening wave of fear, Suzanne said faintly, "What do we do now?"

"Burn the shack when the weather clears, and hope the fire draws attention. These ruins are several years old; a new ranch house may be nearby," replied Rafer with a carelessness she knew was feigned for her benefit. She had not forgotten the horrors and cannibalism endured by the Donner expedition.

The blizzard raged four days until they were virtually buried alive in their snow hut built against a ruined stone wall. Fantasies of warmth, food, and open spaces invaded their minds. Ramsey was deteriorating, his ill temper given way to torpor until his comparative peace was abruptly ended by Rafer's cauterizing his wounds. The scream that filled the hut pressed Suzanne against the ice wall in sickened pity, but he was better that night, less restless and feverish. By morning, he downed three strips of jerky with his customary sang-froid. By late afternoon, the blizzard ceased.

Rafer torched the ruined ranch house at nightfall. Less than an hour later, five riders caromed through the snow drifts. Rafer and Suzanne emerged from the hut to be confronted by rifle bores.

NINETEEN

Daniel In The Lion's Den

A premonition of impending evil crept down Rafer's spine, its serpentine, glassy chill trembling into an almost inaudible, ominous rattle. Like dark birds of prey, the men with the guns hovered about the edges of a malevolent, uncoiling dream. A dream blacker than the reality of the icy night. A slow progress into hell . . . only the hell had no name, offered no reason for his apprehensive, restless anticipation. He was doubly uneasy, having had no forewarning of the bear attack upon Ramsey. He had been preoccupied with Suzanne, his hatred of Ramsey, their perilous situation. Senses that should have been reaching out to his surroundings were blindly focused inward; as a result, Ramsey was mauled. The mistake must not be repeated. Never questioning how he heartshot the beast in the dark, Suzanne presumed he had been lucky: she was more correct than he liked to think. Now his entire being warned him of danger, and he did not know why.

He was not particularly alarmed by the armed riders. Brusquely irritated to be rousted out into the night cold to investigate a burning shack, once they realized the reason, their rifles returned to the scabbards and their manners emerged. Their courtesy was less due to the distressed plight of a beautiful woman and an injured old man than Rafer's mention of Ramsey.

"Ramsey Hoth," mused the foreman, Buck Wheeler, sitting back in his saddle. "He'd be that rich Easterner gallivanting through the Rockies, wouldn't he?"

"Himself," confirmed Rafer in his best Western drawl. "Had to pack him in ice after a run-in with a bear, but he'll keep better in a warm bed. You wouldn't be willing to extend the hospitality of Mi Vida, would you?" He gestured gallantly to Suzanne who stood tensely behind him. "His party includes Mrs. Hoth and myself."

Wheeler motioned a man to dismount and check the hut contents. The cowboy emerged with a nod. "The old coot's chewed up, all right, but he's got one feisty constitution. Says we're to take him to the boss man of Mi Vida and make it snappy."

Masking his wariness, Rafer shook his head with a rueful grin. "Manners and millions. I hope you won't be too offended if Mr. Hoth thanks you with hundred dollar gold pieces instead of handshakes; that grizzly bear kind of embarrassed him."

Wheeler grunted. "Mount Hoth up and tie him to the saddle. I don't want to be digging him out of the drifts every few feet."

On the ride to the ranch house, the windy cold was too sharp to encourage polite conversation, had anyone been inclined to pursue it. Suzanne was exhausted, while Ramsey needed all his strength to stay in the saddle. Turtled down into his sheepskin jacket, Rafer was preoccupied. With each floundering step of his horse through the drifts, he seemed to be moving toward a hideous, yet inescapable destiny; the Spanish called it *muerte*: Death . . . his own.

Festively decorated for Christmas, the huge log ranch house sprawled comfortably against a grove of blue spruce and aspens. The ranch house was an inviting, single-floored manor with two broad wings extending from a high-peaked central living area. Wide eaves supported by massive beams overhung green, shutter-trimmed windows decorated with pine garlands along a stone veranda. Heavy, scarlet-ribboned wreaths cheerily festooned great double entrance doors, which opened in a widening wedge of light as the riders swung down from their horses. Rafer helped Suzanne ease the heavily breathing Ramsey from the saddle. He slung Ramsey's arm over his shoulders as she supported Ramsey's other side.

He turned to encounter a huge figure outlined against the doorway's light as if it were a hellish sun. From the ranch house doors emerged Helmut Banner, his shadow stretching across the snow. Behind him was Bradford Hoth.

Only Ramsey's weight kept Rafer from going for his gun. He abruptly stiffened, Ramsey's shifting bulk making Suzanne stumble. "Dammit, stop jerking me around!" Ramsey swore. "I've had enough . . ." Then he saw Brad at the door. "Well, Merrrry Christmas," he breathed harshly. "We've run the damned prodigal to ground."

Suzanne's head shot up. Rafer heard the sharp intake of her breath; even in the jumble of his panic, he wondered what she was thinking.

Banner was within twelve feet of him now.

I'm dead, dead . . . if Banner doesn't know me, Brad Hoth will.

He had planned this moment for years, but not with his quarry being surrounded by gunmen. They were going to blow him into mincemeat and he had walked into them like a two year old.

He's looking right at me. I can take him . . . even if they kill me, I can take him.

He had a bright vision of Helmut Banner's forehead neatly drilled by his bullet. Fly to hell, you sonofabitch! He saw his own body shaking with laughter even as it was riddled by gunfire. I still win and you lose, Banner! He ached to draw, ached . . . then realized the strain upon his muscles did not issue wholly from his mind. Ramsey was dragging at him, awkwardly pulling him forward.

Behind Banner, Brad's eyes were as round as shiny marbles. He resembled a panicked boxer dog ready to bark.

Then Rafer registered that Brad was gaping at Ramsey and Suzanne. Banner, too, was inspecting Ramsey, the foreman beginning introductions. Rafer felt as if he were ascending to the treetops on ether. Neither Banner nor Brad recognized him! His breath exhalation blasted the inside of his muffler, belatedly reminding him the cloth was high across his face. With more luck than he could imagine, he might walk out of this mess to fight another day. Gingerly, he tickled Suzanne's neck. Startled, her head swivelled, drawing Ramsey's weary attention. "Your show," Rafer whispered. "You two do the honors."

Ramsey was glad to oblige. Rafer prayed he would not provoke Brad into giving away his identity; otherwise, he would provoke an unequal battle to rival the Sand Creek Massacre for Brad knew him as Kimberly Smith-Gordon. Plying her wits, Suzanne gave Ramsey the right cue. "Bradford, darling," she hailed her appalled husband, "you look wonderful! Dr. Holgarth was right to send you to Colorado. Your color is a credit to him!"

"Ah, well . . . fresh air, all that," croaked the confused Bradford, peering back furtively as if an evil genie had conjured her from the night. She must be distracting him so she could rip out his eyes when he least expected it.

Too incapacitated and sly to jump directly for his son's throat, Ramsey wearily addressed Banner. "Sir, I gather you have been kind enough to entertain my son, Bradford, these past months. As Mrs. Hoth and I have come a considerable distance to visit him, I hope you will forbear our arriving in such an awkward fashion. We lost our way in the snowstorm, you see. Our guide, Rafer Smith"—his head inclined ironically toward Rafer—"mistook the address."

"Our Brad Dillon is your son, Mr. Hoth?" Banner's surprise failed to register in his eyes as he turned to Brad, whose pallor rivalled the snow sifted on the veranda. "Well, well, we mustn't waste time on formalities with your father scarcely able to keep his feet, hey? Let's move into the house."

At Brad's vague step backward, Banner cocked his head quizzically. "I expect Mrs. Hoth could use a hand with your father."

The bald hint prodded Brad reluctantly forward. Clearly, he would sooner have approached a pair of starved tigers. Demurely, Suzanne stepped aside to allow Brad to assist

Rafer with Ramsey's weight. With a crocodilian grin, Ramsey gave Brad's neck a sharp squeeze. "I've missed you, boy," he rasped. "Been thinking about you every mile of the way from Chicago."

With a discreet grip on his hair, Suzanne tugged her unhappy husband's head down and gave him a passionate kiss. "I've missed you, too, darling." Then she wickedly purred into his ear, "I could just eat you alive."

Brad was spared the arctic expression in Rafer's blue eyes.

The girl who met them when they entered the house wore no expression at all. Dressed in a green velveteen dress belted in silver conchos, she was a Ute, but not entirely; Spanish blood softened her high-raked cheekbones, and lent her the slender regality of a *condesa*. Her dark-lashed, amber eyes radiated the intensity of a jaguar. Perhaps eighteen years old, she was very beautiful, but Rafer would not have bedded her for her weight in gold. She was the kind of woman who could make love to a man, then breakfast on his liver.

Ignoring the men, the girl gave Suzanne a quick rake of appraisal, which Suzanne as coolly returned. "My housekeeper, Inez Halfmoon," Banner said briefly, waving his foreman to lead them into the west wing. "Inez, we'll need oxtail soup from dinner . . . coffee . . . roast beef sandwiches." He never stopped moving, with scarcely a glance at the half-breed girl. His disregard suggested less indifference than a silent command to the rest of them. Do not look at her. She is part of my world, not yours.

Rafer was glad to abandon the bright foyer for the shadowed hallway. Banner was just behind him, his broad bulk spanning the narrow space. While he had put on weight since Rafer had seen him last, he was mostly muscle, his shoulders formidable. Same chestnut hair, going a little gray like a fox altering camouflage for winter. Same blunt featured, Nordic face, the florid jowls dropped to conceal the iron jaw; with deep-carved smile lines framing the hard, broad-lipped mouth. Same deceptively genial eyes that iced the hair on Rafer's neck. Those gray eyes had bored through his blood-clouded dreams for a decade.

Having Banner at his back was like anticipating a serrated

saw blade's rip into his spine. Snow powdered on his clothing was melting in the heat of the house. He was perspiring. Where was this damned bedroom, so he could dump Ramsey and get out! Once back on the range, he could bide his time, pick his moment. He would be free, like a hunting cougar, not caged, waiting to be skinned alive for bounty. He remembered . . . he remembered . . . The foreman swung the bedroom door open and he catapulted toward it. Ramsey went onto the bed in a sliding pile, tumbling Brad with him. Rafer pulled free, flinched as he brushed Suzanne. Her eyes widened slightly as they met his. *She knows. She sees I'm ready to explode. I've got to get out of here!*

Then abruptly, he realized the muffler had pulled away from his face when he dropped Ramsey on the bed. Having extricated himself from Ramsey, Brad was turning . . . looking full at him and seeing beyond his broken, battered face. Brad's eyes dilated, fixed like an animal waiting for a bullet. *And I'll give you one if you so much as squeak!* Rafer vowed fiercely.

Brad sagged back onto the bed, his face gray. Ramsey gave him an impatient shove. "Get up! You're sitting on my leg!"

Rafer's grip on Brad's forearm brought him up like a sharply released spring. "Sorry, my fault you lost your balance." Letting go of Brad's arm, he touched his hat. "If you folks don't mind," he muttered hoarsely, "I'll head to the bunkhouse. I'm petered out."

Suzanne and Ramsey quizzically eyed him. In his effort not to sound like the boy Banner might remember, Rafer's voice had lowered as if dragging a river bottom.

Fortunately, Ramsey was eager to have him out of the house. "Go right ahead, Rafer," he rasped, pushing up on the pillows. His eyes held a gleam of anticipated triumph and revenge. With his son back under his thumb, he was back on top of the game. Banner was his kind of man, his mature equal; not an upstart con artist flaunting mere youth and muscle. The chessboard was snowed in, nobody was going anywhere, and he was going to win.

Banner glanced at Rafer. "Buck, here, will see you to your quarters and have Cookie roust up some hot chow." Then his attention returned to Ramsey. "Get a good night's rest, Mr. Hoth. We'll palaver in the morning. Your son's quite a boy, you know. We've been mighty pleased to have him around."

The knot in Rafer's middle loosened as Banner continued to compliment Brad. Despite his direct gaze at his uncovered face, Banner had not known him. Banner was a good actor, but not good enough to conceal the shock of meeting a ghost like Jamie Carlisle.

Rafer walked from the room, passed the indifferent Inez Halfmoon in the hall, followed Buck Wheeler through the wreathed oak doors into the open air. Clean air filled his fear and hate-shrivelled lungs. Throwing back his head, he looked up at the stars. I am a ghost. They're all walking through me. Brad Hoth may see me, but dares not reveal what he sees. I can walk among them until Ramsey betrays me, and he will, when the pieces fit together . . . when it suits him.

"Mr. Wheeler," he murmured, "I need to take a whiz. If you'll just point out the bunkhouse, I'll be with you in a minute."

Wheeler jerked his thumb toward the long, snow-covered stone building flanking the corral west of the house. "You can't get lost. About fifty men to steer you back. Afraid you ain't got too much choice in bunks. We're nigh full up."

"Mi Vida must be a fair spread."

"Fair enough. Fifty thousand acres and whatever else Mr. Banner feels like squeezin' out of the Yampas. We got 3,000 head due up from Texas in the spring. Expect we'll expand a mite more." He shoved his mittened hands into his jacket pockets. "Well, don't freeze your pecker off."

Rafer watched Wheeler stride quickly toward the bunkhouse. The barn was too close to the bunkhouse for comfort, the house still lit like a Christmas tree. He might reach his horse after everyone was asleep, but there would be guards, particularly if Banner had been antagonizing the Yampas. Even if he got away, how far could he ride by morning in snow this deep? Ramsey might not betray him immediately, but Banner was a careful man. Taking off like a bat would provoke Banner into discovering why, and a manhunt in this weather put all the odds on Banner's side. Banner's men would have relief mounts, which meant he would have to steal one as well. If he had learned one harsh lesson, it was not to steal from Helmut Banner.

Under the stars, the snowy, rolling hills shone white as a desert: a desert where men died, some dully comprehending, some hideously aware and shrieking in agony. Banner's men. His father and brothers. Bodies twisted and picked by the vultures. Dragged by all the pursuing demons of his nightmares, his mind went back across the years. The horror had all begun with such treacherous, tantalizing simplicity.

His father had returned to camp one night with a broad grin that said they were not going to be living off rabbits and soda crackers for a while. Jane Mock, who ran the Steady Hand Saloon in Breckenridge had a friend with a leaky mouth; a friend named Helmut Banner with a leaky mouth like a steel trap. Years later, after considerable con practice, Rafer put the whole scam together. Jane was Banner's unsuspecting shill, and the mining shipment of gold bullion she described was bait. What better way for Banner to take the shipment himself than tempt incompetent thieves into stealing it? He merely needed to run down the thieves, retrieve the gold, pretend the thieves had escaped with it, and leave no witnesses to offer argument. Everything had run precisely to plan, with two hitches. Jack Carlisle was not an entire fool, and as stubborn as a Tennessee mule.

Rafer heard again the heavy, lumbering rattle of the bullion-laden wagon as they tried to fight it over Ten Mile Range out of Breckenridge. Assuming they would be unable to move the gold fast enough to escape, Banner meant to be right on their tails as soon as the shipment guards worked free of their bonds and reached town. Rafer heard again the squeals of the twenty waiting mules who greeted the hurried loading of the bullion to their backs. The race was on, all the way to Grand Junction with Banner and his men cursing behind them. The exhilarating chase deteriorated into a gruelling strain to stay alive. No matter how they dodged and connived, they were unable to hide a trail of twenty mules. Banner had a dozen men with him, three of them Ute scouts who could follow a trail through thin air. He came to curse the gold, curse his father, but the insanity could only end one way. If Helmut Banner underestimated his father, his father was equally wrong about Banner.

The Grand Mesa Desert was a cauldron of raging heat that sucked down sweaty horses, dying mules. Finally, they hid the gold in a jumble of boulders similar to a thousand others. Banner caught up to them near an arroyo that snaked west after a fork at a red sandstone bridge across an ancient, long-dry stream bed. The gunplay was vicious. Five men were dead by the time the Carlisle ammunition ran out. Will lay wounded with a bullet in his throat.

After that . . .

A retch tore at Rafer's empty stomach. Holding his head, he devoured the icy wind, let it pour into his lungs, freeze his mind. He had to forget . . . long enough to finish the job; otherwise, he would either make a mistake or go berserk.

Time was his enemy; not only the past, but the present Ramsey Hoth could snatch away by uttering a single name to Banner: Jamie Carlisle.

He must decide whether to go or stay, and whether to kill Ramsey Hoth.

Humming to himself, Helmut Banner strode along the west wing hall with a faint, pleased smile curving his lips. His plan was falling into place like clockwork. Ramsey Hoth had been delivered like a Christmas goose. The only thing he lacked to perfect the holiday was Jamie Carlisle served for plum pudding.

Stringing Brad along with an accounting job, Banner pried into his background when a pair of Pinkertons came to Sheriff Oliver Ingram in search of Bradford Hoth. Banner struck pay dirt. The president of Gilstrap and Mather was unwilling to supply information, but an ambitious vice-president leaked a story that could send Bradford to prison . . . and insure his father's support in a railroad venture. Freighting would eventually succumb to railroads, which promised to make his current fortune compare to an anthill.

Although vague about his father, Brad was less so about the swindler who sold him the Coco. Kimberly Smith-Gordon was a blue eyed, blonde Englishman about the same age Jamie Carlisle would be now. Jamie Carlisle had very possibly turned up at last, to remain tantalizingly beyond reach.

Banner shook his head as he continued along the hall. Jamie Carlisle had gotten away scot free with more than the secret of a fortune in stolen gold; he sure as hell was not going to turn up for Christmas. Banner's jaw tightened. After playing the hermit all these years for fear of Carlisle's giving him away, he would give five years of his life to get his hands on the sonofabitch!

Passing a window, he paused, distracted by a man's solitary figure near the *corrida*. Moving closer to the window, he blocked the light with his hands. Tall . . . buckskin breeches. Ramsey Hoth's guide. Rafer something . . . Smith . . . was looking toward the barn. Banner waited to see what he would do. Take a step in the wrong direction, my friend, and I'll find out why double quick.

Smith made a familiar movement, then turned back to the bunkhouse. Banner's lips curved slightly. He was taking a pee, that's all.

Ramsey's door closed and Banner's head turned as Suzanne and Bradford Hoth came toward him. Suzanne Hoth was tired and grubby, but even so, one beautiful woman. A man would need a firecracker in his hip pocket to leave behind a looker like Brad's wife. She had grit to dog him into the Rockies in winter and brains enough to extract him from an awkward situation by inferring he had come west for his health. She would be concerned for his health, all right. She'd probably like to poison him.

With Brad sheepishly trailing her, she advanced with the weary, disciplined smile of a woman who had seen more of life than she liked, but could bite its tail if necessary. She and Inez ought to get on like a pair of bitch bobcats.

"I want to thank you, Mr. Banner, for your hospitality," she said huskily. "Mr. Hoth is resting well, thanks to you. Your housekeeper predicts his wounds will mend with proper care."

"Inez is an accomplished doctor in her fashion. Mr. Hoth

is in good hands"—Banner's lips quirked—"provided he doesn't object to being treated by an Indian."

Stripping off her fur cap and shaking out her hair in a silky spill over her creamy sheepskin jacket, Suzanne regarded him with a quizzical smile. "You're not suggesting Miss Half-moon would greet a lack of chivalry with fatal retribution?"

"Inez is part of the family," Brad inserted curtly, "and dad can be deuced unpleasant when he's ill. She cannot be blamed for refusing him care if he insults her."

Suzanne turned on him. "Your father"—her tone was deceptively mild—"had his expedition broken up in Breck-enridge. He lost several horses and a wagonload of equipment to the Utes near Tysdale's post. A man was killed and we fled in fear of our lives." She looked back at Banner. "If Mr. Hoth should ever appear rude, I hope you will forgive him, sir. He has been under a considerable strain, and in some pain for several days."

"An encounter with a bear doesn't leave a man in the best of spirits," replied Banner in a kindly manner. "Inez may look like a chili pepper, but she's a tame Ute, like the rest of her tribe. She comes from a Yampa band near here. Never cause anybody a lick of trouble."

Brad's subdued expression warned Inez might not be so benign as she sounded.

"And now, Mrs. Hoth," continued Banner mildly, "you must want to retire after your arduous journey. Brad will show you to your room and I'll have Inez prepare a bath for you."

Brad started to say something, then catching Suzanne's eye, held his tongue. Her room would be his room.

Hey, nonny, nonny, what a fitting end to a beastly hon-eymoon. She had the bridegroom to herself at last, and was too tired to strangle him with a bellpull.

Smiling sweetly at Banner, she linked her arm through Brad's. "Thank you, Mr. Banner. You're very thoughtful. Brad has so often spoken of his admiration for you in his letters. I hope you'll forgive him for concealing his identity. He did not wish his family connections to prevent his being treated like the rest of your employees. Being 'one of the fellows' was very important to him.''

Banner amiably studied his protégé. "I didn't know you were such a diligent correspondent, Brad. Appears you've been a man of mystery in more than one way.''

Brad shifted uncomfortably. "I hope you understand, sir, that my deception was not ill meant.''

"Oh, I understand, son,'' drawled Banner. "No offense taken. You run along now. I expect you and Mrs. Hoth have a good deal to discuss.''

With mock adoration, Suzanne gazed up at her husband. "That we have.''

Brad smiled weakly as she steered him down the hall.

The bedroom door closed, shutting them in with their long-festering animosities. Behind her show of pleasantry, Suzanne was irritable; Brad's squirming made her more so. The cad was comfortably tucked away at Mi Vida, while she and Ramsey had battled snowstorms, wild beasts, and savage Indians . . . not to mention Rafer's Machiavellian maneuvers. Her underlying compassion and misgivings at provoking Brad's ruin were submerged in blistering fatigue and resentment. His every guilty flinch made her want to slap him silly. His only spark of spirit was shown in defense of the sullen housekeeper. She wagered that "chili" was not solely employed to ply a feather duster!

Suzanne tossed her cap and muffler on to the brass bed, then surveyed the handsome, timber-walled room with its Navaho rugs and Spanish furniture. "Well," she dryly observed, "the rat has found himself quite a cozy hole.''

"Look, Suzanne, I don't blame you for being angry . . .''

"How gracious of you. We're making a good start: everybody forgiving everybody.'' Ignoring him, she unbuttoned her jacket as she wandered about the room. "Yes, quite a cozy hole; but then"—she turned—"you always know a good thing when you see it.'' She flung the jacket in an elkhorn chair.

He came toward her, his hands extending in supplication. "You don't understand. Dad doesn't understand. I want to make it all up to you . . .''

"You can never make it all up to me, Brad," she replied curtly. "Not the humiliation, your cheap cowardice; not the last, hideous year."

"Believe me, I am sorry," he pleaded earnestly.

"Sorry?" Her temper rose. "I don't doubt you are! 'Sorry' ought to be carved on your gravestone! You are the sorriest example of a man I have ever encountered! You're a crawling cockroach!"

His own temper flared. "What do you think you are? I landed in this mess because I felt sorry for you, even fortunate to save the maiden fair. For once, I was going to do something right and live happily ever after!" His face flushed with self-disgust. "Talk about gravestones. I imagined you to be a flesh and blood woman, but you were a stone angel atop a cobwebby monument to snobbery."

They warmed to the fray, guilt and acrimony splattering off the timber walls. Time whipped by in a scarlet haze of battle until a rap at the door drew them up short, embarrassment draining the blood from their faces.

Brad opened the door a crack. He seemed confused, then murmured something to Inez outside, who announced adamantly, "*Senor* Banner asked me to bring *Senora* Hoth's bath; I have brought it."

"Very well"—Suzanne made a gesture of impatience—"I haven't had a bath since Breckenridge."

Reluctantly, Brad opened the door. Like a princess walking a dog only because she chose to do so, Inez strode into the room with five Mexican servants carrying buckets of steaming water and a copper hip bath. A child bore a tray of sandwiches and brandy. While the servants prepared the bath, Inez waited with the expression of a bored eagle. Suzanne was generally oblivious to servants, but Inez was difficult to ignore as the half-breed's dark eyes appraised her dirty, dishevelled appearance, the unmarred surface of the bed, and Brad's discomfort. Brad leaned against the dresser, his hands under his armpits like a sullen, apprehensive boy unable to escape a well-earned thrashing. When the servants were finished, Inez ushered them out, and imperiously closed the door.

Brad hurriedly straightened from the dresser. "You needn't

help Mrs. Hoth with her bath, Inez. I'm sure she can manage.."

"You will assist your wife?" Inez's sardonically arch tone suggested a hippopotamus might be more adept.

Suzanne was annoyed. Brad had no notion of how to handle servants; one could not expect an Indian to have the polish of a Mayfair maid, but she would not stand for rudeness. "Brad, I should like Miss Halfmoon's assistance, if you don't mind," she countermanded briskly, unfastening her skirt. "Your employer recommends you highly, Miss Halfmoon. I should not wish to miss the benefits of your expertise." Without more ado, she stripped. The first garment hit the floor like a flung gauntlet.

Brad swallowed, darted a nervous look at Inez. Her expression unchanged, she assisted Suzanne in removing her unbuttoned shirt, then negligently dropped it atop the skirt. Next followed petticoats, woolen stockings, long underwear. After the fury and pain of their argument, Suzanne enjoyed undressing in front of Brad, revelled in his discomforted surprise that the modest, naive bride deserted in New York now had the sang-froid of a demimondaine. Dirty as she was, she was beautiful. Let him look, she thought, stepping into the tub; let him see what he would never possess and degrade again. Even more proudly naked before another woman, she saw desire flicker in Brad's eyes as they roamed the slender curves of her figure.

But then, luxuriating in the hot water, she sensed Brad had changed. He was no longer the uncertain bridegroom who feverishly, clumsily bedded her in New York. Having exuded adoring infatuation on their wedding night, he now regarded her with the impersonal, fleeting lust of a stranger. If he had ever been in love with her, she perceived with dull shock, he was not now.

Suddenly, as Inez took up the soap and began to shampoo her hair, Suzanne's fatigue grew overwhelming. Having considered herself finally beyond illusions, she felt foolish, deflated, and disillusioned. What had she expected of Brad? Love? Repentance? A marriage in name only? A divorce? A reconciliation? After coming so far to find him, she was beginning to wonder why she had bothered.

I suppose . . . I wanted to find peace, she reflected tiredly as Inez rinsed her hair. Peace for Brad, peace for myself . . . yet peace seemed to be the most impossible illusion of all.

More peace than she imagined was a great deal nearer than she supposed.

Behind Suzanne's head, Inez was looking at the white curve of her throat with the appetite for a razor. Brad's body tensed, his eyes filled with warning as Inez's narrowed slightly. Her head lifting, she almost smiled at him; not a friendly smile, but a hard curve of contempt and cold fury. She wrapped a towel about Suzanne's head, then poured brandy into a glass and placed it on the portable table beside the bath. "Will you have something to eat now, Mrs. Hoth?"

"I should really prefer to sleep now." Water dripping down her body, she sat up, extending her hand for a towel.

As Inez did not move, Brad quickly handed the linen towel to Suzanne. "Your assistance will be no longer required tonight," he told Inez briefly. "You may go now." When she stared at him defiantly, he thrust the tray into her hands. "Thank you."

Inez appeared to consider hurling the tray at him, then something in his eyes made her think better of the idea. She shrugged, her temporary surrender promising a reckoning. "As you say."

Wrapping the towel about herself as Inez headed for the door, Suzanne rose from the tub. "Aren't you forgetting my clothes, Miss Halfmoon?"

"No," was the careless reply. "I will send Luis to burn them."

As the door closed, Suzanne arched a brow at her husband. "That's quite a lady. I'm rather surprised she allows you to keep your scalp."

"Inez would be far more likely to take your scalp than mine," Brad responded dryly. "She is accustomed to serving men . . . up to a point, but has never waited upon a woman in her life."

Suzanne blotted her skin. "Women never come here?"

"Not since Inez's arrival," he said flatly. "She's Helmut Banner's mistress."

Suzanne tucked the towel about herself. "How discreet of him."

He studied her. "You've hardened since I saw you last. The glow is off the rose."

She laughed ironically. "What did you expect? The rose bed hasn't been precisely thornless. Nothing is the matter with me that . . ."

"Money wouldn't cure?" he cut in swiftly, bitterly. "Well, I don't have any . . . at least, at the moment."

"Really?" she countered lazily, wrapping a second towel about her hair. "What happened to that gold claim you described in your letter, that is, the one before you purported to be dead? Keeping count of your fables might challenge the Brothers Grimm."

He leaned across the table. "I can pay you off: you and dad, if you help me make him see reason."

"Pay me off?" she purred. "Now why do that? You piled up this whole mess for me, didn't you? The lies, the embezzlement, the 'flit'?"

The freckles paled on his knuckles as he gripped the table. "If you didn't want money, why did you come here? You must want something. Revenge? A divorce?"

Her eyes evaded his. "We'll continue this discussion another time. I'm tired and going to bed."

He caught her shoulders as she turned toward the bed. "I must see dad in the morning. I need to know now, Suzanne!"

She thrust off his hands. "Don't push me, Bradford! I'm in a dangerous mood. Have your little chat with Ramsey, and then perhaps we'll talk." Her clefted jaw jutted. "Then again, perhaps we won't. All I've ever had from you is talk, Brad. Air." She threw the towel in his face. When he grabbed for her again, she caught up her sheepskin jacket, jerked her derringer from the pocket and levelled it at him. "You would be advised not to press your luck, Brad. You would also do well to see that I stay in excellent health and spirits because you need me very badly. Placating your father isn't the least of your problems.''

"Will you help me?" he asked breathlessly. "You won't be sorry; I promise."

Her lips curved in a small, bitter smile. "You made a similar promise the night you proposed . . . and 3,000 miles later, here we are." Uncocking the gun, she rested the barrel against her bare shoulder. "Now, I'm going to bed. The whole floor is yours."

She tumbled into bed, crammed the gun under the pillow before settling down, then in minutes, fell asleep.

I could kill her! Brad railed in silent anger. I could smother her, bash in her head with a fire iron while she sleeps, but she's off like a baby! His mind in turmoil, he gritted his teeth. I need strong women in my life like plague! I spent my first twenty-four years being bullied by my father and now . . .

He was trapped. Sixty miles of snowbound passes lay between him and escape. He might as well have been blocked in by stone. Even if he could run, flight would cost him his time and trouble invested in the Coco and Banner. He would lose a good deal more than the promise of a fortune. Curling up on the floor by the lowering fire, he morosely contemplated the fire irons.

TWENTY

The Mulberry Bush

Glaring dawn light awakened Suzanne. She squinted briefly at the open shutters, then at the patterned rug before the fireplace. The fire was out, the room cold, and Brad had already left. His absence left her unruffled. He must be as desperate to escape his predicament as a weasel gnawing a trap, but for once, he was stuck . . . and surrounded. His misery was only beginning; after her round with him, Ramsey and Rafer would take turns, then have a go again, around and around the mulberry bush, the monkeys gleefully outnumbering the weasel. In time, Brad might earn respite, but meanwhile, his tail would grow ragged, indeed. She pulled the covers over her head and went back to sleep.

Suzanne underestimated the number of monkeys after the weasel. Intent on recovering his credibility, Brad breakfasted as usual with Banner at dawn. Aside from revenge, his father and Suzanne must want the Coco claim. Certainly, Rafer Smith would not venture so far to recoup worthless claim shares. He must either expect blackmail money or claim profit. Brad had to persuade Banner to underwrite the mine development now; otherwise, the others would squeeze him out like a runt pig from the trough.

Apparently undisturbed by the prospect of uninvited guests sharing his house for several months, Banner genially waved away Brad's apologies. "I look forward to your father's acquaintance. He's a remarkable man, and I've heard he's accomplished a good deal in Chicago. Also, I'm flattered you took time from your wife to have a cup of coffee with me." He gave Brad's shoulder a roguish slap *en route* from the dining room. "I did expect you to have more appetite this morning. A beauty like Mrs. Hoth must be a hard lady to leave!"

Brad smiled weakly. "She is that, sir."

As Brad pushed his chair back, the servants' bell tinkled in the kitchen. Suzanne had shown no signs of stirring, so his father must be wanting breakfast. Brad's stomach knotted. He went to the kitchen to tell the cook, Maria, that his father would want ham, well-done eggs, and strong coffee. He was relieved Inez was not around; she must have answered his father's summons.

"Your father is a sick man. You sure he don't want porridge and custard?" Maria was asking him when Inez walked in on them. Planting her tray on the table, Inez surveyed him.

Aware of Inez's icy gaze, he assured Maria his father would

like what Helmut Banner would like. Maria glanced at Inez for affirmation, and Inez nodded. Maria cracked three eggs into the frying pan. The grease hissed as Inez turned her back on Brad and went to join Banner. Maria pursed her lips. "Inez is in a bad mood this morning. I hope she don't stuff a dead mouse into the Christmas turkey."

"Heaven forbid," murmured Brad devoutly.

When he carried the breakfast tray to his father, Ramsey was sitting up, his blunt bulk leaning precariously into space as he tried to peer under the bed. "Where's the damned slop jar?" he was muttering impatiently as Brad opened the door. Looking up, he grimaced. "I ought to feed that half-breed wench those eggs; they're probably laced with arsenic."

Subduing the urge to brain his father, Brad set the tray down with particular care. If he let Ramsey provoke him into a quarrel, he could not win it. He must humor the old tyrant if it killed him. "Good morning, dad. I hope you slept well," he said brightly, then to hide his patent hypocrisy, bent to pull the slop jar from under the bed.

When Ramsey faltered in attempting to rise, Brad supported his elbow, but Ramsey shook him off. "When I have to be propped to take a poop, you'll be up to your lily ass in grandchildren."

Brad forced a laugh. "I expect Suzanne will want some say about grandchildren . . . but I hope we can give you a great many."

"Oh, you'll give me grandchildren." Ramsey settled on the pot like a crocodile on warm mud. "You'll damned near have to."

"Then"—Brad uncomfortably averted his eyes from the antelope head mounted over the fireplace—"I take it you prefer that we . . . not be divorced."

Ramsey slanted a bloodshot eye at him. "You divorce her and you're done for, Mr. Slick. You'll be a damned pauper."

"Look, father"—Brad sat tentatively on the bed; towering over his father in such an intimate position made him feel awkward—"if you're thinking of disowning me, you have a perfect right, of course, but . . . Suzanne is extremely angry. She may divorce me. In any event, I can make up the

loss to Gilstrap and Mather if you just give me a little more
time.''

"Time?" snorted Ramsey. "You're up for twenty years
behind bars as it is." He voided explosively and held out his
hand for paper. "You got into this damned mess by yourself;
why should I help you out of it?''

Brad stoically handed him the paper. "If you've been
through Breckenridge, you must know I own a promising
mining claim; I wrote Suzanne about it.''

"Right before you drowned," sneered Ramsey. He threw
the soiled paper at Brad, who angrily ducked.

Fighting for control, Brad shot back the alibi shaped in the
middle of last night. "Who told you I died? Rafer Smith?
Surely you realize by now that the man lies like a dock rat.
He's a cheap swindler named Kimberly Smith-Gordon.''

Ramsey steadied himself on the bed. "What do you know
about Smith?''

At the eager tension in his father's voice, Brad sensed he
had struck a promising tack. "Why, he probably lured you
out here with some mad tale about being cheated out of the
Coco claim." He took a deep breath. "He must have discovered the real worth of the claim. The Coco will bring a
fortune, dad.''

Ramsey's currant-brown eyes were unnervingly bright.
"Let me get this straight. You're saying my guide is cooling
his heels in the bunkhouse in hope of getting a cut of your
mining claim.''

"Something like that," Brad replied carefully. "Who
knows his precise motives? He's as devious as an asp.''

"Yes," said Ramsey softly, "he certainly is." Then his
eyes narrowed shrewdly. "Not that you're a bastion of virtue.
Are you proposing to give me the Coco claim in return for
not tacking your hide to the fence?''

"I'm proposing we become partners, dad," Brad lied. "In
spring, we'll go to Breckenridge and make it legal." Come
spring, he prayed, Banner might stop blowing hot and cold
long enough to underwrite the Coco . . . but even if Banner
came around, how could he prevent Ramsey's taking the

whole claim? He disliked his father's maliciously speculative expression. He almost wished Ramsey would throw a fit of rage. When Ramsey controlled his temper, he was contemplating some scheme that promised ill.

"Hand me that breakfast tray," ordered Ramsey. He carved up an egg and devoured it, then swigged his coffee and peered sardonically at his son. "You think I'm rube enough to travel all this way just to buy some worthless gold claim? Try again, bub."

"It's not worthless!"

"It is, locked up in rock." Ramsey forked another bite of egg. "Besides, you don't own it." He grinned wickedly. "Your wife does."

Brad stared at him, then laughed harshly. "The hell she does! What has Suzanne to do with anything?"

"She had to do with Rafer Smith," purred Ramsey. "She did so well with Smith that he handed her the original and only valid deed to the claim sold him by James Carlisle. As you well know, all other shares, like the ones you hold, aren't worth a red cent."

"My wife slept with that chiseling boozer to get my mine?" Brad's eyes rounded with furious, disbelieving outrage. "I ought to beat her within an inch of her life!"

"I wouldn't try it, if I were you." Ramsey calmly buttered a slice of toast, bit into it, and added with his mouth full, "She'd make sausage out of your balls."

Scarcely hearing him, Brad stormed for a full five minutes with rising volume, then abruptly subsided as if unable to cope with the full damage to his honor. "Why come here," he gritted, "if you knew I had nothing worth trading to evade prison?"

"Well," replied Ramsey thoughtfully, "one reason was to see the look on your face you're wearing now. I expect to enjoy other fringe benefits."

"Including playing cat and mouse with me," retorted Brad curtly. "You smirk while I grovel."

"You've developed a streak of spirit and ingenuity since we last met," observed Ramsey judiciously. "Turned insolent as well as crooked. Doesn't pay to bite the hand that can rip out your gizzard." He plumped his pillows. "Mr. Banner appears prone to little homilies like that."

"Helmut is one of the most powerful men in Colorado," Brad snapped. "He controls governors and property larger than some states. Out here, he's the big bullfrog, dad, and he's your host, so I wouldn't make hasty judgments about him."

Ramsey pushed away his finished plate. "Found a new daddy who doesn't know what a bad boy you are?"

Brad's jaw tightened. "Do you mean to tell him?"

"Maybe. Maybe not." Ramsey's hand folded placidly over his stomach. "Supposing that blood is thicker than water, you'd do well to remember Banner isn't kissing kin. For that matter, you wife is a tad detached. Appears the only way you'll retrieve the Coco is to become a widower."

Brad gaped at him. "You're not suggesting . . ."

"I'm merely suggesting that you unalienate her affections. You've got four months to persuade her you aren't the shit you are." He stretched. "That shouldn't be so hard. Smith managed a similar challenge in four weeks."

He closed his eyes. "And now, if you don't mind, I'd like a bit more nap time. The old man isn't what he used to be."

The hell he isn't! thought Brad furiously . . . but he did not slam the door.

Three nights on the cold bedroom floor did little to improve his mood . . . and his private life. Slamming the ledger with resolution late one afternoon, he determined to find Inez— even if she came at him with a carving knife.

Surreptitiously, he dodged back to the kitchen; her red blanket was gone from the hook by the back door. He retrieved his own jacket, then making certain he was unobserved, slipped from the house and headed for the woods behind the house, his bootprints cutting deeply into the snow, angling away from Inez's smaller prints. Beneath the clear cobalt sky, the woods were silent, the aspens and ponderosa pines dripping with melting snow in silver blue pocks widening to the size of English pennies. Once concealed by the thick mass of trees, he followed the frozen stream bed where

Inez had crossed, and clambered up the bank, his feet slipping on the crumbling snow and dead cattails. After following her tracks for a quarter of an hour, he noticed they were winding in circles. She was vindictively playing with him. "Come out," he called hoarsely. "I want to talk to you."

The snow dripped; the aspen limbs sawed in the silent breeze.

"Inez, I know you're here. If you don't come out, I won't follow you again." He paused, his eyes narrowing as he scanned the dark, unmoving pines. "And I won't offer explanations . . . not ever." Snivelling would lose him the game for good . . . if he had not already lost it. Minutes passed. Finally, his throat tight, he turned away.

She came at him from the rear, all teeth and ripping claws, bowling him to the ground. He rolled, grabbing her hands before she could reach his eyes. The holly she had been gathering scattered on the ground, jabbing into his back. She swiped and his cheek stung. He wrenched her hand away, forced her over on her back, then straddled her, jamming her wrists into the snow. "Stop it!" he ordered sharply. "Stop it or I'll beat the hell out of you."

Her black eyes glaring up at him, she spat.

He shook her until her head rattled. "Listen to me! Did I say we would be married? Eh?" She started to spit at him again and this time, he slapped her. "You will not do that, woman. If you try it again, I will spit on you and your stupid jealousy."

"You did not tell me you had a wife, you pig," she snarled. "Dog of a liar! *Bastardo!*"

He spat on her, slowly, so that it made her wild. Then he held her down until she was exhausted from swearing and struggling.

She regarded him sullenly. "I am going to kill your horse, you pig."

He forcibly curbed his impulse to laugh. Ute women customarily did not attack faithless men, but their horses . . . also the rival woman.

"You will not touch my horse, Inez, and . . . for the time being, you will not touch my wife."

Her attention sharpened to an ironic pitch. "So, it's all right if I kill her later?"

Warily, he released her wrists. "Suzanne isn't my wife in any real sense. We married for convenience. Halfway through the wedding night, I left for Mexico."

Her eyes sparkled maliciously. "You seek a better pillow, eh?" She tried to thrust him off. "You do not look at her like you want to run to Mexico!"

"She is beautiful, no?" He pushed her down again. "A rattlesnake is beautiful, but you don't take it to your bed if you want to wake up in the morning. Suzanne and I hate each other. All she ever wanted from me was money."

Inez searched his face. "Is that why she is here? Because she wants your gold?"

"That, and revenge for my desertion. She was clever to ally with my father, who was furious at the scandal." Neglecting unflattering details was not precisely lying.

Inez toyed with the meaning of scandal, then grimaced with contempt. "You are right; it is all stupid. When Utes tire of being married, they stop living together. Why make such a fuss?" Her silky lashes lowered. "Let me up. You hurt me."

He eased his weight onto his arms. "Does that mean you forgive me?"

"Ask me again when your wife is gone."

His face lowered over hers. "That won't be for at least four months."

She awarded him a cool smile. "Until she is gone, Bradford. Gone to death; gone to divorce."

"But I love you!" He was growing desperate, and this time, was not lying.

"Yes," she said softly, "you love me. I will remember."

"Inez!" His fingers caught in her raven hair spilled on the snow. "Don't do this! You don't belong with Banner any more than I do with Suzanne. We should be together . . ."

"That is your decision," she intervened mildly. "You are the man."

Frustrated, Brad sat up and rubbed his forehead. She was right. He must make a choice: Suzanne or Inez, Inez or

Banner's friendship and all its possible profit. Banner had been kind; there was no man in the world he wanted less to betray.

He regarded her speculatively. "If I asked you to run away with me, would you do it?"

Her eyes veiled. "You have no right to ask such a thing."

He caressed her shoulder where the scarlet blanket had fallen away. "What would give me the right?"

"Why should I leave a strong man for a weak one?" she murmured. "Be strong, and we shall speak of rights. Prove you do not want your wife . . . and that you are fit to be my husband."

Brad was taken aback. He had never considered marriage. Mr. Bradford Hoth II of Lakeshore Drive, Chicago, weds Miss Inez Halfmoon of the Yampa Village on the Eagle River, Colorado Territory. As he searched for some evasion, Inez's eyes turned to ice.

Rising quickly, she brushed the snow from her skirts. "You are pitiful, Bradford," she said curtly. "I would sooner mate a dog."

He came to his feet and slapped her. She did not flinch, her steadfast eyes sealing the injustice. She left silently. Despite his shame, he did not apologize; she had no use for remorse.

Sick at heart, he headed toward the house, then saw something that made him sicker. Rafer Smith was leaning against a silver aspen trunk, casually whittling a minute heart into the bark with his bowie knife. Smith's grin and the sun's slant on the knife blade had the same glint. "Lovely girl, isn't she?"

"Who?" croaked Brad with desperate innocence. The trees prevented them from being seen from the house. If Smith meant to carve him up for the Mexican swindle, he had scant chance to escape being filleted.

Rafer flicked a bark scrap into the brush. "Your wife, of course. Who else?" His amusement acquired a more wolfish tilt. "A practical, if prideful woman, Mrs. Hoth. She will undoubtedly understand your easing the loneliness of your long separation by turning to the attractive Miss Halfmoon.

I daresay she might even find the prospect of an Indian rival beyond comprehension. She should have quite a chuckle with your employer over the whole minor affair.''

Brad's hands went clammy beneath his gloves. He was caught in a nightmare! "Look," he responded urgently, "I'll give your claim shares back, but I used up my money getting to Colorado. You must know the Coco is worthless without a major investment.''

"Couldn't say," replied Rafer easily. "I've never set foot on the property. That claim was sold to me by a fellow I rode with in Mexico until his fatal perforation by the Federales. In the good old U.S. of A., I'm just a guide by the name of Rafer Smith. You don't embarrass me, and I don't embarrass you.''

Brad's attention narrowed sharply. "You mean you don't want the Coco shares?''

"Would I have sold them to you if I did?''

"You sold the damned things nearly a dozen times!" protested Brad with a note of healthy indignation.

"That a fact?''

"Wait a minute," countered Brad suspiciously. "Using an alias proves you're in trouble with the law. You may have something on me, but I have something on you.''

"Perhaps. Perhaps I merely want to sell something." Rafer cocked his head. "Then again, your knowledge of the law may be more intimate than mine, considering the unpleasant difficulty in New York that banished you to Mexico." Placidly, he watched Brad's pallor heighten. He would love to know what Brad had done to turn so white. He shrugged. "However, if a trifling discretion on your part is too much to ask . . .''

"All right," Brad agreed sullenly.

Initials formed on the bark beneath the bowie's deftly applied tip. Rafer smiled amiably as the whittlings dropped into a gathering pile. "I'm glad we've come to a mutually satisfactory agreement, because at the slightest suggestion that your flaccid integrity is slipping, I might be tempted to kill you." With a flare of disgust, he noticed the lurch of Brad's

Adam's apple. That Suzanne was compelled to marry this weakling fool compounded his contempt. Rafer started for the bunkhouse.

"Wait," called Brad hoarsely, "what about my wife?"

Faintly surprised at his determined tone, Rafer halted. "You have nothing to say about her."

"She's too good for you and you know it!"

So, Ramscy had wasted no time setting them against one another over Suzanne. Grudgingly, Rafer conceded Brad a degree of spunk . . . only Brad with spunk might turn dangerous. Brad had fooled him in Mexico with his tame idiot act.

He strolled toward Brad and Brad backed . . . to fall over a fallen tree. Rafer gazed down at him. "Considering that your verdict is mutually accurate in respect to our tainted virtue," Rafer drawled, "but that you share the lady's bedroom while I reside in the tormented celibacy of the bunkhouse"—he kicked Brad swiftly in the balls—"a delicate discouragement to temptation may suffice to protect her from us both." He shook his head apologetically as Brad curled into a ball of agony. "Forgive my directness, but my beating your face flat might draw awkward attention to our differences. Mustn't mar the cheer of the holidays." He tipped his battered suede hat. "Merry Christmas, Mr. Hoth."

TWENTY-ONE

Winter Among The Wolves

"I think you should ask Mr. Banner to invite Rafer Smith to Christmas dinner," Suzanne suggested to Brad. Rafer's being banished like a lackey to the bunkhouse irked her. She

and Ramsey owed him their lives, and she owed him a great
deal more. She deplored Ramsey's spite, but now that Brad
knew about her affair, she would not play the hypocrite.

"The hell I'll invite him to dinner!" Brad exploded. "I
won't have your damned gigolo in the house!"

"The invitation would sound better from you," she returned imperturbably, "but I can ask him myself."

"By God, you have gall," he gritted. "You'd flaunt that
bastard before your father-in-law, your host . . ."

"And my exemplary husband? My dear, considering your
flawless behavior, I can not only flaunt my lover, but run
him up the mast." Affecting a mocking swing to her hips,
she strolled to their bedroom fireplace. "I needn't, of course.
If you are civilized, I shall be civilized . . . and so will Rafer.
He knows a finger bowl from a dog dish."

"So he ought. The dog dish is where he lapped up his
drinks in Mexican bars." He threw up his hands in exasperation. "For God's sake, Suzanne, we've been over this
ground enough. Aside from lechery, the only reason he beds
you is to irk me for outwitting him in Vera Cruz."

"You also robbed him."

"He was robbing me! He considered the Coco worthless!"

"Well, your comparative virtue paid off, didn't it? The
Coco is worth a great deal and you are married to its owner
. . . provided she doesn't show you the connubial door."
Her green eyes narrowed shrewdly. "Your customary greed-
iness wouldn't be the reason for these jealous fits, would it?"
Her lips curved wickedly. "Don't worry. We're happy
enough as we are. Under his rather remarkable tutelage, I've
taken to sin like a pig to mud."

He flushed, recalling her fear and his clumsiness on their
wedding night. "Look"—he pushed his hand through his
hair—"I don't blame you for provoking me; I can't say I
don't deserve it, but you're making a mistake by pressing
your affair at Mi Vida. Haven't you suffered enough embarrassment?"

Suzanne did feel a twinge of compunction. She and Ramsey
had batted Brad back and forth since their arrival, leaving
his nerves understandably frayed. Although nearly desperate

in his attempts to effect a reconciliation, he was undoubtedly thinking mostly of himself. "Why should I fall into line for your convenience, Brad? The newspapers crucified me when you ran off to Mexico, while your father merely sat back and enjoyed the show. He only joined forces with me when he feared you were dead."

"My father came West because he hoped I was dead, and he could get control of my claim," he retorted bitterly.

"I don't agree, Brad. He wants the mine, yes, and he's likely to use any means to get it, but he had no intention of coming West until he believed you might be alive."

Brad gazed bleakly toward the sun-glared window for a moment, then his face twisted. "He hates me. He blames me for my mother's death." He began to pace distractedly. "And now this . . . well, he won't get the Coco." His eyes filled with intensity. "You mustn't let him have it, Suzanne. No matter what. The claim is our only chance for freedom, yours and mine. That's what you want, isn't it? Money to return to the old life?"

"I'm not sure what I want anymore," she murmured, her face pensive. "I do want freedom, but the old life sometimes seems very far away."

"New York and Chicago are at the end of the earth," he asserted harshly. "That's where cities belong. I hate cities; their dirt and meanness. This is clean country, even when it's cruel." Brad hesitated, fearing he had revealed too much. If Suzanne got the idea he did not want to go back, and she did not care to stay out West . . .

"I know what you mean." Suzanne was looking into the fire as if seeing a thousand fires on a thousand nights of star-spangled mountains. "Colorado fills the heart with rock and sky." Her head inclined back. "For the rest of my life, I shall listen for the sound of coyotes in Connecticut."

Relaxing against the mantel, Brad recollected the first time they had talked together of the West back in New York for a handful of minutes that shut out the world for him. Suzanne had been so beautiful at the Astor ball on the eve of his proposal . . . but she was more beautiful now in a richer sense as if an amber glow hovered about her, a quiet strength.

"Do you remember our rainy Sunday rides?" he asked suddenly.

"Yes, of course."

"I didn't think you would, but they're why I wanted to marry you. I knew we could be happy given half a chance."

"Because of rainy Sundays?" she echoed softly, her eyes acquiring a startled, whimsical glow. "Not my venerable ancestors?"

"Well"—he hesitated—"those, too. I thought you very glamourous. A butcher's son has trouble being anyone but a butcher's son, even in his daydreams."

"What about your mother? Ramsey says she was lovely."

"Yes, and very nice, but not glamourous."

"Why does Ramsey believe you killed her?"

He considered how to relate Elizabeth's death in a way that would gain Suzanne's sympathy. For once, she did not appear to harbor the urge to throttle him when no one would notice. He must make the most of the moment. "Dad broke mother's heart, but he blamed me," he began heatedly, then noticed the jaundiced expression creeping into her eyes. "Dad neglected mother until she fell in love with another man. He got rid of him; I don't know how, but I suspect it was messy. Mother never got over it. She had a weak heart. After I visited her one weekend from school, she died and dad said it was my fault."

Suzanne was dubious. He looked too evasive and sounded too noble. Besides, Ramsey seemed to love his wife and Brad looked guilty. "I see." Her tone suggested she did not see.

"You don't believe me," he accused.

She rose from the chair. "You must settle with your father. What I believe is irrelevant."

"We need some foundation for trust if our marriage is to work." Brad's manner altered to wounded anger. "Or don't you care if it works? Do you plan to run off with that bar bum back to Mexico? You sure as hell can't display him in Connecticut."

"Why don't I go to the bunkhouse now, and ask Rafer where he would prefer to go?" Her hands squared on her hips. "Or shall I inform Banner that I should prefer a change of bed partners?"

Out in the barn, Rafer blew into his cupped hands to warm them. His misted breath floated briefly through the air, then disappeared. He could be blown out of existence just that easily if a wrong word detonated the right idea in Banner's head. Suzanne might reveal his identity by mistake; Brad was unreliable, and Ramsey would delight in his destruction upon realizing how to accomplish it. Hanging around Mi Vida made him as tense as a steel trap.

He worked the curry comb over Patch's hide. Activity burned off restlessness and made him fit in with Banner's ranch hands. A quarter of them were Texas gunslingers with pasts that banished them to the fringes of civilization. Defense was mandatory at Mi Vida. On the edge of nowhere, the Eagle Valley was surrounded by Indian tribes. Mi Vida was the only ranch within a hundred miles in a territory given to more speculation than settlement. Agriculture and cattle ranching were mere sprouts in the wilderness.

Why, besides Inez, had Banner settled so far from civilization? he wondered. Unless Banner was afraid of a boy named Jamie Carlisle showing up to expose him. Banner preferred the center of activity . . . but then again, he was also a mustang among saddle horses; in that respect, they were alike. Aside from the danger, Rafer was glad to be back in the White River country. The evergreen tang cleaned the barroom smoke from his lungs, cleared his head, and simplified his priorities to staying alive before and after killing Banner.

"That's quite a horse, Mr. Smith."

At Banner's amused voice behind him, Rafer whirled, his gun snaking out. Banner eyed him quizzically. "Sorry I startled you. I ought to know not to walk up on a man."

Banner was unarmed, but Buck Wheeler at his side was sporting a .45. Slowly reholstering his gun, Rafer slipped into his dumb cowpoke role. "No offense taken. Guess Mr. Hoth's tangle with that bear made me a tad spooky."

"You're a remarkable man, getting a pair of greenhorns through the mountains at this time of year," observed Banner with an admiring twinkle in his eyes. "Where do you hail from, Mr. Smith?"

"The Grand Tetons of Wyoming, Mr. Banner." He assumed a bashful grin. "But I can't take much credit for looking after Mr. Hoth and his daughter-in-law. They're not the usual tenderfeet."

Banner laughed. "No, I expect not." His gray eyes genially studied Rafer. "Still, Mrs. Hoth tells me you shot that bear."

Suzanne would turn him into a dead hero. "Just dumb luck, sir. It was pitch dark; Mr. Hoth was getting chewed, and Mrs. Hoth was yelling. I was too scared to run, and didn't know where the bear was, so I just started shooting and hoped I wouldn't hit Mr. Hoth." Rafer wagged his head sheepishly. "I'm sure glad your boys found us when they did. In another day or so, I'd have lost my fancy reputation."

"You're an honest man, Mr. Smith," Banner approved, "and I expect, a damned modest one. We're having a big turkey dinner at the house this afternoon around two o'clock. The Hoths and I would be mighty pleased if you'd join us."

Tiny, malevolent vultures seemed to dance on Rafer's neck. Was Banner on to him? The big German was entirely capable of killing a man over dinner with the pleasant smile he was wearing now. He was also capable of dispatching witnesses, but although no one beyond Mi Vida would be surprised by the Hoths' disappearance, Banner could not entirely trust his ranch hands' silence. This was a chance to get at Banner inside the house. "I thank you for your kindness, Mr. Banner." He beamed with the gratitude of a coyote at a chicken coop door. "I'll wash up and come around on the dot."

He did not turn his back until Banner and Wheeler left the barn. Then, the knot of apprehensive anticipation in his stomach was released by a coursing thrill of perverse pleasure. Whatever happened, he would also see Suzanne.

* * *

Suzanne greeted Rafer at the ranch house door. Hearing the others conversing around the parlor Christmas tree, he knew she must have been waiting to have a few moments alone. Her beauty struck him like a breathless blow, dazing his senses. She was wearing an ice-blue velvet dress trimmed with Alençon lace that Helmut must have obliged Inez to loan her. She was thinner than he remembered, the flawless bones of her face more evident, her eyes larger and lustrous with delight to see him. She had been through hell, but it suited her.

"I'm glad you came," she murmured as she helped him out of his sheepskin jacket. "I wasn't sure you would."

He handed her the jacket. "Did you put Banner up to inviting me?"

"Brad did"—the blue fires in her green eyes danced with mischief—"after I threatened to ask you myself. He expects to be banished to the kitchen while I entertain you in the bedroom."

He did not share her amusement. "You didn't waste much time hitting him over the head with being cuckolded, did you?"

She drew back. "Ramsey told him; I didn't."

"Well, don't push him. He's as nervous and unpredictable as a greased pig."

Stung by his curt tone, she hung his jacket on the brass hall tree. "Are we to spend Christmas day quarrelling over Brad? This week has been a strain on everyone and"—she gazed wistfully up at him—"I've missed you."

The openness in her eyes hurt him. How could he expect her to know what was happening? If he revealed he meant to kill Banner, she might inadvertently give him away; at the least, she would try to stop him. And if Banner found out about them, he might grow suspicious. If Banner assumed Suzanne knew too much . . .

"I've missed you, too," he said quietly. He silently gazed into her luminous green eyes, wondering how he could ever leave her. His hands almost shook with the need to touch her, to unpin that wealth of hair and let it fall down about them and shut out the world . . . Banner. He wanted to take her to the nearest bedroom and spill those gleaming pearls about her white throat down her soft flesh and bind her to him, about him so he could bury himself in her, hard, raw, and hurting for her like a mateless wolf. He could almost hear the snap of the trap; not just Banner's steel jaws, but the irrevocable snare of love. He had to escape that snare if it meant tearing the heart that yearned for it. "Is Brad sleeping in your bed?"

"No." She smiled faintly. "I'm afraid he may catch cold from the floor drafts."

"Afraid?" he echoed, with a prick of jealousy. "Then you do give a damn about him."

"Brad isn't a monster. He's just weak . . . an unhappy little boy."

"Then he needs a mother, not a wildcat like you."

"I don't need to be a wildcat now," she teased, touching the band of pearls about her throat. "I'm reverting into quite a tame tabby."

Rafer did not trust himself to respond. What would happen to her when he was gone? Her battles were not yet done. If she remained married to Brad, the sneaking sonofabitch would continue to hang around her neck like an albatross.

When he started toward the parlor, she caught his arm, hesitantly, for she was now uncertain of his mood.

"I have a gift for you," she said softly. "It isn't much, but Mr. Banner is teaching me to braid leather."

Reminding him of the stinging lash Banner had once used on him, the narrow hatband she pressed into his palm was as neatly knit as a slim snake and required all his force of will not to fling it away. A braided lash singeing down into his brain like a streak of fire, he carefully laid the hatband on the hall table. "Thank you. I'll pick it up when I leave."

The childlike expectancy drained from Suzanne's face as she preceded him into the parlor to conceal her disappointment. What had she done? she reproached herself. Clearly resentful of being here, Rafer did not want her gift. He must consider her a fool for placing him in the same company with Brad, only . . . she had to see him, know if she was still as crazily in love with him now that they were not caught up in an insane Odyssey. Mi Vida was the real world and she was married to a man who lived in it . . .

Suddenly, she felt Rafer's hands on her shoulders and he was thrusting her into a darkened doorway. His arms went hard around her and his mouth closed over hers, taking away all her breath and misgivings. She pressed against him, felt the quickness of his desire firing hers. His desperate grip was hurting her, and she wanted the pain. She wanted no part of Mi Vida's world; she was his, his! and he was making her know it as if he were branding her. Her heart pounded so that she could hardly hear him when at last he tore his lips from hers. "This is insane," he whispered harshly. "We have to end it, Su. We've come to the end of the journey, and you've found everything you meant to find."

I didn't mean to find love, she thought in panic. I didn't mean to lose you! "Rafer, you don't understand," she pleaded. "I don't want Brad, and he doesn't want me."

"He will," Rafer said harshly. "You'll make him." He thrust her away. "You'll be all right." He flicked the door open and went alone into the parlor.

For some minutes, Suzanne remained in darkness, gripping her sides, straining to hold back her pain. She had known Rafer would someday cut her adrift. She wished he had done so somewhere on the trail, some lonely, fitting place. Here, she felt cheapened, as if she had done something shamefully foolish. Neatly dressed people were singing Christmas carols in the next room! They would be shortly unfolding napkins for dinner.

She had come to the end of the journey.

Years later, Suzanne was to wonder how she ever endured that Christmas day: the false merriment, the pretense of civility by people who longed to fall upon one another like hyenas. Even Inez appeared to restrain some deep resentment. While Banner headed the scarlet-clothed dining table beneath the Spanish silver chandelier, Inez was seated as his hostess. In black taffeta and diamonds from San Francisco, she was more *soignée* than Suzanne, although her attire was suited to an evening affair and fairly screamed that she was being kept.

Rafer, too, was unusually quiet, which was a relief, given his yokelish behavior. He was a stranger, someone she had never seen before, who told silly jokes and forgot to use his napkin. He was drinking again. When Banner led the men into the library after dinner, she noticed through the open door that Rafer had several brandies.

She retired early, even before Rafer left. Brad kept cognac on the side table; she drank enough to drive away whatever dreams might come.

In the study, Rafer unfolded his long legs and pushed up from the sofa, grabbing the arm to steady himself. Pretending to have drunk more than he actually touched he laughed at the bemused expressions of the other men. "Sorry, too much cheer tonight. See myself out." He waved crookedly at Banner. "Many thanks, Mr. Banner, for your cordial hospitality. Have a good'un."

Banner shook his hand. "Merry Christmas, Mr. Smith. I hope we'll see more of you."

Fighting back his revulsion at Banner's touch, Rafer gave his hand a firm squeeze. "Well, I was thinking of maybe heading up to a line shack, if you don't mind." He borrowed Joe Cousins's excuse. "Seeing as I'm kinda fond of the bottle. I'd best be out of temptation's way."

"Of course, if you like," Banner responded, then deferred to Ramsey, "but of course, that's up to you, sir."

"Fine with me," replied Ramsey briefly. His eyes held Rafer's in puzzled relief mixed with suspicion.

Rafer knew Ramsey must wonder about a number of things. As Brad's reaction was only patent relief, Ramsey smiled faintly. "Expect we'll see you again by spring, Rafer."

"Expect you will." If things went wrong and Banner caught on to him, the line shack would give him room to maneuver and keep him away from Suzanne, for his remaining at Mi Vida might prove deadly for them both. "Good night, all," Rafer murmured, then with a nod to Brad, wove gently from the room.

"A very contradictory fellow," commented Banner. "One wonders how so apparently frail a vessel manages to be a successful guide."

"He's a short timer," replied Ramsey. "He does well within his limits, but beyond that . . . I had difficulty with him on the trail. He wasn't always reliable."

Despite Rafer's drunken display, Brad doubted his father's assessment. Suzanne would not choose another weakling for a lover. While he hoped to discover why Ramsey was lying, he was now more intent upon seeing Inez when Banner was occupied with his father. Quickly, he excused himself.

After searching the house, he concluded she had gone out, but as the snow was heavily tracked, he was unlikely to find her before Banner retired. Disappointed, he returned to his room, only to hesitate before the door. What if Rafer was with Suzanne? Anger galvanized him. Suzanne was still his wife; there were limits to the indignities he would endure!

He thrust open the door. Startled, Suzanne lifted her head from the pillow, the dim fireplace light revealing she was alone. Letting out his breath, he shut the door behind him. "Suzanne, do you mean to make me spend the next four months on the floor? I'm coming down with a head cold that I'll likely keep all winter at this rate. Cross my heart I won't touch you, but I need to sleep in a bed."

For a moment, nothing issued from the silence, then with a resigned sigh, Suzanne thumped the pillow. "So long as you stay on your side. Put so much as a toe on mine and I'll shoot it off."

After undressing, he climbed gingerly into bed. Aware she was not asleep and he was not the one keeping her awake, he needed some time to relax. Turning carefully on his side, he peered at her. Tear streaks glistened on her face.

"Stop staring at me like an owl," she growled, "unless you want to be stuffed with the contents of my whole damned pillowcase."

His eyes hurriedly closed.

Rafer slipped his knife from his sleeve, then eased the library door closed behind him. The firelight outlined the back of Banner's balding head, his languid reach for the ashtray, then filtered through cigar smoke above the chair.

Three long, silent steps put Rafer behind him. Cletis, the

big hound, lifted his head beside the fire, then hackles rising, advanced. Blanking his mind, Rafer let it sniff his leg, remembering the scraps he had slipped it beneath the dinner table. The hound took its time smelling his boots, then finally, with a dismissive tail flick, drifted back to its rug. Banner failed to notice, probably half asleep. In five minutes, Rafer would be back in the bunkhouse, with no one thinking anything of his stumbling to bed at this hour. For that matter, none of the hands carried watches. As far as anyone knew, he was asleep when the killing occurred, and had no motive. Revenge upon Banner would be simple.

And murder.

His hand tightened on the knife haft. One quick slice and one less monster would walk the earth . . . leaving another in its place. He had killed more often than he liked to remember, but never murdered anyone.

Perspiration tickled his left temple. Damn you, kill the sadistic butcher! This may be your only chance!

But his hard-core sense of justice rebelled. During the robbery, the chase, and its hideous finish, Banner held the upper hand. Now he would retain the upper hand in his execution. Little men killed big men in the back. He wanted to bring the sonofabitch down face to face. Jack, Will and Jody would want Banner to know who executed him, and why.

On the other hand, the odds disinclined Rafer toward nobility. Open conflict almost guaranteed his being dispatched with his victim.

Banner leaned forward to pick up his brandy glass. His breath catching in his throat, Rafer was torn between fear and craving of being discovered. Turn on me, he wanted to yell. Turn so I can kill you now!

Resettling in his chair, Banner resumed his smoking. When he rose to retire a quarter of an hour later, the library was empty except for himself.

When Banner reached his room, Inez was in bed, her breathing regular. He undressed by the guttering candlelight on the dresser, then crossed to the bed, his bare feet just missing the dampness spreading from Inez's wet moccasins

on the bedside rug. Sliding beneath the covers, he reached
for her.

Fifty yards from the house, an aged Indian with the gaping
fangs of a wolfskin shaman cap bared above his copper brow,
stood watching the light extinguish in Banner's window. Then
he silently retreated into the grove and disappeared among
the pines.

Rafer looked up from sketching as the light dimmed. The
early February twilight was already falling, a few icy pellets
pecking on the line shack's cracked window. The shack was
bitter cold, the wood supply low, giving him an excuse to
fetch coal in a few days. He scanned the pencil-drawn map;
it looked good enough to persuade Bradford Hoth he would
be a rich man. Hearing bridle bits jingle as his two shackmates
returned from their tour of the ranch's west sector, he tucked
the paper into his shirt pocket, then put his feet up on the
table as if he had been asleep in his chair. Short, bandy-
legged Moe came through the door, sweeping his snow-covered hat off his carrot-red head. "Nasty out there," he
wheezed, steam clouding about his short whiskers. "You
were lucky to be inside today." Then he grinned. "Going
to be worse tomorrow when your turn's up."

Rafer smiled drowsily. "Think it'll be too bad to touch
Cookie for coal at the ranch house?"

Tall, lanky Cap barrelled in behind Moe and gratefully
slammed the door. Snow powdering off his worn Union military cape, he fiercely rubbed his hands. "Coal? Mister, you
can bring us a whole barrel of fixings. Tell old Maria I want
a cake. Chocolate."

"And some cans of peaches," chimed in Moe eagerly.
"Smoked trout and . . ."

"Tell you what," drawled Rafer. "You boys fix me up a
nice travois and I'll bring you all it will haul." He grinned
slyly. "If one of you took a day off and loaned me his horse,
I could haul back two travois."

Cap sobered. "Mr. Banner might not like that. He knows
every horse on the ranch. He don't pay us to slack off."

Rafer shrugged. "I can tie the nag in the grove with nobody
the wiser, but it's up to you."

Cap considered. "All right, but don't forget that cake."
"Cap, if Maria's not in the mood, I'll make it myself."

Nearly frozen to the bone, Rafer entered the ranch house kitchen as the mestizo cook and Maria scrubbed the lunch dishes. Over the clink of plates, a piano sounded distantly from the parlor . . . *Schubert's Ode to Spring.* Unless Brad was musically inclined, the pianist must be Suzanne. His chest muscles compressed. A vision of her sitting tranquilly in a silk day dress at the keyboard hung clearly in his mind. He could see the soft tendrils escaping the upswept hair on her ivory neck, the delicate, vulnerable curves of her ears. He could smell her subtle perfume and a faint cedar scent lingering about her dress; he imagined it to be yellow . . . gay, as the halfhearted music issuing from the piano was not. He needed all his restraint not to head for the parlor.

Cookie glanced up from the dishes. "You must be one cold potato today," he observed, blotting his hands on his apron. "You got a list for me?"

Rafer handed him the list, not the one Moe and Cap had given him, but including their fondest wishes. Cookie scanned the hurried scrawl. "Don't know if we can spare this much canned stuff. Got plenty of the dried meat, though. I'm surprised you don't want some fresh steaks."

Rafer pulled off his gloves. "Just didn't think of it. Throw in a few along with the jerky and we'll all kiss your feet."

The mestizo laughed. "Nah, they stink. Have a seat and Maria will give you coffee while I pull this stuff together. That chocolate cake must be for Moe; that'll take some time."

"No hurry," drawled Rafer. "Oh"—he suddenly dug into his pocket as if just remembering—"I found this penknife in the barn on Christmas Eve. I think it belongs to Bradford Hoth, but I forgot to give it to him." He smiled up at Maria as she handed him his coffee. "Would you mind asking Mr. Hoth back to the kitchen so I can return it?"

"Of course, *senor*." She padded from the kitchen to deliver the message. Minutes later, the continuing piano music told him he was listening to Suzanne.

Following Maria through the kitchen door, Brad greeted Rafer warily.

"Care to take a walk with me, Mr. Hoth?" suggested Rafer. "You look pale from all that ledger work."

Brad flicked a glance at the falling snow. "Why not join me in the library?"

"Well, truth to tell, my joints creak from my ride. If you don't mind, I'd like to walk the kinks out."

Brad sighed inwardly. Whatever kinks existed lay in Rafer's devious mind. If Rafer cherished any notions about kicking him in the balls again, he would find a derringer pasted to his teeth.

"All right," he said sharply when they were outside, "I know I lost that knife in the grove when I was with Inez. What do you want this time?"

"To offer a proposition: more exactly, a trade," replied Rafer easily. "I want your wife, and you want to be rich; I think that might be directly managed."

Brad cast a scornful look at Rafer's worn duster and chaps. "You haven't got two dimes to rub together. Why would Suzanne want you?"

"That's my problem; yours is how to make Banner excited enough to bankroll your mining claim . . . or should I say your wife's. Suzanne wants nothing to do with you, least of all to share her claim." Rafer tilted his hat back slightly to impart an ingenuous air. "After that, you've got another problem: your father. With all respect, that sly old vulture is going to pick your bones clean. Even if you get a handle on Banner and Suzanne, Ramsey has a handle on you. Add up all your troubles and you may as well kiss off that claim and set your sights on higher stakes in a game where he isn't holding a winning hand."

"Such as," Brad cut back sarcastically.

"Liquid assets—$200,000 worth. Five days ride away." He blew a perfect mist ring through the frigid air. "For that kind of money, Inez might be tempted to tag along. Big warriors make big coups."

Brad laughed shortly. "Big suckers fall for the same line twice."

"The Coco was real, wasn't it?" Rafer blew another ring. "The $200,000 comes from the same source."

Brad mulled over that possibility. "The friend of yours who was killed in Mexico? What was he doing in Mexico if he had $200,000 cash stashed in Colorado?"

"Two hundred thousand dollars in gold bullion, not cash. Gold's difficult to carry on the lam. He stole it, you see."

Brad was silent for some time. "Why tell me all this?" he demanded finally. "Why not go for the gold yourself?"

"Because I can't have both the gold and Suzanne. If you go, and take Inez with you, your horrified wife will rejoice to see the last of you and marry me. Your father has nothing on me, and I'm an expert at spending a woman's money without annoying her. Besides"—Rafer looked at him levelly—"I care for Suzanne. The money is merely icing on her delectability . . . and I expect 20 percent of the $200,000. A finder's fee, so to speak."

"You imagine I'm going to turn Suzanne over to a lowlife rum pot with the morals of an iguana?" Brad fanned his hand in revulsion. "I don't know how you managed to seduce her, but despite her apparently hard exterior, she's a brave, cultivated lady, and has suffered enough trouble without having to suffer you."

Rafer appraised his vehemence, then gave a sober nod. "Good show, old man. I perceive a streak of moral fiber left in your wavering spine, which I am very glad to see, for I've been sorely tempted to relieve Su of your debilitating presence. She is a lady, and I intend to treat her like one; I do know how, better than you suspect . . . and I won't drop her in some future wayside ditch unless she so requests." His blue eyes glinted shrewdly. "I don't drink all the time, amigo."

Brad eyed him. "No, I suspect you don't. You put on quite an act; I'm beginning to wonder why."

"Staple of the trade." Rafer grinned. "I fear I shall have to go legit once the connubial knot is tied."

"You think Suzanne would marry you?"

"Perhaps not. Without my 20 percent in my pockets, I don't propose to ask her. No dignity in poverty . . . but I expect you've found that out." He drew the map from his pocket. "Meanwhile, consider this wondrous token and reflect that it may be writ in letters of gold." Wafting the map from Brad's reach, he retucked it into his pocket. "Should you wish to reconsider your disinterest, let me know; otherwise, I shall go after the bullion alone in the spring."

"How would you be sure of getting your 20 percent if I went after the gold with Incz?"

"Oh, I mean to come along." Rafer smiled wolfishly. "I wouldn't dream of letting you outwit me twice."

Rafer left without seeing Suzanne. The horizon never looked lonelier than when he set out with his travois. A mile from the line shack, he buried the jerky and dried fruit he had privately added to Cookie's list, and cairned it with rocks and dry straw. Then, he took Cap his chocolate cake.

TWENTY-TWO

The Ferret

Brad was a haunted man the whole of snowbound February. Had he read Hamlet in school instead of punting on the Charles River, he would have recognized classic indecision. Running away with Inez would precipitate a divorce, Banner's unending animosity, end his claim to the Coco, all quite possibly for a nonexistent cache of gold. He would be up the creek without a paddle . . . but he would have Inez. Her withdrawal gnawed terribly at him. Where her dark eyes saw into his soul, they now looked through him, past him as if he were hollow. I was a hollow man before I came here! he wanted to cry out to her. I'm different now!

Only he was not different, not when mere sight of his father tied his belly into knots, not when he was willing to spend the rest of his life with a wife who considered him contemptible. Rafer was right; he might control Suzanne one day, but Ramsey would always control him.

Morosely, he noticed his pen leaking ink on the ledger page, jabbed it back into the inkwell, and stood up. Trying to talk to Inez availed nothing, while Suzanne merely tolerated him. If he meant to make a change for the better, he must discover where he stood, and face his responsibilities; also face down his father.

Ramsey, sitting before his bedroom fire with a copy of Aristophanes' plays on his knee, brandished the book as Bradford came into the room. "You know, I never had much time for this stuff before; it's damned good. The Greeks made the same jokes and mistakes we make today." Elated at his near recovery, he chuckled. "Guess I owe that grizzly bear one."

Well aware of his father's self-read education, Brad sidestepped his pretense of ignorance; Ramsey often used it to disarm an adversary, and their entire relationship had been adversarial. He closed the door. "Dad, do you intend me to run the Coco?"

Ramsey settled back into his maroon rocker. "The Coco belongs to your wife."

"You'll find some way of prying it from her, even if she technically retains ownership." He crossed the room to stand over his father: a rare opportunity as a desk generally separated them. "Do you mean to control the mining development through me?"

"I expect so," replied Ramsey mildly.

"How much say would I have?"

"Not much, but then you don't know much."

"So I'm to be the pygmy, as always."

Ramsey shrugged. "If the shoe fits . . ."

"You hate me, don't you? When I was little, you ignored me, but when mother died, you really hated me."

"You always snivelled, and you're doing it now. I hate snivelling." Ramsey's lips drew back slightly. "Your snivelling killed your mother."

"That isn't true!" Brad retorted hotly. "You killed her, but always tried to push it off on me."

"You told a woman with a weak heart that instead of claiming your inheritance, you wanted to sortie off to India, turn Buddhist, and scull with your tea-assed friends on the Ganges. You informed her that you didn't mean to graduate, having cheated through your courses to cover your laziness and stupidity."

"I wasn't lazy and stupid! I could have passed without cheating."

"Bullcrap."

Brad's weight surged to his toes. "I had no reason to pass! Where would graduation have gotten me but further under your thumb? You have to control everything you touch, just as you did mother . . . and when you lost control of her, you drove her to her death. You gave her the weak heart, not me! You wore her down year after year until she couldn't bear the death of a butterfly. Did you want me to leave without telling her? Without saying goodbye?"

"You could have done your wizened duty by staying!" Ramsey bellowed. "She wouldn't have lived much longer. You could have lasted a year or two. Was that too much to ask?"

"Yes! I was strangling! And if your grip tightened, I would never have escaped. I wanted to go to India to find out who I was. To see if there might not be something beyond your hallowed religion of 'Gimmeee'!"

Ramsey leaned forward. "Well, 'Gimmeee' paid for your fancy ideas, boy. A pauper has no time for esoterics." He smacked his stomach. "This, this has to be kept full, boy, before the brain can produce anything but a groan."

"I embezzled that bank money and married a Maintree to prove myself to you, but even if I'd turned the money into a fortune with nobody the wiser, and Suzanne adored me, you still wouldn't be satisfied. In fact, you'd have been furious. Cheated of your vindictive revenge. That's why you're here now . . . not because you care about me. You want to smash what's left." Brad glared down at his father. "Well, keep the Coco and be damned! You deserve a gold-lined coffin!"

As the door slammed, choler mounted in Ramsey's face,

then shook him. He grabbed for his cane, but his fingers began to shake with unbearable tension as if his whole body were being squeezed, his bones crushed. His mouth opened in a silent scream. This is it! he thought in panic. I'm dying! His skull was jabbed by burning needles. Then the seizure passed, and he dropped back in the chair, his chest heaving to gulp in air. Life. Damn Brad. Damn him to hell.

Brad waited with Inez in the grass near the evergreen-banded river. They had crouched there for some time waiting for the wily ptarmigan. His knees ached, but he had no notion of complaint. He had missed Inez too badly to risk offense. Against a windless blue sky, the tall grass glittered with early morning frost above snow, silent as a waiting heaven. I should die happy now, he thought, gazing at his love's chiselled profile. If she killed me now, among these reeds, I should look at all her colors against this wide sky and be glad they were all I should ever see.

Inez looked around at his shining eyes with her enigmatic smile.

By mid-March, Inez knew all she needed about Brad, the most important being that he loved her. After a first show of reluctance to hunt with him as Banner had suggested, she won him to her step by step, and now all that remained was to make him irrevocably hers.

Each clear morning, they left at dawn when Suzanne was asleep, but in any event, she did not question Brad's explanation of hunting with an Indian guide. She certainly did not imagine his guide was Inez. As Helmut did not enlighten her, and Inez was commonly not to be seen about the house until dinner time, the forays continued undisturbed.

Inez relentlessly drilled Brad with a bow and arrow until he could bring down small game. Graduation would be a deer. His elation in her confidence faded to dismay upon learning he must do so by himself. His lessons were done.

For two weeks, Brad floundered through the drifted forests in pursuit of his prey. His manhood on the line, he grew nearly wild with frustrated disappointment. At length, he ceased coming home, but spent his nights in clumsily dug snow huts. Nearly frozen and hungry for days at a time, he began to understand why Suzanne and Ramsey so detested him.

One twilight, as he waited behind some elderberry bushes where deer tracks were frozen in the river mud, a stag appeared with velvet ragging from its antlers. The stag poised against the skyline, its nose lifted to test the breeze, then moved gingerly down to the water, and lowered its head to drink. With his heart hammering against his ribs, Brad raised his bow with stiff fingers and took aim.

That night, when he travoised the stag to the ranch house steps and saw the look on his father's face, on Suzanne's, and Helmut's, was the proudest moment of his life. By the bloody wool bandages on his fingers; his gaunt, bewhiskered face, they knew what he had done. His bow was strung across the saddlehorn. Some of the ranch hands drifted over to grin in approval. Whistles shrilled. "Our tenderfoot's done got himself a buck with his damned toy slingshot," they joshed.

Helmut ran his hand along a six point antler. "You've done all right, boy." Surprise lingered in his eyes.

His father grunted. "Took you long enough." Clamping down on his cigar, he went back into the house.

"Congratulations, Brad," Suzanne said quickly in an attempt to cover Ramsey's rudeness, and he saw she meant it, but her relieved admiration did not make up for Inez's absence.

He hauled the stag around to the kitchen door, but refused to let the cooks unload it. "Tell Inez to come and see it," he told Maria.

"Inez is not here," she said. "She went out a little while after dinner."

Not caring who might put two and two together, he went after Inez. She found him. "I heard the cheering," she said, emerging from the grove before he crossed the clearing.

"I got a stag." He looked down at her small ramrod figure. "You weren't there."

"Show me," she said softly.

He showed her. She silently surveyed the big, limp-headed

carcass, then nodded. "It is well." Her silky lashes swept up. "Ute warriors must prove their hunting skills before they claim a woman." Then she walked away into the house.

Brad lay awake beside Suzanne that night. Suzanne's hand was outflung, so near him she must be asleep. He slipped out of bed and pulled on his breeches, then crept from the room. Helmut's bedroom was opposite Ramsey's at the end of the hall, while Inez's bedroom was decorously located midway; her door was unlocked. In a heartbeat, Brad was inside the room.

"Always you have asked if you might come to me," she murmured from the darkness. "Tonight, you did not ask."

"Tonight, I did not need to ask," he replied quietly. The dark curve of her head was barely outlined on the white, moonlit pillow. "I have proven myself to you."

When he touched her hair, she caressed his hand. "What you have done, you have done for yourself. I needed no proof of your prowess; you did."

"I have decided to tell Helmut about us, Inez; it's the only honorable thing to do. He'll be hurt, but I think he will understand." He sat on the bed and kissed the back of her hand. "I want to marry you, if you'll have me." Almost as he spoke the words, they congealed in his throat. Her palm had stiffened with the urge to push him away.

"Say nothing to Helmut," she said tersely. "He will understand only that he has been humiliated and cheated. As for marriage"—her voice softened—"do you understand what marriage outside your race will mean?"

"I've learned things worth having don't always come easily. I don't want a life without you." He was silent for a moment, then said slowly, "I gather you don't want me."

"We will be together. Soon."

"But how?" he protested. "We can neither live in your world or in mine. Wherever we go, will require a good deal of money. I don't want to live as either a clerk or a cheat."

She smiled. "Do not worry. If you really wish to be with me, you will think of a way."

He moodily stared out at the bleak, snow-swept terrain, then his head lifted slightly. "There is one possibility, but it's probably not worth a damn." He described Rafer's gold bullion proposition.

Inez slowly sat up, her hair falling in a satin sheet about her bare shoulders. "This Rafer Smith," she murmured with a note of intensity, "would be about the right age."

"The right age for what?"

"He may be a liar, but he does not lie this time; gold from such a robbery is hidden in Grand Mesa." She leaned forward, her eyes filling with light. "He says he has a map?"

Brad nodded.

"Have him to bring it to you."

"He refuses to let me see the map until we're on the trail."

"Then you must somehow steal it just long enough for me to see it." She eyed him quizzically. "Why did he tell you about the gold in the first place?"

"He wants Suzanne," Brad said briefly.

For the first time since he had known her, Inez laughed.

At twilight, Inez waited in the grove. Just as the last mauve light faded, the gray figure of an old Ute shambled from the aspens, an antelope-horned wolfskin shrouding his head. He carried a gallon tin, punctured with air holes. From beneath the cover came an agitated scratching. "You found what I asked?" she questioned urgently.

With a nod, the shaman handed her the basket. "You have five days."

"You have done well, uncle," she breathed. "Where is the cage?"

"Below the willow stand. I have covered it with leaves and snow."

Followed by the shaman, Inez carried the tin to the scrap metal cage, carefully freed the can's contents, and hastily slammed the cage door. A small furry body hurtled against the bars with a manic chittering that chilled her blood. The old man shrank from the cage. Behind the bars raved a rabid ferret.

That night, Suzanne discovered Brad missing from their bed again. Determined to discover why he was so often gone of late, she slipped into a cashmere wrapper, and headed silently toward Ramsey's room. From behind Ramsey's door came only familiar snoring. Helmut's door evinced nothing. The next two rooms were empty, which left only Inez's room in this wing. Inez must be with Helmut . . .

But what if she was not?

Suzanne halted *en route* to her bedroom, then slowly turned back to Inez's door. From the other side came low murmurs, then soft footsteps. With horrid fascination, she stared at the turning doorknob. Brad opened the door with Inez behind him, her hand on his shoulder. They froze at Suzanne's appalled face.

Suzanne bolted back to her own room. She was unable to breathe. Her hands went to her head to fight back the unbearable, pounding pressure mounting in her temples. I hate him! she screamed silently. The vile, sneaking cheat!

Inez caught Brad's arm as he started after Suzanne. "Silence her before she raises a hue and cry," she said harshly, "Helmut Banner must not hear of this."

Even in Brad's agitation, he caught an unfamiliar note in Inez's voice. She used Banner's name as if he were a stranger . . . as if she were terrified. Propelled by her desperation, Brad hurried after Suzanne. As he swiftly closed the door, Suzanne flew at him with fists flying. He caught her hands. "What did you expect?" he hissed. "You didn't want me! You've spent months mooning about a man who repels me as much as Inez must you!"

Her face white, she stared at him, her hands suspended as if she suddenly did not know what to do with them.

"Well?" he whispered angrily. "Did you even care where I was these last weeks while hunting? Who I was with? As long as I showed up now and again to demonstrate that I hadn't escaped my cage, did you once wonder whether I was alive or dead?"

"I wondered," she replied huskily, "but somehow, I thought you'd survive, just as I did all those frozen miles after Georgetown." Her hands dropped as if collapsed by exhaustion. "I want a divorce," she said dully. "I won't carry on this pathetic charade for the rest of our lives. If you leave quietly, I'll cede you a 10 percent share of the mine free and clear, but nothing more. Ten percent is not enough for your father to manipulate, as I do not propose to sell him more than 30 percent. You will certainly never control my portion as my husband.''

''You appear to have given this ultimatum some consideration,'' he replied. ''Why grant me anything? You can cite me for adultery, unless you don't want my correspondence with an Indian made public.''

''That's part of it, and yes, I have given my decision a great deal of thought.'' She dropped wearily into a chair, the wrapper falling slack. ''Perhaps I also feel you deserve something.''

''What?'' He laughed ironically. ''Why so suddenly turn charitable when you've dragged me through the coals?'' His tone altered slightly. ''Not that I didn't deserve retribution to some extent, but . . .''

''You deserved it royally.'' Her head lifted. ''But at least, I know now why you did it. You never really loved me, did you? I was a collector's item, something to impress your father. You meant to defy him, make a great deal of money, and take a fashionable wife, then spread it all before him like a grand, Persian carpet. When your plan failed, you couldn't face him. You ran more from Ramsey than the police, didn't you? You also ran from me.''

Leaning against the door, he scrutinized her intently. Finally, the lines along his mouth softened. ''You're mostly right, but you weren't merely a collector's item. At the time, I was convinced I . . . loved you. You were an impossible dream made possible. I wanted to help you, and help your father because I knew him to be a good man . . . far better than my father . . . far better than me. I hoped I might grow into a good man by marrying you. All I had to do was make you happy. Somehow, I thought in the end, I would win my father's respect.'' His lips twisted. ''The grand illusion.''

''Do you love . . . that girl?'' Suzanne forced a rephrase. ''Inez?''

"Yes," he replied quietly. "I love her. She taught me to be a man, if not a good one, then at least one with self-respect."

"Does she love you?" Suzanne asked softly.

"I think so. I don't know why, but there it is." His steady eyes relayed none of their usual facile charm. "I'm proud of her loving me. She's a remarkable woman."

"I'm sure she is," Suzanne replied grudgingly. Honestly.

He smiled. "You're remarkable yourself; even my father is forced to admit it, and that's a concession I doubt he would make to any woman other than Catherine the Great. I think if I hadn't met you first, he might have married you."

On that precarious note, Suzanne decided to end their discussion. "Then you'll give me a divorce?"

"At no charge. A mere 10 percent of the Coco will do nicely."

"Make it 15 percent. You did try to bail me out when I had my back to the wall in New York." She rose from the chair and shook his hand. "Friends?"

"Friends."

"Good," she replied briskly. "Now you can either sleep on the floor or with your lady."

He flushed slightly. "I'll take the floor, but I had better wish her good night."

"A wise precaution; otherwise, both of our scalps may dangle from the bedposts ere morn."

Inez unemotionally listened to Brad's description of his agreement with Suzanne. "Good," she said at last. "She is sensible. When you were quiet for so long, I thought you might have killed her; that might have upset Helmut."

"Upset Helmut! That's a rather bland assumption, isn't it?"

"Nothing is bland about Helmut when he is upset," she replied dryly. She abruptly changed subjects. "You must go for the map tonight."

He frowned. "Why tonight?"

"Because if Rafer Smith is the man I think, the map could be genuine." She placed her hands upon his shoulders. "You would like to have $200,000 in gold, wouldn't you?"

"How did you know how much is out there?" he asked warily.

"Bring me that map"—she kissed him lightly—"and we shall see how much I know."

The next morning, Inez took Banner's dog, Cletis, for a walk as usual while Banner rode out with the hands. After an hour, she saw Brad and Rafer Smith advancing on horseback across the sodden snowmelt toward the ranch house. Brad waved; she did not wave back.

She continued with Cletis into the woods. Cletis whined, catching the scent of a rabbit, then pulled against the leash as Inez neared the cage by the willows. She curbed him sharply; unused to a leash, he barked, lunging toward the willows. She dragged the dog back on his hindquarters and forced him to pace along with her back and forth across the snow until he was frantic to reach the scent summoning him. Inez was in no hurry; when the moment came, the dog must not hesitate.

From the windows, Suzanne watched the riders dismount. Gripping the sill, she pressed close to the glass, then turned away, her heart pounding. Brad was bringing Rafer into the house. She went quickly to the piano, but her fingers were so tremulous and uncertain upon the keys that she spun on the bench to look for a book, anything not to appear to have been waiting. Waiting all the long days and nights of winter.

And then Rafer was in the room, seeing her flushed as if on the verge of flight. Summoning her control, she smoothed her saffron silk skirts and rose. "Welcome back," she said simply.

Rafer pulled off his faded hat. His mustache was bleached, his beard stubble dark along his jaw. The high altitude sun had tanned his face to mahogany so that his eyes burned bluer than ever as he drank in her loveliness. "Good to be back, ma'am," he said softly. "You look mighty pretty today, especially to a man reduced to admiring jackrabbits."

With a crooked smile at the glow on Suzanne's face, Brad pulled off his jacket, then held out his hand for Rafer's. "Suzanne, why not pour aperitifs for us while I have Maria set an extra place for lunch?"

Rafer shrugged out of his sheepskin, and handed it to Brad with a quizzical look.

Brad's eyes met his levelly. "I may be a few minutes. I want to see how Cookie's dressed out that stag haunch for dinner." He left the room.

Rafer looked at Suzanne. "Am I mistaken in supposing we are being given carte blanche?"

"I asked Brad for a divorce last night," Suzanne replied quietly.

Rafer's tanned face was a mask, not revealing whether he was relieved or dismayed, but she sensed he might be both. "Am I cited as correspondent?" His tone was hard.

So he was not glad.

"Actually, Inez is the correspondent," she replied stoically. "Although that fact will not be mentioned in the proceedings."

His face lost its ambiguity. "I'm sorry, Su," he said softly, sympathy darkening his eyes.

She did not want his pity, particularly as Brad had left her for months without a word. She had been in agony thinking Rafer would not return and she never wanted to feel such pain again. "I'm not sorry, and neither is Brad. A sham marriage would have been miserable for us both. He has a chance to be happy now."

"What about you?"

She crossed to the liquor carafe. "I shall have what I always wanted: freedom and the money to enjoy it." She uncorked a stopper, firmly seized a carafe, and poured.

"And beyond that?"

She handed him the aperitif. "There is no 'beyond that.' " She clicked her glass against his. "You taught me one thing: practicality. The difference between realism and the ridiculous." Her green eyes deepened slightly in hue. "Women who pursue inappropriate men are ridiculous. Now I have no need to pursue anybody."

"You mean to return to Broadacre?"

"Broadacre is where I belong . . . or at least, feel comfortable."

"Don't you mean safe?"

"What I mean is what I mean." She tossed off her aperitif. "Crossing half the Rocky Mountains in the dead of winter makes 'safe' relative."

"Don't go back to Connecticut, Su." He took the glass from her.

She took it back. "If you're going to California, then I'm going to Connecticut, which is as far as I can get from California."

"You're that hurt?"

The look in his eyes made her want to run. "Not hurt, just tired . . . and bored; I've been at Mi Vida long enough. I want to go home."

"You want to go to prison where the condemned's last meal is served on English porcelain."

"Don't preach to me!" she flung back. "I haven't noticed you breaking any damned dishes lately!"

Brad returned to the parlor to find Rafer alone on the piano bench, picking out "Onward, Christian Soldiers." Brad settled beside him with his back to the keyboard. "I take it my wife's delight at your return got the better of her."

Rafer hit a wrong note. "Suppose we discuss business instead of Su. That's why you brought me back, isn't it?"

"Indeed, it is. As a gesture of good faith, I've persuaded Helmut to put you up in the house for a few days. He grinned. "I advised him my father wanted to make sure you stayed sober before guiding us out of here. I advised him my continuing to hunt with Inez may cause difficulties with Suzanne: a pretext, of course. She hasn't the slightest interest in me." He leaned back against the piano. "When were you planning to go after the gold?"

"Within forty-eight hours if the thaw holds." Rafer swivelled on the bench. "If Inez doesn't come with us, the deal is off. I want Suzanne's complete lack of interest in you to be reinforced by 24-carat jealous rage. Divorce guaranteed."

"Deal. And one other thing"—Brad rose from the bench—"Suzanne will be alone tonight. You're in the room across the hall." Whistling softly, he headed for the library to work at his ledgers.

His eyes narrowing to cold, blue slits, Rafer rubbed his

stubbled jaw. He could do with a shave before lunch time; a pity he couldn't spend that time beating Suzanne's pimp of a husband to a pulp. With a muffled oath, he went outside to get his saddlebags.

Outside in the grove, a cord jerked, a cage door ran up, and Helmut Banner's hound plunged into the cage at the small, frenzied shape that should have been easy prey. The ferret went for his muzzle like a shrieking magnet. Cletis yelped but did not turn from the kill. Seconds later, the bloody ferret twitched as the dog worried it. Inez let the dog work out his excitement, then tied him. She tossed the cage in the melting creek, and buried the ferret while Cletis whined. She patted his head.

TWENTY-THREE

The Last Dangerous Game

Lying across his bed, Rafer listened to the midnight silence of Helmut Banner's house. The only sounds were a distant coyote's halfhearted howl, and on the other side of the wall, Banner's whining hound. The muscles of his bare torso tense, he sat up, unable to delay the moment his body craved, yet all his soul resisted. He must play out yet another lie that must hurt Suzanne terribly. No one would be the victor after this last, heartless charade. Certainly not the Carlisles for whom it was to be enacted. He might win the game, but in the end, must lose.

For months, he had dreamed of her, with all her shimmering aurora of bright hair and green eyes ablaze like the dazzling light on the snow fields. She was the day's flaring largesse of diamonds; the night's cool, caressing moon. She was the spirit who had come to inhabit him. His impossible love, melting away like quicksilver.

I love her, he thought, rising to walk barefoot across the moonlit patterns restlessly shifting on the floor. Like a worn-away man loves the peace of his end, I love her.

In the hall lingered a murmur of voices from the library where Ramsey and Helmut were still arguing the railroad debate begun over dinner. Brad had left Suzanne's door slightly ajar when he went to Inez; once inside the bedroom, Rafer slipped the lock. Brad could look after himself. Suzanne was lying on the bed, her red-gold hair spilled over the pillow. He cast off his buckskin breeches. She did not move as he came toward her, but her eyes were open. Lovely wells of resigned sadness, they lured him down. Silently, he lowered himself upon her, and silently she welcomed him. Their lips met gently as their bodies fit surely together. His slow caresses shaped her as her fingers wound into his hair. The night was theirs. He buried his face in her throat as her touch floated over him . . . rediscovered the bare, gathering tautness of his wide shoulders and back, the hard curve of his buttocks. Their kisses deepened, luxurious and languorous, a prologue to their hunger. His sex was full, heavy with need of her. He rolled over and invited her to lie upon him that he might feel her length, her weight . . . his hands slipping gently over the ripe thrust of her breasts, the heat of her against his tawny skin. She was ivory silk, sliding through his hands, upon his nakedness. Her hair brushed his nipples as her lips trailed down his body, explored him, found the pulsing heat at his core. Without hesitation, she tasted his sex sensitively, intuitively, knowing how to make him wild for her, delighting in his gathering tension, the raggedness of his breathing. "Now, *querida*," he whispered at last, his arms tightening about her. "I must have you now."

The moment of his entry was a sweet rush of heat, a slow surge of ecstasy. She cocooned him with her body and with her hair, embracing him with a tenderness that captured his wild heart like a snared hawk who had lost his will to fly. Her body straining against his, she mated him as he mated her, their soaring spirits entwined in pristine currents that gave the impression of fallen angels poised in their fall of luminous glory, to be wrought in endless yearning in the immortal poetry of flesh and sensory impatience. Her hands clasped in his, their arms winged out as if reaching for that impossible, glowing height for which they yearned. Her hands tightened upon his with each surge of his sex within her, each quickening, soaring beat of her heart. His dark skin intertwining her pale one, he lured her into the tempest rising within him, impaling her with the delicate lightening that played between them . . . let it slowly, rhythmically rise into full force until she cried out against his lips, her body arching like a white, whipping light extending from his source. Her light burst, scorching him in iridescent, showering splinters. His own shattering power returned upon him, shaking him until he clung to her to save himself, destroy himself . . . her . . . nothing mattered anymore but the leaping, devouring love between them. His body cording, he caught her swiftly down to him, bruising his hoarse, despairing cry of lost felicity in her soft flesh.

When they lay quietly, she cocooned him again as if protecting him, sheltering him. She was soft tonight, softer than he had ever known her, and he sensed jealously that the change had to do with Brad.

Ramsey Hoth might be a randy ogre, but he was better than his four-flushing son any day. Nothing less than a grizzly bear intimidated the old fart.

But at that moment, Ramsey was being mauled by a benign-looking creature much deadlier than the grizzly.

"So you propose to head back to Denver by the end of this week," reiterated Banner, peering over his cigar at Ramsey. He stretched his legs out more comfortably. "I'm sorry to hear that. I've not only grown attached to Brad, but to you and your beautiful daughter-in-law."

Ramsey laughed. "I should think you'd be glad to have the house quiet again without my monopolizing your Milton collection. In appreciation for your hospitality, I'd like to send you my personal copy of Dante's *Inferno* when I reach Chicago."

"You're more than generous," replied Helmut amiably,

"but to tell the truth, I'd prefer a less expensive memento than the *Inferno*. Why not provide me a little backing from the railroad angle? No money, of course; just a good word with the right party, perhaps information at an opportune moment."

"Of course," Ramsey agreed readily. "You scratch my back; I scratch yours."

"Good. First off, I'd like you to pry into General Palmer's Denver and Rio Grande spur line."

By the time Helmut elaborated, Ramsey balked. "You don't want information; you want me to delay the line, not just politically, but with hard-case sabotage, so you can step in ahead of Jay Gould. I won't get in Gould's way for God himself."

"I don't pretend to be God, but then your son does pretend to be honest . . . doesn't he?"

An hour later, Ramsey left Helmut, his footsteps faltering along the hallway. His face pale, he paused outside his son's door. You fool! he railed impotently. You incompetent fool! Banner knows you're an embezzler! You couldn't even keep your mess confined to your own kennel! His hand poised above the doorknob, then jerked away. Lie in your own muck; I'll see you choke on it!

Pulling the covers high, Rafer nestled Suzanne against him. Her face buried in his golden chest fur, she was still for a long while. She was no more asleep than he, her breathing irregular. "We shall regret becoming lovers again," she murmured at last, "yet at this moment, I feel like Icarus before the plunge. Although my feathers are being burnt away, I cannot resist flying nearer the sun. I feel like both a fool and a god, yet am a dismally mortal woman with a mortal lover. The sun has set; it is night, and cold." She gazed pensively into his eyes. "All I see are blue, unreachable stars set upon a course that lies a dark universe from my own."

"The distance may be deceptive." Rafer caressed the moonlit, gossamer cloud of her hair. "Even the stars move in time; nothing is written in them forever." He saw she did not believe him, would never believe him. He saw her as she must have been once, a child whose brave illusions and vaulting courage were stifled beneath the dust of ceremony. She broke his heart. "Suzanne . . ." he whispered, then the words hovering on his lips died stillborn. Come with me, he had wanted to say. Whatever happens, I'm willing to take the risk if you are . . .

But he was not willing to take the risk, for if his scheme to destroy Banner went awry, the forfeit to Suzanne would be far more horrible than the prospect of their coming to hate one another: horrible, in the real, immediate sense of dying in a way that shrivelled the imagination. He could not risk taking her with him . . . even if she agreed to go. And she would not, because she knew as well as he, they could not live together. He could not pretend she loved him. To her, he was freedom, excitement, a poke in the nose of confining tradition; that kind of love faded before the reality of grimy hotel rooms, all-night poker games, the hot breath of the law. They could have no children, no permanent home. In time, the fickle benevolence of Lady Luck would become a beckoning, demonic cheat.

Broadacre might be sterile, but it was better than anything he had to offer her.

Better she learn to hate him now, than later.

He left after she fell asleep. Once in his room, he checked his saddlebags flung over a chair back. As expected, the map left in the bag was gone. The last, deadly game was in play.

But not in the way he supposed.

Helmut Banner went to bed late. The brandy in his belly was warm, like the success of making another strong man bend his knee in homage. Hate often accompanied the homage, but in this case, he could not insure one without the other. He lit the lamp. The sudden light startled Cletis's head up from his forepaws. His eyes yellow-red from the kerosene lamp's reflection, the dog stared at him, but made no effort to come and be petted. Just before supper, Banner had cuffed the dog soundly for snapping at him. The skin had hardly been broken but Inez had been quick to bandage the small finger on his left hand.

Cletis must be tired from rambling with Inez. Inez had not wanted Cletis in the house as a pup; like most Utes, she considered dogs in a dwelling bad luck. Now, she and Cletis were almost inseparable, despite her refusal to sleep in the same room. When she shared Helmut's bed, Cletis was banished to the library.

Come to think of it, Cletis had been lying on the bedroom pad while he had dressed for dinner. Once in a while the dog would aimlessly pace, then resettle. Loosening his collar, Helmut patted his thigh. "Come here, Cletis."

The dog's head lowered to its forepaws.

The hound must be ailing. Banner finished undressing, pulled on his nightshirt and went over to scratch the dog's head. Other than a few minor muzzle cuts, Cletis was uninjured. As Helmut's hand withdrew, casting its shadow over the indifferent dog's face, Cletis snapped again. The graze stung a wire of blood from a scuffed groove on the back of his hand. Startled, Helmut automatically cuffed the dog's muzzle; Cletis's teeth bared. Thoroughly irritated, Helmut grabbed Cletis by the collar and dragged him, now growling and resistant, to the kitchen door and shoved him out into the sloppy snow. Sliding in the mud, Cletis whipped around, his forelegs spread and hackles high. Helmut picked up a stone. "I'll smack you one, boy!"

The dog slunk off into the shadows.

Troubled, Helmut shut the door. What was bothering that mutt? He was genuinely fond of Cletis, but if the dog had turned mean, he would have to be shot. He had better have one of the boys find it in the morning.

With a sudden pang of loneliness, he did not want to spend the night in an empty bed. He went to Inez's room to find her bed not only empty, but still made. His stomach tightening with a cold lurch, he shut the door. His mind moving at a dead, he cruised the silent house. Inez might be outside; she was as nocturnal as a bobcat. Then again . . .

He went to Brad Hoth's room. Suzanne Hoth was alone, asleep.

Light still shone beneath Ramsey's door. He knocked. Ramsey opened the door, his face baleful. "What is it?"

"Where's Brad?" Helmut grated.

"How should I know? He's too old to sleep with me,"

was the curt reply. Then, perceiving Helmut must have already been to Brad's room, Ramsey's eyes narrowed suspiciously. Malicious glee, then uneasiness flickered across his face. Helmut wheeled blindly for Rafer Smith's door. His fist slamming against it, the door sheared open to reveal another empty bed. Smith's saddlebags were gone.

He ran back to Inez's room. Her clothes were still there, but her Spanish silver jewelry was missing . . . the emerald necklace from Columbia . . . the sapphires from Belize. Everything of value he had given her that was worth a damn was gone.

With Ramsey sharply monitoring his progress, he barged into Suzanne's room, and ignoring her muffled cry, he threw open Brad's armoire; only useless city suits dangled from their hangars.

Brad must have paid Smith to guide him and Inez out of the mountains. Unable to track them until dawn, Helmut had four hours to build on an already cold determination to kill them all.

Alone, and in no hurry, Rafer rode due west from the paling horizon. His phoney gold map had sent Brad and Inez northwest to Rio Blanco as decoys to occupy Helmut Banner. Inez would elude pursuit for days. She and Brad might even escape Helmut altogether, but he doubted it. By the time nip came to tuck, he would have staked out the gold in Grand Mesa, then cut north to pry Helmut off their backs. By then, Brad should be scared green.

Suddenly, his grim speculation was cut short by sight of hoofprints made by four horses and a pack mule in the spring mud. Two horses were unshod Ute mustangs, one was a thoroughbred by its stride length; the other, one of Helmut's mixed breeds; the last two were spares, and all moving at a dead run. The thoroughbred was Brad's; Rafer had notched its rear left hoof before leaving for the line shack in December. Keeping track of a man one cuckolded usually paid.

Rafer's brow furrowed. Why the hell were Inez and Brad on this trail when they should have been miles away? They were on the right trail at the wrong time . . .

And leading Banner right to him.

Two hours later, Rafer spurred his paint from the trail up an embankment, then dismounted and shoved loose shale down to cover his tracks. Above were the high buttes of Red Table Mountain; far behind, the dust trails of approaching riders. By the time he reached the butte crest and pulled out his field glasses, the riders were moving along the valley floor. The Indian scouts would have picked up his trail overlying that of Brad and Inez's and, if casual, assume he was with their quarry. They would soon realize his tracks had disappeared, but might be unable to guess precisely where. Apaches would not be deluded. He was lucky his old Taos mentors were not on Banner's payroll.

He waited half an hour, the flat, sharp-edged rocks digging into his body. If the Yampas sniffed him out, he wanted to know now. Scraping horses' hooves on the valley floor rocks echoed up the butte. He twisted the field glasses' focus. The Yampas were passing his departure point without missing a hoofbeat; twenty yards behind them rode Banner, Ramsey, and dammit to hell, Suzanne! Her hair was a red blaze among the mass of riders, even at this distance. Swearing violently, he lowered the field glasses. Would she never give up chasing that idiot husband of hers, even when he ran off with another woman? This was a royal mess! If Banner caught up to Brad and Inez, he would turn ugly.

Still fuming, he clamped the field glasses to his eyes again. A Yampa was lagging, his attention on the trail sharpened. He had noticed the missing prints. Tensely, Rafer waited for him to summon Banner's attention, but instead, the Yampa resumed his regular pace, shifting in his saddle to converse briefly with his fellow scout. The other scout's head lowered, then he gave a single nod. The whole exchange lasted less than a few seconds.

What the devil was going on? First, Brad and Inez ignored the map; now the trackers were ignoring him. Something was wrong. Deadly wrong.

He rolled over to stare up at the fathomless sky. He must change his plans.

* * *

Inez was already pulling the blanket off her own mare to switch to her spare mount when Brad slid off his horse. He unfastened his saddle cinch with an impatient jerk. "Will you tell me now why you're ignoring the map after I risked my skin getting it? The thing might as well be rubbish!"

She glanced at him with patient affection. "It *is* rubbish."

His fingers froze on the cinch. "Why not say so back at the ranch!"

She gave the other animals oats from a parfleche. "Because this was as good a time for me to leave Helmut as any . . . perhaps better." She smiled mysteriously. "The map may be false, but from your description of Mr. Smith's behavior in Vera Cruz, he is genuine."

Exasperated, Brad flung his saddle on the fresh mount. "What has that flea-bitten crook to do with anything?"

She unhooked her canteen. "If we are still alive tonight, I will tell you."

Suzanne rode between Helmut Banner and Ramsey; while neither of them wanted her there, she flatly refused to be left behind. Brad was in another ugly scrape but she could no longer hate him for his desperate illusions. Wisely or unwisely, Brad loved Inez, but he had dishonored a man who had befriended him, and made the dishonor public. She was distinctly uneasy about the aura remaining in his wake. Ramsey was furious, overwrought . . . and fearful. Confrontation with savage, unpredictable animals might frighten him, but men did not; yet Banner alarmed him. Banner was too calm.

After Banner stormed into her room, he abruptly quieted upon discovering Brad and Inez were beyond reach. He became charming and polite, deprecating his loss. Inez and Brad might have been two foolish children to be retrieved before injuring themselves. He evaded Ramsey's request to join the pursuit; only when Ramsey became adamant, and Suzanne added her insistence, did he reluctantly relent.

And now, behind them rode twenty men in pursuit of the two foolish children.

* * *

The night dropped quickly, drawing the inky blue remains of the winter cold closely over the Red Table Mountain country. The flaring stars seemed close enough to touch from the stark black reaches of the earth. Brad was glad of Inez's warmth beside him in the moonless, wind-swept heights. While she would not permit a fire, he found the cold more bearable than he did before claiming his stag. Weeks in the icy woods had stiffened his spine.

His back against an unyielding boulder, his arm tightened about Inez. Although her eyes were directed toward the eastern horizon, she laid her head against his shoulder. They had only a few hours to rest, as she was determined to reach Grand River as quickly as possible, but his mind was still nagged by her mysterious knowledge about the hidden robbery gold in Grand Mesa where the river would take them.

Sensing his unease, she looked up at him. "You begin to wonder if I know what I am doing, eh?"

"You know what you're doing," he said simply. "I just don't know what you're doing."

She laughed, then was silent for some time. When she spoke again, her voice had sobered. "The story of the gold is not one to make pretty dreams. Perhaps you should not hear it until we are out of reach of Helmut Banner."

He frowned. "If Helmut is dangerous, I should know why"—his eyes sharply searched hers—"unless you're afraid I'll run."

"You are already running, but so be it," she replied softly.

Some of the story originated from her grandfather; the rest she had learned after coming to live with Helmut Banner. At age twelve, she had gone to a mission school in the south to learn to read his notebooks and ledgers . . . before she became his mistress. Before he ever met her. "He did not choose me," Inez informed Brad gravely. "I chose him."

"But why?" he demanded jealously. "Helmut's an old man!"

She smiled. "Among the Chinese, age is respected; among the Utes, also. I went to one old man because I respected another: my grandfather, Two Bows." She continued her story, and in minutes, Brad was as intent as if it issued from Two Bows himself.

Inez was White River Ute, not Yampa, as she led Helmut to believe. In midsummer of her twelfth year, her grandfather, Two Bows, had ridden into camp. He was ill, exhausted and half-starved. The horse was also in a bad way, so the squaws killed it and gave some to the old man, who was very depressed. He ate as if the food choked him. For two days, the women tended him until he was strong enough to speak with his family, the shaman, and the chief. Nothing of his account ever passed beyond the teepee.

"I was Helmut Banner's friend and scout for twenty years," he said. "My son died in his service during the great war between the whites. My grandson, Tall Elk, assumed the place of his father. Now Tall Elk is dead."

The women began to wail, but Inez was confused in her grief for her favorite brother. Tall Elk was only eighteen years old. He was strong, brave, and merry. He was also clever; that was why Two Bows chose him to succeed as Banner's scout. She could not believe Tall Elk was dead.

But Two Bows left no doubt.

Men had stolen gold from Helmut Banner, and Banner had pursued them with many *vaqueros* and two scouts. The chase was very hard and long, into the Grand Mesa country. Two Bows's heart was no longer strong, and he became ill. His grandson, Tall Elk, made him a camp and went on with Banner, who was impatient to catch the thieves. As the days passed, Two Bows's heart mended, but Banner did not return. Then from a high distance, he saw Banner coming back alone with only his foreman, the man who was now Sheriff Ingram. Two Bows was greatly disturbed, for to lose so many men and return with no outlaws ran against Banner's relentless nature. He hid himself, and let Banner think he had wandered from the camp and died. This was a wise precaution, for Banner and Ingram searched for him with their rifles ready as if seeking an enemy.

When Banner and Ingram were gone again, Two Bows set out upon his grandson's trail. The trail was old and many

days long, but the weather was dry, and Banner's and Ingram's tracks were still fresh. At a place white like dust in
the far Grand Mesa bordering the Uncompaghre and Unitah
countries, he made a terrible finding, so terrible that it pierced
his heart like an arrow, and he feared he must die in the
desert.

Banner had found his quarry. Two Bows found marks
where stakes had been driven into the ground and four men
tied and tortured. Bloodstains and bits of skin were faded
upon the rocks where the ants were still busy. There were
other marks: many boot and horse prints, horse tracks lightened of saddles and packs heading toward the south, fresh
earth and rock spilled down an arroyo. Pulling his knife, he
went to dig in the arroyo. In time he found nine bodies; three
of five that he recognized as Banner's men were shot at close
range in the back of the head; two more in the face from
several yards away. Tall Elk was one of these.

Two Bows wearily shook his head. The bullion robbers
were also in the arroyo. Skinned alive. The youngest, with
heavy blood loss from a throat wound before his capture, had
died quickly; the other had taken longer, much longer.

One thief was missing . . . surely he who had done this
thing. Two Bows dug in the arroyo into the night, until he
knew the ghastly faces by touch. One by one, he excavated
the bodies. A thief was still missing. With his heart doing
mad things in his chest, Two Bows crouched in the arroyo
as the sun rose red. His mind churned with a nightmarish
whirlpool of evidence that gradually centered upon one conclusion. Many different boot prints marked the torture site.
The face-shot men had died unsuspecting, shot at close range
by someone they did not fear. Banner's three *vaqueros*, shot
in the back of the skull with their wrists tied behind their
backs, had died after the robbers. Banner and Ingram had
escaped without injury, and had come to his camp with their
rifles drawn before seeing he was gone. They carried gold.

Banner and Ingram had killed nine men.

Two Bows reburied the bodies, then went back to reex-
amine the place of the torture. Two tequila bottles were
dropped near the scene. A widened peg hole revealed the

missing thief had worked loose a peg. When night fell, he must have undone his bonds while his captors were preoccupied with the tequila and crawled away. Two Bows followed the trail even after realizing the fleeing robber was a boy in no condition to shoot anyone.

With dogged patience, Two Bows trailed the boy well beyond the point where Banner and Ingram had halted. At the river, the trail ended. Two Bows found no emerging tracks for miles on either shore. The river would take him deep into Uncompaghre country, and if the boy had not drowned, he was far beyond reach . . . also beyond reach of Helmut Banner.

The trek cost Two Bows; he barely survived the journey home. He had tried to find the site of the hidden gold. To steal the gold before Banner returned would be rich revenge. Before the white men's disappointment faded, the Utes would fill their mouths with their own entrails.

Although the white men's tracks wandered through the rugged canyons and arroyos, casting this way and that about the place where the robbers sidetracked to hide their unwieldy load, Two Bows knew Banner never found the gold. Banner and Ingram were good trackers, but not so good as Tall Elk; their inability to find the gold because they had murdered his grandson was justice; also a puzzlement. If the robbers had died without revealing the gold, Banner had no reason to kill witnesses . . . unless one of the robbers had revealed something just as dangerous for the witnesses to know.

Two Bows was now too weary to think. Now others must think. He went home.

As Two Bows lay dying in the teepee, the question was decided by the chief. The Utes must not become involved. The robbers were tortured by Indian methods; who was to say all the men dead in the desert had not been killed by Indians? The bodies must remain hidden . . . as must the wicked, worthless gold for which so many had brutally died. The vengeful spirits guarding the gold would be too strong and dangerous to disturb now.

But Banner must die by a Ute hand, as if by accident so that no Ute would be blamed. His death must be a bad death.

He must suffer the shame and torment of the men he murdered.

Inez listened, then gave them the way. A Ute must come close to Banner; not a White River Ute, whom he might suspect, but a Yampa. This hidden one must learn his secret thoughts and needs. In this way, his death would be chosen, that it might strike him to the heart. For the hidden one, this would take time, and the wiliness of Coyote.

What Yampa will do this for us? protested the others. And how can an Indian come so close to Banner?

Two Bows had looked long at Inez's hard, beautiful little face. My granddaughter will be the hidden one, he said slowly. She will be Coyote.

So it was done.

Unable to speak at first, Brad had difficulty comprehending the coldblooded, revengeful intrigue that Inez and her people had patiently wrought about their prey. "You've lived with Banner for three years, just so you could pick the right moment to kill him?" he breathed in horror.

"To shame and kill him," Inez corrected gravely.

"You used me to shame him!" He thrust her away and came to his knees.

"I loved you," she corrected again, this time gently. "I could not leave with you unless I killed him. It is true that I began with you to shame him, but I might have chosen another man . . . any one of his men. I did not."

"You chose me because I was the most convenient!" he flung back.

"I used you, it is true," she replied calmly, "but not with a cold heart. I loved you because you were nothing like Helmut."

He caught her violently by the shoulders. "You love me like a wolf does some stupid rabbit. You're using me as bait for a troll who skins people, for Chrissake!"

He was furious, his fingers digging painfully into her shoulders, yet she was gazing at him as if she longed to comfort him against her breast. She had given him no answer about Banner and he knew there would be none. She was simply waiting for him to decide whether he would stay.

At length his arms tightened about her. And his decision had nothing to do with the gold.

TWENTY-FOUR

The Chase

Suzanne ached in every bone. After months of housebound inactivity, her body bitterly protested being recalled into severe service. She must adapt to the rugged pace of thirty miles per day; otherwise, Banner would have her returned to Mi Vida. Ramsey was more fatigued than she, but his jaw was set with implacable determination. When the trackers called a halt after sunset, Ramsey was slow to dismount, and walked as if his leg troubled him. After the bear attack, he used a cane on uneven ground: a necessity Inez predicted might be permanent.

And for a customarily collected man, Banner was unable to stay still. He kept pacing erratically, not even pausing long enough to listen to Sheriff Ingram and Buck Wheeler debate tomorrow's direction. He prowled about the men unsaddling their horses as if they might suddenly need supervision until several fumbled with their tack, then furtively peered after him as his prowl continued. Although he sharply reprimanded a man for losing oats from a frayed feed bag, he seemed distracted as if in a particularly bad mood. His speech issued in a quick stream that occasionally lost its flow almost in mid-sentence.

Suzanne surreptitiously rubbed her saddle-sore bottom. Acquaintance with Brad was sufficient to drive anyone to bizarre behavior, even strong-minded Helmut Banner.

Personally, she was inclined to sob like an abandoned pup. Not because of Brad. Brad was Brad.

And Rafer was Rafer. She should have guessed an alliance had developed when Brad brought him back to Mi Vida, but why would Rafer agree to guide Brad and Inez unless he saw Brad as a gullible soul to finance his trip to California? Brad was sly, but not in Rafer's league. And while Rafer might dump Brad in the desert out of revenge for his tricking him in Vera Cruz, she doubted if Rafer cared enough about the con to bother. Unless . . . he wanted Brad dead. She could be widowed much more efficiently than divorced.

By midnight, Rafer was five miles ahead of the Banner party. His reins in his hand, he crouched amid the rocks near the tree line of Red Table Mountain. Here, he would rest for a few hours. The fugitives were a short distance ahead of him. Inez was dictating the route; it led unhesitatingly toward Battlement Mesa for the Grand River. Leaving a clear trail, she appeared simply bent on outrunning Banner to Grand River, then following into Grand Mesa. If she and Brad lacked river transport, they were wasting their energy. The upper Grand might be spring flooded too high to wade across with horses, not to mention being used to cover their trail.

He would not have traded places with Brad right now for every hockable jewel in the British crown. On the other hand, being placed between Brad and Banner was scarcely more appealing, but if he did not occupy the position, Suzanne, sooner or later, would.

She probably figures I'm tarting off again—he settled uncomfortably down in the rocks. But hell—he plucked a fist-sized lump from beneath his rump, then tilted his hat over his eyes—this is as noble as I get.

Tired as he was, Rafer awoke before the morning sun's first rays pried beneath his hat. The rugged country about him was softened to grayed mauve by the first whisper of dawn where stars still sleepily flickered. The air was still as if it were also lingering in sleep. For a few moments, he did not move, his breathing timed with that of the earth, his eyes filled with starry dawn. Banner seemed far away, but Rafer knew better. After a brief stretch of cramped muscles, he saddled his horse and dug into his saddlebag for jerky. Chewing a sliver, he hunkered down to scan the ground. Perhaps six feet away, shod hooves had left whitish scratches on the rocks. Inez and Brad were headed for the Grand River, all right. He vaulted into the saddle. If they had a canoe waiting, they would safely outdistance Banner and free him to head deeper into the canyon country after the gold cache. He could not have set out a more convenient route to the gold had he planned it himself.

Brad and Inez reached the Grand. Rafer discovered the spot where the raft had been landed; also the soft-soled tracks of the Indian builder, now on the river with Brad and Inez to lend enough manpower to negotiate the muddy, treacherous torrent of the lower Grand. Inez must have coordinated this escape some time ago. She was wise to prefer the river's mercies to Banner's.

His horse moving at a steady trot along the riverbank, he began to follow their course downriver. Disembarkation above Uncompaghre Apache country would bring them to shore somewhere around Grand Junction. Whether they left the river or not, he was continuing west at that point. It had been dangerously long since he had friends among the Apache.

The nasty feeling between his shoulder blades also warned him Banner was too close. He prodded the paint to a canter.

"That's it, boss," said Buck Wheeler, flicking his reins against his thigh in exasperation as he viewed the riverbank marks. "They've taken to the river. We've lost them."

"We'll follow the river," said Banner briefly, regarding the muddy sweep with aversion. He rubbed at his hand distractedly as if he had suddenly touched a hot stove, then tucking it awkwardly under his armpit, hastened up the bank. "They may run into trouble."

Portly, mustachioed Sheriff Oliver Ingram mopped at his pink, perspiring neck, knowing better than to argue. Banner had been short-tempered most of the day. They would not be making camp tonight if they hoped to outpace the Grand River current. As he followed Banner and Wheeler to the horses, he noted Ramsey sagging wearily in his saddle among the other riders. The old Easterner was a tough bird, but would be unable to maintain the pace. The woman would likely fall behind, although she had held up like a trooper so far. Her eyes were set like impenetrable jadestone in her pale face and her lush body concealed a strong backbone. There would be plenty of volunteers to escort her and the old man back to Mi Vida. Banner must have known they would have to turn back before he caught Brad Hoth. Banner had something on every man who worked for him; they were not going to talk if young Hoth and the Indian bitch got their just deserts. If old Hoth and the missus raised a stink, well . . . nobody would be surprised if they disappeared. The escort could have one fine time with the woman before cutting her throat. Maybe he should dispense with the volunteers and impose his official services. His pale gray eyes bright with anticipation, he smiled up at Suzanne as he passed her horse. "No need to worry, Mrs. Hoth." He swung up on his horse and fell into line beside her as the riders moved out. "Everything's going to work out just fine."

Appraising his mealy-mouthed stare, she gave him a cool look that made him feel like a lizard. "The Grand River may have other ideas, Mr. Banner."

Just wait, bitch, thought Banner as she spurred ahead to join Ramsey. One day soon, you're going to want to talk to me real bad. I bet you can beg just as pretty as you look.

Brad was feeling fine. The sun was high, the water fast, his muscles acquiring the tone that he remembered from his days of sculling on the Charles. Paddling a raft was far easier than balancing a scull and Inez's uncle White Stone was an expert stern man. They were making excellent time with the current behind them. Banner had to rest his horses sometime. If they held this speed for the next forty-eight hours, he would never catch up, particularly once they hit the faster current downriver.

Inez was less certain. "The Eastern rivers are not the rivers of the West," she advised with a rare lack of assurance. "We will not risk the lower river. Horses await us with my cousin at Plateau Creek. From there, we will cross into the canyon country."

Although he trusted her judgement, Brad wondered if it now was shadowed by her hate and fear of Banner. This section of the Grand River was nearly flat and mostly inferior to the breadth of the Mississippi. Both rivers were brown as paint; the Utes generally called the Grand the "Great Muddy." Sheer, rusty canyon walls and buttes towered above the water with the intervening plains a grand sweep of crumbling shale piled for as much as one hundred and fifty feet up some of the buttes, which were being dismantled by time and the restless, roaming spirits of the winds. Endlessly through the millennia, the wind and river shaped forth mammoth sculptures to be once more relentlessly reduced to rubble.

This is as close as a man comes to eternity on earth, reflected Brad, yet the earth is only a speck among the stars where small, wizened man seeks to become master.

God, how I love this empty, manless desert. If I were to die here, I should have a sepulchre to overwhelm that of Napoleon . . .

"*Per Dio!*" cried Inez.

His stomach knotting in horror, Brad flung a look back over his shoulder. Despite a mounting roar, the river was placid . . . until he spun back around to see a fifteen-foot-high wall of savage log jam fanged with trees and debris combed from hundreds of miles of river. Piled between boulders that reared over their raft, it blocked the river ahead.

The log jam wall smashed into the raft, shoving it under, then curling it high. Inez was screaming at him, her eyes black with fear, but he could hear nothing, his mind frozen. A tree trunk sheared between them as the wall dropped. He heard a horrible sucking, then the ugly grind and tear of the raft as it spun over, flipping him underneath into stunning cold. He clung to a log, trying to breath over the spuming surge. Mercilessly torn loose, he rolled to the river bottom, his arms and legs jangling, Gnarled tree roots clawed his face, careening him into a rock, then another, and something inside him cracked. The river was becoming shallow, the bottom scraping him raw. His lungs screamed. Wildly, his brain blackening, he clawed for the snarling surface. Suffocating brown abruptly became blue as he rocketed up, the air tearing into him with a terrible sound. He grabbed at the looming bank, his fingernails tearing, fingers clutching, slipping, holding, and he kicked hard, dug his boot toes into the bottom to propel his body from the sucking, starving water. Mud filled his mouth and nose, and he blew it out, only to choke again. Until he could not remember breathing any more

Until he was looking up into his father's angry face. Defeat was almost as stifling as the river, now faded by dusk. He must have lain unconscious on the bank for hours, long enough to be caught. Three men were standing on the ruddy clay bank, their clothes muddy. Banner was some distance further up the bank under a cottonwood stand budded green enough for a picnic setting. Clouds spun in mares' tails raced across the cobalt sky overhead like a free-running herd of dreams he would never catch. Rearing up beyond the cottonwoods was a rusty canyon wall as massively impassive as the first day primitive man split an enemy skull with a stone axe beneath its frowning rim. Despair washed over him. "Where's Inez?" he croaked, too exhausted to lift his head. White Stone must be dead. If Inez were dead, he wanted to die. Dazedly, he tried see past Ramsey's boots to the river. He must get back into the river.

Then, "Brad!" came Inez's faint, spent cry. A hundred feet away, across the shallows, she was trying to push Sheriff Ingram away so that she might come to him. She was soaked to the skin, her hair sticking in long ropes to a bruised face scraped from hairline to jaw on the right side. Fury filled him as Ingram caught her by the hair, his grip tightening around her neck, as he dragged her forward.

"Take your hands off her, Ingram," he yelled, trying to get to his knees.

With a startled gasp, he caught his breath, his chest feeling as if it were stabbed by daggers. Someone . . . Suzanne, helped him keep his balance. Now he glimpsed a shadow of the devastation he had left behind. In her eyes lingered the same suffering and disappointment unbearable in his mother's. He wished passionately that he had done better by her. "I'm sorry, Suzanne," he murmured hoarsely, "but if I hadn't taken off, dad would have eaten me alive."

Suzanne squeezed his hand as Ramsey bent over him in fury. "Oh, it's my fault as always that you're a damned spineless worm, is it?" His big, gnarled hand lifted Brad's head by the hair, and in a split second, his other fist broke Brad's nose.

Flinging herself between them, Suzanne grabbed Ramsey's arm as he aimed a blow for Brad's blood-streaked mouth. The momentum of his fist carried her back atop the sprawled Brad. Clamped to Ramsey's arm, she hauled him down with her and rolled with him away from Brad. When he tried to get up, she locked her arms and legs about him. "If you don't stop, I'll bite your ear off, you vindictive old sonofabitch!" she hissed in his ear. At his wrench, she tightened desperately. "You'd devour your own cub to stay king of the mountain. Well, this is Banner's mountain, remember? You have to face him now!"

Ramsey's face was scarlet, blood vessels distended in his temples. He looked as if he wanted to kill her . . . anyone in reach, but uncertainty underlay his rage. Brad had contrived a situation Ramsey might be unable to control . . . people might start dying.

"All right," he wheezed, his eyes growing more uneasy as his breathing steadied. "All right. Let me go now."

Tentatively, her grip eased until he disengaged. He shot Brad a look that promised more than a broken nose if they were ever alone again, then with an effort rose to his feet. "Get up, you misbegotten whelp," he growled at Brad. "Whatever happens, take what comes on your own two legs for once." His hand cupped to his streaming nose, Brad struggled to rise, but his knees would not cooperate, and he looked as if he wanted to retch. With a grunt of impatience, his father reached down, grabbed his shirt, and with an effort, hauled him up.

Ramsey slicked back his grizzled hair, then straightening his clothes, he climbed the bank toward Banner. His balance was awkward without his cane, but with each step, he became more assured and by the time he reached the claybound bank top, Suzanne could envision the swaggering strikebreaker who had faced down mobs and swung billy clubs with the worst.

He did not mince words. "All right, Banner, do what you like with the Indian girl but I'm taking my boy back to Chicago. I'll pay $10,000 in damages and you can beat the shit out of him for interest, but I want him breathing and his kneecaps in one piece when we leave."

Banner smiled ironically, but no one ever knew what he would have said, because Brad said it for him.

"I'm not going back to Chicago, dad. I love Inez, and I'm not leaving her here." His voice was uneven, but adamant. He was shivering in his wet clothes, his feet spread to maintain unsteady balance.

More impatient than angry, Ramsey had more on his mind than Brad's adolescent idiocies. "You can't stay here, so keep out of this." He might have been slapping aside a whining child.

Brad shook his head. "It's my choice, my life"—he looked at Inez—"my girl. And my decision."

"So much forthrightness is admirable," rasped Banner, "if belated. Don't you fear the least bit for your kneecaps, as your father so pithily puts it?" His pupils were tiny, ominous.

Brad's freckles stood out on his pale face. "I know reasonably well what you can do to me, Mr. Banner: maybe better than anybody here except Inez, so I'm sure as hell not leaving her to you." He was not rash enough to elaborate. If he started talking about nine men buried in the desert, nobody would walk out of here alive, not him, Inez, Ramsey, or Suzanne. They did not guess what he was talking about; for the moment, he had them off guard. There would be no escape this time if he opened his mouth, and if he remained silent . . .

His father cut in, talking quickly . . . too quickly. "Look, Banner, the boy's brains were rattled in the river. Let him go and the railroad deal's yours; that's more than his hide's worth any day. Hell, I'll thrash him for you," he added with a note of joviality. "He's long overdue for a cinch in his saddle."

Don't start to beg, Ramsey, thought Suzanne in mounting apprehension. Look at Banner's eyes. He isn't buying it.

Banner's attention had drifted to Inez, as Ingram gave her a final shove almost into their midst. Her eyes were nearly black with hatred that did not quite hide her fear. Inez knows Banner better than we do, thought Suzanne anxiously, and her behaving as if she were facing the jaws of hell is damned unsettling.

Inez had more spine than anticipated. Her chin came up. "Tell your dog, Ingram, to let me go, Helmut. You know I will not run, no matter what you do. This doing was mine, so deal with me."

Banner stared at her for a moment, then almost indifferently motioned Ingram to release her. The moment Ingram's hands dropped, Inez turned and slapped him. "That, for your smell of rancid pig." He reached for her, but she was already ducking beyond him and striding toward Banner.

"Do as you please with the boy, Helmut. He was against the idea from the first, but"—Inez smiled tauntingly—"you know me. I always get what I want." Her derision mounted. "He felt so badly that he wanted to ask you for my hand in marriage. You had treated him better than his own father, he said." Her feet in the shallows, she halted, ignoring Brad's anguished eyes. "Why not come and hit me, Helmut? Don't you feel well?" She cocked her head. "What's the matter? You can swim. Surely you're not afraid of the water." She began to back away, her fingers beckoning, her eyes maliciously flirtatious. "Come on, big man. Think I'll throw you in?"

Venomous hate now glittered in Banner's gray eyes. Inez laughed as he took the first step toward her.

"No!" cried Brad. "Leave her alone. She's lying, don't you see?" He sounded as if he were trying not only to convince Banner, but himself. He stumbled forward, then turned to his father, his voice strained. "I'd rather die, can't you understand that? Whatever Banner does to me, it's better than being a nothing . . . it's better than crawling." At the sober anxiety overcoming Ramsey's face, Brad steadied. "I'm a man now, dad. You have to let go." His tone was almost gentle.

Suzanne watched Ramsey. Did Ramsey himself know why he had struggled so far to find Brad? Now the answer must emerge, if ever.

Ramsey's face was tight, his lips locked in so set a line that he seemed to be trying to keep them from trembling. "You don't know what you're talking about, boy," he warned urgently. Ignoring the sound of Ingram's rifle cocking, he placed his hands on Brad's shoulders. I can't help you if you buck Banner. He's not going to let you walk away with that girl. I know how a jealous old man thinks; he doesn't think; he grabs and smashes . . . and if he thinks, he can be more dangerous than a snake." His grip tightened. "You've cost me, son, but I don't want to see you hanged. You keep quiet for now and we'll talk about what you want to do when we're safe out of here."

Brad was silent for a moment. Ramsey had not called him son since his mother's death. His lips curved with a trace of sadness. "Next you'll be saying you love me."

Ramsey looked startled. He started to pull away, but then his hands stayed tentatively on his son's shoulders. "I expect maybe . . . there are times when I do," he conceded awkwardly.

"I wish I had known, dad," Brad said simply. His eyes glistened, but his voice was steady. "I guess like everything else, love has a price." He appeared to consider saying something else, then continued, "What about Inez?"

"Nobody can do anything for her," Ramsey reiterated flatly, "most especially not you. The longer you stay, the worse it will be for her."

Brad remembered the bodies in the arroyo. Whatever happened, Banner must never touch Inez. "I'm not abandoning Inez, dad," he said quietly. "Tell him."

Sick at heart, Ramsey knew a final decision when he heard one. Not trusting himself to speak, he nodded.

As Ramsey turned toward Banner, Brad snatched the revolver from his father's waistband and pushed him flat. He swung on Banner, but even as the revolver cracked, Ingram put a thumb-sized bullet through Brad's skull.

No one even realized Banner was wounded at first; all eyes were on the sprawling, twitching figure whose quixotic gallantry was denied a decent ending. Nothing was noble about part of a head missing, and whatever Bradford Hoth might have meant to say to his father was soaking into the shale.

Ramsey was stunned, and at the sight of his sick, wild face, Suzanne's own horror galvanized. She leaped toward him even as he went for his gun. Suddenly, gunfire was coming from everywhere. Ramsey went down again with a big red splotch on his chest and his own gun firing. He hit two men, but another two red blobs appeared on his body. Thrashing like a broken-backed animal, he stopped firing. Suzanne dropped to the ground to frantically squirm toward him. Not until she saw Banner's men also hitting the dirt did she realize someone was firing from the rocks overhead. Anyone retaliating was abruptly dropped, the sniper in the rocks raking the terrain with the quick-firing deadliness of a Gatling gun. She reached Ramsey; he was no longer thrashing, but breathing in short, spasmodic gasps. His face was frustrated, baffled, wild with grief. He was aware of her, but his eyes were already glazing. "G . . . out of here . . . go!"

Her own eyes stinging with tears, she peered over Ramsey's chest to find Ingram. Banner's men had no chance in the open with no place to run. Some of them dropped to the ground with their arms over their heads. Ingram was alive, mad, and scared stiff, but firing steadily toward the sniper's ledge. Banner was inert on the ground, a bright patch of blood covering his face. Inez was slithering away from Ingram toward a .45 lying on the rocks. Suzanne snatched Ramsey's gun from his useless fingers, but abruptly the firing from Banner's men stopped. Hastily, the exposed men began to throw their guns to the ground and their hands into the air. Three more shots from the rocks spat a neat triangle about Ingram, forestalling any second thoughts of retaliation. "Lose all your guns, boys. The Lord doesn't like this much racket on Sunday."

Suzanne's heart leaped. Although unable to see the sniper, she recognized that silky, threatening drawl as Rafer's.

When guns bounced across the shale, Ingram's was not one of them. His gray eyes looked almost white with rage in the sunlight as they needled over the rocks, looking for a breath of movement. Rafer's manner lost its mildness. "Drop your gun, Ingram, or you're dead where you stand!"

For a moment, Suzanne thought Ingram was not going to obey, then at the slow cock of a rifle from above, he suddenly cast away his gun with a contemptuous jerk.

"All right, boys, strip."

Nobody moved.

A shot sang out at Ingram's heels. "You first."

Suzanne shivered at the look on Ingram's face as he unbuckled his belt. Clothes and gunbelts followed the guns.

A faint, croaking laugh emerged from Ramsey. "Hot damn, I could almost . . . get to like that rascal. Did you ever . . . see so much smelly chicken flesh in your life?"

She might have laughed, had Brad not lain five feet away. Glad Ramsey was becoming too erratic to remember clearly, she clasped his hand; it was limp. He was already dead.

Rafer had saluted him out of life with the humiliation of his enemies.

The tears came hard now. Ramsey had been a selfish, mean-tempered man, but in his way, he had loved her. Sometimes he learned hard, slow, and late, but he usually learned; this time, the learning had taken too long . . . and ended in death.

Ignoring the nude, shamed men about her, she wound Ramsey's pocket handkerchief about his face. Then, she shakily rose and went to kneel by Brad. Averting her eyes, she unfastened his gay western neckerchief. If one looked only at this side of his face, he resembled a boy playing at being a desperado . . . but when he died, he was a boy no longer.

He died with courage . . . as recklessly as he lived, but with heroism. She started to wrap the kerchief about his face, then caught sight of Inez. Her arms filled with the men's clothing, Inez resembled a harried young laundress, her eyes like dark holes in her pale, pinched face. Her customary boneless grace was now full of bones, protruding and sharp; no part of her seemed to move at once, but in fits and starts like a very old woman . . . or a rusty machine. Three times now, she had passed Brad's body without looking at it on her way to the river. Moved by pity, Suzanne rose from the body to block her path. She held out the bandanna and started to relieve Inez of the clothing and gunbelts.

Inez stared at Suzanne in disbelief. "Because of you, your man is dead, but you do not claim him even in death," Inez said bitterly. "How like you."

Suzanne recoiled in anger that Inez should so willfully misinterpret her generously meant gesture. "Whether wisely or not, Brad loved you. I assumed you would want to pay your respects."

"I share nothing with you," spat Inez. "Do what you like with the body; the living man was mine." She strode off toward the river, rage returning her old hauteur.

Suzanne glared after her. Of all the . . .

Her indignation was cut off by Rafer's abrupt order. "Finish it, Su, then give Inez a hand. We need to leave here directly."

His accuracy did not lessen Suzanne's anger. Her grief mounted as she carefully laid the bandanna in place. This was not the time to mourn, but Brad and Ramsey deserved something better than a rag to temporarily hide their eyes from the vultures.

Steeling herself to raid the dead and wounded, she hurriedly collected the last gunbelts and hurled them in the river, then noticed Inez had buckled on a gunbelt and was strapping another over her shoulder. She ran to Buck Wheeler's horse to pull his Remington from the saddle scabbard, then stuck it into her own scabbard. While Inez dumped all the other rifles into the river, Suzanne ran off the horses, except Banner's which she begrudgingly saved for Inez. "Here"—she tossed the Indian girl the reins, then added tartly—"don't fall off."

Rafer stood up on the rocks to grimly survey the men squatting like pale pink peonies on the riverbank. Banner lay sprawled, his face a bright splotch of scarlet against the clay. Rafer ordered Inez to make sure he was dead. She squatted down and poked a finger against Banner's jugular, then rose and neatly kicked in Banner's ribs. "Dead," she shouted.

Rafer waited for a sense of triumph, but felt only anger. Banner's death had been too quick. The sadistic sonofabitch had not even known what hit him.

So what were you going to do with him? Rafer wondered dully. Extract his brains through his ears with a crochet hook? Try to outdo him as a butcher? Better to kill him clean . . . but God, where was the satisfaction? After a decade of waiting, he felt as empty as a dry canteen. Inez's vindictive exaltation roused only his revulsion. Imagine sleeping with a woman who hated your guts. Rafer had loved only one woman, and she was now walking among dead bodies with a white, careful look on her face. One misstep and she would sink into the horror he had created.

Her husband lay dead. And Ramsey, who had loved her.

Then realism gripped him. He was not responsible for Brad and Ramsey. He had simply timed their inevitable choices to his own advantage. Without his interference, Suzanne and Inez would also be dead, but that did not make Brad and Ramsey any less so. Once, he would have cheerfully seen Ramsey killed, but today he would have given every dime he would ever see to have the old man up and roaring again. Rafer was unable to hate a man who loved the same qualities in a woman. And in the end, Brad was as much, and perhaps more man than his father.

Rafer felt Ingram staring up at him, but Ingram was unlikely to recognize his hat-shadowed face if Banner had not know him at his own dinner table. The sun gleamed on Ingram's bald skull. Ingram was as guilty as Banner; if he lacked the stomach to kill him, Inez would not need much urging to finishing the job. Inez was done with dumping the guns; now she was watching Ingram, too. A man who perspired even on cold days, Ingram was beginning to sweat.

"Look here," the chubby sheriff shouted, trying to cover his privates, "you've got witnesses! If you kill us all, the territorial governor will initiate a federal manhunt. You won't even be safe in Bolivia!''

"What will you care, with only ants inside your skull?'' taunted Inez fiercely. She advanced on him, her rifle coming up. Colorless now, Ingram squeezed against the rocks.

Her lips tightening, Suzanne raised her own rifle. She could not let Ingram be murdered in cold blood. Just as she started to warn Inez, Rafer curtly intervened.

"Leave him be, Inez. Ingram didn't kill Brad; Banner did. Shoot him, and I'll put a bullet through your scheming little brain.''

She glared up at him, braced against the boulders. "Ingram is a pig, the same as Banner!''

"All the same, back off.'' He was not going to gun down an unarmed man, and besides, killing a sheriff meant trouble.

Scowling, she lowered the rifle, then strode to Banner's horse and mounted. "So,'' she snapped, "we go.''

Suzanne mounted. Rafer covered her and Inez as they cantered southward along the bank. As soon as they were out of sight, he ducked back into the rocks to retrieve his own horse.

His eyelids slitted against the glare, Ingram peered up, and the moment Rafer's turning face profiled against the sun, Ingram remembered.

Like an attacking shark, he jerked clothing from a dead body. The other men rifled the dead, but not enough clothes were left. Starting to hesitantly strip Banner, Buck Wheeler suddenly recoiled as if bitten. "Shit, he's alive.''

Ingram stiffened in mid-wrench at a pair of too-tight pants up his thighs. Cramming on the pants, he slowly advanced to Banner's side. Banner stirred, licking his lips and grimacing vaguely at the taste of blood, then flung out a hand. Ingram involuntarily jerked back his bare foot. Banner's red-rimmed eyes opened, his face like that of a bloody, resurrecting corpse. Nobody wanted to touch him. He gaped upward, then focused. "What the hell are you all looking at?'' he croaked.

"You.'' Ingram's tone was displeased. "You ain't in any shape to go after Carlisle.''

"Carlisle?" whispered Banner, then his eyes narrowed. "What are you talking about?"

"Hoth's damned guide was Jamie Carlisle. He's taken both women and you can damned well guess where he's gone."

Banner sat up, then thrust his hands into the dirt to keep from falling back again. One of the men tried to help him, and he spat, "Don't touch me, you blasted idiot!" He put his wounded head down between his knees. "Get me some whiskey . . . my head . . . feels like a railroad tunnel's been rammed through it."

Having no whiskey, Wheeler brought muddy river water in his cupped hands; when it dripped on Banner's bloody face, his scream could be heard for miles.

TWENTY-FIVE

Under the Claw

Suzanne missed the Grand River; she longed to drown Inez in it.

For two days of heat, dust, and smelly horse sweat, she endured Inez's silent air of cold accusation. Intent on putting as much distance between them and Colorado as possible, Rafer did nothing to mitigate the tension. She was unable to share his concern. Where could fourteen men in their birthday suits go but on a two-day hike into Grand Junction? Even if Ingram reorganized a pursuit, they had a daunting headstart to California.

Rafer was a brooding stranger, but a stranger she recognized from the days after Frock's death. He was like a clock from which she could elicit no more than an occasional tick. She did not want to talk to him; if she did, she would begin to scream accusations of his having lured Brad into the desert. So, like everyone else closed in upon his own grim thoughts, she said nothing. Instead of trekking across a desert with boundless horizons, they might have been enclosed upon a ship in the shape of the abandoned Carlisle cabin, with mounting snow without and the echoes of madness within. For the first time, she sensed the extent to which the spirit created its own prison. With Ramsey and Brad dead, she was a castaway upon a sea of sand; by all events, free; but not only unable to swim across a sea of sand, too stunned with grief even to consider doing so. As indifferent as one of the dead, she followed Rafer.

Only mounting resentment of Inez kept a spark of fire alive within her soul. Inez's attitude was damnably superior, with some reason for she was perfectly adapted to her environment. Knowing how to finesse a cotillion did not compare with the ability to finesse a rattler barehanded. While Suzanne was bewildered by the desert vastness, Inez seemed to know every stone. They glared at one another like territorial lionesses forced to drink from the same waterhole; only interests of survival kept them from clawing one another raw . . . that, and a certain respect for their common misery.

Although grief soon gouged circles beneath her eyes, Inez did not weep for Brad. The first night on the trail, she concentrated her agony into a dance of mourning. Her face blackened with campfire soot, she danced, and wailed, and tore her hair. Her body was all angles, her shrieks like a stricken animal's. Like a stone, Suzanne sat and watched her.

After some time, Suzanne blackened her own face. Inez froze, her face twisted with fury as she faced her rival across the fire. "No!" she spat. "You have no right! You cared nothing for your husband when he was alive and you will not mock his spirit now!" A knife flashed in the firelight, and like an adder, she went straight for Suzanne's face.

Swift as Inez was, Rafer was faster. He grabbed her from behind, jerking her kicking and clawing off the ground. "Enough!" he said curtly in Ute. "Will you fight like carrion eaters over the dead?"

"You are the eater of carrion, James Carlisle!" spat Inez.

"You lured my man to his death with false promises of wealth because you wanted his worthless woman! Now you have the pale, greedy bitch! Wait and see how long she takes to turn on you as she did her husband! She will cheat you of your blood money and see you hanged!"

He wrenched the knife away and jerked her head back. "What do you know of James Carlisle?"

Inez suddenly realized that in her fury, she had revealed too much, enough for Rafer to silence her for good. She had already lied about Banner being dead, for his head wound was only a bloody crease. If he found out that . . . Her eyes narrowed, turned cunning. "Nothing . . . but I can guess. Perhaps you meant to kill two birds with one stone, eh?"

Rafer sensed Inez knew more than she was telling; otherwise, she would not have ignored the false treasure map. But how could she possibly know? . . .

He lacked time to speculate for Suzanne was already rounding on him. "What does Inez mean, Rafer?" she demanded. "Did you use Brad to bait Banner for some reason?"

"More or less." He shoved Inez away. "Inez is just peeved because I was a step ahead of her . . . and don't bother to screech," he snapped as Inez started to deny it. "We all used Brad for one reason or another, just as he tried to use us."

"That isn't good enough, Rafer," Suzanne said tautly. "If you had Brad and Ramsey killed . . ."

"Banner killed them over Inez," he replied tersely. His blue eyes bored into the Indian girl's. "Didn't he?"

Inez's gaze faltered. Given the shameful fact of her own guilt, she dared not bring up the hidden gold. James Carlisle's icy blue eyes implied he could be even more dangerous than Banner. He had outwitted Banner, which meant he might be able to outwit her.

Ironically, Suzanne Hoth was her only ally. Inez began to realize Suzanne had been unaware of Carlisle's plot, and he wanted her to know nothing of it now.

Four days beyond the Grand River, they rested beneath saddle blanket shades as the horses drowsed in the shadows of the great buttes. They did not travel by day now for the heat was too great. Rafer lay beneath his own shade, his eyes fixed on the eastern horizon. Inez could not fathom his endurance; even Indians slept sometime, but this man's eyes never seemed to close. Although he was tired, he never slacked the pace, never dozed in the saddle . . . never gave her the chance to cut his throat. She would have liked to cut his throat. Not only had he made a fool of Brad, he had robbed her of Ingram.

Inez wondered cynically how long Rafer would want Suzanne once she became a liability. He wanted Suzanne very much now; Inez could see it in his eyes when Suzanne was unaware of his attention. He was a man sick with desire, but he desired more than a woman. Inez smiled tightly. She would have revenge for Brad. She would see that Carlisle would be unable to have both the woman and the gold.

Inez glanced toward Suzanne. Her eyes were closed, her gold-red hair unstirred by the breathless heat. The nights were cold, but day made an anvil of the red, smouldering earth. Hell occupied this place; few whites ever recognized it was also heaven. Inez stretched peacefully, only to notice that Suzanne was watching her beneath her lashes. "How curious you are," Inez drawled. "Do you suppose Indians change color in the sun?" Her head turned lazily. "You're wondering how your husband ever loved a woman who can eat grubs without calling them *escargots*, aren't you?"

"Not any longer," replied Suzanne quietly. "You're quite a woman: not one I like, but quite a woman."

"Ah . . . you have come to deal with reality on that point, at least, but you are less perceptive about your lover." Inez glanced at Rafer. He did not stir. She was beginning to suspect he was asleep with his eyes open, but he was twenty feet away; if she kept her voice low, he could not hear her. With an eye on Rafer, she continued, "But perhaps I am mistaken. The two of you have little to say to one another these days, do you?"

"Rafer and I never spent much time in conversation," Suzanne retorted dryly.

"And now, even less, hm? What is he to you, a temporary amusement?" When Suzanne did not reply, Inez fanned herself idly. "I suppose it does not matter. You strike me as a

woman who is too preoccupied with herself to be serious
about any man.''

"Unfair, and untrue," Suzanne replied tonelessly. She had
grown inured to Inez's barbs these last days.

"It is true. Brad could have been the strong man you
wanted, had you given yourself to him wholeheartedly, but
you made conditions. Was it any wonder that he could not
face you when unable to meet those conditions? A woman
must have loyalty to her man.''

"What about a man's loyalty to a woman? replied Suzanne with a stab of pain. No man had ever stood by her
when she was in need of succor; every one of them backed
away. Even Rafer had not come after Banner to protect her;
as always, he had an ulterior reason.

"You are still making conditions; as long as you continue
to do so, you will be disappointed." Inez studied Suzanne's
pensive face, then glanced at the immobile Rafer. "Still, you
might do well not to trust that one too far. A fire rages in his
heart that has nothing to do with a woman. If I were you, I
would find out what kindles it, before you are burnt. He has
faith in nothing; such men are never reliable.''

"You tell me this, of course, because you wish me well,"
replied Suzanne with a sad, ironic smile.

"I tell you because I do not wish Bradford to have died
for nothing.''

With a glance at the lowering sun, Inez crossed to Rafer
and prodded his boot. "We go now.''

He tilted back his hat, his blue eyes expressionless. "Sure
I won't drop you down a canyon, Inez?''

She shrugged, uncaring that he had heard everything. "You
will do what you will do, and I will do what I will do.''

Suzanne rose, dusted off her skirts, then joined Inez to
gaze down at Rafer. "Why did you tag along after that manhunt, Rafer?''

He stretched, then uncoiled. For a moment, she did not
think he was going to answer, then his eyes met hers levelly.
"Because I wanted to kill Banner." Then he looked at Inez,
and her eyes held his. For the first time, they understood one
another perfectly.

                              * * *

"Shit," muttered Rafer, his grip tightening on the field glasses. He swiftly motioned the women to the horses.

"Posse?" queried Suzanne tersely as he jumped to the ground from the boulder outcrop.

"Uncompaghres."

"Apache," Inez enlightened Suzanne with a grim smile. "They will like your red hair."

"Save the fashion commentary," said Rafer curtly as he swung into the saddle. "It's the rifles they want." At Inez's sardonic laugh, he shot back, "If necessary, I'll toss in a woman."

. No matter how fast they rode, their distance from the Apaches stayed the same. Perspiration poured into Suzanne's eyes, blinding her. Her horse was beginning to labor. She had heard of Apaches from Banner; they drove bone needles under women's fingernails.

Rafer knew they could not outrun the Uncompaghres, who must be a wandering band from the camps farther south. There were nine of them and they would not be satisfied with a rifle this early in spring. In another ten minutes he would have to shoot the women.

The gap steadily closed. The taste of metal galled Rafer's mouth. Inez knew what must be done, but Suzanne did not. He would have to shoot her first; otherwise, he would never be able to kill her. Her hair was spilling like a flame on the wind, her fear evident, but her hands were steady on the reins. She was vital, beautiful, and he loved her more than his life. Now he was going to have to turn her into carrion left on a barren plain. If the Apaches got her, the end would be the same, only it would come slowly and hideously. Instead, the cheated Apaches would have him, and by the time they were done, the buzzards would be repelled.

Inez glanced back, her face tight. When he slipped his .38 from its holster, she violently shook her head. Oh, hell, she was going to make him do it the hard way . . .

"No!" she screeched, then flailed. "They're turning away!"

Suzanne's head jerked around. She saw the gun, and he

almost squeezed the trigger. Another screech from Inez made him hesitate. Involuntarily, he darted a look over his shoulder and the pent-up breath in his lungs collapsed. She was right. The Apaches were fading left and right as if scattered by an approaching locomotive. What the hell?

He shoved his gun back into the holster, and grabbed for the field glasses. The urge to cheer died in his throat.

"What do you see?" yelled Inez. Suzanne was less inquisitive; she was still thinking about the gun.

"Banner," he said tersely, "risen from the dead. He's up front, fanning eight men." He saw Inez's eyes light, the bloody-minded bitch. He might want Banner's head, but she craved haunch and hindquarters as well.

Inez peeled off like a hawk after a chicken. In seconds, her horse was thirty yards away to the north. He might have suspected she was trying to escape Banner, if not for the gleam in her eyes. Whatever she planned, how far could she run on a winded horse?

Then he saw she had no intention of going near Banner.

"She's leading them away!" cried Suzanne.

But only part of them. Two riders cut out after Inez; the rest kept coming, including Ingram . . . and Banner. That told Rafer something that made his mouth go dry again as he whipped out his rifle.

His paint stumbled; it was going to founder.

Howls splintered the air. The Apaches were back. Having seen the Banner party split to manageable numbers with desert on the side, they swooped onto the main group. Gunfire rattled through the screeches.

Suzanne's gelding abruptly caved and Rafer's paint blundered into its rear end, then went down atop it. Rafer and Suzanne hit the ground almost together. Despite the cushion of her body, his shoulder was dislocated. Suzanne lay face down, unmoving, then her head lifted slightly. Rafer, gasping with pain as he clutched his shoulder, kicked the scrambling paint away to keep her from being trampled. Her own horse was dying. His teeth gritted, he crawled after the rifle. He snatched it up and fired point blank as two Apaches bore down on him. The first Apache went down, but the stock

kick from the first shot hitting his ribs threw off the second
shot. The second Apache was on him like a rat . . . only to
develop a third eye when Suzanne shot him in the face.

Still on his knees, Rafer grabbed the Apache's reins as the
pony lunged away. The horse pulled Rafer onto his face, but
he held on. Her hair wild, Suzanne added her grip to the
reins. His face white with pain, Rafer vaulted onto the horse
and hauled her up behind him. "Let's get the hell out of here
before somebody notices our kidneys are still working!"

By the time the dust settled, Rafer and Suzanne were several miles away atop a mesa. Sweat burst out on his face as
she jerked his arm back into the socket. "Christ," he
breathed. "I wish I knew Latin."

She eyed him worriedly. "I don't suppose Latin would
summon an extra horse."

Rafer squeezed his eyes shut. "Patch'll be along when he's
had a breather. He knows I have the closest water."

"Had the closest water," she corrected. "Your canteen is
on his saddle, remember? And if he encounters an enterprising
Apache, he may prove enterprisingly fickle."

Rafer smiled crookedly. "God, you're a New England
pessimist. Get up on the wrong side of the rocks this
morning?"

"Oh, go to hell," she muttered. She tore off her shirt
sleeve and ripped it into strips to immobilize his shoulder.

"Nice shot back there," he observed. "If you were a giddy
sort, the coyotes would be running off in sundry directions
with my wits. That Apache had a sharp axe and a clinical
eye."

"No self-respecting coyote would want your wits . . . or
mine," she retorted. "We should have cut north. Inez must
have relatives enough up there to cover an elephant's tracks."

"Trust Inez, would you?" he jibed with a grimace at his
meager bandage.

"She's no more treacherous than you." Suzanne hesitated,
then knotted the bandage with more force than necessary.
"Perhaps I should vilify her in the past tense. She's probably
been killed because she tried to save our lives."

He laughed shortly. "Inez would have served us to the

Apache on toast, if she hadn't meant to cheat Banner. And I wouldn't count on her being dead. Banner only sent two men after her.''

Her perspiring brow knitted in puzzlement. "That doesn't make sense. Inez is the one who betrayed him. Why should he be more interested in us?''

He rose with a wince. "If we hang around here much longer, you can ask him. Those Apaches are probably wishing they'd never meddled with him.'' With an effort he mounted and held down his hand to her.

She gave him a weary look. "Do you know I've lost nearly ten pounds since I met you?''

He grinned. "I prefer lean and hungry.'' His eyes taking on a less amused glint of desire, he grabbed her hand, and hauled her up.

When they finally stopped that night, Suzanne was slumped half-asleep against Rafer's back. He swung his leg over the horse's neck, dropped to the ground, then turned to catch her as she toppled after him. His good arm around her, he let her soft weight sag against him. Her head fell back. Her eyes dazedly opened, then shut again. He kissed her, heard her moan a sleepy protest. She was too tired to think, far less push him away. His mouth covered hers again, still guarding his hunger as he lowered her to the ground.

Suzanne felt Rafer's fingertips graze her throat, her breast, then his lips trace its curve. His touch was like the stars, warm and swirling about her, soothing . . . She was so tired, so tired of fighting. She wanted to be held, loved, allowed to sleep, and fear no more. She could scarcely remember what she feared . . . yet she felt as if she were being swallowed by some nameless dread only Rafer's touch could banish. Something was pursuing her; something was always pursuing her. Like a small, sharp-toothed weasel, the fear ran . . . quick and snapping when she could not keep it at bay.

Rafer's hands and mouth were like velvet. His sex, coming inside her, like velvet. He was saying soft things, quieting her frightened whimpers, moving to her slowing heartbeat, filling that black, nameless void inside her. Making her bind him close and cry out to him. Tears were on her face when the blindingly bright stars lit her emptiness. "Love . . . love," she whispered as they dimmed away. "Oh, stay . . . please . . ." Then darkness came again, and the stars were just a dream.

Suzanne awoke with Rafer entangled about her. As he had predicted, the paint pony was back, his nose practically in her hair as he slept on his feet, hanging over Rafer. The pony smell was strong, but Rafer's scent was on her, gathering as the heat of sunrise dispelled the desert night's biting cold. His weight anchored her, warmed her. His sleeping face buried in her neck, he looked exhausted, the sun lines cut deep around his eyes and mouth. His eyelashes were nearly white, catching the first long glints of the sun swelling over the rocky, alien terrain. His breathing was heavy, his fair hair soft. Her skirts were up around her thighs and he was still inside her as if growing there. Not for the first time, she wondered if he had given her a child: part of him to keep. An ache grew in her throat. He was no good to her, no good at all, yet she wanted some part of him. Her arms tightened around his neck. She had to be crazy to want trouble like Rafer all her life. He took what he wanted by hook or crook. Having desired her, he had simply waited until she was too tired to say no. Ramsey and Brad were less than a week dead because Rafer had to have his way and now he had her. She remembered little about the night, and even now could scarcely summon energy to hate him. She could hate herself.

She pushed at his shoulder. "Get off me."

His breathing scarcely changed.

She pushed at his dislocated shoulder. He caught his breath, stirred, then went slack again.

This time she pushed and yelled at the same time, "Rafer, get off me!" The paint pony threw up its head and backed off a few paces.

Rafer's eyes flickered open, slits of blue as uncomprehending as an infant tom cat's. "What?" he whispered, his voice slurred with fatigue. Then he realized where he was. She had never seen a tired man move so fast. He was on his feet, his gun out before he was completely awake. When he saw nothing stirring except the returned paint pony, he looked down at her in some puzzlement, then realized his buckskin breeches were still open. "Oh," he said softly. He was silent for a moment, then added even more softly, "I didn't mean to make you cry."

Paling, she touched her wet face; she had not known she was weeping.

They saw no trace of Banner that day; by noon the next, Suzanne croaked, "Rafer, we need to rest. The Apaches must have finished Banner."

"No." He said it without stubbornness, any emotion whatever. "Banner's alive, and as long as he is, we have to keep moving."

"We can't!" she protested. "We're doing nearly eighteen hours a day. The horses are dropping."

"They'll hold until we reach the Green River tonight."

She grimaced at the name; she hoped the Green River was more promising than Muddy Creek where they had last re-filled their canteens. Her brain struck a discord. There was water, but in the wrong place. Banner had a territorial map above his study fireplace. Westward after the Colorado River came the Green River, then Muddy Creek . . . unless one were headed east! In this wild, twisted country of multi-colored buttes and fantastic rock formations, they could be headed in the wrong direction.

The blood drained from her head. She stared up at the sun; it was high in the sky, but directly in front of her. Just now, they were headed south as surely as Mexican homing pid-geons. Why had she not noticed Rafer was going the wrong way until now? She was not Inez, but she knew the sun sank in the west every night.

Holding her tongue with considerable effort, Suzanne dis-covered by sunset why she had noticed nothing. Rafer had placed all their rest sites facing west . . . but when they were on the move, the sun was all over the place. They were not headed to Mexico at all, but erratically wandering. Her throat nearly closed with fear. They were lost in Apache country!

Panic rose. Furtively, she peeked at Rafer. Beneath his bandanna, a worried frown creased his brow. He must have been trying not to worry her.

She saw one rocky arch twice, but they reached the Green River precisely at sunset. And suddenly, as she dipped her canteen into the water, she had the nasty suspicion that Rafer knew precisely where they were.

Her forbearance dissolved. "You sonofabitch!" she screeched, grabbing him by the hair as he lowered his own canteen. "Where in hell are you dragging me this time? You're leaving a trail like a Mexican jumping bean!"

It took a while, but he finally got her straddled on the bank, then he just waited until she stopped screeching.

"Where did you think I was going?" he queried mildly.

"California!"

"I never said that."

"You made me believe it! This is Apache country"—she was nearly sobbing—"and you're damned well going to get us fed to the ants!"

"Who told you that?"

She tried for his eyes again. He ducked, then eyed her soberly. He had never really seen her scared. She had probably been scared half the time since first meeting him in that Vera Cruz bar brawl, but she had never let on . . . until now. "Listen," he coaxed softly. She shook her head, then began to cry helplessly, her sobs rasps of exhaustion. "Listen to me, baby." He cradled her then, rocked her. Then he told her the truth about Banner, why Banner had not gone after Inez; at least, he told her most of the truth. Torture was a word few people could comprehend; elaboration would not improve her nerves. "My dad hid the gold out here, Su, and Banner still wants it back. Now, he's not only pissed about Inez, he knows who I am . . . and he knows I've come for the gold. There's just one problem."

She stared up at him. "You've forgotten where it is."

He nodded.

"Let me up," she breathed.

"No, darlin', I won't find podunk with my eyes scratched out."

"The last thing I want to do is touch you," she said quietly.

He released her. She got to her feet, turned her back to reappraise the situation, then whirled and fiercely slapped him. "You selfish, rotten sneak! Banner's as bad as the Apaches, and you're risking both our necks so you can lord it up in some castle in Spain! Don't you ever think of anyone but yourself?"

"Who's selfish?" he shot back. "You were ready to sell your soul for some damned castle in Connecticut! Well, I handed it to you along with a whole trigging gold mine and now you're howling like a singed saint. You've committed about every crime short of murder, just to end up tucked away in a dusty reliquary!"

"Me, criminal?" she rounded on him. "Who dragged me into every crooked scheme he could think of . . . and I didn't steal the Coco like you Carlisles stole that bullion shipment. That bullion got Brad and Ramsey, and God knows how many other men killed, and now it's my turn!"

"I had no say at all about stealing that shipment! Even when I was twelve, I didn't need half a brain to see my father would end up on a hang rope, and take me and my brothers with him. I could have run away, but I stuck . . . a hell of a lot better than you'd ever stick to anyone." Mercilessly, he ignored the dart of pain in her eyes. "And as for Brad and Ramsey, I had nothing to do with the way they died. I used them, just like you used them; no more, no less. Brad ran like he was bound to do, sooner or later, because Inez sure wasn't going to share him with you. And she had her own game to play. No matter who was moving the pieces, Brad was a born pawn"—his vehemence faded into regret —"until the end, when just for one move, he turned into a king."

He frowned, his thoughts distracted. "One thing's certain, my phoney map didn't bring Brad out here; Inez did."

Suzanne threw up her hands. "So now you believe Inez is after the bullion, too! Why can't you forget the gold long enough to live to spend it? You've thrown away half of your life to chase revenge and that gold; now it's chasing you! Is it worth dying for?"

''My father and brothers thought so,'' he said grimly, ''and I'm too close to back away now.''

''Stupidity does run in your family,'' she spat.

He rounded on her. ''I hate you rich, sanctimonious son-ofabitches! Hoth, Banner, all those insufferable sods in England who wiped their feet on my father!''

''Your father was a failure like my father, and my husband . . . and you!'' she yelled back. ''Your sort wants to fail. Failure keeps you free to avoid honor, love, responsibility . . .''

''What do you think you're out to win, besides a cold bed and a colder heart? You'll be the biggest loser of any of us. But you're wrong about me. I'll run Banner's ass off!''

''What good will that do? He won't give you time to take a leak, much less find that gold!''

A bee sang past her left ear; Rafer grabbed her wrist in mid-swat and shoved her toward the horses. ''There's no honey around you, babe! That was a bullet!''

Whining its nasty song, another bullet spat splinters on the boulder where Rafer's head had been. Dodging bullets like flushed ferrets, the two of them reached the horses, but while Rafer's paint stood its ground while he mounted, Suzanne's horse had a failure of nerve. Shrilling and plunging the instant she grabbed its bridle, the gelding snapped at her shoulder. Inspired by panic, Suzanne snatched off her hat and in one fell swoop, covered the horse's rolling eyes. With two more bewildered kicks, the Apache mustang fell into a hushed state of trembling, whereupon she vaulted aboard, whipped the hat off, and gave it an Attila-like kick in the ribs. The beast surged forward as if pronged by a cactus. Bullets whistling around her ears, she galloped after Rafer and swore if she ever caught up to him, she would geld him with her bare teeth. Only seconds out of range did Suzanne remember Rafer had been shielding her with his body while she was mounting. Dear Lord, what if he had been hit trying to save her!

She dug in her spurs in an attempt to reach him, but he was picking out such a precarious route up a mesa that a mountain goat could not have outdone. She was compelled to concentrate on her own riding to keep the gelding from breaking a leg in the treacherous tailings of shale footing the mesa. Rafer certainly looked intact; riding with easy, unerring instinct, he had swung his rifle out of its scabbard as if even his dislocated shoulder had ceased to trouble him. Once on the high ground, he swiftly dismounted behind a mass of boulders. Her perspiration-soaked shirt clinging to her ribs, she fought the gelding up the tailing. Just as she slid from the saddle behind the boulders, she heard the metallic crack of Rafer's rifle. At her horse's uneasy snort, she clapped her hat over its eyes again. Hanging on to the reins, she stole a desperate glance over her shoulder. Rafer was emptying saddles with the accuracy of a low barn door. Two out of five men went down like dropped sacks. The speed of the three other riders abruptly became less audacious. They veered away from the mesa and headed northeast.

"Where are the rest of them?" Suzanne asked worriedly. Nothing moved on the bleak landscape but the trails of dust from the retreating riders.

"Behind us, maybe." Rafer squinted up at the grim, trackless face of the mesa. "They couldn't be much higher, though, unless they've sprouted wings."

Suzanne's spine prickled. Surrounding them was an endless warren of ambush niches. Being shot at was like being reborn in reverse; she could practically feel the impact of a .45 bullet entering her head. "How much ammunition do we have?"

"Enough for an army." He gave her a sly grin. "Brazilian chocolate, too."

She let out a sound of exasperation. "When did you plan this shindig? Last Christmas?"

"Something like that." If he kept her irritated, she would remain distracted. He wasn't bleeding much, but the bandanna he had stuffed under his shirt was slipping. He pressed against the rock, trying to work the bandanna back into position while Suzanne was intent on the fading riders. Although his dislocated shoulder hurt like the devil, the slug that had settled near his spine was still more or less asleep on a cushion of shock; when it woke up, he would not be much longer on his feet. The entry point angled like a flesh wound, but the bullet had gone deep. The bandanna was back in place; he surreptitiously stuffed his shirt more tightly into his breeches to help secure it there until he could resume his saddle. A bandolier was furled in one of his saddlebags; if he strung it on over the wound, he could camouflage his injury for a while longer. He had to get Suzanne back to Muddy Creek. If he hung around here with her, Banner and Ingram would show up with more *vaqueros*. They might not be able to pry him out for a couple of days, but now time was on their side. All they had to do was wait until he weakened.

He just damned well wished he knew where Banner was right now.

"They've cut back to the Muddy," observed Ingram, squatting over the tracks.

Banner barely stopped to listen. Like a bulldog sniffing after a rabbit, he stolidly kept moving. Buck Wheeler sighed, but held his tongue. Nobody had talked much for the past three days; Ingram was doing enough for a labor lobbyist. Personally, he'd had enough of this shit. At first chance, he was going to fade. Banner wouldn't touch the canteen water; kept complaining it was foul until his lips cracked and Ingram persuaded him to suck some cactus. The head wound must have addled him, and he was getting worse. They had trusted his strength and judgment . . . up until the Grand River episode. Now twelve men were dead, five deserted, and nearly forty guns and twenty horses lost over an Indian whore who was probably halfway to Tucson. Buck spat a thick stream of tobacco juice and wiped his chin. Banner ought to be pissed at Smith, all right, but when Bill Harvey suggested they give up, Banner tried to shoot him right out of the saddle; if that weren't bad enough, he missed by a mile. And now when he and Baker had returned to report nearly killing Smith and the Hoth woman, Banner had gone berserk. Even bland-tempered Ingram was furious. "You leave 'em alone!" he snarled. "You were told to bring back a report, not scalps! We'll run 'em down soon enough." Then Ingram delayed nearly an hour to placate Banner.

Buck would rather follow a mean man than a peculiar one,

and this whole show was turning peculiar. He disliked the malevolent way Banner kept looking at him. Banner's predatory gray eyes were almost white in the moon's silver dark; the lack of difference between their whites and irises made him resemble a blind man . . . except for his large, luminous, restless pupils. Black pupils like holes in the night. Wheeler wondered what was creeping through those holes.

Tears of frustration springing to her eyes, Suzanne swivelled violently in the saddle. "We're back at the Green River, Rafer!"

"Yes." Keeping his back to her, he slid off the paint. There was no hiding the blood now. He stood still for a moment, hovering, unsure of his balance. "This is where you cross," he explained with an effort.

"We're going back into Colorado?"

"You're going back. There's nothing out here . . . for you, anyway."

She stared at him, her anger mixed with confusion, then stunned anguish. "I don't understand. You're not leaving me here to find my way back alone?"

"You'd better believe it, baby." He put a chill into his eyes a catamount would envy.

"Rafer . . ." Her choked voice gave him more pain than the seeping hole in his back. "Please don't do this."

"You're slowing me down, Red. Time to say goodbye." He nodded northward. "Just follow the river for two days, then head toward the rising sun until you strike the Grand. If you don't see Grand Junction in a couple of days, turn around and go the other way." He gingerly eased the bandolier off his shoulder and tossed it to her. "You'll make it."

"I hate your bloody guts," she whispered, the tears coming now.

"Yeah, well, you never did have much luck with men." He forced a sardonic smile as she fiercely swiped the back of her hand across her dusty, tear-streaked face. "Don't give up, though; jinxes come in threes, so you're due for a change in the cards.'' His voice softened. ''You're also a hell of a lady. Enough lady to face down Lady Luck. One day, you'll look back at the likes of me and laugh when you rake in your winnings.''

''You're not that good a joke.'' Suzanne strapped on the bandolier and rode off without a backward look.

Rafer watched her for a while, then hooked his arm around the saddlehorn and leaned against the saddle, his stubbled cheek hot on the hot leather. Well, here he was again, free as sin and twice as sorry. Bloody fucking alone as usual . . . for good, this time. He would not be coming out of the desert. If Banner failed to get him, the bullet the ride had loosened would. He had been shot before, but not like this. He felt as if a torpedo were buried in his back. His head was beginning to pound. He had to get on the damned horse, divert Banner from Suzanne. He tried to mount, then swallowed hard, wanting to retch with pain. You're not just losing your ass, you dumb sot; it's your heart. Your damned heart is falling out. You had to keep messing with a redheaded woman who's pulling it out of you.

Get on the goddamned horse. She could still die, you shit. They could still get her, the desert could get her . . . How could a lady with beauty, guts, and heart enough to be queen of England ever love a chickenshit drifter like you? You gave her nothing to respect. All you ever did was fuck her and hurt her. The saddle was wet against his face when he pushed himself up.

By sunset, he knew where he was. He was in hell, familiar as the horror-filled dreams of years upon years. The subtle smell of his own blood was in his nostrils. Dead men lay in the path of his horse, but he moved over them to the place where his nightmares were born. Where death rasped like a cricket and the wind hollowed the mouths of shrieking things like monstrous embryos born before their time. He saw the thing that had been his father, the still things that were his brothers. The terrified, bleeding, pleading thing that was himself. And the horror. The horror of knowing he would have told Banner anything, anything, if he could have remembered . . . Now, half a lifetime later, he remembered. How could he have writhed atop $200,000 in gold and not recalled where it was?

At last, he knew where the gold was hidden . . . and the shame. The weight of the memory bore him down like a waiting succubus.

TWENTY-SIX

Mad Dogs And Englishmen

"We've got him, Helmut," said Ingram in dry jubilation. He prodded Rafer's inert form with his boot. "We've finally got him."

"What's left of him," amended Wheeler, misunderstanding the occasion's significance. He hunkered down to pry open Rafer's left eyelid, then expertly assessed the sodden scarlet stain widening down his back and side. "He ain't going to last another half-hour."

"I want to touch him," murmured Banner.

With a grimace, Wheeler moved out of the way. Banner stooped and felt the blood, then put his fingers to his nose. He smeared the blood across his mouth and chin, then upward across the rest of his face.

"What the hell? . . . ." was all that Wheeler got out before Ingram shot him in the back of the head. He wasn't about to let Wheeler hear what Carlisle had to say under torture about the gold.

Then Ingram pulled out his knife.

Suzanne camped six miles upriver. She had made poor time, having left pieces of herself along the way. She hugged her knees on the riverbank and rocked as if she were the only living thing on the moon. She was dehydrated; no more tears would come, but the ravaged sounds of weeping still emerged, hollow and wild in the desert silence. She forced herself to stop; the sound would carry. She might die of her own grief, but what the hell, she thought. She had made an Odyssey that could have ended in no other way than her own death; her body might survive, but her spirit: never. She resembled Midas in a garden of gold, whose every leaf rattled with the sound of golden, deadly metal.

Suzanne stared across the white emptiness glowing beneath the round, trackless moon. Finally, even Ramsey recognized the ultimate need to love and be loved; a realization which cost him life, but she doubted if he regretted it. Rafer was right about her being a loser. Unable to love, she could not bring herself to say the word aloud, least of all to the man she loved.

For what he was worth. Rafer had abandoned her like an ill-fitting shoe . . . and not for the first time. He always came back for one reason or another: convenience, necessity, a new angle. She could not bear to hope he had a deeper reason, for each time he returned, he hurt her again. Loving Rafer was like begging for a knife in the heart. If he loved her, he would not keep leaving her.

But then, why should he stay? She never wanted him. He did not, and never would, fit into her life. Her ideal of a proper mate had been Marcus Hampton; chosen like settee upholstery, he came apart at the seams the first time she had put any weight on him. Brad was a footstool; Ramsey, a billy club. Her father was an umbrella.

Rafer had never let her use him. He made her stand on her own, offering a hand only when she was in danger of plunging over a cliff. He gave her independence in spades. Only, now she was in a fearful fix, and where was he? Chasing rainbows as usual, and leading a batch of cutthroats a merry dance as if it were May in January.

Away from her.

Given the condition of his horse, Rafer needed his field glasses almost as much as a rifle; why had he given them to her?

To retrieve the gold, Banner must find Rafer. With sudden, fearful clarity, the calculated pattern of scars on Rafer's body traced itself upon her mind. She almost felt the slit of the knife: Banner's knife.

Suzanne's scalp prickled. No wonder Rafer hated Banner. No wonder he avoided the ranch house. No wonder he wanted Banner nowhere near her now.

She scrambled to her feet. She must find Rafer. Whether or not he loved her no longer mattered. Gold or no gold, he meant to have a showdown with Banner, and he was out numbered. If they caught him, they would torture him to death. He would be unable to tell them anything, even if he wanted to.

Torn by panic, she mounted. How would she ever locate him? He was swallowed in endless miles of desert. After leaving the river, she might never find him . . . and never find her way back. She would die; worse, she might encounter Banner.

Rafer awakened, shaken by his own scream. The pain was worse than before, that distant long ago, that split second ago that ripped into him as if time were a dagger. His darkened vision sharply cleared, then slid out of focus as the obliterating blackness closed over him again.

Ingram swore with a trace of impatience as he withdrew his glowing knife flat from Rafer's shrinking flesh. After a fast, rough job of digging the bullet out of Rafer's back, he had cauterized the wound to keep him from bleeding to death, but Rafer's color was bad. He had been riding around too long with the bullet in him. "Sonofabitch is liable to stay out of his head, then die without a wheeze. We got to wake him up real good before jerkin' his short hairs."

Pacing restlessly, Banner took no interest in Ingram's prattle. Occasionally, he stumbled against a rock, and wavering, caught himself. Once, Ingram had to thrust out an arm to keep him from tripping over Rafer. Banner was stone blind, which suited Ingram fine; but less happily, he was a lunatic. If Rafer Smith died without revealing the gold, Banner was an ace in the hole. Bringing the big man back to Grand Junction would make him a hero. The question was whether he was crazy from his head wound or lack of water; his swollen tongue made his delirious mutterings incomprehensible. He sounded like an animal. Ingram could always force water into him if he started to croak. After all, he just had to show up with Banner. If Banner died directly, fine. Ingram would also be the man who had run down the last of the Carlisles.

Sitting back on his heels with a satisfied grunt, he surveyed the distracted Banner. Banner considered him stupid, but he never played a losing hand. Let the big players risk their shirts; he always came out of the game with something. He knew his limits and wasn't greedy, but this time he just might take the whole pot.

The next morning's sun rose huge, with a pale, sullen promise of heat. Tethered to a stake, the blind madman rolled and howled, while Ingram sipped coffee. Rafer was lax on the opposite side of the fire. Ingram finished his coffee then dashed out the hot dregs across Rafer's face. He stirred fitfully.

Ingram picked up his canteen, then with utmost care, trickled Banner's share of the water between Rafer's lips. Rafer coughed; the water ran out. Ingram waited until noon, then tried again when Rafer began to mutter in delirium. The water stayed down. Ingram tenderly changed his bloody bandages; the new one, cut from Banner's shirt tail, remained unstained.

By the next morning, Ingram knew Rafer was awake because he was pretending not to be. The pulse in Rafer's neck jumped when Ingram's boot tip tapped him in the ribs. That boot belonged to a dead gunslinger and rubbed Ingram raw. He had more than one bone to pick with Rafer.

He placed his knife in the fire to heat, then took the canteen over to Banner, climbed onto him and poured water down his throat. Ugly thing, a maniac close up.

Almost casually, he glanced over at the fire. Predictably, Rafer was trying to reach the knife, but he was too weak. Ingram smiled just as Banner bit him. With a shriek of pain and revulsion, he pounded Banner in the face with the can-teen, trying to beat him off; when that failed, he picked up a rock and knocked Banner cold, but had to break his jaw to make him release his arm. Gripping his bleeding hand and swearing, he lurched over to the fire and kicked Rafer away from the knife, then trod on his hand bare inches from the haft. "That's it, dammit!" he gritted. "I've waited ten years for my piece of your hide, Carlisle!"

Rafer did not know which was more horrible: Ingram's murderous grin, Banner's frenzied howling, or his own pain. Ingram's fit of temper done, he was a patient man again. Rafer clenched his teeth as Ingram's knife delicately retraced another scar . . . another memory of agony that mocked his limits.

He was not going to scream . . . he was not. If only Ingram would shut up. A silent Apache would have been preferable to Ingram's ceaseless, mindless chatter. Just let me at him, Rafer swore as the knife made his muscles cord again. Let me at him long enough to rip out that lip-licking pink tongue!

He passed out. Not long enough. The sun stopped. He drowned in darkness, then in unbearable light. He thought he was going as blind as the raving Banner. Banner's being mad as a hatter was little consolation, for Banner was unaware of what was happening to him while the last surviving Carlisle was a child in hell again.

No . . . no. He was a man. As long as he could hold his tongue and his sanity, he was a man. Ten years ago, shock and terror had made him less than human. He forgot not only the gold, but for nearly a week after his escape, his own name. He had broken his own arm to chew through the rope cutting into his wrist; a broken arm was nothing compared to being butchered like his father and brother.

Ingram's knife made his memory acute. Pain like a tooth of lightning snaked through his arm and shoulder into his skull.

Black again. Then light, and Ingram was babbling again. He remembered what Ingram wanted; at least, he thought he remembered. Ingram bent to catch the drift of his mutter.

"Shut up," he whispered. "Do the bloody hell whatever you want . . . just shut the hell up, you cretin."

Ingram turned the sky red. Night mercifully cushioned him when he revived. Through a haze of returning consciousness, Rafer smiled up at Ingram. "Anything for a bit of quiet."

After that, Ingram did not care anymore about killing him. His blade angled toward Rafer's throat.

Until a Sharps rifle settled into the back of Ingram's neck. "Drop the knife," said a frozen voice, "or you're going to be ladling up your brains with a sieve."

Ingram stiffened, his eyes bulging. Perspiration drenched his palm. "I'll slit his gullet, lady," he said quickly.

"Go ahead and try," Suzanne breathed. "If you're faster than me, I'll mount one of your ears on a cactus in memoriam."

"You're bluffing."

The Sharps's jab bloodied the back of his skull. "I may even wash the hairy little thing if I can find it."

Ingram's Adam's apple bobbed as he dropped the knife.

"How good of you." The rifle butt brained him senseless. "You pig."

Rafer gazed up at Suzanne with not quite so bright blue eyes. "Don't tell me . . . you're more attached to me than Ingram is to his ear."

She swallowed hard, trying not to look at the blood covering him. "I'm . . ." The word stuck, along with the bile in her throat. "I'm in love with you." Her emerald eyes were defiant, terrified, a trifle glassy.

His eyes cleared, then acquired a mischievous twinkle that dismissed his condition. "But you were going to wash his hairy little thing . . . not mine."

With a muffled sound of exasperation, she caught up Ingram's canteen, then jerked off his bandanna and began to swab at Rafer's chest. There was a lot of blood, too much. Overcome by fear and self-consciousness, she was unable to look at him for a minute. Did he love her? Preoccupied with falling stars, the spangled, ancient sky gave no answers, just as Rafer had given no answers when she confessed she loved him. No answer was: no. No, Suzanne Maintree Hoth. You

are on your own, forever and always . . . so, don't damned
well cry about it anymore.

She did some more sopping. "You're not as badly off as
you look, give or take a thousand stitches," she said finally,
bandaging him with strips ripped from Ingram's shirt.
"You're lucky Ingram is a nitpicker."

He grimaced in agreement. "Banner cuts more of a swath.
Last time . . . he didn't even leave my fingernails."

With a shiver, she glanced at Banner. He was less lively
now, his eyes rolled back in his head. He had gnawed through
his tether, but seemed to have little inclination to go anywhere. His head jerked as he lay on the ground. "I think
he's dying," she murmured, "as horribly as your father and
brothers must have done."

Rafer's head turned slightly to follow her troubled gaze.
"No . . . but it'll do." His attention focused on Banner's
foaming mouth. "How's our water?"

"Enough to take us back to the river if we don't loiter."

"Help me up, *querida*."

She tried, and he tried, but his face turned white and he
fell back. "Come on," she urged desperately. "We're not
that far from the river. You can do it . . . try!"

For a moment, he lay with his eyes closed, then gave her
a twisted grin. "Sorry . . . neglected to mention . . . there's
a wee bullet hole in the other side. Ingram's . . . rather a
lackluster surgeon."

She paled. "Rafer . . ."

He patted her hand. "Now, now, don't fuss. Prod Ingram awake. Make the bloody troll . . . hoist me into the
saddle."

"Are we going to leave him without water?" she asked
faintly.

"No, darling," he replied softly. "I love you too much
to turn you into a murderer."

"What did you say?" she asked even more faintly.

"I'm too . . . fagged out . . . for encores. Give our thug
a dainty kick in the teeth, please."

She kissed his cracked lips. "Yes," she breathed, "oh,
yes. The loveliest kick in the world."

But when she stopped kissing him at last to give Ingram a prod, Ingram already had the rifle. He fixed her with a yellow eye. "If'n you don't recall the whereabouts of that gold, Carlisle, I'm going to peel this bitch like a turnip."

"You were sitting on the bullion ten years ago," Rafer replied slowly. "You practically buried the men you killed with some of it."

Ingram frowned in bewilderment, then realization dawned. "Hell," he exploded, "you bastards buried the stuff under the campfire?"

"And ran the mules off."

Ingram's jaw worked. He rose and swept down on Rafer. "You sonofabitch, you made us sweat all these years."

"Stop it!" cried Suzanne. "You know where it is now, don't you?"

"Yeah," whispered Ingram, gun barrel resting against Rafer's face, "now I know."

"So you have it all to yourself," she said swiftly, "and you have me."

His teeth bared in an unpleasant smile. "Sure. How dumb do you think I am?" He jerked his head toward Banner. "That drooling idiot over there thought I was dumb and look at him. His brains are fried and I'm going to end up one of the richest men in the state." He backed toward Banner. "Hear that, big man? I've got your gold and you're goin' to foam yourself to death like a crazy dog!" He whooped and danced before Banner. "Come on, old man, get up on your hind legs and bark! You're no better than my damned hound dog now!" When Banner paid no attention, Ingram kicked him. "Bite me, you sonofabitch."

His eyes flaring with demonic rage, Banner went for him. Ingram danced out of the way, singing, "Come on, hound dog, come on!" Banner blindly attacked again and Ingram laughed, leading him toward a ravine. "Think you can fly, dog? Let's see if you can fly."

Banner lunged again, Ingram's responding titter giving Suzanne the shivers. Sinking down by Rafer, she breathed in horror, "They're both insane."

Rafer gaged the distance to the ravine edge. "Sidle toward Banner's horse," he whispered. "His rifle's in the scabbard."

She did not look at him. "Ingram will shoot me."

"He'll do worse if you don't kill him first."

Stiffly, she rose . . . edged toward the horse. Catching the flicker of movement, Ingram wheeled. At the same moment, Banner was on him. In a bizarre embrace, they sailed backward over the edge, hovering impossibly before they dropped utterly out of sight. Ingram's scream rose to a squeal until it abruptly flattened.

Suzanne ran to retrieve Banner's rifle, then hesitantly looked over the side of the ravine. Ninety feet below on the rocks, Banner still clutched Ingram. Their bodies resembled smashed dolls.

With an effort, Rafer lifted his head. "Are they dead?"

"Grotesquely." Suzanne turned, her voice unsteady. "I want to go home now, Rafer." She began to walk toward him. "I've really had quite enough murders and massacres. My nerves are frayed." She settled beside him like a child whose first effort to walk has dropped her into a nasty mud puddle. Her lips began to tremble. "How big is the hole in your back, darling?"

Mercutio's "not so big as a church door, but 'twill suffice" speech flickered through Rafer's dimming mind. "Well, if you don't mind . . . assuming the dominant position for a few days, we should be . . . making love in the grand old style by the time we reach Utah."

"Utah!"

"Practically tourist season up there. Hundreds of lovely people making a beeline . . . for California. With your smile and my charm, we should manage to ride the rails . . . right to the brass door of the Clarendon Hotel in San Francisco."

Her eyes narrowed. "And forget the gold bullion?"

"Not exactly. The site is on the way . . ." He smiled winningly, aware of her splendid reserves of energy when provoked. "Practically around the corner."

"I thought you forgot where it was," she replied tightly.

"I remembered."

"Good. You just keep recollecting until we reach the Clarendon, because if you don't die, I may strangle you in front of the doorman." She wormed her rifle stock beneath his back and pried him up.

TWENTY-SEVEN

Rosebud

Suzanne stretched luxuriously. The Clarendon had opulent sheets, opulent service . . . a pity Banner's money was running out. Rafer had encouraged her to do a bit of pocket picking before heading for San Francisco. His advice was revolting but practical.

She closed her eyes, recalling Rafer's blithe description of the westbound traffic crossing Utah. They never reached Utah. If that band of mule skinners had not cut through the Roan Plateau, the sand would have been decorated by two new unnamed skeletons. She could smell the stench of the skinners now: dirty rascals with language that paled the San Francisco stevedores. She fully expected them to kill Rafer, rape her, and steal Banner's grubstake, but they proved to be gentlemen, in their earthy way.

She stroked her bare toe fondly up Rafer's bare leg. Sleeping like an innocent babe, he was sprawled over most of the huge, white satin-draped bed. He had nearly died the first night on the trail. She never anticipated getting him alive to the Dirty Devil River, one hundred and twenty miles to the point where the skinners found them bloody with sunburn and babbling about honeymooning on a polar icecap.

Winding an arm around Rafer's neck, she pulled his head up and kissed him. Without opening his eyes, he fitted her to him and himself into her. Then he made love to her sleepily, sweetly, his sex as opulently upstanding as the hotel. She sighed happily.

Rafer's lips curved. She was humming: Mozart, this time. In two weeks, he had heard her full repertoire from "Oh, Suzanna," to Beethoven. She hummed a little flat, but with pure pleasure. Nuzzling the peak of her breast, he lifted her musical register a little. He was nearly healed but not quite yet up to the high notes; although holding back was difficult. Suzanne had such delectable skin, glorious hair, fathomless eyes . . . such energy. As for range of imagination, she could lilt the tilt of a man's kilt had he been dead a century.

Even when she hummed "God Save the Queen," he adored her.

Sometime later, Suzanne looked up at him earnestly, her hair tumbled over the fat pillows. "Rafer, this is all very lovely, but aren't you ever going to make an honest woman of me?"

"My sweet girl, if I wanted to go to bed with Abraham Lincoln, I should desecrate a national monument."

"I'm serious, Rafer. Do you mean to marry me?" Her sea-green eyes were enormous with longing and apprehension.

"Darling, I said I loved you," he said softly. "I didn't say I'd marry you."

Her gaze faltered, then levelled again with all the determination of a poker player ready to stake his last shirt. "Don't you want to marry a prosperous lady?" she countered. "As Brad's widow, I may inherit the whole Hoth fortune."

Rafer gave her a knowing grin. "Not legally. You were a virgin that night I bounded into your riverboat cabin."

"You wouldn't know a virgin from a Bourbon Street lamp post . . ."

He delicately laid a finger across her lips. "Darling, you were as tightly sealed as a baby tea rose. You even bled daintily on the sheets."

"There are ways . . ."

"That you employed while rowing madly up the Mississippi to escape my lustful embrace." He kissed her thoroughly. "I'm so glad you caught the boat, darling."

She fidgeted. "All right. I was a virgin. On our wedding night, Brad was . . . well, we were both . . ."

"Nervous."

"Yes." Flushing with embarrassment, she hesitated. "At first I thought he was . . . peculiar, but after I saw him with Inez, I wasn't so sure. I don't know what I did wrong, but he wasn't . . . he didn't . . ."

"Rise to the occasion."

Defeated, she wistfully perused his dusty boots on the French rug beside the bed. He had not worn them since they climbed into bed five nights ago. They had to abandon the bed for the bathtub while the maids changed the sheets, but then he had taught her flexibility, having made love on the rug, in the chairs, on the settee . . . Every day, huge arrangements of roses arrived with breakfast, only to be mysteriously dismantled during the course of the day. The maids wondered at all the flowers scattered on the bed and floor, but giggled outright at the ones Rafer wove into her hair. She was Pompadour; then, Chloe; another day, Guinevere. Today, she was Suzanne, confronting dusty boots that were soon to walk out of the door . . . yet again.

"I suppose," she managed faintly, "I wasn't the woman Brad wanted, that you . . ."

"Darling, if I wanted you any more, I should be blueballed from your social register." Rafer brushed tiny kisses along her hairline. "You and Brad didn't do anything more peculiar than scare each other silly." He nuzzled her porcelain ear. "I shall be eternally grateful that shy nature eventually took its course."

"But Rafer; no one knows Brad and I never consummated the marriage. Even Ramsey didn't know; Brad never would have admitted such a failure to him. I am the sole, direct heir."

Rafer smiled ruefully. "Try claiming the old tyrant's loot with him and his first heir shot, while you're shacked up with the only survivor." She heard the dusty boots in his bleak voice. "It's no good, Red. You've even lost your backer for the Coco; while you may still turn lucky there, it makes no difference. I adore you poor, but I won't saddle you with a penniless fiddlefoot. And if you are rich, I won't be your hairy lap dog.''

Her face grew glum. She slid out of his arms and went to sit in the rocker near the fireplace. The rocker squeaked just like the one in her New York bedroom, the one where she had mourned Brad and all her lost dreams more than a year ago. She had come all this way for nothing. Only to lose, to lose . . .

Suddenly, the chair halted. She slowly rose, strolled to the bed, and kissed Rafer's stubbled jaw. Gliding into bed, she tugged him beneath the covers. "About that gold you left lying around the desert . . .''

EPILOGUE

New York: November, 1871.

His ears blue with cold beneath his dockman's cap, Edward Maintree dejectedly surveyed his tattered coat. Another button lost last night. He might have conjectured that someone was slicing the buttons off as he slept, for he was never able to find them in his sleeping nest of newspapers. He was careful to button them all before lying down at night for the temperature sometimes dropped to forty degrees. His cough had worsened, but this week, he felt better. Teddy Lascowitz had promised him a busboy's job. No one from the old days went to Teddy's, and he would not have to keep orders straight, so he could keep the job if his strength held. He had a hard time remembering these days. Hunger made him lightheaded; sometimes, he sounded drunk when he was not. He had begun to drink; not much, but whenever he could get it for the liquor warmed him. Free meals at Teddy's should help. If his health improved, he might be promoted to waiter; then he could afford a room and endure until spring.

Spring made him think of Suzanne, how lovely and gay she had been in the garden at Broadacre. He smiled to himself. Suzanne should live in a tree, her hair, eyes, and skin all sunlight and vivid, dappled vitality. When spring came, he missed her so much he wanted to die. He did not, only because he feared she might be more ashamed of him than she was.

Hearing a slight clink by his knee, Edward flinched, his pale blue eyes flying open. He saw a gentleman's cashmere coat sleeve. The owner's leather-gloved hand was emptying his whiskey bottle. Edward started up angrily, then sagged back onto his newspapers, dumbfounded as the man tucked a furled hundred dollar bill into the bottle neck. A sharp judge of character after two years on the streets, Edward saw he was mistaken in first taking his benefactor for a gentleman. Despite his polished bearing and expensive attire, he was a rake, probably a gambler flush from an all-night game. His features were too hard, his tan too weathered for a man who made a predictable living. His disconcertingly blue eyes were friendly and a trifle amused now, but Edward perceived he might as easily turn as coldly dangerous as a Viking vaulting the gunnel of an enemy ship.

Edward reassessed the $100 bill. Why not accept it? He felt a certain camaraderie with a man who made his living from luck and the roll of the dice. Then, another bill matching the first slid into the bottle. Another bill followed. Edward's heart began to pound. Was this a cruel joke? A fourth $100 bill pushed the other three to the bottle bottom. The bottle filled, until with subtle finesse, the blue-eyed man corked the bottle and placed it before Edward as if presenting a fine year in champagne.

There was too much money. Edward shook his head.

A woman's slender, silk-gloved hand wafted a fine Havana cigar beneath his nose. On her third finger was a diamond-mounted emerald wedding ring that might have provoked Cornelius Vanderbilt to burglary. Her hand daintly pressed the cigar between his lips, then lit it with a $1,000 bill. Despite the sulfurous flare of the match, Edward smelled something else that startled him more than a thousand dollars going up in hot, bright seconds. Through the air delicately sifted the perfume his wife had worn; that Suzanne wore. Now he knew why he was being offered money. Tears stinging his eyes, he removed the cigar from his lips, extinguished it, and began to gather up his things. He must disappear again. No job at Teddy's.

"I have the honor to present Mr. Rafer Carlisle, papa," said a soft voice that tore at his heart.

"With your permission, sir, I'd like to remarry your daughter this afternoon," Rafer Carlisle said quietly. "When we were wed this summer in San Francisco, we missed both your blessing and your company."

Edward was unable to look up. He fought to answer levelly, but found himself so choked, he gave it up.

"I do love him, papa . . . flush or flat."

Startled at her turn of phrase, Edward tentatively glanced up. Suzanne was in love, all right. Rainbows looked duller. He drank in her radiant face, then appraised Rafer Carlisle's steady blue eyes, and those eyes told him what he needed to know. The warmth in his heart making him momentarily forget his numb extremities, Edward nodded. "You have my blessing." He pushed himself up, and began to ease away. "Of course, I must purchase a proper suit for the wedding. Not properly tailored, mind you"—he laughed self-consciously, his steps quickening—"but never fear, I shall be there . . ."

"Where, papa?" Suzanne's question softly reached out for him.

"Why . . ." Realizing his mistake, he turned a trifle wildly toward the open street. "Never mind, never mind . . ."

He was too slow. Suzanne's ermine cape settled around his shoulders. This time the warmth penetrated further than his heart. "I do mind, papa," she murmured as she kissed him. "I mean to have both the men I love on my honeymoon."

As sunset flamed the New York City harbor, a sleek yacht steamed steadily past Staten Island toward the North Atlantic bound for the Mediterranean. On the white kid cushions of the rear deck sat Edward Maintree, dressed from head to toe in a warm beaver coat and hat. From his broad smile jauntily spiked a Havana cigar, its smoke wafting over the mahogany stern emblazoned with gold and green script. Two miles out, the throb of the screw ceased and the sails billowed up with a snap. *Naughty Suzanne* had the luck of the wind.